Goodnight, Whoever You Are

VICTORIA COOKE

Goodnight, Whoever You Are

Copyright © 2024 by Victoria Cooke.

Goodnight, Whoever You Are is a work of fiction. Unless otherwise indicated, all the names, characters, businesses, places, events, and incidents in this book are either the product of the author's imagination or used in a fictitious manner. Any resemblance to actual persons, living or dead, or actual events is purely coincidental or fictitious.

For information about this title contact the publisher:

Native Red Bird Books, LLC
nativeredbirdbooks.net
info@nativeredbirdbooks.net

ISBN: 979-8-9894933-0-2 (paperback)
ISBN: 979-8-9894933-1-9 (eBook)

Printed in the United States of America
Cover and Interior design: 1106 Design

In memory…

of my friend, Barbara, whose journey inspired part of this story,

of my parents, who helped me see the funny moments,

of Conrad, our first son, who taught me how to parent,

and of my Aunt Georgia, who loved me and my writing, and

who prayed for me every day!

*For my husband, Michael,
and our very blended family…*

ONE

1959

The first time I ever saw Marty, I had my pants down around my ankles. I was seven years old. Bucky Malone had bet me fifty cents I couldn't climb to the top of the telephone pole and zip-line down. Midway up the pole, my pants snagged on one of the pegs and the elastic popped. My pants came down. I climbed to the top anyway with hot tears streaming down my face and I zipped down that line. Fifty cents is fifty cents. I could face Bucky Malone *and* his bunch pant-less, but I wasn't going to lose that bet.

That was the first of many moments in my life when I wouldn't back down, determined to carry out something I had no business doing. Marty was usually close behind, picking up the pieces. When I made it down to the ground that day, Marty had made them all stop laughing by squirting them with icy cold water from the garden hose.

Bucky Malone was ticked because he was wearing a new shirt. He threw the fifty cents on the ground and ran home with his cronies close behind him. Watching him run away made me happy, but it also made me shudder. Bucky Malone had been held back two years because he was just plain mean. He lived down the street in a big ugly house that was the color of baby poop. Nobody liked Bucky Malone, but they were afraid *not* to hang out with him because he might paper their houses or leave gross stuff in their mailboxes.

Marty, a head taller than the rest of us, took one look at me and smiled. Sweat was rolling off me in the August Oklahoma sun and my light brown ringlets were soaking wet. I was clinging to my pants for dear life. Marty fished a large safety pin out of his front pocket, rescuing my pants. He also handed me a handkerchief from his back pocket.

"Thanks," I said, wiping my face and blowing my nose, hoping my tears didn't make my green eyes look like two frog pools. "What's your name?" I asked, looking at my white knight with admiration.

"Marty, Martin Greene," he said. His dark brown eyes smiled. His hair was even darker. "I moved across the street this weekend—from New York. We love it here because we used to live in an apartment and here we can have a house!"

"Oh, that's great! Welcome. I'm new too but we lived in Oklahoma in the country. This is city for me!" I said, smiling. "Thanks for all your help. I'm Lizzie Littleton, Elizabeth when I'm in trouble. How old are you?"

"Seven" he said proudly, "almost eight."

"So am I," I lied. Well, I was almost seven.

"What grade are you in?" he asked.

"Going into second," I said.

"Me, too,"

He walked me back to my house, talking the whole time. I remember thinking how odd it was to have a boy talk to you like this. I had just met him and already I felt like I could tell him anything. He told me he was the only boy and had three sisters. His mom, like mine, was a homemaker.

I told him about my sister, Claire, who was my mother's favorite. I explained she was a jerk to me most of the time. I told him about my dad and how we did a lot of stuff together like fishing and fixing things and about my mother, who loved me but worried that I wasn't more like my sister and girly. Marty thought I was *just* right and girly enough. I felt ten feet tall and forgot all about my pants, now held firmly with a Martin Greene safety pin: true security.

I knew two things when I watched Marty walk across the street that hot August day in 1959 as surely as I knew it all those years to come. I knew he would be my best friend for life, and I knew I was going to marry him someday.

◆　◆　◆

1964

"Do you *like-like* Marty Greene?" Ginny Glamercy, a.k.a. "Glam," asked me as she stuck her long legs in the air and examined her newly polished toes. Glam was one of my best friends. She had always been glamorous, with her long "enhanced" blonde hair and her dangly pierced earrings. My mother said only gypsies had pierced ears. Glam's mother was a model for different stores at the new shopping mall and had pierced ears. My mother's response to this information was silence. Okay.

We were at a sleepover at our friend Betsy's house. Betsy was cute and giggled a lot. She was blonde, like Glam, but her unshaven legs were half the length of Glam's and her hair was truly blonde where Glam's was out of a bottle. My mother was appalled at this fact, since we were only twelve or thirteen. In the early sixties, *nice* girls didn't color their hair, according to my mother.

"We're friends," I said agreeably, talking about Marty truthfully while trying to think of something cool and exciting to say. I could only come up with, "He's kissed me." I said it with a shrug like it was an everyday occurrence.

This new information met with a round of loud gasping, laughter, and faces buried in pillows.

"Did he stick his tongue in your mouth? Did he *French* you?" Gloria asked, wide-eyed.

Gloria was a *Negress*, as my mother referred to her, and she was one of my best friends. When I first heard my mother say "*Negress*," I thought it had something to do with grass on Gloria's knees. In those days, at Central High School in downtown Tulsa, "the better Negroes" as my mother would say, made up about ten percent of our school. Gloria's father managed some really nice apartments where they lived near the school and her mother worked in the school kitchen.

"Well," Gloria said, putting her thin cocoa brown arms on her hips in a huff, "Are you going to answer my question?"

"NO!" I said, "I'm not *that* kind of girl."

"My sister says it's the same as going all the way with you for a guy," Betsy said knowingly. We figured her sister knew what she was talking about; after all, she was in ninth grade and we were only in sixth.

"I'm never doing it," Gloria said, looking up at the stars. We were in Betsy's backyard on sleeping bags amid the chiggers. Her cat, Gus, as big as a bus, was asleep on my right leg. Her schnauzer, Dooley, was lying on his back, snoring.

"Don't you want babies?" Betsy asked.

"I guess so. Well, maybe I'll do it once or twice to have babies. Can they put you to sleep while he's doing it?" Gloria asked.

"I wouldn't know," I said.

"*My* sister says her husband is so boring, she sleeps through it," Susan Winter said from the other side of Glam. "I overheard her telling my sister Casey the other night."

"Well, good," Gloria said, rolling over, "maybe it won't be such a big deal."

"I wonder if it hurts," Glam said, staring at the sky or her toes, whichever was farther away.

"I guess it hurts the first time," Gloria said thoughtfully. "I guess it depends on how big the guy is."

"Do they come in different sizes?" Betsy squeaked, followed by uncontrollable giggling.

"I don't know. It's not like I'm an expert. But people come in different sizes, so it stands to reason those things do, too," I said, trying to sound convincing.

There were many squeals and groans at this thought.

I decided to pull my dead asleep foot away from Gus and try to walk around a bit. We were all in pajamas by now and nature was calling. I went inside the house to Betsy's mom's little powder room under the stairs. It smelled like fake roses, which made me gag a little. The slanted wall was covered with wallpaper scattered with roses, and Betsy's mom had glued plastic roses all around the door and the mirror. The guest towels were embroidered with red roses and the toilet was black with a red plastic seat that squished when you sat down. It was quite the little bathroom. Okay, time to go now.

I opened the door to three expectant faces watching me with glee in their eyes.

"What?" I said, drying my hands. "What did you guys do?"

Betsy giggled uncontrollably, put her hand over her mouth, and ran into the next room.

"Shhhh," Gloria said, "Betsy, you'll ruin everything."

Glam shrugged as she walked into the den and turned on the television. There was no remote. "Let's just sit and watch some TV," she said casually.

I plopped down on the sofa and leaned back on a pillow. Betsy was giggling so hard; she crossed her legs and ran into the bathroom, which I had rechristened "the flowerpot."

My hand slid under the pillow. I felt something wet and icy cold. I pulled back the pillow and saw my padded bra frozen solid. The cups looked like twin Pike's Peaks with snow on them. My mother had just purchased this heavily padded bra to create what others would think was an ample bust, of which I had very little. I was horrified that my friends discovered my secret. I burst into tears.

Not expecting this reaction, the room grew silent.

Gloria spoke first. "We didn't mean to upset you, we thought you'd laugh and think it was funny."

My sobbing sounded like someone was choking me.

"You're not the only one with a padded bra," Glam said. "I have one boob bigger than the other and my mom makes me wear one."

"My mom makes me wear one, too," Betsy's high-pitched voice chorused from the flower pot.

"Not me." Gloria shook her head sadly. "My mama said there's plenty of time for all of that later. I'm stuck with an undershirt over these babies."

I stopped crying, realizing we were all the same, even though we were different.

It didn't matter who was bigger or smaller, who was glamorous or who was plain, we were friends, and we were just trying to grow up. Those voices echo in my heart now, but at the time I was too caught up in my own insecurity to fully understand the sweet innocence of those conversations.

My mother said boys wanted to have sex all the time and I must be very careful and wait until I was married because that's what nice girls do. I pondered the merits of being a nice girl and what that really meant. I *was* a nice girl. We were all twelve, and no matter what we *thought* we knew, we knew almost nothing. I figured the girls in school who were really wild, the ones who sneaked out of the house and went drinking with high school boys, didn't have fathers like mine. I couldn't bear to disappoint him. Every time I walked into a room, he would look half amused, as if I were going to say something funny or do something crazy.

Even though he never said it, that look of amusement told me he loved me. No sir, if it meant disappointing my father, I would be a nice girl for life.

◆　◆　◆

1968

"I have a confession to make," I said, my eyes darting at Marty and back to the road.

"What's that?" he asked, trying to look relaxed, but I saw him gripping the door handle.

"Well, when I go around a curve…"

"Yeah?"

"I just close my eyes when I'm making the curve because it's too scary to watch it all the way," I said, looking at him for approval.

"You've only had your license a week, Lizzie," Marty said, shaking his head. "I'm thinking maybe you need a little more practice."

Getting your license is a big deal. We both got ours the very day we turned sixteen. It followed a long and grueling summer of driver's education taught by Coach Renner. He was the basketball coach because he was over six and a half feet tall. He barely fit in the metallic gold Pontiac Firebird the school used to teach us how to drive. That would be the closest I would ever get to driving a cool new sports car.

Coach Renner liked to joke a lot, but when I drove, he didn't say much. He kept his fist in his mouth the whole time and would periodically pound the brake on his side of the vehicle. The first time I drove, I went so slow you would have thought I was ninety. But after that I had a bit of a lead foot.

My father would agree with Marty. I needed more practice. I'd already dinged my mother's black Catalina Pontiac on the driver's side twice.

Marty had a '66 Mustang convertible his dad bought to share with him. It was dark green, and we thought it was a pretty cool car. We spent most evenings out in Marty's car, but sometimes his dad took it for a spin. He'd often take it to work when he went into the office on Saturdays.

It wasn't until our senior year that we figured out that sharing the convertible wasn't all it was cracked up to be. Marty called me, his voice shaking, and asked me to drive him to church.

"How come we can't use your car?" I asked.

"Can we just go in yours?" he demanded.

This wasn't Marty. Marty was always Mr. Even Keel. This was somebody else.

I drove us to the church, and he was silent. His eyes were teary and his fists were clinched. I pulled into the parking lot and said, "Okay, what's the deal?"

"Mom was putting the new insurance card in my glove box and found a pair of panties," he said, sighing heavily.

"You're kidding? Whose were they?"

"Well, when she started screaming about it to me, I told her I didn't know whose panties they were, and she slapped me."

"She SLAPPED you?" Marty and his mother never fought.

"Yes," he said, hanging his head, a tear dropping on his thigh.

"Did she say she was sorry?" I asked.

"Well, Dad came home, and they got into it. He told her they were probably your panties and boys will be boys."

"MY panties! Why would I leave *my* panties in your *glove box?*" I asked, totally blind to the situation.

"Because they think we're having sex," he blurted out.

"But we're not," I said.

"I know, but somebody left them in there and because you're the only girl who rides in my car, my mother suspected you. After that, my mother went to the store and I was in my room…" His whole body stiffened and he looked away.

"What? What happened?"

"Dad came in my room and said, 'Son, we both know those weren't Lizzie's panties and just keep that between us, okay? I don't want your mother getting upset,'" Marty said, choking back the words.

"What does that mean?"

"I think my dad's been having an affair. I'm never getting in that car again."

"An affair! Gosh. Are you sure?"

"Yeah, I heard him calling someone in the bedroom and he kept his voice low, but I heard him telling her that she'd have to be more careful, and then I stopped listening."

"Do you think your parents will get a divorce?"

"No." Marty's voice was hard. "It happened before when I was little. Mom doesn't have any skills but being a mom and Dad makes too much money. She'll look the other way."

"Promise me if we end up together that you'll never cheat on me, Marty," I said.

"I promise," he said solemnly.

We went into the church. In those days churches were open all hours of the day. We knelt at the altar. We both prayed silently, holding hands.

I opened one eye and watched Marty after I'd finished. He was praying fervently, head bowed, his eyes moist with tears. When he seemed to be finished, he looked over at me.

"Do you want me to say anything out loud, like an out-loud prayer?" I whispered, as if the empty pews would hear us and pass judgment.

"No, that's okay," Marty said, "I think I just gave God the full load."

◆   ◆   ◆

1970

"I think I'm going to throw up. Bucky Malone just asked me to the prom," I said, slamming my locker door shut, sticking the silver combination lock through the hole, and giving it a spin.

"What did you tell him?" Marty asked.

"Before or after I threw up on his shoes?"

He grinned. "Take your pick."

"I told him I was going with you," I said, purposefully not looking at him.

"I haven't asked you yet."

"I know, so technically I lied."

"I think God will forgive you in the case of Bucky Malone," Marty reasoned.

"That was my thinking."

"Well," he said coyly, "what if I asked another girl?"

"Two things: first, I would rather stay home and sew with my mother and sister, which you know I'd rather have my blood drained first, than to go *anywhere* with Bucky Malone, much less the prom, and two, you wouldn't ask another girl because the whole time you'd be thinking how much fun you could be having with me."

"Well, aren't we full of ourselves?" Marty said, trying to keep his smile under wraps. "So what if I'd asked that cute new girl in our science class? She's nice."

"She *is* nice. I like her. We could take her with us," I said agreeably.

"I already ordered your corsage."

"How do you know what color I'm wearing?"

"Your mother told me she's making you a pink chiffon dress from a Vogue pattern and she's hand-covering the buttons."

"Like you'd be interested," I said, handing him my books to carry.

"I was, I mean, I am."

"Right," I said, rolling my eyes.

I began walking a little ahead of him because he kind of shuffled his feet when he walked. I think it was because his mother starched his jeans.

"Do you want me to surprise you or tell you what I ordered?" he teased.

"Tell me. That way if it doesn't match, you can still change it."

"My mom says orchids would be beautiful with pink."

"Are you kidding, orchids? Aren't they expensive?" I said, absolutely floored.

"Yeah, big time. I'll get them paid off by prom. Whoever heard of a corsage with installment payments?"

"You're kidding."

He chuckled. "Sort of."

"I'm worth it."

"I know."

I put my hair up with a fall. Falls were big. Falls were made from real hair that you clipped onto your own hair. My mother meticulously curled my fall into ringlets, and we matched my other hair in ringlets. I sort of looked like Medusa with all those ringlets, but my mother thought I looked like I was going to the Academy Awards.

We only had one prom at our school, *the senior prom*, and there were several hundred kids in my senior class, so lots of people attended. There was a big senior banquet before the prom. Then they opened the doors of the ballroom at the Mayo Hotel. Everybody oohed and aahed, and there was the prom. All the appropriately elaborate decorations had been lovingly placed by the junior class. There were crystal balls and colored tissue paper flowers. It was very exciting and would have been a breathtaking moment if my mother hadn't given me her emerald rose ring to wear.

My mother wanted my night to be special and the only "nice" piece of jewelry my father had ever given her was a frosted gold emerald ring in the shape of a big rose. It was pretty ugly, but my mother thought it would be perfect for my special evening.

Knowing the importance of the ring, I accepted, but I had a problem. I couldn't get my full-length white gloves with the little pearl buttons on OVER my mother's ring. So I thought it would be cool just to slip that baby over the finger of my glove.

Everyone admired the beautiful ring while we were seated at the table. They began serving the food and some idiot thought everyone loved fried chicken, so they served it for dinner. Who can eat fried chicken in white gloves and who can remove a white glove with your mother's ring on your swollen finger?

Marty took one look at my predicament and decided to pour cold water on it, which got all over my chicken. Glam thought butter would help, so she buttered my glove.

"Hey, Lizzie," Bucky said, his mouth full of food, "got any honey for that finger? Get it?" he roared, nudging his buddies.

Marty kept me from chucking my roll at him. Besides I was starting to cry a little because my finger hurt like a big dog, as my dad would say.

I excused myself and went back to the kitchen where a very nice lady found a pair of scissors and cut around the material of the finger of my glove and pulled it off. My mother's ring went flying in the air, but Marty was right behind me and caught it.

I made the presentation for most popular teacher, which ended up being Coach Renner, *without* my elegant gloves on and Marty very sweetly rolled them up and put them in his deep coat pocket since my tiny little evening purse could only hold a dime for a phone call, a Kleenex, and a lipstick.

As Marty and I danced, I leaned my head on his shoulder. He smelled strongly of British Sterling, which Marty thought was sort of like being James Bond. I guess that made me Miss Moneypenny with her "gold finger" missing from her white glove.

◆ ◆ ◆

Summer of 1970

"Jinx-pinch-poke-you-owe-me-a-Coke," Marty said, teasing, whipping his thumb faster than anybody I knew. He was the Jinx-pinch-poke-you-owe-me-a-coke champion thumb player.

"I always owe you a Coke. How can you drink coke with pancakes? It's too much sweet," I said, making a face.

"I don't care," Marty said with a shrug. He shifted his almost six-foot frame sideways on the cushioned booth seat. "I wish they'd fix the rip in this thing, it's uncomfortable."

"Do you want me to sit there?" I offered, knowing he would never agree.

"No," he said, "but thanks for offering."

Marty and I were dating. It was logical as we spent all our time together. Marty was taller than me. With his natural dark hair and eyes, he sort of fit a girl's dream of tall, dark, and handsome and could have been a member of the Beatles.

Girls liked Marty. He had played a little basketball in high school to please his parents, but Marty's passion was his art. He sculpted amazing lifelike sculptures in all kinds of mediums—paper-mâché, clay, and even some metal. He could also whittle wood and would make little figurines out of things. He could paint, too, but he really liked working with his hands and creating the pieces.

I didn't have this gift. I could see things, though, and loved to take pictures. Mom gave me her old brownie camera, but I wasn't allowed that much film, so I'd just pretend to take pictures most of the time. I started working at Molly's TALL shop in the mall so

I could buy a camera and save money for college. Marty worked in the tuxedo shop around the corner. There was a back walkway for mall employees only. That's where we'd meet sometimes, sit, have lunch, and talk about people. We didn't even make $2.50 an hour.

Marty always had more money though, because he sold a lot of his artwork to rich people at art shows. He'd grown a mustache and would put on a little black beret. We found Marty some thin black leather boots, European-looking clothing, and cool sunglasses. He'd sit with a cigarette in a holder perched on top of some ashes in a fancy little ashtray he'd designed. People stood in line to buy his stuff. "Martinique" sold out at every art show.

Marty got a full ride to the University of Oklahoma in the art department, and I got a scholarship in the journalism department. For two Tulsa kids, we were going to be two hours away from home, which was heaven to us.

We lived in the same building but on different sides. It was the early seventies, so there were summer flowers mixed with the pungent smell of marijuana floating on the gentle serenades of Judy Collins and Joni Mitchell. People were protesting the war in Vietnam and the female population, including me, had stopped wearing bras. My hair was long, golden brown, and curly. Once, I'd tried to bleach it and it turned green. I looked ghastly for an entire summer, but Marty was encouraging. He'd simply said it made my green eyes brighter.

I know you're probably wondering if Marty and I had any big romantic weekends with rose petals and candles. We did the candle thing in the woods once. I don't know why Marty picked the woods. We were actually at Lake Thunderbird, and we didn't think anybody could see us. We weren't naked or anything, just sitting on a blanket with candles around us until a little breeze started blowing and snuffed out the candles. We sat there for a moment in the dark with the bugs buzzing around us and who knew how many snakes and bears! (Okay, no snakes and bears.)

"Did you, uh, bring a flashlight or anything in your purse?" Marty's voice rang out among the crickets and cicadas.

"No," I said, fishing around in the cavern of my purse, feeling loose change and sticky gum wrappers. I landed on something long that might work. "We could set fire to my tampon. That sucker would probably burn enough to get us back to the car!"

"Super or regular?" Marty expertly asked. He did have three sisters.

"Super. I come prepared when I go to the woods. I was a campfire girl."

"Matches?" he asked, somewhat urgently.

"A lighter," I said smugly.

"Where'd you get a lighter?" Marty asked incredulously.

"I stole it."

"Where?" He sounded shocked.

"You remember the other day when we were at that place on Campus Corner and Bucky Malone was the cashier?"

"Yeah, I didn't even recognize him until he started making all those noises with his mouth."

"He did the big cough a loogie on his hand, then gave me change. So I took a Kleenex and put the money in his tip jar. When he wasn't looking, I stole his lighter."

"You didn't," Marty said. I knew he was smiling even though it was pitch-black outside. "That's my girl. Did you wipe off the loogie?"

"Yup. I put the lighter in a plastic ziplock bag in my purse so it didn't accidentally leak. I just had a feeling it would come in handy. I'm sure Bucky cussed a blue streak when he found out it was missing. It's a cheap plastic thing, but as the fluid goes down, so does this lady's shirt on the inside of the lighter. Only Bucky would have a lighter like this."

"I want one," Marty teased.

"I'll give it to you after we light these two tampons."

"You have TWO!" Marty shrieked.

"I told you, Greene, I came prepared," I said smugly, and produced the two Super Tampons with a wave of my hand.

"Let's stick them in these pop bottles for holders just in case they burn faster than we can get back to the car."

"Good idea," I agreed. We stuck them in the holes, holders and all. Marty pulled me up, which was a good thing because I was starting to get creeped out sitting in the dark. We lit the tampons and carried our tiny torches ceremoniously across the woods and back to the car. I think most people, had they known what we were burning, would have gotten a good chuckle out of this sight. Except, of course, Bucky Malone.

◆　◆　◆

1973

I knew Marty was going to do something really clever and terrific for our last Christmas in college, because he couldn't keep his enthusiasm under wraps for a minute. I was stumped about what I was going to do in response. I'd given him Bucky's lighter, which he considered a prize possession, but I knew I'd have to either spend some money or think up something super sweet.

I was now a photographer, so I could do some cool things. And of course I'd taken a bunch of pictures of Marty. I had this idea. I called his mother and made a special trip home when he was away on an art trip. I gathered up some old pictures, raided a few books of my mother's, and worked hard to make a montage of our lives. The pictures were mostly in black and white. I found a cool piece of wood, glued them all down on the wood, and meticulously shellacked the surface. I took four gallon-size yellow Charles Chips cans and glued them at the base to make the legs. Then I steamed off the labels from wine bottles we collected and I shellacked those on the legs. It was a work of art when I finished. It was our life together from the time we were seven and eight to now, at twenty-one and twenty-two.

Marty decided to give me my present at my house on Christmas Eve. We had all returned from Christmas Eve services—my mother and father, my sister, Claire, and her husband, Dork (real name, Malcolm). I didn't really like him, so I conveniently forgot his name and never used it. I don't think my father had much use for him either, because Dad was merely pleasant to him and didn't talk to him much. My mother had knitted him a sweater.

So here we were, all in our good church clothes because my mother stood on every occasion with formal attire.

Mother dutifully passed out pajamas to Claire and me. That was always the Christmas Eve present so you'd have something decent to wear in the morning. This year she gave Dork a pair of plaid Christmas pajamas because last year he'd come downstairs in silk boxers that said "Santa's secret" across the front. From the looks of things, even though Dork was a Dork, he had a pretty big secret.

My mother was horrified and went back upstairs with a migraine. She whispered to my father to "Do something about it!" So he took Dork aside and told him to get dressed before coming downstairs to be with the family. My mother said Dork must have been born in a barn, which I thought worked nicely with the Christmas theme.

I dragged out the table I had made Marty. I had wrapped cardboard around it and covered it with red paper, then I put white paper across the top and bottom and glued wooden paint stir sticks on the side to make it look like a big drum. I didn't know what to put on the card. I had considered putting "Bang Me," on the drum, but thought the double entendre might be too much for some in the room. So I had a nutcracker lying on top holding a Christmas card for Marty.

He took his time opening it. Marty loved Christmas and spent a lot of time decorating both our parents' houses—inside and out. My mom liked vintage decorations, and Marty's mother went modern with an aluminum foil Christmas tree and shiny green balls in all sizes. The tree was on a rotating stand in their living room window with a color wheel at the bottom that went from red to green to blue.

His eyes teared up when he finally peeled away the drum and saw the table.

"I love this," he said, shocked. This clearly was better than things I had gotten him in the past, and he knew I'd spent days on it.

My parents hadn't seen the table. My father was amused and thought it was very creative. My mother said it was "interesting," which was her word for things of which she didn't approve. In her way of thinking, a nice sweater would have been more appropriate.

Marty handed me a box wrapped in newspaper with my name in magic marker on it and a pre-made bow taped to it. I tore off the paper, and there was a box of Aunt Jemima's pancake mix.

"I thought you could make us all pancakes tomorrow," Marty deadpanned.

This was followed by some uncomfortable silence on the part of Claire, Dork, and my parents, and my slight amusement because I knew this wasn't all of it. It would be pancakes and tickets to something. Inside the box, in the middle of all that thick white pancake mix, was a homemade card from Marty. On the front, there was a stack of pancakes in front of two people sitting at a restaurant booth. They looked exactly like us. Inside the card it said, "Have pancakes with me for the rest of our lives. I love you, Marty. P.S. Keep digging!"

Marty had stopped acting and his eyes were shining reflections of every Christmas light on our tree.

"Go ahead," he urged, "dig."

I shoved my hand in the pancake box and grabbed a small black velvet box. It was from my favorite jeweler on campus. We had passed it a dozen times or more. They specialized in helping you design your own jewelry.

I shrieked when I opened the box. Marty had obviously designed this himself because the band was intricate swirls of gold with three tiny diamonds clustered together. It was unique and lovingly made, and I thought it was the coolest thing I'd ever seen.

"Oh, Marty," I cried and rushed to give him a big hug. "It's beautiful! I love it!"

"Well, what's your answer?" my father said, looking at us both with a big smile.

"Yes," I said, "yes, of course!"

TWO

1974

I don't know why I was afraid of sex. Maybe it was all of those lectures my mother had given me over the years. I truly thought something would happen to me if I had sex, like everybody would know because the mark of the beast would suddenly appear on my forehead.

Marty and I never had sex before we were married, but it was discussed.

"Marty," I said, "don't you want to have sex *before* we're married? I mean, everybody is having sex."

"No, that's not right. You're a nice girl. I wouldn't do that to you."

"Don't you think we ought to mess around a little? I mean, aren't you even curious to know what these girls look like?" I asked, indicating my less-than-voluptuous breasts.

Marty sighed. This was not a good sign. Marty sighing was like the weight of the world being sucked out at a vortex.

"I want to wait," he said simply, dismissing further discussion on this matter. "We just graduated! The wedding is less than a month away. Don't you have things you could be planning?"

"Are you kidding me? My mother has been planning our wedding for the last ten years."

We both laughed and I dropped it. We were always so busy we didn't think about it that much. Well, Marty didn't think about it. I thought about it all the time, probably because Glam talked about it all the time like she was some expert. In truth, when we were in high school, she had only seen three you-know-whats. One was her brother's, which she saw when she walked in on him while he was peeing, so that didn't count. The second one was her cousin Barry's; he whipped it out whenever the parents weren't looking. Glam said it was pretty small and unimpressive, and finally, her boyfriend Sky's, which was pretty nice, as you-know-whats go, according to Glam.

Gloria, on the other hand, had learned all about sex from some of the basketball team. She swore she'd never gone all the way, but she let those boys show her their stuff.

So my "experts" weren't really experts and my mother certainly never talked to me about sex. Her idea was to buy me some books. She told me to read them when she left the house to do her volunteer work. Mom never worked. She volunteered. She made a few investments with her spare grocery money, which is why we always had the same meals all the time. Mom was a basic cook, and like many women of her day, she baked all her own bread and made her cookies and cakes from scratch. She would make these elaborate desserts or a vat of cookies. Then she'd tell me not to eat them because I would get fat. I was always bigger than Claire and Mom constantly compared us.

Claire was no help either. She just would giggle and say, "You'll learn about sex soon enough!"

Mom would tell me in detail how to make a tuna casserole, but she never talked to me about sex, except to say that men want to "do it every night" and that my father's sex drive "didn't slow down until he was in his forties, and then we only did it about four or five times a week." Who wants to know that about their *parents?*

So, armed with the idea that I came from sex maniacs, I felt *almost* confident to marry my best friend. At the end of June, after our graduation, Martin Greene and I were to be married in the sanctuary of our neighborhood Methodist church.

I wore a white floor-length satin dress with a daisy-covered empire waist. Daisies were big then. I pulled my curly brown shoulder-length hair up in a French twist. My floor-length veil had daisies in the crown and fabric daisies glued to the train. My big sister was my matron of honor because she and Dork had been married five years. She didn't look like the big sister. Claire is short and a petite size 4. Mom had insisted on wearing a gold dress for the wedding and Claire wanted to wear deep blue, while the bridesmaids (Marty's three sisters) wore baby blue. Glam and Gloria were really my bridesmaids of honor, if there is such a thing, because I just wasn't crazy about Marty's three sisters. They were nice to me, but basically treated both of us like we were nine.

The wedding should have gone off without a hitch. Marty's niece and nephew were the flower girl and ring bearer, dressed in cream and blue. His nephew wore a little blue bow tie. I just didn't anticipate my sister's indigestion problems (which caused her to burp like a truck driver) and Marty's allergies. Actually, we made it down the aisle with a semblance of dignity. It was standing for a long period of time that got to everybody.

"Dearly beloved, we are gathered here…" Pastor Bob said in his slightly nasal voice. (Allergies.)

Somewhere in the middle of the description of marriage, my sister burped.

"Good God," Marty's father bellowed, "did a bomb go off?"

"Oh, Jack!" My mother turned to my father in a loud wail, "I told you not to feed her before the ceremony."

My father defended himself in a loud whisper, "I didn't feed her! Dork must have fed her something."

"Did you call my husband 'Dork?'" my sister screeched, turning around to face our parents sitting in the front row.

"Sorry, Claire, slip of the tongue." My father almost laughed, realizing his natural mistake. He winked at me since that was "our" name for him.

"Is it okay if we get back to the wedding now everyone?" I asked, looking at my family. I was beginning to sweat, or as my mother would say, "*perspire.*"

Marty began to wheeze.

"Could I just get my inhaler? Excuse me, uh, it's all the flowers," he said, wheezing and sneezing at the same time. It wasn't pretty. His mother rushed forward, pulling the inhaler out of her purse, but a couple of wadded up wet tissues fell on the ground and her lipstick rolled under Glam's shoe.

"Where'd it go?" Glam said, bending her tall frame. This action revealed her ample cleavage and drew approval from all the groomsmen, who immediately got down on the floor around her to help look for the lipstick. Dork helped, of course, because he was one of the groomsmen, along with Glam's boyfriend, Sky, Gloria's boyfriend, Fred, and three of Marty's cousins on his mother's side. They were close to his age. We liked to call them Hewey, Dewey, and Louie. They all looked alike and sounded like ducks when they talked.

"It doesn't matter, it wasn't very expensive," Marty's mom said, dismissing the boys and Glam. "Let's get on with the wedding."

"Thank you," Pastor Bob said through a deep sigh. "As I was saying, marriage…"

"Found it!" Gloria said, at the top of her voice, picking up the rolling lipstick and reaching over to return it to Marty's mother.

"Are we married yet?" I asked, realizing my foot was for sure asleep.

"I don't think so," Marty said, after a few short puffs on the inhaler.

"Can we just…do this?" I asked, looking at my family and the minister.

Everyone nodded and somehow, about ten minutes later, he was pronouncing us Mr. and Mrs. Martin Greene.

It was an afternoon wedding, and we had the reception at the church, so there was no booze. My mother's friends made lots of food though, and we ordered the cake from Safeway. We danced to records and had a friend who wanted to be a disc jockey play music.

"I guess I should have kept a closer eye on that kid when he was building forts in my backyard," my father joked, as he made his toast. "Seriously, we love Marty. I know I'm not losing a daughter, I'm gaining the son I never had."

Everyone applauded. Marty smiled and hugged my dad. I could see the tears in Dad's eyes.

Marty's mom, wearing a navy suit, blew her nose loudly and put her newly coiffed head on Marty's dad's shoulder. Marty's dad absent-mindedly patted her hand. I think he might have been checking out Glam, but it could have been his thick glasses. The poor man was less than attractive when he looked at you because his eyes looked three times their size. I asked Marty why his dad didn't wear contacts to the wedding and Marty mumbled something about his mother accidentally stepping on one of them. Everyone knows you can't just wear one contact.

The reception was fun. I was encouraged to call his parents either Mom and Dad or Bill and Edna which was hard because I was raised to use Mr. and Mrs. Everybody, and Marty was supposed to call my folks Jack and Helen. Both families got along as neighbors. The reception lasted until we had to go to the airport at five.

"How come you had Glam take us?" Marty whispered, jammed in the half seat next to me. "You know she drives like a bat out of—."

"I know, "I whispered back, but she offered, and I thought it wouldn't be that bad."

"I just hope she doesn't kill us before we get there." Marty winced as Glam shot in front of a semi- and we were serenaded by his horn and a hand gesture. We made it though and got to the airport with half an hour to spare.

Marty and I didn't get drunk until later. We didn't have any money. And in those days, middle-class kids had average weddings and simple little honeymoons. We flew to Kansas City, which was Marty's first time on an airplane, and he threw up from all the excitement. We had scrambled eggs and toast at the International House of Pancakes and Marty won the jinx-pinch-poke-game again. We stayed at the Ramada Inn at the Plaza. We walked around a little bit, then went up to our room and drank two glasses of bubbly from our complimentary bottle of champagne. I took a hot bath, rubbed lotion all over myself, and slipped into my new yellow floor-length peignoir set with little yellow daisies on the yoke and cuffs.

"Wow, you look beautiful," Marty said, his voice catching in his throat.

"*Sank you,*" I said demurely, trying to sound like Elke Sommers or Eva Gabor, someone sexy and glamorous.

It didn't work. Marty doubled up laughing. I didn't think this was funny. This was my wedding night. Little girls wait a lifetime for this. Long story short, I didn't lose my virginity on my wedding night, and it barely happened before we came home. He used everything for an excuse, the booze, his asthma, sunburn (we sat by the pool for a couple of hours), and getting used to married life.

"Shouldn't you take my nightgown off?" I asked. "Shouldn't we sleep naked?"

"Oh no, you keep it on. You look so pretty in it. There's plenty of time for the good stuff later. I'm kind of sleepy right now. Let's get some sleep. We have our whole lives to do this," he said. He kissed me awkwardly and pulled off all his clothes except his briefs. He slept in his briefs. I didn't even get to see his you-know-what on my wedding night.

He had so many good qualities; I told myself it was just honeymoon jitters. It was more than that, of course, and I wouldn't really know the reasons behind his hesitations for a long time.

My mother had always mused out loud, "there's something different about that boy," and she was right. I wouldn't find out just how right until after we had Michael, who would become, like his namesake in the Bible, a warring angel and very, very different from his father.

THREE

1980

It took us six years to have Michael. Marty was so proud when we finally got pregnant. After all, it takes only one time and our sex life averaged about two times a month. Marty wanted to help me shop for maternity clothes and even stuck a pillow under his shirt to see what he would have looked like pregnant. He painted the nursery jonquil yellow and made a hand-carved cradle for the baby. It was a special time for us. I thought everything would be perfect, except for the no sex part, but you can't live in denial forever.

Michael Martin Greene whooshed into this world weighing almost ten pounds. I had to have a C-section. That was a great opportunity for Marty to bond with Michael, because I couldn't lift him. Marty did everything: he bathed Michael, walked the floor with him, and sang to him. They adored each other. I was so happy to have them close, and I felt relieved that I could get some sleep from time to time.

Because I'm a photographer, we had a jillion pictures of Michael around the house, wonderful pictures of Marty and Michael, and a few of me with both of them. From the outside looking in we were a perfect little family.

Our ten-year high school reunion was held in the summer. It was a dress-up deal with tuxes and fancy dresses. We let Michael spend the night with my parents and we got a room at the hotel. Our plan was to party hearty.

Marty was seated next to Mr. Cool-Blond-Buff-Grady-Spencer, one of his former basketball teammates. Grady, a confirmed bachelor, had inherited millions from his grandfather. He had recently purchased several buildings on Fifteenth Street and wanted to make one of them an upscale restaurant and bar with an attached gallery. He was looking for artists to show their work and wanted to hire Marty to help design the gallery as well as show his art.

This was extremely good news. Marty was a great dad and helpmate, but he wasn't the best breadwinner. I had the steady job and the insurance as a camera person shooting news and documentaries for the ABC TV station. I even had a few still photographs published in the *Tulsa World* and *Tulsa Tribune* from time to time. Marty was a part-time waiter and did some substitute teaching. He also did some odd jobs for people and painted window scenes around town.

I was seated next to Cecil Tribbey and his wife, Libby. Can you imagine? How did you say that name in bed? Libby was stocky with over-sprayed hair. She badly needed to have her upper lip and eyebrows waxed and a touch-up on those roots. She hadn't gone to school with us. She was from St. Louis, which might explain everything. Cecil was very bald, fat, and drunk. He decided to go for a little footsie. He knocked off my black high heel sandal. I leaned over and reached for the shoe, which drew some odd looks from Libby and an alarmed look from Marty.

"Something wrong?" he whispered. Grady looked annoyed at the interruption of his elaborate plans, then a polite, gleaming white smile quickly took its place on his perfectly tanned face.

"Lost my shoe," I said, a little too loudly.

"Your strap is loose, Lizzie," Marty whispered, motioning to my shoulder with his head.

I stumbled to the ladies' room and waited a century in line. I saw quite a few people I knew, including Glam.

"Why aren't you sitting with us?" Glam demanded, as she put her lipstick on with a pout. "You look great, by the way. Nice black dress, makes you look much thinner."

I am always trying to look thinner, because all my friends are thin and I'm just okay. I am an average five foot six. Glam has almost four inches on me, and in the high heels she always insists on wearing she towers over me by about eight inches. Her legs are so long, her waist is where my boobs are. When we walk together, I take two steps to her every one step.

"You look great too," I said. "Great green dress! Where are you guys sitting? Believe me, I'd rather be with you. Marty's been talking with Grady Spencer all night and Cecil Tribbey won't stop flirting," I rattled. Babbling is a bad habit when I'm stressed.

"What a dweeb," Glam sympathized. "Grady Spencer, huh? I always thought he was kind of cute."

"Well, you go girl, you're single and he's single and rich. He inherited millions and is building a restaurant, bar, and gallery."

She winked. "You're kidding. I just happen to have lots of experience in the restaurant business and am looking for a job."

Glam was always looking for a job. Right now, she was working as a sales rep for a builder because he was hot. But Glam had experience at everything, including multiple jobs and men. She could fix a car engine, cook a gourmet meal, and tell you about the time she went to bed with the Flying Flamingo Brothers. (One at a time of course; Glam was no slut.)

We emerged from the ladies' room just in time to see Marty and Grady arm-in-arm, weaving past us toward the men's room. Grady seemed to be steering Marty, who was having trouble standing up.

"Is he all right?" I asked Grady, somewhat alarmed.

"He just suddenly acted like he was going to pass out. I thought I better get him to the john," he said, giving me a look like he was in charge.

"He can't hold his liquor," I said, shaking my head, and feeling the room spin a little.

"Cold water is what he needs," Grady said confidently. "I'll get him fixed up."

"Be careful of the tux," I said, adding sheepishly, "it's rented."

"Ohhh, of course," he said, laughing, and they disappeared inside.

"He's still pretty hot," Glam commented. "Tall, too, I need that in a man."

"You need anything with a—"

"Shhh, Lizzie, he might come out and hear you."

I timidly knocked on the door to check on Marty. Somebody else opened the door and I saw Marty leaning over the sink while Grady splashed cold water in his face with his left hand and his right hand had disappeared down the back of Marty's pants. I thought this was a little odd.

"Hey," I shouted, in my typical brilliance.

Grady turned around looking startled and amused; his eyes had almost a dreamy look. He slid his hand up, grabbed the back of Marty's pants, and pulled him away from the sink. "Just trying to hold him up and keep him from drowning himself." He managed a smile.

"Thanks," I said, pushing through the door. Several old classmates were standing at the urinals. One waved. I averted my eyes. "I think I can take it from here."

Marty turned and flopped an arm over my shoulder. He was unsteady on his feet but could walk. His rented shirt and satin lapels were damp.

"Sor-ry," he mumbled.

Glam walked with us to the elevators. Grady stayed back at the table.

"You're staying in the hotel, right?" I asked Glam as I pushed the button, carefully balancing Marty against the wall.

"Yeah, me and Gloria."

"I didn't know she was here!" I said, disappointed.

"You ought to see her. She wore a gorgeous red dress with beads and sequins. She really looks good," Glam exclaimed.

"Is she inside?" I asked, indicating the large, hot, decorated room we had just left behind us.

"Well, she hooked up with a couple of her old drama buddies and I think they're in the thick of it playing charades in one of the rooms and doing the remember-when-thing. She'll be around later. Do you want to join us after you drop off Mr. Party?" Glam said, smiling.

"I don't know. I may just call it a night."

"Who knows, you might get up there and old Marty will sober up and you could get lucky, start on a little sister for Michael."

"I doubt it," I said to myself, but not out loud. "You never know," I said, smiling back.

I poured Marty into our room, helped get him to the bed and shuffle out of his clothes. I covered him with a sheet and blanket.

"Thanks for tucking me in," he slurred.

"Marty, why did Grady have his hand on your butt?" I asked.

"What hand?" Marty opened one eye.

"Well, when Grady was helping you, he had his hand on your butt."

"I don't know." Marty shrugged sleepily, and his face became a big snore.

Sometimes Marty's passivity bugged me. I looked in the mirror and saw a fairly attractive woman, late twenties, never as thin as I thought I should be, but yes, attractive. I looked good in this black dress and heels. I wondered if Marty would ever be attracted enough to me to just spontaneously want to make love. I was always the initiator in that department, and I only rarely succeeded.

We had a good life. We had a beautiful child, and we were best friends. Was that the problem? Should we fight more? Should we not know so much about each other? Was I living with a brother instead of a husband?

Reunions are important occasions, but I didn't realize it would be pivotal in our marriage. Seeing Grady again had launched a whole new career path for Marty. It meant more money for us. We moved to a neighborhood with sidewalks where Michael could ride his bicycle and have little friends over for peanut butter and jelly sandwiches. His new school was just across the street, and he joined a little soccer team. It was Americana at its best.

But just two short years later, a bank in Oklahoma City would fail and the rumblings would be felt across the nation. I didn't know it could affect us.

FOUR

When Penn Square Bank in Oklahoma City failed in 1982, it had grown from \$62 million in assets in 1977 to \$520 million by 1982. Of the \$470.4 million the bank held in deposits, only \$207 million was insured. Oil and gas prices were falling. This resulted in the largest bank failure in FDIC history. Like a giant earthquake, the tremors were felt all over the country and extended for years. Oklahoma was especially hit hard. Bankruptcies filled pages in the local papers daily. Divorces, suicides, and all the ugly things society does under stress ramped up.

Ironically, it was the availability of buildings through this bad time that had caught Grady's eye. He invested heavily in several areas near Utica Square in downtown Tulsa, and downtown Oklahoma City. People will always eat, but the expensive sandwiches and upscale food had to be modified to fit moderate budgets. People were not investing in new art. Why should they? They could buy other really expensive things everywhere for a song.

Grady decided to change the gallery to a video rental store. Video rentals were becoming *the* thing and he had Marty run it. Marty loved movies, so it wasn't like he was selling burgers, but it was a dash to his dreams as an artist.

I was still working as a cameraperson at the local ABC affiliate. Our documentary team suffered severe budget cutbacks, so

I was assigned to the news department. My work bounced back and forth from the mundane to the magnificent, depending on the news day.

I had learned the mechanics of film editing and shooting at OU, but it didn't prepare me for the pace of a newsroom—or the magic. Editing video and integrating still photos using slow zoom techniques to make a story always took my breath away. When I hit the final edit button, I just loved it.

I tried to manage my schedule so I could shoot and edit and still make some time with Michael and Marty…well, with Michael. Marty was working longer hours. They stayed open until ten on weeknights and midnight on Friday and Saturday. I would wake Michael, make him breakfast, and get to the station by seven or seven thirty. Marty would get him to school. I would work and get all my editing done by three and be out the door. I could be home in time to meet Michael as the final bell rang and watch him bounce down the walk with his little red backpack in hand and his red OU ball cap askew. If anything required me to return to the station later, I'd drop him off with one of the sets of grandparents or have the teenage girl who lived next door watch him. We were happy, and this setup worked for us.

I don't know why people pick holidays to tell people bad news. Maybe it's the pressure of getting together with family; maybe it's too much pie. I don't know, but Marty picked Thanksgiving night to drop his little bomb.

The video store was closed. I had cooked a huge meal and had everyone over. Both of Michael's grandmothers had made the pies, but I had made the turkey, the sweet potatoes, the mashed potatoes with-the-peels-off-thank-you, the green bean casserole, the homemade fresh cranberry ring, regular *and* cornbread stuffing, and sugar cookies that looked like turkeys for Michael.

Marty's three sisters showed up with their husbands. They brought macaroni and cheese, cake, orange Jell-O salad, and a big green salad. Claire doesn't cook, so she brought the rolls. Claire and Dork were playing ball with Michael in the yard and Marty was looking all over the house for batteries because, heaven forbid, the batteries were dead in the remote and the men would turn blue without sports.

My mother kept complaining about her pie.

"The meringue fell. It just doesn't look like my lemon meringue pie, Jack."

"It all goes down the same. It's fine. The pecan looks perfect."

"I picked those pecans myself," she said, looking proud.

"I know, I cracked them." He smiled and patted her back gently. "It looks good, hon."

I liked seeing my parents like this. My mother was in her vulnerable state. She was always a little nervous when she baked and it didn't turn out well. She didn't have a job. This was her career.

I had gotten up at dawn to finish thawing out the 20-pound turkey and wrestle with pulling the neck and giblets out of the stupid thing without getting freezer burn. (According to my mother, you had to boil the slimy stuff inside the turkey with celery and onion to make the gravy.) Michael managed to throw up on the kitchen floor *before* the meal because he'd eaten too many black olives and drank too much Gatorade. The televised ball games had gone into overtime, which meant the meal was delayed. That made dinner kind of a hit-and-run with the men. Going around the table and telling what we were thankful for drew many blank stares and some eye rolling.

It took forever to clean the kitchen and of course, we had to burn candles because we didn't want that vomit smell in the house. My mother became overzealous and sprayed Lysol in the air, unaware of the burning candles, which caught my kitchen curtains on fire. Luckily, I had the big roasting pan soaking in soapy water in the sink. Marty was walking through the kitchen carrying the trash out when the curtains started to blaze. He dropped the trash and put out the fire with the soapy water. I never liked those curtains anyway. His mother had made them, but she reassured me she could make me another set.

It was almost midnight when they all went home. We finished cleaning up, locked the doors, turned out the lights, and went to bed. I was worn slick. My back ached, my feet hurt from standing on that tile floor all day, and I had eaten too much. I was so tired that it felt like my body was vibrating. I was just about to drift off to sleep when Marty said, "I'm a woman."

"Hear me roar," I mumbled.

"I'm not kidding, Liz, I'm a woman."

"Really? That's funny," I said, "and here all the time I thought I was the woman."

"I'm not kidding, Lizzie," he said softly.

"Marty, I'm the one with the female parts. I'm the one who carried Michael and nursed him for nine months, and I'm the one who stood on my feet all day and cooked Thanksgiving dinner. I'm the one who makes the lunches and does the laundry and—"

"I don't think you understand what I'm saying," he said, turning on the lamp.

"Ow," I said, immediately squinting.

"Sorry, but I thought it would be better if we could see each other."

"It'll take me a minute," I said, blinking and rubbing my eyes.

"Lizzie, you're my best friend since forever," he began.

"I know," I said, trying to focus. "That's part of our trouble. You don't think I'm hot," I said hollowly. I had never said this out loud.

"I love you with all my heart, but I don't think you're hot because I'm not attracted to you. I'm attracted to men."

Men. The word echoed in my brain. I felt a stab in my chest that pierced my heart. For a moment, I couldn't breathe. I couldn't talk. This was like something out of a bad movie. All the ugly names for homosexuals rose to the surface of my mind mixed with flashes of Truman Capote. I didn't really know any homosexuals, did I? I didn't even understand all the things men did together, and I didn't want to know. It was a foreign world to me.

"So, you're g-gay?" I stammered.

"I'm not gay. I don't want to *be* a man. I've always felt like a woman inside and have wanted to do women things," he said.

"I didn't see you in the kitchen cooking today," I said sarcastically.

"I try all of the time to bond with guys," he said, leaning forward.

"I guess so, if you want to sleep with them," I said, hating myself.

"I don't want to sleep with all of them! I try to bond with the dads. Look, ever since I was little, I've felt different. I liked pastels and wanted to dress up in girls' clothes and play with dolls and have babies. When you were pregnant, I was jealous that I couldn't carry Michael. I have those longings."

"This is weird, Marty. We've been married for twelve years," I said, feeling tears roll down my cheeks.

"I know it is and I'm so sorry. I just can't pretend anymore, Lizzie. I've been in therapy for about a year now and…"

"Therapy? I didn't know that. Why didn't you tell me? How can we afford that?" I asked, cringing.

"Well, Grady is paying for it," he said quietly.

"Grady!" I spat out the name. "I should have known he's behind this. Is that who you're sleeping with? Sick, Marty."

"It's complicated."

"Twelve years of marriage and all the years we've been together and you tell me it's *complicated*?" I said, raising my voice.

"Shh, don't wake Michael," he hissed.

I ran into the bathroom and threw up. I looked at my tear-stained face, puffy eyes, and matted hair and wondered how any man could love me. I wanted to break the mirror and break everything in the bathroom over his head, but I didn't. Instead,

I splashed cold water on my face, dabbed it with a towel, folded it back neatly, and returned to our bedroom to see Marty sitting upright and cross-legged in our bed, his head in his hands.

"So do you want to move in with Grady or just go out with him on Saturday nights?" I said bitterly.

"Okay, let me talk, okay, and listen for a minute. Pretend I'm your best friend from forever and just listen. I love you with all my heart and I always have, you are and will always be until the day I die, my best friend," he said, touching me gently as I sat next to him in the bed.

I flinched inside at his touch, but I couldn't move. I didn't say anything. My eyes were full of tears and my throat felt like it had a rock in it.

"Grady is gay. He is crazy about me, in love with me he says, and he wants us to be together. I think he's attractive, I always have, but I don't want to be a man, Lizzie, because I'm not a man inside. I want to be a woman. Grady won't be attracted to me when I'm a woman because he's gay. And even though he says he loves me, it won't matter. I've got to be a woman or I'm going to end up doing something awful because I hate myself so much!"

I sat next to him, hugging my pillow for sanity, and looking at the pain and anguish on his face. I ached all over. My feet ached from standing in the kitchen all day cooking, but that was eons ago, and my body ached from being tired, and my heart ached from this horrible news. I felt something jar itself deep inside of me, like a split. Suddenly I ached for myself *and* for Marty because he was in so much pain. And Michael. I couldn't even go there with Michael.

"What do you mean you hate yourself?" I managed to whisper.

"I hate my body. I hate my hairy chest, hairy legs, and armpits. I want to have smooth skin and a woman's body. I want to have a manicure and long hair."

"You have long hair," I said, matter-of-factly.

"Yeah, but not like a woman. I hate my voice. I'm a woman inside and my body doesn't match my soul. I've tried to paint it out of myself, I've tried to sculpt it out, I've tried to macho it out, I've tried to be a good husband and father, and I just can't fake it anymore. I'm thirty-five years old. Half of my life may be over, and for all those years I've been pretending, living a lie. I've got to change or die."

"Was our marriage a lie?" I asked feebly.

"No, not in the sense of love and faithfulness. I've never cheated on you, even though Grady has begged me to. Michael was a wonderful gift and I love you both with all my heart, but I'm a fake. I don't make love to you the way I should and the way you deserve because I can't. Every time we make love, I feel weird, but I know it's something I should do to satisfy you and I know that I'm not really making you happy, but I don't know what to do." He began to cry, and he cried like I've never seen any human being cry. It was anguish so deep and sad that I reached out and held him to me.

"What do we do now, Marty?" I asked softly after his crying subsided.

He blew his nose a couple of times and wiped his eyes.

"Well," he gulped. "That's up to you. I'd like to stay here for a while. I could sleep in the spare bedroom. You can have the house, of course, and I'll pay you whatever you need. I don't want this to get ugly with attorneys."

"So, of course, we're talking about divorce," I said flatly.

"You deserve a real man. I've completed my first year of therapy. This next year, I begin living my life as a woman. I'm going to be having hormone shots and I have to go to an electrologist and get my beard removed. I have to pick out clothes and decide on a hairstyle, get a wig, proper shoes, and so forth. I have to pass acceptably as a woman for at least a year, and probably two years before the doctor in Colorado will consider doing the operation."

"Operation? What operation?"

"It's called 'sex reassignment' surgery. I don't know exactly how to explain it. You can come to the doctor with me if you want. But when it's over, I'll be a woman and can have a normal sex life as a woman."

Maybe it was the normal sex life part of the sentence that got me. I started laughing. I couldn't stop laughing, and when Marty would say my name, I would laugh even harder. I fell off the bed laughing, like this was the best joke I had ever heard, though of course, it wasn't, because it was really happening, and it was my life.

FIVE

There are no self-help books for women whose husbands decide to become women. At least, I haven't found any. I'd never even heard of this before. How do you tell people? Family? Friends?

On a practical basis, we had to decide what to do with all of Marty's clothes, because he had gone out and bought an entirely new wardrobe. I'd helped him. He gently told me that while what I chose to wear looked nice on me, he wanted more feminine things, like lots of pastels with eyelets and ruffles. Just an observation: he'd have to wait on the eyelet until he got rid of all his chest hair.

I helped him buy the makeup. We were quite a pair at the drugstore in the makeup section. The first time he put it on, he used way too much and looked like he could work a street corner, but he kept practicing. I showed him how to steady his hand to put on eye liner and open his mouth when he put on mascara. He loved wearing lipstick, too.

Shopping for wigs was something. We decided on a color about two shades lighter than his natural dark hair, something with a little shot of henna in it. I thought the straighter one, but Marty wanted the shorter one with the curls. He bought both. He had Grady's Mastercard.

We had to go to the tall shop for pantyhose. We bought starter shoes at Payless. Marty wanted all high heels; I told him it would kill his back. He'd need sensible shoes for work. I wondered what this change in Marty would do to his business, but some people don't even look at the person behind the desk. At least, that was Marty's argument.

The undergarment shopping experience was dicey. Marty had to have a bra with falsies until he could get implants. Cringe. He also wanted lacey bikinis, but I told him I didn't think the band would hold his dangle. I suggested full brief style underwear with a little Lycra. He wanted to go to a sexy lingerie store, but I vetoed that idea. I wasn't ready for all of this and only agreed to help him because he's my best friend and the father of my child. Also, it had to be done. When I set aside the weirdness of it all, it wasn't too bad. Marty and I had always shopped together, and this had a quality of shopping for a costume. It seemed natural for us to be shopping together because we shopped together for Michael. In fact, we bought him a few things while we were out, which we paid for ourselves.

Speaking of Michael—there had to be the inevitable conversation. Michael was full of questions when he saw all the boxes and wondered why Daddy was moving into the guest room. I had told Marty it was okay for him to stay with me, but he said when he became Martha, he wanted to have her room and not even sleep in the same bed Marty had slept in. He told me it was nothing against me, but once he started dressing up, getting the hormone shots, and shaving until he could have all the hair removed, he was Martha, and he didn't want to confuse himself.

We decided the guest room stay wouldn't be permanent, but it would be Martha's room when "she" stayed over for Michael's sake. I told him I didn't want Michael spending the night away from home unless it was at the grandparents', and I didn't want him at Grady's house overnight. Marty started to protest, but then conceded.

"Did you get me anything?" Michael wanted to know, peering into the sacks and boxes. "Who is all this stuff for? Is it Grandma's birthday?"

Marty was immediately insulted. I stifled another inappropriate laugh.

"We did get you something, Pumpkin Boy (he was born in October), and we hope you like your new shirts. One of them has Spiderman on it!"

Michael was pumped.

"Are there any toys in here?" Michael said, grinning. "Wow, look at the size of those bazookas!" he laughed, pulling out the bra and falsies.

Marty was mortified. He snatched the bra and pads out of Michael's hands and snapped, "Give those to me and get away from this, Michael."

The wide grin was replaced with a look of shock on little Michael's face.

"What's the matter, Dad? I was just being funny."

Marty left the room.

I told him Daddy just wasn't himself right now (the understatement of the year) and that it would probably be a good thing if he went downstairs and watched a movie or caught a cartoon.

I went into our room. Marty was sitting on the bed with his head in his hands.

"Did you think it would be easy, Marty?" I said, feeling the full power of motherhood behind me. "When you sat in your therapist's office and talked with Grady, did you think that it would be all shopping for heels and going to the prom? That's a flesh-and-blood little boy downstairs, *our* little boy, and he thinks his dad is the guy who can help him kick soccer balls and shoot baskets. This isn't going to be easy for him, especially when he gets older. Does he have two moms now? I don't like the sound of that."

"No, the therapist suggests that he just call me Martha or Marty and he can refer to me as his … aunt," Marty said hoarsely.

"We've taught him not to lie and that's a lie," I said firmly.

"Well, my whole life is a lie, Lizzie. I don't know what I'm supposed to do."

"What if we went to the pastor, Marty? We have been kind of hit-and-miss at church. What if we get counseling? I did a little reading up on this. Some people think it's a spiritual attack," I said.

"I wish to God it were a spiritual attack. I wish people could lay hands on me and I would be a man who loved to screw and drink beer and fart in public, but I'm not made that way. Six weeks into gestation all fetuses are female, then your brain gets the signal if you're supposed to be male that you're male and you develop male genitalia. Well, I developed the male genitalia, but my brain, my psyche, never got the signal I was male. Also, I had the genetic testing done a year ago, and I'm different. I have more female chromosomes than male. I never developed an Adam's apple. I am female. I just have a birth defect," he said sadly.

"So you can't fix this with therapy?" I asked, fumbling for the right words.

"No. I tried."

"Oh Marty, this is awful."

"I know. I wouldn't wish this on anybody, much less the people I love. I even thought about killing myself, but I know that's not right. I don't want to do that to you or Michael or my parents."

"What about Grady?" I said, hardly able to say his name.

"I know you have strong feelings against Grady, but he has been very kind to me, and he truly loves me."

"I'm angry you told him before you told me," I said weakly. "I deserved to be told first."

"I know," he said, moving toward me. I involuntarily took a step back. He stopped.

"You did deserve to be told first. You didn't deserve this. Please understand, I started coming to terms with this a year or so ago and then I was so panicked by everything, I just dove into work. I thought about quitting and finding another job away from Grady, but it isn't just about Grady, I've been attracted to men for years, since we were in high school, and I was attracted to *him* in high school."

"I see."

"No, you don't, or maybe you do, I don't know how you can."

"I'm trying to understand," I said.

"I know you are, and I love and appreciate you for it. But I knew changing jobs wasn't the answer. I had to face myself, so I went into counseling. Grady had professed his love for me. I told him that I loved you, but I was struggling with some things and explained how I felt. He said he would pay for counseling and has kept his word. He said he'd pay for the operation too and that I would owe him nothing, so I'm doing some sculptures for the restaurant and his place to make up for it."

"I bet," I said bitterly.

"I haven't had sex with him," he said matter-of-factly.

"There has to have been something going on," I said, looking at him evenly.

No response.

"It's not always the actual act, Marty. It's still adultery."

"I have my own code."

"I'm done," I said. "Take the clothes and your things to Grady's or wherever you're going to stay. You can sleep in the guest room when you watch Michael if I'm out of town, but I don't want Grady over here. I never liked him. I know he was kind to you, but I blame him for this, Marty."

He sighed. "If it hadn't been Grady, it would have been someone else."

"Yeah, but maybe that guy wouldn't have footed the bill and made it so easy."

"It's not going to be easy for me. Physically, it's quite grueling, and emotionally it'll be tough to tell everybody. I've hurt you and I'll be hurting Michael, and it will kill my family. The list goes on, but I couldn't live with myself anymore. I *had* to do something."

"This is something," I said quietly.

"If you had a big dark mustache on your face and had to face yourself everyday with that big ugly mustache, what would you do?" he demanded.

"I'd shave it off, or get it removed," I answered.

"Well, there you go," Marty said.

SIX

Marty didn't start being Martha until the New Year: 1987. We had muddled through the holidays. Marty slept over at Grady's big house in a guest room, or so he said. He told Michael he was working late for the holidays, which was true. He came over every morning before Michael got up and spent as much time with him as possible before he took him to one of the grandparents' houses so we could both work.

Marty told his parents about the changes that were going to happen in his life after Christmas. He told his mother first. She said she didn't understand, but he would always be her child, and she loved him. His father just left the room and didn't talk to him. His sisters thought it was a joke at first until the youngest one, Missy, remembered he used to try on her clothes. They didn't understand and were preoccupied with their own lives. They added that they loved him and good luck with it, but they were still going to get their mom's china, crystal, and jewelry.

In January, we sat Michael down for "the talk."

"Michael," Marty began, searching for the words.

"Dad, after we do this, can we go play ping-pong in the garage? I've been practicing at Andy's house and I'm real good. We haven't played anything in a while, and I bet I can beat you, Dad."

Marty choked and his eyes filled with tears.

"Okay, well, I won't try that hard. It's okay, Dad. I'll let you win."

Marty put his head in his hands. I just sat there, and we waited.

Michael gave me a worried look. "Mommy, I'm sorry. I didn't mean…"

"Michael, it's not you, honey. You haven't done anything wrong. Daddy is just going through some changes right now," I said, aching inside.

"What kind of changes? Is he going to *die?*" Michael whispered the last word.

"No, nothing like that," I soothed, "just some changes."

Marty lifted his head and looked at his son.

"Michael," he began and choked. "Michael, I love you very much."

"I know," Michael said, looking scared.

"I'm going to be staying over at Grady's house for a while."

"Can I come? He has an indoor pool. We could go swimming."

"No," I heard myself say.

"Why? I can swim good," Michael said, starting to tear up.

"This isn't going well, Marty," I said, looking at him.

"Look, Michael," Marty said, taking both of his hands and squeezing, "Daddy is going to stay at Grady's house. I'm going to be going through some changes. I'll be dressing differently."

"Like a costume? I could wear my Halloween costume. Me and you could be pirates, Dad."

"Well, I'm going to be dressing up like a lady, Michael."

"How come? Is Mommy going to dress like a man?" he asked.

"No. See, Michael, Daddy is a man on the outside, but a woman on the inside. I mean, I feel like a woman and so I'm going to a doctor to help me look like I feel on the inside."

Dead silence.

"The doctor can make you well again," Michael said, after some thought.

"The doctor *is* going to make me well. He's going to make me into a woman like I am on the inside."

"But who'll be my Daddy?" Michael said, horrified.

"Well, I'll always be here for you, Michael; I'll just be a woman," Marty said.

"No, no, I want you like you are, Daddy!" Michael started crying. He leaned into Marty's chest, sobbing.

"I can't be the same anymore, Michael. I have to be who I am on the inside."

"I'm not a girl on the inside, am I? I'm a little boy."

"You are a little boy," I said quickly and put my arms around him. "This is a lot for all of us to understand."

"It's like a mistake," said Marty.

"Did God make the mistake?" asked Michael.

"No, but something got messed up when Daddy was in Grandma Greene's tummy," I said.

"Is it her fault?" Michael asked.

"No, it just happened," Marty said.

"I have to go to the bathroom," Michael said. He went into the bathroom and closed the door.

"Marty, here's the difference in men and women … excuse me, you and me, Marty," I said, keeping my voice low, "I could be a man inside with balls down to my knees and I'd stay that boy's mother the rest of my life."

"You're not making this any easier," he said, sighing.

"This is *your* deal, Marty. I just have to try to pick up the pieces."

"He'll understand more when he's older," Marty said.

"No, he won't," I said flatly. "This is a lot to swallow. He may be able to intellectually handle it, but he will never forget this hurt. I hope you can stay in his life and if you do, always own this, Marty. Don't play the victim or put this off on anybody else. This is your decision, and no matter how it turns out I will love you. But I don't know if I agree with this. And if you kill yourself, I'll be really angry."

"I won't kill myself; I promise."

"Go talk to your son," I said.

I couldn't hear everything he said, but at some point, Michael stopped crying. As time went on, Michael seemed to shut down around Marty. We both went to counseling, but there's just not much you can do when someone you love decides to make this kind of change. You can choose to cut them out of your life or leave them in. Michael and I decided to leave Marty in our lives, but we never could call him Martha.

SEVEN

After six months of watching my husband gingerly walk up the steps at my house in drag wearing four-inch heels to pick up our son, I decided to go ahead and quietly file for divorce. Marty didn't contest it and agreed to let me have total custody. I agreed to let him see Michael if he kept our agreed requirements for the visits. Marty and I still talked on the phone several times a week, but I had trouble seeing him and didn't hang out with him much. It was just too hard. I was going through things myself: like would I ever be attractive to ANY man and how it was affecting my son?

Michael stopped saying "Daddy," and one night, we put all the pictures of Marty as we knew him in a special photo album. Michael pointed out that Daddy might change his mind about being a girl and we'd have them, just in case.

Michael had asked Marty to not take him anywhere where we knew people, so a lot of times they'd get a hamburger at a drive-thru or go to a movie across town. Marty was grateful for any time that Michael would spend with him and kept his visits limited to a couple of hours. I still wouldn't let Michael go to Grady's house. I was angry at Grady, and I wasn't sure what kinds of things Michael would find there. I didn't want that influence on Michael. This was uncharted territory, and if I let my imagination run wild, the picture became sleazy. I preferred to think that Marty wouldn't go there, but I didn't know what Martha would do.

One day, Marty called and said he was moving into his grandmother's house by himself. Granny was going into a nursing home and was not expected to live very long.

I had heard his grandmother wasn't doing too well from his mother, but I hadn't thought through this turn of events.

"What about Grady?" I asked wryly.

"I decided to terminate our relationship," he said quietly.

"Well, what about your job?" I demanded.

"Mom and I bought the store," he said.

"Really?" I asked.

"Yeah, she's a silent partner. She gave me money from granddad's trust fund that supposedly matured when I was thirty-four, but I think she just did it. Anyway, I bought the store from Grady for a very reasonable price and it's mine. I just didn't want to be with Grady and his friends anymore." He laughed. "My tastes run to more normal people, if you can believe that."

"Where *do* you see yourself in a year, Marty?" I asked. "I mean, you've got to be thinking past the next set of treatments."

"I am," he said, "that's why Mom and I bought the business. I'll make more money now. I'll be living at Granny's house for nothing and I'm going to try to buy it from Mom someday. It's a great little house in a nice neighborhood and it's still in Michael's school district."

"You're right," I agreed. "Is your dad still giving you the silent treatment?"

"Yes. I hope he'll change, but he probably won't for a long time."

"What about from other people—strangers or customers? Is anyone giving you a hard time?" I asked.

"No, I have read articles about people who have been bullied, but I am relieved to say, it's never happened to me. I think it's because people haven't heard of it, and I am not going for a flamboyant look. I'm more subdued. Maybe my customers think I'm my sister! Anyway, on the house deal, I'm good with my hands. I'm going to fix it up and make it beautiful. It has a nice yard. Granny had a vegetable garden at one time and lots of flowers. I can get those going again and maybe Michael will want to help me."

"He would probably like that," I said. "I would let him spend the night over there as long as it is just you and other family there."

"I know. I don't want that flashy life, Lizzie. It's not me. I just want to be married to someone or have a partner. I miss you terribly. I loved living with you, but I knew it wasn't normal for either of us."

I shuddered at the thought of Marty having a husband. I sniffed my response, feeling the familiar tears.

"Anyway," he sighed, "I feel good about this change."

"What about your sisters? Are they jealous?"

"No, they could care less. They all have much more money and live in bigger houses, and they think it's nice that the weirdo has someplace to live. People in the neighborhood just think I'm another grandchild. They haven't made the connection."

"Well, that's kind of like a fresh start, then."

"Speaking of fresh starts, have you started dating?" he asked.

"No, but I don't think I could talk to you about that, Marty, if I had."

"You can talk to me about *anything*, Lizzie. You're still my best friend."

That phrase haunted me daily. Marty had always been my best friend, but so were Glam and Gloria.

One warm Saturday while Michael was spending the weekend with Marty, the girls and I caught a cheap flight on Southwest to Kansas City and stayed at a hotel on the Plaza. We shopped until we dropped and got seriously inebriated on two large bottles of Chardonnay.

"So, when are you going to start going out again?" Gloria demanded. "Your divorce is final, isn't it?"

Glam laughed. "No kidding," she said. "I started making a list of the eligible men I knew and went out with three of them just to see if they were any fun,"

"Did you sleep with them?" I asked. "I'd like a heterosexual male this time, please."

"Only one of them," she mused, "and he was just so-so."

"We've got a new Assistant DA who is cute," Gloria said enthusiastically. Gloria was a paralegal down at the DA's office. "He's tall, built, and blond."

"Is he single?" I asked.

"Yes. He just moved to Tulsa from someplace back East. He's moved back to take care of his dad. He's an only child."

Glam frowned. "Man, you don't want any part of that. Every time I've dated an only, they only think about themselves. They're so spoiled and are usually mama's boys."

"His mom is dead," Gloria said.

"Good, then you don't have to deal with a mother-in-law," Glam replied glibly.

"Hey, guys. I'm sure not getting married anytime soon and I don't know if I'm ready for dating. I don't think I'd know what to do. Besides, who would date me? The only man in my life is about four feet tall. Most guys probably don't want someone with a child. They probably want someone who is younger and has no baggage. Face it, my baggage is sizeable."

"Most guys would kill for a little boy like Michael. He could use a good male role model in his life," Glam said, gulping her Chardonnay.

"Girl, don't gulp that stuff, you'll have a headache as big as Dallas," Gloria chided. "Well, I don't think he's dating anybody. I can't tell if he's nice. I just know he's smart."

"Smart is good. So is nice. Would sexy be asking for too much? I'd settle for reasonably good looking, but male of course. Well, so what's the guy's name?" I asked, beginning to see two of Gloria.

"Who?" she asked, obviously trying to concentrate.

"The new guy," I said.

"I can't remember, but he's hot." Gloria laughed at herself.

"Ah," Glam laughed, almost choking, "Stick with us, little girl, we'll get you a man."

Gloria giggled. I downed the rest of my Chardonnay and decided I'd better eat something, so I reached for the cheese and crackers, when the phone started to ring.

"It's probably room service," Glam said. "I'll order up another bottle and a bellhop!" she joked. She put the phone to her ear. "Hello? Oh, sure. Yes, she's right here."

She handed the phone to me. "I think it's Marty," she mouthed.

"Hello?"

"Lizzie, it's me," Marty said on the other end. "Can you catch a plane? Michael is in the hospital."

EIGHT

If you've ever had bad news and had to take a plane ride some-where, even if it's a short distance, it can be hell. The taxi had a flat tire on the way to the airport. The plane was delayed. The stewardess, excuse me, "flight attendant," spilled a drink on me and the fellow sitting next to me had excessive flatulence. I cried the entire trip.

When I got off the plane, they had lost my luggage. I filled out the forms in triplicate and headed for the parking garage where I discovered the police had impounded my Toyota because they thought it had been used to smuggle drugs. The parking attendant, who had the unpleasant aroma of cigarettes and ten-day-old body odor, leered at me through greasy locks of hair. He handed me an official looking letter from the Tulsa Police Department telling me where I could pick up my automobile. It included a weak apology at the end.

"Don't worry, they paid your parking bill," the attendant said, with a toothless smile.

"Great." I groaned and started to cry again.

The attendant hailed a cab for me and wrote his phone num-ber on the back of the police letter envelope. He managed to pat my butt as I got in the car. The cab driver, a horsey bleached blonde woman with a butch haircut who probably weighed a svelte 350, turned to me with cigarette in hand and said, "Did he just pat your butt?"

I nodded.

"Why didn't you slap the crap out of him?" she growled, throwing down her cigarette. "You want me to do it?"

"No, thanks, I have to get to St. John's Hospital," I said. "My little boy is in the hospital."

She handed me a couple of rank smelling tissues and a smeared little hand mirror from the front seat.

"Don't worry, honey. I'll get you to the hospital. What's wrong with your little boy?" she said.

"I don't know," I said sadly. "His dad, uh, the person who called me, didn't elaborate."

"Well, it's probably just his tonsils. My tonsils were always bad as a kid, and they finally took 'em out. They don't take them out like they used to when we were kids."

When *we* were kids? This woman had to be in her late fifties, early sixties.

"My name's Rosie," she said, raising her voice to be heard over the country music playing on the radio.

"I'm Liz," I said, struggling to smile and be polite. The woman was trying to be kind.

"So where have you been?" she asked.

"Oh, Kansas City, just a quick trip," I said, trying to concentrate on anything but the picture in my head of Michael lying in a hospital bed.

"I like Kansas City. Had an aunt who lived there, but she was murdered. I only went there once to see her and then for the funeral. I don't really like her kids, but I did a little shopping there. I like that Plaza place."

"That's where we stayed," I said flatly.

"Oh? Well, that's real nice there, lots of shops. Do you like country music?" she asked, turning up the radio.

"It's okay," I said. "I like Reba."

"Everybody likes Reba. She's our girl, isn't she? I had a little sister who looked like Reba with red hair and all. Well, she wasn't as tiny as Reba, she probably weighed about two fifty, but she was the smallest one in our family. She died. A bus hit her."

I put my head in my hands. Couldn't this woman stop talking?

"Oh, it's okay, I'm over it now, that was a long time ago. I have other sisters left; there were eight of us girls and four boys. My daddy just couldn't get enough of my mama," she laughed.

Dear God.

"My daddy bought an old school bus, one of those short ones, you know, like for special kids, to haul us. He had to fix it first because it was in a wreck," she said, glancing in the mirror.

I started fantasizing about lying on a beach on a private island. It wasn't working.

Interpreting my silence as interest, she rattled on. "Daddy loved that old bus and drove it around even after we were all growed up. He used to overhaul all kinds of engines. It was kinda sad though, Daddy was working on an engine one day, lit a cigarette and blew himself up. Damn cigarettes," she said, sniffing. "I should give them up. They'll kill you; you know, they killed him."

"I'm so sorry," I said.

"Oh, that's okay; it's been a long time ago. My mama died last year of the breast cancer. Have you had your boobies checked?"

I could only nod.

"Well, that's a good idea to have those boobies checked. Of course, my boobies, they have to get a grain elevator to lift these girls up for those mammygrams. I hate those things. They squish 'em like a big old pancake. I bet a man invented that machine. I don't know why they couldn't make it like a cone. You'd just stick your boob in there and it would check it out. I have a distant cousin who works for a doctor. I might call her. Oh wait, I can't call her, I forgot. She died last year of a parasite. They got her body mixed up with some old lady's body and everyone was shocked when they went to the wake, but they got it straightened out for the funeral. You gotta have your pappy smears, too. A lot of people don't get those because they figure their monthlies are regular, so who needs them, you know? Are your monthlies regular?"

I just stared at her.

"Well, it doesn't matter if they're regular or not, you need your pappy smears. Pappy smears are important and can save your life! I have first-hand experience. If my neighbor Beulah's sister had one of them pappy smears, she'd be alive today. But she just put it off and boom, got the cancer. It was quick, but ugly. You know what I mean? She was deader than a doornail inside of six months. She didn't even get her Christmas wreath on the door. Well, here we are. Boy, that was a short trip!"

Rosie shut off the meter and turned to look at me.

"I don't wanna charge you for this trip, but I have to 'cuz the meter's been running. Tell you what, since we hit it off so well, I'll give you a free trip somewheres around town when you want to go someplace, how'd that be?" she asked, smiling.

"That's very nice of you," I said, managing a smile. I handed her the fare with a liberal tip and returned her mirror and tissues. "Bye now."

I trudged up the steps to St. John's Hospital dreading what I would find. Once I was in the lobby, I asked the nun behind the desk where Michael Greene's room was.

"Pediatric floor, room twelve," she said.

The elevator seemed to take an eternity. Once inside and oddly enough, all alone, I pushed the button for Michael's floor and leaned back to just breathe. As the doors opened, I turned right to go to his room.

"Excuse me, ma'am, for security reasons, we check the people who come and go, who are you coming to see?" the khaki uniformed security guard asked kindly. His smile was comforting.

"Michael, Michael Greene," I said, trembling.

"Oh, his mother is with him down the hall."

"*I'm* his mother," I protested.

"Oh, I must be confused," he said. "I'll just follow you and we'll get to the bottom of this."

"No, it's okay," I said, realizing what had happened. Marty had probably not wanted to do a lot of explaining. "It's okay; she's a relative and probably just said that because of the insurance card to save time."

"Oh okay." He nodded. "Well, here it is."

I opened the door to Michael's room and saw a worried Marty sitting at his bedside. Michael looked small and pale, asleep on the big set of pillows. A green blanket was tucked under his chin.

"I'm sorry," Marty said, rising as I came in. "I was so upset, I should have told you more, but everything happened so fast…"

"What?" I said, crying, rushing to Michael's side, "what's the matter with him?"

"Spider bite, big spider bite, a brown recluse," Marty said sadly. "I don't know if he picked it up in the back yard or inside. We had been outside. We came in and I made him some lunch. He was lying down, watching one of his favorite shows and I was loading the dishwasher. I came back in and he was having a seizure and he was feverish. I called an ambulance and rushed him to the hospital. I called you when I got here, but they had to have me sign him in and go into the emergency room with him. I was frantic. I'm so sorry, Lizzie."

Marty was such a girl! I knew she was upset and scared, but I needed her to man up here. I needed a shoulder to cry on. I needed someone to hold me. I needed someone to get back my car for me and take care of things.

"What did the doctor say?" I asked, stroking Michael's forehead. He was in a deep sleep.

"They're running tests. They've gotten the fever down. I expect him any minute."

Just then, the door swung open and the most gorgeous man I'd ever seen walked into the room. He must have been about six-four with dark hair that was gray at the temples. He looked around forty, with a great body — he obviously worked out.

"Mrs. Greene, we have the results of Michael's lab tests," he said, holding the chart and looking up at Marty.

"I'm Ms. Greene," I said, feeling irritated.

Dr. Gorgeous looked confused.

"We're both his parents," I started to explain.

"Oh, I see," he said, stiffening.

"No, we're not lesbians," I said, annoyed, my voice rising.

"Lizzie," Marty said in a hushed voice, looking miserable.

"Well, this is none of my business," the doctor said, looking at me and trying to contain himself. "I will need a signature on these labs, and I just wanted to go over Michael's condition with you. By the way, I'm Dr. Pendleton."

Pendleton. Liz Pendleton. It sounded like the merger of two great clothing companies. We'd have the bridesmaids dressed in Tartan plaid. "Of course," I said, straightening. "How is he?"

"Well," Dr. Gorgeous said, all doc, forgetting he was a hunk. "Michael has sustained quite a large spider bite. His white count is way up and we've brought his fever down some, but we'll just have to wait and see how he continues to react. We've given him mega doses of antibiotics to fight the infection, but since it's in the lymph node area, we're concerned."

"Where did he bite him?" I asked.

"There, on the right shoulder," he said, gently pulling back the covers. I could see the redness and the marble marks on Michael's skin.

"Typically, patients will have a high fever anywhere from ten days to a month and will feel terrible. The skin will fall off to the bone and, depending on how much falls off, you may have to have a plastic surgeon graft it back on. He's pretty young, so it may just grow and regenerate on his own."

I felt sick. I wanted to throw up and die at the same time. Every muscle ached and the weight of the day was pounding down on me.

"Would you like to sit down, Ms. Greene?" he asked politely. "We could get you a cold drink."

"I just need a minute," I said, trying to hold my head up. I turned and went into the bathroom, ran the water, and threw up. Then I splashed cold water on my face and dried it with a towel. I rinsed my mouth out and turned off the water. I found a compact in my purse, dabbed some powder on my face, and smeared some lip-gloss on my chapped lips. I didn't know what I could do about the puffy eyes, but I ran my fingers through my hair to smooth it out a bit.

I looked like a train wreck, but better than before. I found a mint in the pocket of my purse, vigorously chewed on it, and used my earring stud to pick the food out of my teeth. I replaced the earring and hoped the doctor had left the room when I went back. No such luck. He was standing there with my drag queen ex-husband whose hair and makeup looked perfect, but Marty's wig might have been on a little crooked. Both had expectant looks on their faces, as if they thought I might fall into a million pieces at any moment. To be honest, I wasn't sure I wouldn't.

NINE

As he had my entire life, it was Dad who helped me. I slept by Michael's side all night in an uncomfortable fake leather chair. The next morning, Dad picked me up when Marty came to give me some relief. Dad didn't say much after we left the hospital room because he could barely be civil to Marty. He just couldn't look at her. Dad blamed himself for "letting me marry him" and he was angry at Marty for hurting Michael and me. I tried to explain it all, but Dad didn't believe in "those excuses." He was of a generation that stuck with things, which included your gender and basic genitalia.

Dad and I drove to the place where they impound the cars and found my little red Toyota Corolla on the lot. We gave the letter to the officer at the desk and waited.

"Oh yeah, that Tie-yoda," the officer said, rolling his eyes. My father stood silent, staring at the man. My father was a man's man. He was about five foot ten. He hunted and fished and had been a rancher for twenty years before he moved us to the city. Now he ran a little hardware/feed and grain store. It did a good business because he had the good sense to put it in a rural area. My father wasn't timid. He wasn't one to pick a fight, but he could hold his own. He'd fought in World War II and didn't take guff from anybody.

"Has there been any damage done to the car?" my father asked.

"Well, we had them drug dogs go over it pretty good and Pete relieved himself in the backseat," he said.

"Who is PETE?" my father asked, his anger rising. I was beyond words. My car would smell like urine. My ex-husband was a woman. The list went on.

"Pete's our lead drug dog, but he's kind of old. When he can't find drugs, he just pisses, uh, excuse me, urinates, on the place and leaves. That's how we knew there wasn't any drugs in the car," the officer said matter-of-factly.

"*I* could have told you there weren't any drugs in the car. It's *my* car and the only ones ever in it are my little boy and me. This is ridiculous, now I have a car that smells like pee and…"

"Yeah, and we had trouble putting those side panels back, plus there are a few rips in it. We thought Pete had found something, but he was just hungry and was trying to get them gummy bears that had fallen between the cracks. Pete loves gummy bears," the officer said, chuckling.

"I need to see your superior officer, the person in charge," my father said, taking off his sunglasses so the man could see he was serious.

"Dave hasn't made it in yet 'cuz he's picking up the donuts. We take turns you know."

"Take us to the car, please," my father said quietly. This man didn't know my father. If he's yelling, you're probably okay, but when he gets that quiet steely little voice, you better be careful. You better hide, because he's liable to deck you or take your head off or something.

"Sure, no problem," he said. "I got the keys right here. I'll have Tuck bring it around. It's parked kinda far back because of the smell."

"Oh, great," I said, wondering when this lucky streak would stop.

We followed the man outside and waited in the heat while "Tuck" brought my car around. Tuck turned out to be a kid of about seventeen, and his face looked like he'd eaten a thousand lemons. He left the engine running, threw it in park, and jumped out of the car. Tuck's black curly hair was damp and his glasses were fogged over.

"Man, that thing STINKS!" he said, handing the officer the keys.

We could smell the car from where we were standing.

"I'm not getting in that car," I said to my father.

"Neither of us is getting in that car," he said quietly. He turned to the Barney Fife standing next to us and simply said, "You'll hear from our attorney within twenty-four hours."

I knew what that meant: my cousin Tommy. Tommy was a really smart trial attorney and loved a fight. He'd take this on for the pure pleasure of it. Besides, we were family.

Dad drove me home, where my suitcase was waiting for me on my front porch. The airlines must have delivered it last night. He waited while I showered, put on fresh clothes, and threw in a load of laundry. I grabbed some of Michael's stuffed animals and a couple of his favorite storybooks. I blew my hair dry and made a feeble attempt at putting on makeup.

We were back at the hospital by eleven. Marty had left to open the store and my mother was there in her place. I have to say this about my mother: she could be annoying and self-involved, but she was a great mom when I was little, encouraging my every step from toddler to teenager. She made costumes, my clothes, and every curtain and bedspread I ever owned until I was almost thirty. She adored Michael. She was reading to him when we came in and she had made them each a puppet. Michael's puppet covered his hand that lay across his stomach. He was watching her with sleepy eyes and a soft smile.

"And then, the wolf said, lowering her voice, I'll huff, and I'll puff, and I'll blow your house down!"

Michael mouthed the last five words with her.

"It looks like someone is feeling better!" I smiled, feeling genuinely relieved.

Michael turned and looked at me.

"Hi, Mommy!" he said weakly.

"Hi, Pumpkin Boy," I said, feeling the tears tickle the edge of my eyes. "Mommy slept here all night with you, do you remember?"

He nodded in the affirmative.

My mother was glad to see us, but I knew she wanted Michael to herself. She liked the attention, and it made her feel good to entertain him.

"That good-looking Dr. Pendleton stuck his head in the door a while ago to check on Michael. He said he'd be back later. He's single, you know."

"How did you know that, Mother?" I asked warily.

"He wasn't wearing a ring, so I worked it in the conversation."

"I bet you did," I said, shaking my head.

"It wouldn't hurt you to go out with a real…"

"Mom," I said, overriding her sentence and tossing a glance at Michael. I didn't want her badmouthing Marty in front of Michael. He had enough to deal with and he wasn't feeling well.

Dr. Gorgeous came in behind me. I smelled his cologne first. I turned around and stared into his large brown eyes.

"Dr. Pendleton," I said, sounding school girly and breathless. I lowered my voice an octave, "It's good to see you here."

He smiled at me. I didn't think it was all professional, hoped it wasn't, but I couldn't tell for sure. He smiled warmly at Michael and looked at his chart. "This little fellow is a trooper and is responding well to the antibiotics. We are trying to keep him well hydrated, which is why he has to stay on the IV, and we want to keep him here for at least a week because we want to watch that bite. When the skin starts to slough, there's further chance of infection and we need to have 24-hour care keeping the wound clean."

"Thank you," I said, feeling grateful.

"May I see you outside?" Dr. Gorgeous asked.

"Me?" I responded. Did I just say that? Why couldn't I have responded with something witty?

"Yes," he said, nodding and smiling, "you."

He held the door open as I walked through it, and he walked with me down the hall without saying anything. He waited until he saw an unoccupied waiting room and indicated we should sit down.

I looked at him and held my breath, not just because he was devastatingly handsome or that his cologne made me weak in the knees, but because I was afraid. I was afraid he would tell me that Michael wouldn't recover properly or something I couldn't even face.

"Even though he's doing much better today, Michael is still very sick," he began. "When the skin begins falling off, it will probably get black and ugly and possibly fall off all the way to the bone. This is painful, it stinks, and he'll still be running a fever. We'll have nurses taking care of him, but you—or whoever—will have to watch him. We'll keep him fairly sedated so he won't want to be so active. It could run longer than a week, it could be a month."

I thought about the little bit of vacation time I had left.

"You and the other Mrs. Greene may want to trade off," he said politely.

"Marty was Michael's dad until six months ago when he decided to change his way of life and become a woman," I told him.

"I see," he said, his expression guarded. "Are you still married?"

"No," I said, "it was just too much. But we're still friends. We've been friends since we were seven years old," I said sadly.

"That's good," he said. "I mean, uh, the friends part. This is kind of a unique situation. I bet it's been hard on you and Michael."

"Very hard," I said, nodding.

"Maybe you could use a nice dinner out somewhere," he suggested.

"Is that your professional opinion?" I asked with a smile.

"My prescription for good mental health," he said, grinning. "How about some evening after Michael goes to sleep, I finish my rounds, and we grab a bite to eat somewhere?"

"Really?" I asked, not believing my ears.

"Sure. Doctors eat, even overworked ones, and I imagine photographers eat, too, or is that the right label for what you do?"

"I am a photographer/camera person. I shoot film and video, but how did you know that?"

"I saw your station key ring and remembered the name and some of your work from Channel 8. I saw that documentary you did on Greenwood and the one on the Oil Barons. That series won some award, didn't it?"

"One state, one regional. Nice plaques on a wall. I don't want to brag."

"Well, I'd like to hear all about it. Let's go out tomorrow night. You look beat and I think you need some sleep. Go home tonight and rest. You can't sleep on those chairs very well," he said.

"I just can't leave him," I said, shaking my head.

"Then I'm having him moved to a suite, where you can have a proper bed and sleep next to him," he said. "I guess if I get here early enough, I'll see what you look like first thing in the morning."

TEN

Michael was in the hospital for almost a month. It was a terrible experience, one made much better by Dr. Gorgeous, uh, George. Dr. George Pendleton: witty, charming, incredibly good looking, intelligent, and rich. One night, while Michael was still in the hospital, he brought me to his house for a candlelight dinner. We had broiled lobster, a wonderful, marinated salad, fresh asparagus, and that crunchy bread from the bakery. He made hot fudge sundaes for dessert. I had a very large glass of some expensive merlot and mellowed out.

His house was amazing. I'd been in lots of these old houses around Utica Square when I was growing up, but this was one I hadn't seen. It faced the Rose Garden, and the yard was covered with beautiful magnolias, pears, maples, and tall pine trees. When you walked in the front door, the stairway spiraled up to the second floor with richly carved cherry wood banisters and a beautifully woven burgundy-red paisley patterned carpet.

The furniture was mostly soft leather and smelled extremely masculine. The tables were cherry to match the wood, and the artwork was tasteful and colorful—some city scenes and some countryside pictures. The high tin ceilings held huge ceiling fans. They looked original. The mantel in the living room was old travertine marble and the end irons were true antiques. All the doorknobs were glass, and the kitchen had a polished black-and-white tile floor with an antique six-burner stove. Everything was immaculate.

"Would you like to see the upstairs? It's a little messy," he said apologetically.

"Well, uh…" I hesitated.

"I promise not to take advantage of you in any way," he said, smiling warmly.

Why not? I thought. This was my best and only black skirt and this blouse had cost me forty bucks.

"Okay," I said, and smiled demurely.

He led and I followed, which was good, because I didn't particularly want him following me up the stairs. Sometimes lobster makes me toot, and how would that be?

The upstairs was lined with cabinets with expensive ornate brass pulls. The hall bath had a shiny red claw-footed tub on brass legs with thick navy striped wallpaper. The mirror over the pedestal sink was antiqued gold. The sink looked new, but authentic, and the cabinet next to it was weathered. The shower curtain matched the paper and was pulled back with a brass tie. There was a tiny skylight above the sink area and a small window over the tub.

"Here's the hall bath," he said proudly. "I had to redo a lot when I moved in. I put in the skylight and refinished the windows. I made that half bath under the stairs because there was no bathroom downstairs and this one was pitted out."

"Do you like to do this kind of thing?" I asked.

"Yes, when I have the time. I worked my way through medical school doing handiwork and carpentry, so I have experience. There are four bedrooms up here, my bedroom and two guest rooms and a project room. My study is downstairs."

"Projects?" I asked.

"Yeah, like if I want to make something or work on something, I do it in there."

I surveyed the bedrooms. They were tailored in style: one was in greens and the other in reds. The project room was just as George had said: a project room. He had some wood and a saw-horse in the middle of the floor. There were drop cloths piled in a corner with some cans of paint and a couple of small pieces of furniture that looked like they were in the process of being refinished.

"Now I want to show you *my* room," he said, a huge smile spreading across his face.

I felt a little weak at the knees, but of course, I followed him. I was slightly buzzed, and half wanted something to happen. Who was I kidding? I hadn't had sex in forever and the only time I'd ever had it, it was with a woman-man. What would lovemaking be like with someone like this? I held my breath.

He turned the rheostat, and the darkened room was suddenly bathed in warm light. The ceiling fan gently swirled over a huge king-size mahogany four-poster bed covered with a plush burgundy corduroy comforter. The windows had dark plantation shutters on them. The room felt cool and serene.

"I made the bed myself," George said proudly.

For a split second I almost wisecracked him. I mean, Michael makes his bed every day and he's a kid.

"You're kidding?" I said in a slightly mocking tone. "You *made* this? How long did it take you?"

"Oh, it took about a month because I still had to work. I sanded everything down and it has several coats of stain and then the finish took a lot of coats. I had to wait for it to dry."

Okay, so I'm an idiot. Maybe he hadn't noticed I was mocking him. He didn't seem to. Even doctors aren't always swift.

"Wow, this is wonderful. Your room looks great," I said, thinking of things I needed to stash away before he ever came to my place, like my ceramic goose collection Marty had started for me when we were married. Screw it; I couldn't get rid of that. That's what was missing. There were no collections or pictures of people.

"Did you do all of this yourself? No girlfriend or wife in the picture?"

"I did it all myself."

"Have you ever been married?"

"Twenty years ago. We were young, and it didn't last long," he said.

"Well," I said, taking note. "You must be very proud of this place."

"I am. It took me a long time to get this. There were a lot of us growing up and although we lived in a pretty big space, we didn't have anything nice."

"Tell me about your family. Where are you from?" I asked, genuinely interested, setting aside that I was standing near one of the most gorgeous men I had ever seen with a king-size bed just inches away.

"Not much to tell." He shrugged, putting an arm around me and escorting me out of the bedroom. "I was the second oldest of a bunch of kids. I left home when I was seventeen with my big brother who was nine months older, and we never looked back."

"You mean you've never been back home again?"

"Nope," he said, his jaw firm.

"What happened?" I asked as we got to the bottom of the stairs.

"Nothing horrible. My brother and I just thought it was time to go. My parents had a lot of kids, and we were two more to feed."

"How many kids?"

"I don't really know now. My mom was having the third set of twins when we left. Twins run in my family. It usually skips a generation, but there are twins on both sides, so it doubles. Anyway, when I left there were twelve of us, with two more on the way."

"Catholic?" I asked.

"Morman," he said. "I could care less about any of that now."

"Religion or the family?"

"Religion."

"Do you believe in God?" I asked, hoping he'd say yes.

"Yeah," he said as if somebody were asking him if he'd like to go for pizza. "I mean, I'm basically a science guy, but I've seen some unexplainable things happen. What about you?"

"Yes. Always. I've believed in God since I was a little girl."

"I don't have anything to do with those people anymore. Better get back to Michael."

It felt like someone had dumped a bucket of ice between us. George definitely didn't like talking about the past and he didn't like talking about religion. I should have left it alone, but as a journalist, I'm always curious. Look what it did for the cat.

As we got closer to the hospital, the dark clouds passed, and he started being his old self again. As our relationship progressed, I would see those dark clouds only a few times. I learned what to say and what not to say to bring on the storm.

ELEVEN

1987

Here's why you're supposed to wait to have sex until you get married: it's not because you'll get pregnant, although that's always a possibility, and it's not because everyone will know, because you can't always tell despite everything my mother told me. Basically, it's because it just confuses things. I know this from firsthand experience with Dr. Gorgeous.

We had been officially dating for several months. He had passed the test with Michael. He'd been wonderful and even played pirates with him on his birthday. Between George and my father, they gave him every boy toy one could imagine for a seven-year-old. He got full fishing gear and a toy rifle from my dad, much to my disapproval. George gave him an entire big box of sports stuff. Marty gave him a set of paints and an easel, which was fine. Michael loved it all: the perfect little diplomat. George had won Michael's approval, not just because he gave him gifts, but also because they had bonded during his sickness.

Michael still had a pretty bad scar. He seemed a little more sensitive now, afraid that something would hit his wound. George practiced with him and slowly worked Michael through his fear. I was grateful to George for that.

It was Thanksgiving weekend. I had Marty over to the house because she couldn't go to her parents' house. My parents were tolerant of Marty and had kind of gotten used to her. I had decided to give in and refer to Marty as a female, but I asked Marty not to wear anything flamboyant. For once, could she wear something simple with jeans and sneakers so that it wasn't so … so flaming. She complied. We all dressed casually. I sat Dad at the head of the table and Mom on the other end. I put Michael between Dad and Marty. George and I sat opposite them. I was close to the kitchen. Claire and Dork called and decided to come at the last minute. Glam called and asked if she could come because she was fighting with her parents. Okay, I had a big table. We'd just sit closer. I kept folding chairs in the garage.

Ironically, we had all prepared the meal. Marty had spent the night in the guest room, so she helped me make the stuffing and stuff the bird early in the morning. Mom and Dad brought the pies. As per tradition, Dad chopped the pecans. George brought several bottles of different wines and all the raw veggies with a dip. Claire brought the homemade cranberry ring and the green bean casserole. Glam brought store-bought rolls, which were kind of squished because her Great Dane, Daisy, sat on them in the car. She also brought Daisy. It wouldn't have been so bad, I guess, if Daisy hadn't been in heat. The Saint Bernard next door jumped the fence and we had to shoot the hose on them. Thankfully, the water wasn't frozen but it was still quite cold. Mom kept Michael busy when all the ruckus was going on, as the backyard activity was rated "R."

We made it through the meal with a few unpleasantries.

My sister, Claire: "Oh, it's so nice to see that Lizzie is dating a *real* man. I bet you're rich, too, since you're a doctor. How much do you make?"

Glam: "Lizzie's *extremely* inexperienced in the romance department, so don't take advantage of her."

Mom: "Does it make you uncomfortable to sit at the table with a man dressed as a woman, Dr. Pendleton? If so, we can have Marty removed."

Dork (a.k.a., Malcom): "Just what do they do to you, Marty, old man? Do they cut it off? Ouch! Your boobs look pretty real." (Fortunately, Michael was out of the room.)

Still, all in all, it wasn't a total disaster. Marty held her head high and didn't dignify the unkind remarks with an answer. She did tell Dork if he wanted to know the procedure she would undergo in January, she'd be happy to give him some literature to read. Dork looked kind of sheepish and declined the offer.

George took it all in and tolerated everybody with good humor. I watched his face for the storm clouds, but they never appeared. My mother grilled him about his family. He said they were all celebrating at home today, but it was too far to travel. This casual comment made me uncomfortable. I knew he hadn't seen them in over two decades, so why did he act like he'd talked to them this morning? Oh, let it go, Lizzie.

After the dishes were done and the football games were watched and everyone had gone home except Marty and George, I saw George put his arm around Marty and ask if she were going to stay the night. Marty said she didn't care; she could stay if we needed her to or if we wanted to go out. George told her he thought I needed a break.

"How about you go up and get out of your turkey outfit, slip into something comfortable and let's take a drive, maybe hang out at my place for a while?" George asked me. Who could resist that gorgeous smile?

"Sure, but we have a tradition," I said.

"What's that?"

"Christmas lights at Utica Square. They turn on the lights and sing carols to start the season and it wouldn't be Thanksgiving if we didn't go. Michael's been every year since he was little."

"Okay," George agreed, pleasantly. "Do you want to go, sport?"

Michael agreed. "Can Marty go?"

"Of course," I said, smiling.

We took two cars. Michael rode with Marty, and George and I took his little Mercedes convertible. He put the top down and the air was a bit icy, so I bundled up in my coat, hat, and scarf and I was fine. In fact, I was more than fine, I was perfect.

We all saw the lights come on and sang the carols. This was a new experience for George. He turned out to be an amazing tenor. I noticed Marty wasn't really singing, just mouthing the words. It made me a little sad. He/she had always sung the carols before. Poor soul, there were so many transitions for her, so many transitions for us all.

Marty and Michael went home after the concert. George and I went to his house, and he built a big, roaring fire. I stretched out on his leather couch and eagerly accepted a large glass of Merlot. George slipped off my shoes and started rubbing my feet.

"You've had a hard day," he murmured. "You deserve a massage. Did I ever tell you I put myself through school as a masseuse?"

"I thought you put yourself through school doing handiwork and carpentry."

"That was medical school. When I was in undergrad, I was a masseuse."

"Where'd you go to school again?" I could feel my words began to slur a bit.

"Shh. Lay down on that rug and I'll rub your shoulders."

I complied. This was glorious. I felt myself drifting down into this wonderful abyss. I was warm, mellow and…asleep.

I woke up in George's bed, naked with a smile on my face. The smell of bacon and eggs wafted up the stairs. I remembered last night before I went to sleep and when I was awakened in the middle of the night. The man had skills—and all for me.

Breakfast arrived on a black tray with a single rose, fresh orange juice on ice, bacon and eggs, and the most important part: George in a black silk robe with nothing on underneath it.

I would experience this kind of wonder throughout the next few months. George occupied most of my thoughts and I had a new subject to photograph: George. I gave George some photographs I had taken of us framed and he put them on his desk, the only personal photographs in the house.

Things were heating up big time. I felt like I was going to burst. Lust can be a scary thing because it occupies your thoughts, and you forget to think. You just feel. That was the way it was with Dr. Gorgeous. I would think for a little while and then I'd forget to think and frankly, it felt great *most of the time.*

TWELVE

1988

In January, Marty had surgery, after successfully completing two years of therapy and a year of being a woman, except for the genitalia. For the surgery, Michael stayed with my parents and I flew to Colorado to be with Marty. I was all she had. Her mother had the flu, and her father still wasn't talking to her. Her sisters were too busy, and the few friends she had at the store needed to stay and run the store.

We almost didn't make it to Denver. They closed the airport right after we got there. I was worried sick because I didn't want us to both die and leave Michael an orphan. We had recently redone our wills and Marty had upped her life insurance policy in case she didn't make it through the surgery.

The doctor was kind and very professional. He couldn't believe I was there, especially when he discovered our relationship. Marty proudly told him I was her best friend and the mother of our child. The doctor looked at me with admiration.

The operation took eight hours. Apparently, Marty lost a lot of blood. After four hours, one of the residents came out and explained the situation. I gave blood right then. I called George, and he was reassuring.

"I don't want Marty to die," I whispered, hot tears clouding my vision.

"I know, baby. Marty is a good person…a gentle soul."

That was a good description of Marty. I thought back to our growing up together and our marriage. I remembered how he struggled with intimacy with me. He was affectionate but never passionate. Poor guy, he was just a misfit his whole life. I waited and waited. I called George one more time, but he was busy with patients.

At the end of a long day, Marty came through the operation. I slept in her room the first night but stayed in a hotel the rest of the week. After seven days, she was released and we flew home. She stayed at our house for recovery, which took a while. Michael read to her every night.

I knew she was feeling better because she was putting together the packet to send to New York to change her birth certificate to to reflect her new status as a woman. She had a letter from her therapist in Tulsa, a letter from the doctor in Denver who verified her gender reassignment, and luckily, the doctor's sister worked in state records in Albany where they recorded the birth certificates. Marty and her sisters, Mary, Mollie, and Missy, were all born in Albany. Their father had a contract there for almost a decade before he took another job in Tulsa.

Once Marty got this new birth certificate back, she could live her life as a woman and even remarry.

By February, I was ridiculously in love/lust with George. We talked on the phone a couple of times a day and when we were apart at night, which was pretty often because of Michael, we talked for a couple of hours on the phone.

Now you'd think with all that talking that we knew everything about each other.

Nope. George asked me a lot of questions and I talked his ear off. I would ask him questions and he always had a way of turning a phrase or changing the subject. He could tell me in detail how to build something or how an operation was done or why the Sooners could play football so well with that wishbone thing, but he never talked about his childhood or his family. That was okay. What difference did it make?

George was extremely busy at the hospital but managed to get Valentine's weekend off. Marty stayed with Michael, and we flew to New York. We stayed at the Plaza. I had never been to New York. We rode in a horse-drawn carriage, we took limousine rides around the city, and we went to museums and the theater. George and I shopped at Saks and Lord and Taylor. He wanted to buy me some new clothes and wouldn't let me look at any of the prices.

On Valentine's night, we went to the top of the Empire State Building. The night was clear. We could see the twinkle of lights across the city in all directions. George held my hand tightly and kissed me.

"I want to give you the world," he said passionately.

"I don't need the world," I said, my voice almost hoarse. "I just need you."

He reached into his pocket and held up my hand to his lips.

"Will you marry me?" he asked, looking deeply into my eyes.

"Yes!" I said, and with that he slipped a ring on my left hand. The stone was so big; it was blinding…a two-and-a-half carat emerald cut diamond.

I was mesmerized by it. I had never seen anything so beautiful and repeatedly told him so. George grabbed my hand and took me back downstairs where our limousine was waiting. We returned as quickly as one can in New York to the Plaza and didn't leave our room for two days until we had to fly back home.

We set the wedding date for the end of April, when the weather is pleasant, but not too hot. We decided to have the wedding at the Philbrook Museum of Art in the garden, with a reception at the museum. George insisted on paying for everything. He wanted it to be magical for me.

Marty helped me shop for a dress. George had set up an account at Miss Jackson's for me and insisted that I buy the dress and trousseau and put it on his tab. Marty was like a kid in a candy shop and so was I. I had never really shopped at Miss Jackson's because the T-shirts are forty bucks and I could just never pay that kind of money.

We chose something elegant and simple, with a beaded bodice. It was candlelight white, which the bridal consultant said was appropriate. I didn't wear a traditional veil but had a ring of fresh flowers for my hair with a shock of tulle that dropped almost to the floor. The dress had soft, flowing chiffon sleeves. The dress was slightly Victorian in style with a built-in train.

Since we were going to Jamaica for our honeymoon, and the store had a full array of cruise wear, I decided on lots of tropical colors. I bought beautiful sundresses and soft shirts and shorts. George had said Marty could pick out something, so she chose a pink Channel suit.

Glam and Gloria were my bridesmaids this time. Well, Glam was a bridesmaid; Gloria was the matron of honor. Claire was feeling defiant toward our mother for the umpteenth time, so who knew what she'd wear or if she'd even show up.

This time the flowers were purple irises and yellow roses, but no daises. The dresses were in those colors. Mom wore her same gold dress because she could still get into it and thought it was a waste not to wear it again. I didn't care.

George looked handsome in his tux, and I felt beautiful in my gown. The flowers were rich and fragrant. Since we hadn't been going to church, I asked Gloria's now husband, Fred, pastor of a local Baptist Church, to perform the ceremony. Gloria can sing like an angel, so I asked her to surprise me and sing something. She told me not to worry, she'd take care of the music.

I never dreamed she would go so far. George had hired a string quartet to play while people were mingling and arriving.

The delicate flowery music echoed against the museum's gleaming tile floor and elegant surroundings. Once the processional started, everyone floated in. When we were all in place, we looked expectantly at Gloria for the solo. She turned to the organist and said, "Hit it!"

Suddenly, the halls echoed with the sound of the entire church choir, all ninety-seven of them, whom I understand had made quite a commotion out front when they arrived in three big yellow church buses. Well, now they were here, in flaming orange choir robes, singing the theme song from *Cabaret* at the top of their voices. Once the choir was all in place behind the congregation and on either side, the formerly somewhat sedated crowd happily applauded.

"Liz and George, we wanted to kick off your marriage the right way. Remember, with us, you've always got a friend," Gloria said, smiling. With this, Glam and Marty moved in close to Gloria, whipped out portable microphones, and began singing, "You've Got a Friend" by Carole King. George looked a little embarrassed, but pleased, and I was so touched. After their song, I hugged all three of them. Then Gloria and Fred dedicated the final song to us, "Tonight, I Celebrate My Love," backed by the string quartet. It sounded like Roberta Flack had come to the wedding.

The entire room was emotional after this presentation. George and I were so moved by the music and the moment that we were trembling. We managed to get through our vows. Fred led us with flair and enthusiasm and even had us repeat the vows in a big voice, which made us both laugh.

Thankfully, it didn't rain. With the infusion of a hundred more people at the reception, things were pretty lively. Everyone loved the food, and although I had worried briefly that we might have a shortage, Gloria assured me she had taken care of it ahead of time and had warned George. He was happy to do it. I was sad that nobody came from George's family. He hadn't invited them. My mother kept asking questions. I told her it was none of her business.

One of the other photographers from the station shot the wedding for me. Michael looked like a little man in his suit as George's best man. His two other groomsmen were fellow doctors.

Marty cried. It might have been the new hormones.

"I'm so happy for both of you."

"Thank you. You did a pretty good job up there singing," George said sincerely, squeezing Marty's shoulder. "I have you to thank as well as Liz for making me the happiest man on earth."

This was one of those awkward moments that we slid through. Marty smiled and then made some excuse about finding Michael.

When it was over, we caught the limousine home. We spent our first night at George's house. Michael and I would move in after we got back. I was going to rent out my house to Glam for a song.

"Can you believe you're Mrs. George Pendleton?" he asked, nibbling on my ear.

"It's like a fairytale," I whispered. I looked at my ring for the thousandth time.

"Life is a Cabaret, my dear," he sang. "You don't have to work now, you know, you can just stay home."

Shock.

"No, I have to work," I said.

"Well, I have enough money to provide everything you need and you won't be so tired."

"I don't work just for the money, George. I work because I love it."

"Okay baby, we'll see."

I could barely sleep that night. Maybe it was because I was so excited from the reception and the beauty of the day and maybe because that "we'll see" was nagging in the back of my brain. George quickly made me forget any doubts I had at that moment. It would continue to be a series of one romantic moment after another until we got home from Jamaica.

THIRTEEN

George didn't really want us to move much of our stuff into his house because it was already furnished. Michael moved his toys and things in, I moved in clothing and toiletries, plus my desk and photography equipment. Even though I shot film and video for the station, I still liked taking and developing still photos. Let's face it, I was basically giving a furnished house to Glam.

George's house had a guesthouse in the back that was attached to the garage. I moved my desk, books, and equipment in there. George hired someone to make me a darkroom. We hired someone to knock out the low ceiling and finish the beams. This made it a great studio for me.

We moved Michael's things into the bedroom next to the bathroom. His room was bigger in this house and he had a larger closet, so this was an upgrade for him. He loved it.

When people move in together there are always adjustments, and we were blending a family as well. George got along pretty well with Michael. Michael was one of those children who never gave anybody any trouble, so the blending process was easy.

I think I was having more trouble than Michael. A little boy is happy anywhere he has his toys and his mom. Marty came by from time to time when we wanted to go out, but Marty didn't want to stay at George's, so Michael spent the night at Marty's. I was fine with it. Marty hadn't met anyone yet, so there was not the adjustment to a new person.

I know you caught the fact that I keep referring to "our" house as "George's" house. That's because it was George's house. It was still in his name. The phone was in his name, and he didn't really want me to have anything of mine in the house except for a few personal items. I felt like a guest, and as the days passed, the darkness of the house got to me. I felt a longing to paint a room yellow or at least rearrange the furniture to make it mine.

But I didn't. I didn't because I didn't want to invite the storm clouds. I kept telling myself that it would take time for us all to adjust to each other. George suggested that I quit my job again, but I refused. Nicely of course, but I refused.

"What would I do all day?" I asked him.

"There are civic organizations. Lots of the doctors' wives work in the gift shop."

"George! Do you know me? My documentaries have won awards. Do you really see me working in a gift shop with the other wives? Next, you'll have me playing golf all day and joining the Junior League."

"It was just a suggestion," he said, his eyes becoming playful. "You're cute when you're mad."

"Don't," I warned.

"Come on, Liz, don't be mad. You don't want to be mad at me," he teased.

It was true. I didn't want to be mad at him. What was I feeling? I didn't know and really, he had done nothing wrong. It was just a silly conversation.

"Let's take Michael for pizza," he suggested, knowing going places with Michael always made me happy. I loved feeling like a family.

"Okay," I agreed.

It was always like that with us. Wanting to keep the peace, I never really blew up. I might power-up a bit. Then George would diffuse anger, or his storm clouds would gather, and I'd change the subject. However, that dynamic changed on our first Fourth of July as a married couple.

The Fourth of July is special in my family because it's my father's birthday. We always have a big cookout and invite family, friends, and neighbors. We make hot dogs and hamburgers on the grill. Mom makes homemade potato salad. I make the beans and the gigantic double chocolate cake, and my sister makes the layered Jell-O salad. We take turns cranking homemade ice cream. Yes, we still have Mom and Dad's old ice-cream maker because he won't hear of getting the electric kind. His *is* better; I've had both.

We had decided to have the celebration at "our" house this year because we live closer to the Arkansas River and there would be the inevitable fireworks. We had already planned our course of action. We'd park our cars at George's friend's house along the river so we wouldn't get towed.

People started arriving about four. George was on call during the day, so he was at the hospital. He planned to join us around 5:30 or 6:00 p.m., long before it would be dark and his hamburger would get cold. Michael and I had put red, white, and blue citronella candles at all the tables, which were decorated with red-checked vinyl tablecloths.

Marty was the first to arrive. She had on a simple red, white, and blue striped blouse, white pants, and red pumps. I warned her to forgo any sandal wearing. Any way you looked at it, her feet were still man feet—minus the hair. I didn't care how many layers of polish you put on those babies; they were still ugly.

Mom and Dad arrived carrying stuff from the car. Dad hauled in bags of ice. Mom carried the food. They were dressed in matching American flag shirts mom had made from double knit fabric.

Mom wore a pair of navy pants with red-jeweled sandals. Dad had on a pair of red shorts with white sneakers. If you can't wear red shorts to your birthday party, when can you wear them?

My sister arrived with Dork and his two nephews. My sister had yet to conceive. Jason and Justin were two years apart, but Justin, the youngest, was as tall as Jason. They were nine and eleven and both kind of pudgy. My mother was already suggesting the boys should eat the salad instead of birthday cake. Jason started to tear up, but Justin just rolled his eyes and they both went and played with Michael. Claire looked after them with a smile. She was wearing her size four red tennis dress with stars-and-stripes Keds.

Can I just say that I've never been big on holiday wear? Michael and George had bought me some Uncle Sam earrings as a surprise, which George thought were priceless, so I was wearing those, and a white T-shirt, jean shorts, and brown sandals.

The hours are a blur now, but it seemed the time went by swiftly. Dad had fired up the grill and was cooking. We probably had about twenty people in the backyard, ranging from seventy to seven.

At first, I figured she was just another friend of someone's, so I didn't pay much attention. The gate was already open. Glam and Gloria were sitting at the closest table to the fence, and I had just left them to go refill the lemonade pitcher.

"Excuse me," she said, clearing her throat. I turned around to see a young woman with dyed jet black hair, dark makeup, and long dark red nails standing in our yard. She was wearing a black lace shirt with black pants and an oversized stuffed knapsack on her back.

"Yes," I said, "are you lost or are you here for the party?"

"Does George Pendleton still live here?" she asked evenly, almost defiantly.

My heart skipped a beat.

"I'm George Pendleton," I heard George say, coming through the back kitchen door.

"Well, hello everyone," she said, with a wicked smile. "Hello, Dad, I'm Kendra, remember, your daughter?"

There was stunned silence.

Then I did something I'd never done in my life: I fainted.

FOURTEEN

Why my mother felt a need to dump a bag of ice on me, I'll never know. What kind of maternal instinct is that? Anyway, it woke me up and George's daughter-I-never-knew-about was still standing there with an icy glare on her face. George, obviously figuring I had enough people to help me, decided to retreat inside the house. What kind of doctor instinct is that? Maybe he was looking for antiseptic; I had skinned my legs.

When I could move and ignore the pounding in the back of my head, I sat up on my elbows. Glam handed me some paper napkins and I wiped my face. I was sopping wet from the ice.

"Helen, I don't know what made you think to dump ice on her," Dad said angrily as he helped me to my feet.

"I thought she'd get brain damage if she stayed out too long," Mom retorted.

"Well, the only brain damage around here is yours," he muttered. "Are you all right, sweetheart?" Dad patted my shoulder. My mother, miffed at Dad for yelling at her in front of people and at me for fainting, huffed off to find my sister to be consoled.

"Who are you? Are you the girlfriend or the latest wife?" Kendra demanded, looking at me with her hands on her hips. She snickered. "I bet you didn't know about me or my brother."

"Your what?" I asked, my head pounding.

"I have a brother a year younger than me. He may fly out this week if I give him the go ahead. I decided to fly out here today because it's my eighteenth birthday and I wanted to celebrate my independence from Dad."

"Where are you from?" I asked, seeing double of her.

"Sunny Florida. My mom moved us down there. Dad sends child support every month. I'm surprised you didn't know. I'm sure you have access to his precious checkbook," she sneered.

I didn't even know where his checkbook was. He paid all our bills at his office. That wasn't that big of a deal, but two children I had known nothing about was a *big* deal.

"Oh my," my mother said, sitting down, speechless for once.

"Old Georgie boy is going to have some 'splainin' to do," Glam said quietly.

I looked at Marty, maybe out of habit, maybe because we had been through so much together. She had tears in her eyes.

"Well," I said, "this is a nice surprise. I'm Liz; I'm your dad's wife, so I guess that makes me your stepmom."

"I've had so many. Well, he usually doesn't marry them. I wouldn't know though. He left when I was five and I've only seen him twice since then. You probably don't know about Natalie's boys by Dad—twins, they're nine. We met them last year. I understand there's another set of twin boys by someone named Sarah; they're about four. I think she lives in Oklahoma."

My head was pounding.

"You'll want to come inside and freshen up after your long trip," I said.

"Oh, I don't mind sitting out here and meeting the new fam," she said, mock smiling at everybody.

"Excuse me," I said, looking around at my gaping family and friends. I took off across the yard and went inside. George was sitting in his study having a stiff drink.

"Six kids, George? When were you going to tell me? I didn't even know you ever had children. George?" I demanded.

The storm clouds had returned. George was muttering and mumbling to himself.

"George, talk to me," I demanded. "I feel like you're a total stranger. What have you duped me into here?"

"Nothing's changed," he said after a long moment of silence.

"What do you mean, nothing's changed? You have a living, breathing, teenager out there and I think she plans on staying here with us."

"Well, she can't stay here," George said. "We have no room for her."

"We have room for her," I said. "What's the matter with you? She's your daughter."

"I have more feeling for Michael than I do for her," he said stoically.

"I don't know what to say to that," I said, glaring at him. "How can you not have feelings for your own child?"

He faltered a moment. "I don't love her mother anymore."

"So? She's still your daughter—and what about her brother? Is it true? Are there six kids?"

"Yes."

"Are there more than six?" I asked, incredulous.

"No, just six that I know of."

"Well, where are they? Do you see them?"

"No. You know me. I like order. I don't want kids around here."

"What about Michael?"

"Michael's different. He's a great kid."

"Well, maybe some of these others are too. And what if we have children?"

"I didn't know you wanted children. I thought Michael was enough. He is for me."

"I guess so, Dr. Half a Dozen. I just don't know you, George. I mean, I can't believe you have six kids and you don't see them."

"I didn't marry all the women, just the first one. The last two thought they'd trick me into marriage by getting pregnant, and I showed them. I pay child support though, to every one of them."

"You could probably buy a yacht with what you're spending on child support," I said.

"I make a good living. I don't see you *or* Michael wanting for anything," he said, narrowing his eyes.

"Hey buddy, in case you didn't notice, I wasn't the little match girl when I married you. I don't know what the other women were like, but I have a career and I'm good at it." I was furious.

"I didn't plan on falling in love with you," he said in an angry tone.

"Well, same here. We probably did this all too fast. I didn't really ask enough questions and…"

"Oh, you asked questions, all right. That's all you do is ask questions," he said, his arms flailing in the air.

"And you avoid answering, George. You're a master at it."

"Well, maybe some things are private," he said.

"Like not telling your wife about your SIX children?" I yelled. I never yell, but I did then.

"Hi kids, having fun?" Kendra interrupted, with a devilish smile on her face.

"Go upstairs to your room," George bellowed.

"And where would that be? I don't even know where the stairs are, Daddy Dearest. Remember, I've never been here?"

George sat miserably on the edge of his overstuffed leather chair.

"It's not her fault," I said, "she's just a kid. The least you can do is to make her feel welcome. You haven't seen her in all these years, and you haven't even hugged her."

"Who are you to tell me what to do?" George demanded.

"I'm nobody, George, I'm nobody," I said quietly. I passed Kendra on my way out the doorway and up the backstairs. "Excuse me,"

I whispered. Kendra studied my face and for a moment looked almost sympathetic. Then her face hardened.

My head was pounding. I went into our bathroom and threw up. I looked out the bathroom window at my family and friends below. They were quietly disassembling the party and making their way to their cars. I didn't have the heart to stop them.

There was a soft knock at the bathroom door.

"Go away for now, please," I said.

"It's me," Marty said quietly.

I opened the door to see her concerned face, my best friend standing there in red pumps. She hugged me and I cried.

"He has six kids and he never told me," I said, gulping for air.

"I know, I heard," she said, rubbing my back. "Do you have any idea what you're going to do?"

"No," I wailed. "My whole life changed in the last half hour. I feel like I'm falling over the edge of a cliff."

"Well, you and George talk it out. He may have had his reasons for not telling you. Maybe he was afraid you wouldn't marry him."

"Why is this happening to me?" I cried.

"I don't know, Lizzie, but you'll figure it out. Give yourself a little time. Don't make any rash decisions. I'll take Michael for a few days until you can work through all of this. He doesn't need to hear a lot of this stuff."

"I agree. Thank you, Marty," I said.

"I love you, you know," she said.

"I know. I love you, too."

Marty went downstairs to take Michael to the fireworks. The others must have quietly left when our fireworks erupted inside. The backyard was now empty.

I went back to the bedroom and sat down beside the bed. George must have come up here for a moment before going back downstairs. He'd obviously tossed the mail we had missed from yesterday on the bed. A letter addressed to me peeked through the stack. It was from my doctor's office, my lab report.

I opened it and read through it quickly. Everything was normal, blood pressure, cholesterol, thyroid, and the white count was normal for a *pregnant female of forty-five days.*

I felt a sinking in my stomach, and something pierced my heart. I must have missed a pill. Surely this couldn't be happening now? I wanted to take Michael and get as far away from this dungeon as I could. I pulled the covers back and stretched out on the bed. If only my head would stop pounding. Just a minute or two to close my eyes …. George and Kendra could work out their differences. Maybe Kendra and I could be friends. Maybe George and I could work things out. We could go to counseling. We could all start going to church. He had so many secrets. What else didn't I know? Let's face it. I'd married Dr. Jekyll.

FIFTEEN

George spent that night and all the next day at the hospital. I discovered this from his note on the bed that simply read, "Gone to the hospital, can't deal with all of this now. We'll talk in a few days when I've had a chance to think."

Nice. I woke up puffy eyed and nauseated. I threw up in the bathroom and washed my face twice. I was a wreck. My hair was scraggly, and I had a hormonal zit—two, in fact—and my boobs hurt like nobody's business. I looked at my stomach. My periods had always been irregular, and I hadn't noticed the tardiness of this last one. I had thought I was just gaining a little marriage weight. Duh.

I dabbed a bit of cream on my face and put on some makeup base. I slapped mascara on the world's shortest eyelashes and brushed the grunge out of my teeth. I threw on shorts and a T-shirt and went down the hall to the room where Kendra was sleeping. The bed was unmade and her clothes were on the floor.

I smelled coffee and went downstairs.

She didn't look any better than I did, bless her heart. Her dark eye makeup was smudged from crying. Her hair was a rat's nest and her long T-shirt had a stain on it.

"Good morning," I said.

"Good morning," she replied.

"How'd it go with your dad last night?" I asked, opening the refrigerator.

"It went."

I poured myself a glass of Michael's chocolate milk and grabbed some crackers off the shelf.

"Interesting breakfast," she commented.

"How about you, have you eaten something? Toast? Juice?"

"I can just do coffee right now," she said.

I nodded. There was a not-quite-awkward moment of silence.

"I'm sorry I messed up your family's party. I thought about it and felt bad for your dad. It was his birthday, wasn't it?" she asked, knowing the answer.

"Yes." I nodded and teared up. It wasn't because of Dad's missed birthday, although that was upsetting, but I'd missed the whole holiday with Michael. Oh, and then there was that small thing about being pregnant and my husband having six kids.

"Hey," she said, "you seem pretty nice. I was so mad at Dad; I didn't think about anything else. It didn't go like I thought."

"What did you think would happen?" I asked, sliding into the chair next to her.

"Which fantasy do you want to hear? There's the fantasy where he scoops me up in his arms and tells me how much he's missed me and that I have always been his little girl and he loves me. Then there's the fantasy where he gets on his knees and begs my forgiveness for missing every soccer game, recital, school program, and dance I've ever been to, not to mention graduation. Then there's the fantasy where I just shoot him, and he lays there dying and begs my forgiveness. But that last one isn't feasible because I don't like guns. You can't kill someone with a pair of eyebrow tweezers."

"I bet you could make him hurt, though," I said, half smiling. We both started laughing and crying.

"I'm sorry," we both said at the same time.

"This is a mess," I said, shaking my head.

"I didn't mean to cause you any trouble. I didn't know Dad was married again."

"We just got married," I said, "in April."

"That's a beautiful ring. He must love you. That's encouraging … that he loves *anyone*. I mean, it's a good sign, maybe you've changed him," she said wistfully.

"I don't know," I said, thinking out loud. "After last night, I don't feel like I know him at all."

"Well, my mom always said Dad was very, very smart and he was always generous because he never had anything as a kid, but he's emotionally unavailable."

I thought about that for a minute. I hadn't really had any problems since we'd been married or together. I remembered when I'd called about Marty, upset that he might die. George had been sweet then. But George was a doctor, and though he was sympathetic, he wasn't highly emotional.

"How long were they married?" I asked.

"Five years. They were in school."

"Is your mom Morman?"

"No, why?" she asked.

"I just wondered." I shrugged. "He told me he used to be Morman."

"Oh, yeah, I vaguely remember that. Nobody is religious in my family. I never went to church much."

"I grew up Methodist and we always went to church. I miss it. I think I'm going to start going back. I think I'm in a bit of a pickle here and I need some divine help," I said, chuckling.

Kendra smiled. She really was pretty. I could see some of George's features in her face. She had his eyes, but her bone structure was more delicate, probably like her mother's.

"Did you ever meet your grandparents or any of his family?" I asked.

She shook her head no. "None of them, and neither did Mom. Even when my brother and I came along, he didn't want to have anything to do with them."

"I wonder what happened there," I said. "What would make him so unavailable to his family and then unavailable to his own children?"

"I don't know. Mom never could figure it out either, and it really hurt her. Because when they got a divorce, he just left and never came back. They were living in Massachusetts then. He had started medical school and was working as a carpenter."

"He told me about the carpenter part," I said. "I'm famished. How about some pancakes?"

"Yes!"

"I put cinnamon in my pancakes. Do you like them that way?"

"Sounds good. I'm not used to somebody cooking for me. Mom just married an older man and they travel a lot. He doesn't like teenagers, so Mom has asked us to keep out of sight."

"Really? What about your brother?"

"Now that it's not going to work out at Dad's house, I think he's going to live with his friend at his friend's parents' house. They're pretty nice. Hunter, that's my brother, says it's like a real family with grandparents and everything. That's what made me feel bad yesterday after I dropped my bomb on everybody. You have a real family with grandparents, and I think that little boy that looks like you, that little kid, he looked sweet."

Michael. I hadn't even called him.

"He is sweet. He's staying over at, uh, a relative's house."

"Do you really think your dad won't let you stay here?" I asked. "As far as I'm concerned, it's okay."

"He told me last night I could stay for the weekend since it's a holiday weekend and hard to get a flight, but he'd book me a first-class ticket back home in a few days. I've never flown first class. That might be interesting; except I don't really have much to go back to. I was going to try to take some courses while I was here."

"What interests you?" I asked.

"Photography and graphic design. Mom says it's a waste of time. Nobody would buy pictures and drawings."

"I'm a photographer/camera/video and film person, and I do it for a living," I said.

"You do? That's awesome."

"I'm a photojournalist, actually, at our local ABC affiliate. I'll take you to work with me on Monday if you like."

"That would be incredible," she said, her face brightening.

We made the pancakes together and each ate a stack. I couldn't bear the smell of eggs, but I thought some bacon sounded good, so we browned some. Later, Kendra went up and showered and made her bed without my asking. Her clothes were picked up as well.

I called Michael, and he was fine. He wanted to spend the weekend with Marty. I decided to take Kendra around the city, show her the station, and take her to Utica Square for lunch. Seeing that she had only brought a backpack of clothes, I decided we'd go shopping. I bought her some new clothes, suggesting she wear a little bit of color for the summer. The lady at Miss Jackson's gave her a full makeover, showing her less is more, and we had her hair cut and styled at their salon. She toned down the dark and put some highlights in it. All of this went on her dad's account. I figured it was the least he could do.

Since the hospital was across the street, I suggested we stop by and show her dad her new look. She really looked like a different girl, and she was stunningly beautiful. Kendra was hesitant about going up to the hospital to see him, but I insisted we both go. The Pollyanna in me felt that all would be better today and that, with love, all things are possible. I still loved George and I knew we could make this work with Kendra.

We went into the hospital and rode the elevator to the fifth floor. I was encouraging Kendra every step of the way and she was feeling so proud. Nobody had seen George for an hour or so. They suggested I check his office. We took the walk-through over to his office building and rode the elevator again. The halls were pretty quiet. Most people had already gone home since it was after five.

Looking through the glass, I could see the lights were on in the reception area, but the door was locked. I had George's spare set of keys, so I used my office key and we walked in. The door to George's office was ajar. I put my finger to my lips in a motion of quiet to Kendra. She looked terrified, but excited.

I gently pushed open the door and there was George, standing with his shirt unbuttoned, his pants down, and his secretary, Brenda, with her skirt hiked up and her legs wrapped around his waist.

I quickly blocked the doorway, but it was too late. Kendra had already seen them and had run out of the office.

"Liz!" George looked up, shocked.

"This really is the icing on the cake, George. You might want to know," I told Brenda, "that the married man you're screwing has SIX children and one on the way."

"What?" George said, shocked. "Liz, wait," he shouted after me.

"Don't bother coming home tonight, George," I shouted as I slammed the door. I could hear Brenda swearing as I left the office. I was pretty sure she wasn't swearing at me.

I ran down the hall after Kendra, who was crying. I put my arm around her protectively. I was too mad to cry. I hadn't expected this of George, but for some reason I wasn't horribly surprised either.

My maternal instinct kicked in. "He's not worth your tears, Kendra. He's just not worth it. I'm sorry you had to see that."

"What about you?" she said, sobbing. "Why didn't you tell me you were pregnant?"

"I was going to, but I thought I should tell the father first, silly me," I said, wryly.

"What are you going to do?" she asked with a frown.

"Don't worry about me," I said. "*We'll* get through this." I lifted her chin with one hand and wiped away a tear.

We walked in the elevator arm in arm. I thought I heard George's footsteps coming down the hall as the door closed, but I didn't care. I think he even called my name, and he sounded pretty choked up. I was moving out of George Pendleton's house, and if she wanted to come, I'd take Kendra with me. But first, I was going to make a call to my cousin, Tommy-the-attack-lawyer. He'd know what to do.

SIXTEEN

I looked at the rock on my finger, remembering our wedding vows. I think George did love me in his own way, or maybe he was just in love with love. I think I had loved him, but not the way I loved Marty. It wasn't fair to compare a lifetime of love with Marty to feelings for a man I'd loved for only a year or so. Maybe I had confused lust with love, because the man was the full enchilada when it came to what you'd want in bed. He could also be tender and kind out of bed.

I thought about this little life I was carrying and wondered how having a parent who didn't care would affect him or her. I had seen what it had done to Kendra. Maybe George would change. Who was I kidding? Marty wasn't exactly your traditional other parent, but she was an adult who was connected to Michael and who loved him. Michael seemed to be doing okay. I still had *that* conversation ahead of me. I think he would be all right with moving as long as I was around. He liked George, but he would adjust.

"I found more boxes," Kendra said, coming through the door of the guesthouse. "Dad had some in the garage."

"Great," I said. "I don't think it will take us long to pack this up. I thought I'd take a few personal days from work to resettle and get my life reordered."

Kendra nodded. I watched her as she carefully kneeled down and started packing. Her hair was like George's hair, thick and chestnut brown. The salon had restored it to her natural color and the highlights were lovely in it. It fell softly on her shoulders and swished when she moved. We had grown so close in such a short time, and I felt her need to have someone in her life who actually cared. We had decided she would move in with us and babysit in exchange for food and rent.

Glam had told me on the phone that she was going to have to move anyway because of Daisy, her Harlequin Great Dane. She was a fence jumper. Glam was dating a veterinarian, Vince, from Sand Springs whom she'd decided to live with and would very probably marry. He had forty acres near Lake Keystone, where they could ride horses and enjoy their animals. This domestic departure from Glam's world of clothes and shoes was interesting to both Gloria and me. The world was changing. I predicted the vet's business would grow because Glam was his new office manager.

We finished packing before noon. Three Brothers Movers was just that: three brothers who moved stuff. They were Bif, Bob, and Barry. They looked like the three bears, one just a little larger than the other, and all of them were about the size of a regular refrigerator. They lifted and hoisted for a little over an hour and it was done.

Kendra and I thoroughly checked the garage and guest house and then took one last walk through the house. I left the key on the kitchen table and locked the bottom lock on my way out. I held on to the credit card he had given me though. We were still married, and I might need it.

We drove to my house where Glam had all her stuff moved into the garage. She was standing in the garage doorway, hands on hips.

"Sorry about the house, you didn't give me much notice!" she said, looking worried.

"We didn't have much notice either," I said, "sorry. If you can leave a path for the movers, that'd be great, they'll be here any second."

Needless to say, I was disappointed when I walked into my house. Daisy had obviously been inside, which wasn't part of our deal, and my couch was virtually toast. She had chewed up three of the cushions. One of my draperies was missing, and the other was hanging on for dear life.

"This place is pretty bad," Bif said, carrying in four boxes of books. "How come you're moving out of that mansion into *this* place?"

I didn't really feel I owed the mover my life story.

"Temporary insanity," I said, managing a smile.

He shrugged and grunted as he put down the boxes of books in the living room.

The kitchen was pretty clean, but the pots were just thrown in the cabinets. Glam was a careless cook. I had forgotten. Ants were having a family reunion in the corner by the door. They were feasting on a piece of dog food.

The bathroom was not too bad, except for poop in the toilet. Judging from the size of it, it might have been Daisy's. I flushed and braced myself for the upstairs.

My bedroom didn't look like the room I left. The plantation shutters had been used as teething rings and Glam must have bathed Daisy in my bathroom because the walls were spotted like a Great Dane had done the twist. Plus, it stunk, and the shower was leaking.

"She didn't pee anywhere, she's housebroken," Glam said defensively.

"Glam, my house is trashed," I said.

"Well, I had short notice you were coming. I was going to get someone in here to clean and replace stuff. Here's three thousand dollars. That should pay to replace the couch, draperies, and fix the walls and any yard damage. I'm sorry, Lizzie. Let me know if it costs more," Glam said, tearing off the check. I didn't feel bad taking it. She'd lived here almost four months for just the price of the utilities and there was a lot of damage.

"Is Daisy still here?" I asked.

"Backyard, but she goes when the truck pulls out, I promise," Glam said, raising her hand as if taking an oath.

As the truck pulled out, I saw Daisy's enormous body sitting next to Glam in her little MG.

"This place is a wreck," Kendra said, "but I can see where it once was nice."

"Excuse me, ma'am, where do you want all of this stuff?" Barry asked. His voice was kind of squeaky for a big guy.

"Put the bedroom furniture up here but keep it about two and a half feet from the walls, because I'm going to have to get painters in here."

I stepped through the debris and braced myself as I walked through the backdoor to the yard. It was a disaster. Every bush had been eaten or totally destroyed. There were large yellow patches all over the yard and the grass was gone. The little waterfall Marty had built remained, but the angel's arm was broken. My lawn furniture that once had tropical cushions was cushion-less and the birdbath had been toppled. Daisy had been tall enough to get the birdhouses down, so there remained only the chains and some splintered wood. Huge mounds of horse-size poop were all over the yard; the fragrance was staggering.

I sat down in the chair and cried. Kendra put an arm around me and said, "Don't worry, we'll get it fixed up again, I promise."

This sweet gesture brought me to my senses.

I paid Bif, Bob, and Barry with George's credit card and gave them a generous tip on the card. They were thrilled.

Barry, the one with the squeaky voice, gave me a big bear hug before they left.

I tried calling Marty, but he and Michael must have gone away. Gloria and Fred were at Fred's high school reunion, so that left just one place to go. I knew the food would be good; they'd have plenty of room and, as always, plenty of advice.

I locked the back door, held up my car keys and looked at Kendra.

"What?" she asked, looking at me expectantly.

"Brace yourself," I said.

"What now?"

"We're getting in the car and going someplace," I said as she followed me dutifully out the door.

"Where are we going?" she asked.

I sighed. "We're going to my parents' house."

SEVENTEEN

t doesn't matter if you are family, friend, or foe, when you're going to my mother's house you have to call first. I stopped at her neighborhood Safeway and dialed her number.

"Hello?" said my mother's cheery voice on the other end.

"Mom?" I said.

"Oh, hello, Lizzie."

I could hear lots of hissing and noise in the background.

"What are you doing?" I asked.

"Your father went to Sapulpa today and bought a bunch of peaches from a farmer's truck. We have bushels of these peaches, so we're canning. It's hot work, but we're going to have lots of peaches put away for the winter. I might even make a peach cobbler for dessert tonight."

My mouth began to water. It was one of her best desserts, next to the homemade baked fudge and lemon meringue pie.

"Would you like some help?" I asked.

"Sure. I've been meaning to call, but I figured you'd call me when you were ready," she shouted. Apparently, my father was dumping bushels of peaches in the sink. I heard the water run.

"It's been pretty crazy. I need to talk to you. I thought I'd bring Kendra with me, George's daughter."

"That funny looking little teenager with all that dark makeup? Oh, no, dear, I don't think so. I didn't relate to her very well. She was rude to break up our party," my mother said.

Great. I looked at Kendra, who was standing on one foot and looking around while I was on the phone. I covered the mouthpiece.

"Kendra, could you go get us a quart of vanilla ice cream?" I asked.

Nodding, she headed for the dairy section.

"Mom, she's coming with me. Be nice. She's really a great kid. We won't stay long. I just thought maybe we'd have a little dinner."

"Well, I guess that would be okay. I hope you don't expect much."

"Dad can go get hamburgers from Goldie's. I'll buy."

"I have an idea. Why don't you bring them? I'll make the cobbler when I'm finished."

"Okay, bye Mom."

We weren't big on the "I love you's," my mother and I. I always had to start it. I was irritated with her. Why couldn't she just accept people? She had always been this way.

"If my mother says anything rude, overbearing, or unkind," I said, as we got in the car with our ice cream, "just ignore it or smile at her like she's a child."

Kendra giggled. "Is she that bad? She looked nice."

"She can be perfectly nice and wonderful, or she can be the queen mother of all B's. I never know with Mom. It's been a lifetime of love and guessing. She was nice when I was growing up most of the time, though I often perplexed her because of my size. I guess I take after Dad's side of the family."

"You're not big, you're just fine," Kendra said. "You have a lovely figure."

"Not according to my mother," I said. "I'm a size Attila-the-Hun."

Kendra laughed and started fiddling with the air conditioner in my car. It was a typical July day in Oklahoma.

"So, are we going to stay there tonight?" she asked.

"I doubt it," I said. "I know we have our bags in the car, but I think we'll either stay over at Marty's house with Michael or go to a hotel. I don't want to stay at my house. It's gross and it smells. I'm going to have to get a cleaning and painting crew in there. I can't do it myself because I'm pregnant and the fumes are bad."

"I've never been around anybody who was pregnant before," she said, looking thoughtful.

"Oh, I'm just a barrel of fun. I throw up every day for the first couple of months. I fall asleep in mid-sentence. My boobs swell up and resemble watermelons and my legs and feet swell so I can't wear shoes. I get too hot and then I get too cold. I'm moody and I cry all of the time. Are you in?" I asked, smiling.

"I'm in," she said, laughing, and offering her hand for a shake.

I pulled into Goldie's Hamburgers, a Tulsa tradition that started on a golf course in the sixties. Every Tulsan knows Goldie's and usually doesn't want anything else. I explained this as we loaded up on the pickles to go.

The aroma in the car was heavenly. We each stole a French fry before we got to my folks' house.

We were met by the garage door opening and Dad stuffing the trash can with peach pits and broken baskets.

"Hi, hon," he said, giving me a hug. He shook Kendra's hand warmly. "Let's go through the front door, You know how your mother is."

Only on a rare occasion did you come through my mother's back door and NEVER if you were bringing a guest. My mother believed in first impressions, and she wanted people coming through the front door properly. We usually sat with company in the living room, but it was hot today and we were with Dad, so we'd probably go back to the den.

This wasn't a large house, but it wasn't small either. It was somewhere around two thousand square feet, which is a nice size.

The carpet was very dated, at least twenty years old. The trees in the yard were the same age and the furniture was even older, with new slipcovers, of course.

Kendra and I followed Dad to the den. We inhaled the peach aroma. Kendra was taking in the Native American art Dad collected, all painted by local artists. She gasped when she saw the Longhorns over the mantle. Dad had hung little flags over them for the Fourth. At Christmas, homemade Christmas balls graced the horns.

Kendra looked particularly upset at one of the Native pictures, which was a massacre of an animal. I always hated to eat in the den and having to look at that.

"Sit down, Lizzie, Kendra. Do you want anything to drink?" Dad asked. He was such a sweetie.

"Thank you," Kendra said politely. "I'd like a soda."

"What does she mean?" Dad asked me, as if Kendra were speaking Spanish.

"She means 'pop,' Dad. Dr. Pepper or something," I said, translating.

"I've never had Dr. Pepper, what's that?" she asked.

"You'll have to try it," he said, smiling. "It's pretty good."

He got up to fix the drinks. Mom came in, wiping her hands on her apron, and shook Kendra's hand.

"I just put the cobbler in the oven," she said, out of breath. "Hello, again, Kendra. I'm Mrs. Littleton and this is my husband, Mr. Littleton. My dear, you look so different. I love your hair! You look so much prettier than you did in all that black. You're really too young to wear that black."

"Thank you," Kendra said, "I like it, too. Uh, I'm sorry I broke up your party, Mr. and Mrs. Littleton. I was upset with Dad, and it wasn't very thoughtful of me to do that."

"Well, what a darling you are," my mother said, hugging Kendra to her small bosom. "I can understand why you were upset. We all were upset when we heard what you had to say about all your brothers and sisters. We had no idea George had children."

"Mom, sit down," I said, easing on the sofa sitting next to Kendra. "I have something to tell you and Dad."

Dad came in and handed the drinks all around and sat opposite of me in his green vinyl recliner. Mom leaned over and picked up some crumbs off of the hooked rug in the den and put them in the trash. She got cocktail napkins from somewhere and passed them out. They had turkeys on them left over from Thanksgiving.

"Sit down, Helen," Dad said, irritated with her fussing.

"All right," she said, settling into her chair, her back straight, looking at me expectantly.

"Well, first of all, I'm divorcing George," I said, firmly.

"Tommy called me this morning," Dad said, nodding.

"You didn't tell me," Mom said, shooting him *the look*. "Elizabeth. I think this is way too rash. So he has a few children. This girl seems nice. You can get along with anybody. Michael needs a father. He's a doctor; you should stay married to him."

There was an uncomfortable silence.

My father looked at me and then looked at his Dr. Pepper. I didn't know if he knew or not.

"Say something, Jack. She'll listen to you. She has social position now and money. She can't let all of that go."

"It's not our decision, it's Lizzie's," he said, looking at Mom.

"Excuse me, perhaps I left out a valuable piece of information. He's screwing his secretary."

"Don't talk like that in front of this child," my mother admonished.

"It's okay," Kendra began.

"No, it isn't. I don't like that kind of talk in my house."

"Mom, did you hear me?" I demanded. "George is having sex with his secretary. We caught him in the act last night!"

"Oh how horrible!" Mom exclaimed. She jumped up from her chair and ran into the bathroom. I could hear the water running. She was throwing up. Some things are hereditary.

"Well, you don't have to put up with *that,*" my father said in a low, angry tone. "Tommy will put together the right team of lawyers and we'll get this thing settled for you. Don't worry about the money."

"I won't," I said. "I'm pregnant."

"What?" Dad looked shocked. He obviously didn't know whether to hug me or cry.

"You're what?" Mom asked, as she came back, wiping her mouth.

"Pregnant," I said, sighing.

"Well, for the love of…this is certainly a mess, isn't it, Kendra? Do you like your Dr. Pepper, dear?" (Shocking news shoved aside for the sake of propriety.)

"Yes, ma'am," Kendra replied.

"We brought hamburgers," I said, waving the bag, knowing my parents needed the tangible instead of the abstract thought at that moment.

"Goldie's?" Dad asked.

"Let's eat," I said, looking at Kendra.

"I'll get the TV trays," Dad suggested.

I glanced at the Native American scene. "Let's eat in the kitchen."

"I just got it all cleaned up," Mom said, "I'll get the napkins."

She returned with four brightly patterned red, white, and blue napkins. "We always use cloth napkins in this house, Kendra," she began, as if explaining how to color for the first time to a three-year-old, "because we are the nicest people we know and we deserve cloth napkins. Now I'm going to give you a napkin ring, dear. When you finish with your napkin, put it in the ring and then we'll save it for you when you eat with us the next time, so that I don't have to do a lot of excessive washing."

"It costs a lot of money to run the 'warsher,'" Dad agreed. He never left out the extra "r."

Kendra was staring at my mother, blank-faced. She nodded and smiled, remembering my previous instruction.

We ate our Goldie's hamburgers and Mom's peach cobbler as it came out of the oven. I had left the ice cream on the counter by mistake, so there was a mess to clean up in the kitchen. Dad said it was okay and scooped the runny vanilla on his cobbler. "It all goes to the same place," he joked.

"Do you want to stay here tonight?" my mother asked. "The twin beds are made up." I thought about my mother's muslin sheets from 1962. *No thank you.*

"We are going to Marty's house tonight, Mom, but thank you. I haven't seen Michael since the…uh…party."

"Oh. What's wrong with your house?" she demanded.

"I am having some things done to it," I said.

"Well, we've enjoyed having you," my mother said dismissively, which meant it was time for us to leave.

"Thank you for having me, Mrs. Littleton, I enjoyed the Dr. Pepper. It was good. And the cobbler was great! You cook just as well as my grandma," Kendra said sincerely.

"Oh, well, isn't that nice. I'm glad you enjoyed it Kendra," she said, in her best hostess voice. "Goodnight."

Dad walked us to the car and thanked us again for the burgers. Mom had made two cobblers and sent one with us so Michael and Marty could have some. Dad squeezed me around the shoulders and said, "Anything we can do, hon, you just let me know." I fought tears.

"Goodnight, Mr. Littleton, thank you for being so nice. I'm sorry about messing up your birthday," Kendra said.

"You didn't mess up my birthday, honey. It was your birthday, too. Next year we'll celebrate together."

"I'd like that."

"Goodnight, Dad," I said as we got in the car. I was exhausted.

As we backed out of the driveway, Kendra turned to me and asked, "Are we going to Marty's house and who is Marty?"

"Let me explain," I said, taking a deep breath.

EIGHTEEN

When we pulled up to Marty's house, we saw Michael and Marty in the driveway painting a large refrigerator box. The base had been painted white and they were carefully painting American flags on the corners. We got out of the car to inspect their work.

"Hey Mom!" Michael said excitedly. "We're making a spaceship! See, here are the windows. We already painted the inside yesterday," he said, opening the door of the ship to show me the inside.

"Wow, a control panel and earth!" I said, scooping him up in my arms.

"Who's your friend, Mom?" Michael asked, smiling at Kendra.

"This is Kendra. You might have seen her the other day at the party."

"I kinda remember. Sorry, I was playing."

"That's okay," Kendra said, smiling. "Can I go for a ride after you?"

Michael was thrilled. "Sure!"

"I'm Kendra," she said, extending a hand to Marty. On the ride over she had been fully briefed on my life with Marty and her various changes.

Marty returned the handshake and patted her on the back.

"Your hair looks great!" Marty gushed. Kendra looked pleased. "Michael, let's take a break and go inside. We need something cold to drink. It's hot out here."

"Aww," Michael said, surveying his work. "Just a couple more stars and I'm done."

"Okay," Marty agreed.

We went inside. Marty's house had been her grandmother's cottage-style house, so it fit her new life perfectly. Everything was in order, with Marty's flair for the artistic. The walls were soft gold with cream-colored draperies tied back with ribbons of gold, purple, and green.

Marty's paintings were all over the house. Some were whimsical, some were serious, but all of them were delightful. Her sculptures were lit from underneath in the various corners of the house.

"Gosh," Kendra said, looking around, "this place has so much character. I love it."

"Well, I'm kind of a character," Marty said, smiling.

We followed Marty to the kitchen, where she had a cold pitcher of iced tea waiting in the refrigerator and a pitcher of Kool-Aid for Michael. She filled some sparkly glasses with ice and poured the tea. She retrieved Michael's special glass that said, "Michael's brew" on it for him.

"Can we stay here for a few days until I can get my place cleaned up, Marty? Daisy has destroyed my house," I asked.

"Sure, sugar," she replied. "The deal with George is over, I guess?"

"Yes, but not just because of the six kids I didn't know about. If they were all like Kendra, I wouldn't care if they moved in," I said, tossing a nod in her direction.

Kendra flushed, embarrassed, then grinned.

"I caught him with his nurse in a compromising position, shall we say. Unfortunately, we both caught him."

"Ohh," she winced. "I'm sorry, Liz. So, what's the plan?"

"Well, Kendra doesn't really have anyplace to go and we've become friends, so she's going to live with Michael and me. There's some more news…I'm pregnant."

Marty's eyes lit up. "You're kidding!"

"Nope."

"Well," Marty said, not knowing exactly how to react, but being Marty, always putting on the positive spin. "That's wonderful. We'll have a new life to welcome into this family and Michael will have that little brother or sister he's always wanted."

Speaking of Michael, he walked in about that time with paint on his hands.

"Is it okay if there's only forty-seven stars? I got the lines kinda crooked and couldn't get all the stars in," Michael asked seriously.

"Sure," said Marty. "People will get the general idea and I bet they won't even count them. Guess what?"

"What?" Michael replied, reaching for his Kool-Aid and slurping a drink.

"You, Mom, and Kendra get to stay over here for a while!" Marty said, with a big smile on her face.

"Why aren't we going back to George's house?" Michael asked.

"Well, we're not going to live there anymore, Michael," I said.

"What about all my stuff?" he asked in a panic.

"Don't worry, Kendra and I packed it carefully and we had the movers move it back to our old house."

"What about Aunt Glam?"

"She's moving to the country."

"Is she leaving Daisy? Can we keep Daisy, Mom?"

"No," I said, "Daisy is part of why we're staying here. She messed the house up, so I'm going to have somebody clean it and paint it."

"Let me do that for you," Marty said, giving my hand a squeeze. "There's a duplex next door and two brothers live on either side with their wives. Oscar and Orville are in their sixties. They have a painting business and the wives have a cleaning business. You can trust them, and they'll do a thorough job. Let me do that for you," she insisted.

"Thank you," I said, suddenly feeling exhausted and needing a nap. "Can I lie down for a while? I think it's the heat."

Marty nodded knowingly. "And other things. You can lie down in the spare bedroom or in my room. I think Michael has toys all over his bed."

"You and I will be sleeping in the spare bedroom," I told Kendra and went in to see two neatly made twin beds with soft blue coverlets on them. They had belonged to Marty's grandmother. The beds were Jenny Lind style, in cherry wood with spindles. The room was filled with many of Marty's grandmother's antiques. I remembered her fondly, her tightly curled gray hair, her laugh, the tiny gold cross she always wore around her neck. She'd had lilacs growing all around her yard.

At the end of each bed was a gently worn quilt in shades of lilac. I stretched out across the bed and pulled the quilt up to my chin, even though it was about 103 outside. It was cool and comfortable in here, and it felt so comforting to have his granny's quilt up next to me.

"Mommy," Michael whispered, standing at the door. "Are you asleep?" he asked, with wide, brown eyes.

"Not yet, buddy. Come here and see me." I held out my arms.

Michael crawled up next to me.

"So how come we're moving out of George's house?" he asked. "Did George get tired of me?"

"Of course not, George loves you," I said, thinking about the sweet times George had with Michael. "It's just that some things have happened that have made me feel like I made a mistake marrying George."

"Really? Is George a woman like Marty?" Michael asked, playing spider with his fingers.

"No, George isn't a woman. He didn't always tell me the truth about some things," I said, wading in deep waters.

"Like what things? Did he lie about his age like grandma?"

"No." I smiled. Michael was pretty sharp.

"Did he lie about how fast he was going to the policeman like Aunt Claire did that one time?"

"No," I laughed. "I can't believe you remember that."

"I remember," he said, looking twice his age. "Well, did he lie and say he didn't eat cookies when he did?"

"No, it was more important lies. He never told me he had any children, like Kendra and her brother and apparently four other kids."

Michael counted on his fingers. "He has SIX kids?" he asked, wide-eyed. "Why didn't he tell us? I could have been playing with them all this time. That's *good* news, Mom."

"It's complicated, Michael. I just don't think George and I can be together anymore."

"Well, I liked George's house," Michael reasoned, "but I like it here and at our house, too. I don't care, Mom, wherever you want to live."

"Thanks, Michael. Would you like to go find Kendra or Marty and play with them while Mommy sleeps a little bit?"

"Are you sick, Mom?"

"No, just kind of tired. I just need a nap, like you do when you've stayed up late and haven't had enough sleep."

"Oh, I know how that feels. Okay, Mom. I'm glad you're here and I like Kendra."

"She's very nice and she's going to live with us for a while."

"Is she your girlfriend like my friend Jessie's mom has a girlfriend?"

"What do you mean?" I asked.

"Well, Jesse has two moms, but not like I have two moms, although I don't tell people Marty is my mom, I just say he's my aunt, but Jesse has two moms because they're sort of married and sleep in the same big bed and hold hands and kiss and stuff. Jesse says it's kind of weird."

"No, this isn't like that. Does Jesse have a dad?"

"Yeah, I think so, but he's gone a lot, so he lives with his moms."

Michael gave me a sloppy kiss, crawled off the bed with a bounce, and left the room. I rubbed the warm spot he left with a sigh. It was so complicated growing up in these times for kids. I felt pretty confused myself.

"I'm sorry Michael bothered you," Marty whispered, standing at the door. "I'll shut the door so you can get some sleep. By the way, that Kendra is a doll, isn't she?"

"I thought so. I just can't figure out why George deserted her and the rest of his children. This is so screwed up, Marty."

"I wanted George to work for you because he seemed like everything anybody would want in a man: handsome, rich, talented, smart, and nice. I thought he accepted me pretty well," Marty said, looking thoughtful.

"I did too."

"But you know, there was sort of an aloofness about him. Maybe he shut himself off from feeling things."

"I don't know, but he was sure feeling his secretary, Brenda."

"That's so sad. Have you talked to your cousin Tommy?"

"Briefly. I'll go see him in a day or so. I wasn't married that long and it's not like I want to take George to the cleaners, but I am having his child and I expect him to help financially."

"I think George will help in that way," Marty said. "He's always been pretty generous. I just don't see him going to plays and tossing the ball in the backyard."

"You're right. I guess you spoiled me as far as ex's go," I said, smiling.

Marty laughed. "Honey, when they made me, they broke the mold!" He said, "I was thinking about something just now when I was cleaning up the kitchen, it's just an idea, okay?"

"Okay, I'm listening."

"On the fifteenth of this month, I'll make my final payment on this house," Marty said proudly.

"You're kidding, that's great! Since we took out a fifteen-year note, you should have about two more years on your house, right?"

"Actually, I've been making extra payments. I think it's less than that," I said.

"Well, what if I pay off both of the houses and…"

"Marty, are you doing that well with the video store?"

"Business is booming. Ever since we made it movies and music, we're doing a huge volume of business," he said.

"That's wonderful."

"Okay, what if we took some of our equity out of these houses and bought a really big house someplace else and we could all live there together? We could use the rent from the houses to make the house payment, or help make the house payment, or we could sell those houses, put a huge chunk down on the house and work to pay that off. Kendra and I could both help with Michael and the baby," Marty said, obviously excited about the idea. She sat down on the bed and patted my legs.

"I don't know, Marty. Sometimes I need my space. I did love having that little guesthouse in the back of George's house. I think I might miss that more than George!"

"What if we found a house with a guest house or loft with a darkroom? It could be yours. What do you say, Lizzie?"

"I've kind of liked our arrangement," I said, quietly.

"It wouldn't be as lonely, and we'd all have our own space. If the house isn't perfect, we won't take it, or, we could design it and build it the way we want it."

"That's a thought. But what if you get into a relationship? What, if, God forbid, I get into another relationship? What happens to the house? This could get dicey."

"Well, that's something to consider." Marty thought for a moment. "I guess one of us could buy the other out or we keep our old houses so we'd always have a place to go to, no hard feelings."

"Let's talk about it some more when I'm not so tired and not around Michael or Kendra. I have so much to think about now, Marty. I'm not sure I can handle one more thing. I might just want my house cleaned and painted for now."

"Okay, sweetie. I love you," Marty said. "I don't want to stress you out."

"I love you, too," I said. "I know it's lonely for you when Michael's with me."

"All the time," Marty choked.

"I'll think about it," I promised, and Marty left the room.

Marty…George…Kendra…Michael…the baby…George…Cousin Tommy…George…my mother…the station…the documentary I was working on…George…George—my head was swirling with thoughts and I felt like I was spiraling down a long, dark, staircase. Sleep, that's what I needed. And for just those few moments, sleep is what I would get—until the phone rang.

CHAPTER

NINETEEN

"**D**id you think you could hide from me forever?" George asked in a steely voice.

"I'm not hiding from you, George," I said, sighing.

"Well, don't you think you moved out a little prematurely?" he demanded. "We could have worked this out, maybe gone to counseling."

"Would we bring Brenda with us or would she have her own therapist? What about the other mothers? Do you think we could get a group rate?" I asked, hating myself.

"Look, Brenda means nothing to me. It was a one-time deal to work off a little stress," he said, in a low voice.

"Most people go to the gym or for a drive, George. You should try it."

"Liz, I want you to come back home," he said.

"Do you know what I realized when I walked back in that house, George? It was never my home. I had my clothes and a few personal items there. Michael had more stuff in that house, than I did."

"Michael has more stuff than most of us," he said in an attempt at humor.

Silence. "I just don't think we can fix this, George."

"What about the baby? *Our* baby? Doesn't that baby deserve a good home?" he asked.

I shifted the phone to the other ear and rolled on my side to try to get comfortable. I burrowed farther down under the quilt.

"They all deserved good homes. What happened, George? Do you ever see *any* of those children?"

"NO!" he shouted.

"Were you there in the delivery room with them?" I asked.

"No!" George shouted.

"You're a *doctor*, George. You're supposed to be compassionate and caring."

"I am compassionate and caring," he defended himself.

"Not with your own kids. Why? Why? I can't put the pieces of this puzzle together."

"My dad had four wives, Liz," he began.

"Well, in a way, so have you," I said.

"No, Dad had them all at once. The twelve kids were by *my* mother. My Mama Sharon had seven, my Mama Terry had six, and my Mama Dorothy had nine, all before I left. That's thirty-four kids by one man. Male sons were required to leave early, the females had to stay and help with the younger children. He beat all of us, including my mothers, into submission. I tried to get *my* mother to leave, but she wouldn't. The last thing I gave the bastard was a box of condoms."

Well, there it was: why George was aloof, distant, and dysfunctional as a man. Defective goods, this one.

"I'm sorry," I said sincerely. It was all I could think to say.

"The thing with Brenda is over. Can't you come home?" he almost whined.

"No," I said and sighed. "I have to have time to rest and think, George."

"You're not going to file for divorce right now, are you?"

I didn't answer because I didn't know what to say. I didn't know what I wanted to do except sleep.

"Well, if you do, Liz, don't expect to get your hands on my money. Everything is in my name. I have more money than you and I'll hire big name attorneys."

"Well, so much for reconciliation," I fired back. "Was that you being nice and sweet, because it didn't sound like it. I don't remember saying I wanted your money, George, and if you knew me, you'd know the answer to that. But just so you'll sleep better tonight, my attorney is my cousin Tommy-the-shark-Littleton, who eats attorneys like whomever you could hire for breakfast, and he's family, so he won't charge me a dime. He'd probably go after your money if I let him because he loves big settlements."

"Liz…"

"George, I'm tired because I'm in my first trimester of pregnancy. If you'd stuck around long enough, you might remember how this affects women. The heat makes me very testy and so does throwing up all day. So George, the next time you decide to call me, stick your finger down your throat and make yourself throw up, because that's how you make me feel."

I hung up on him. I don't think I'd ever hung up on anybody in my life except a couple of obscene phone callers, well, most of them. Some hung up on me because I asked so many questions.

Part of me felt triumphant and part of me felt mean and low and very, very sad.

I lay in Granny Wilcox's twin bed with her soft homemade quilt and cried. I tried to grab enough tissues to keep from getting my mascara on the pretty pillowcase, but I knew it was too late. Marty wouldn't care. The one thing Marty knew was laundry. He was one of the few former men-turned-women on the planet who pre-treated. Maybe it would be good to live with Marty again. It would be good for Michael, and Marty would be sweet with Kendra and the baby. Marty could rub my back with those nice long, sculptor hands. He gave the best back rubs. Now that he was a woman he had long acrylic nails, so he could scratch, too!

Was this really my life? What happened to the fairytale weddings and the promises? I'm smart. I graduated at the top of my class. I have good ideas. I have a great eye for composition, and I'm an award-winning journalist. Why can't I have these same accomplishments in my day-to-day life? I'm a pretty good mom. I'm a good friend. I'm a so-so daughter, depending on which parent you ask, and I've been a good, faithful wife to both husbands.

Oh, God, I've been married *twice*. What does that make me? Would people see me in the grocery store and say, "So sad. Her first husband was a woman and the second was that handsome doctor. I bet she's, you know, *frigid*."

I hated pity. I wouldn't be a victim and this situation was kind of making me one, so I'd just have to get past it. Should I live with Marty in a big house? Would that work? Or should I move home to my Daisy-demolished house? Maybe Michael and I should get a new house, a house in one of his friends' neighborhoods. I hate moving. There's something so pitiful about putting all your belongings in a box. If I did move, I was calling the three bears movers again; they were very nice and didn't break anything.

Marty popped her head in the door.

"I knew you couldn't sleep after he called," Marty said. "Why don't you bring Granny's quilt and come out and lie on the sofa? I made popcorn and we're going to preview some new kids' movies I just got in. You always fall asleep during movies. I'll even rub your feet."

Deal. I pulled Granny's quilt from the bed, dragged it into the living room, and stretched out on the sofa. Michael had piled a stack of pillows from all over the house in the middle of the floor. He and Kendra were passing a bowl of popcorn back and forth, and each of them had a Sprite can next to them. (We didn't let Michael drink caffeine drinks.) Marty and I sat on the dark green corduroy couch and she pushed the remote to start.

So, this is the way it would be if we all lived together. It was nice, really. I felt safe and comfortable. I could relax. That wouldn't be such a bad way to live, would it? Marty wouldn't push me into making any rash decisions. We could stay here until my house was done. What to do? I liked my privacy. I had plenty of it with George because I had my own little haven out back and he worked so much that Michael and I often hung out alone. Would I ever have alone time again when the baby came? Could I ever just sit and read a book? It would be hard to be a single parent, and who would take care of George's offspring? How much was a nanny? Going back to George wasn't an option at this point, and he'd certainly never help with care*giving*. George was a *taker*. I'd have to work.

Had I known what I would find out in six short weeks, I would have just watched the movie and not wrestled with any of these heavy decisions.

TWENTY

"We're going to do an ultrasound," Dr. Hall said nonchalantly. "I want to check on a few things."

Sometimes it was hard to take Dr. Hall seriously. He was short and looked just like Gene Wilder with a 'fro. He was gentle and funny, chief of obstetrics and gynecology at St. John's Hospital, and I adored him.

"So, how's George?" he asked, glancing at my ringless finger. In truth, I had taken it off because of the swelling.

"Okay, I guess," I said, hedging.

"I heard," he said, lowering his voice. "Working in a hospital is like working in a small town."

I considered this, but Dr. Hall sees women all day. He always had the latest information, and because he had such a warm presence, people told him everything. I found myself ready to spill my guts. I fought it for a moment, contorting my face.

"Am I hurting you?" he asked, alarmed. He was just listening to my heart.

"No, I'm just uncomfortable."

"With me?" he asked, surprised.

"No, just uncomfortable. This pregnancy is different from my first."

"Well, you're a little older, that makes a difference," he reasoned.

"It's weird, I throw up in the morning and then in the afternoons and evenings, I'm ravenous."

"Every pregnancy is different and when you're going through, uh, difficulties, those hormones can really rock and roll. I noticed George has been staying up here a lot."

"His interests are here," I said pointedly.

"I think he fired her about six weeks ago because she came up here looking for a job," he said.

"Why didn't you hire her?" I asked with a grin.

"My wife does all of the hiring for this office," he chuckled. "Brenda's qualifications didn't fit the job description here."

It was true. Dr. Hall's wife ran the office, and everybody looked matronly. All of them were regular and married or old and married. The only hot young thing in the office was Dr. Hall's niece, and she was engaged.

"I think George has been staying here day and night," Dr. Hall said, looking at my chart, and then looking at me. "He's a very driven man and someone who is in a lot of pain, in my estimation."

Here came the tears. It was the hormones. Dr. Hall put his arm around me and I cried. He just let me.

"I ca-can't go back." I stammered. "I have a son to consider and this baby."

"I understand. You have a lot on your plate. I want you to take it easy."

"I work."

"I know, but I don't want you lifting those heavy cameras or anything. Let someone else carry them for you," he said.

"Okay."

"Let's go to the ultrasound lab and see that new life forming in you. But first, drink as much as you can of this gallon of water."

Don't get me wrong, ultrasound is an amazing boost in our technology and has enabled doctors to catch problems ahead of time and save lives. It also helps when you're decorating the nursery to know what sex the baby is going to be. In 1988, ultrasound was still relatively new, so it was kind of scary. It must have been invented by a man, because no woman would design something where you have to drink a gallon of water and have some fool push hard on your abdomen with a cold metal gooey thing while you try not to pee all over the table.

I did as I was told, drinking maybe a little over half of the gallon of water. The technician, who was a young guy, and I think was Dr. Hall's niece's fiancé, helped me up on the table.

"I'm Zach," he said. He was average height and had blondish hair with a cute smile. "We're going to press this on your tummy, okay?"

"Okay," I said, trying to return the smile.

He put gooey stuff on me and the silver thing that took the pictures, relayed the message, or whatever it did.

"Do you keep this in the refrigerator?" I asked sweetly.

"I know, it's cold," he apologized.

We could hear a really fast heartbeat and I watched as the black and white images came on the screen. He clicked the button over and over and took all kinds of pictures.

Someone knocked softly on the door. Marty stuck her head in.

"Dr. Hall said I could come in, if that's okay with you, Lizzie."

"Sure," I said, kind of relieved to have her here. Dr. Hall knew Marty from my first pregnancy and had followed the progress of our lives. With George being so absent, Dr. Hall must have thought it would be nice for me to have *someone* here who cared.

"Why is the heartbeat so fast? Is there something wrong with the baby?"

"Well, actually, the heartbeat isn't that fast," Zach hesitated, reading the monitor. "It's just that…"

"There are *two* of them!" Marty said, staring at the monitor behind Zach.

"Well, now that the cat is out of the bag," Zach said, smiling. "You're hearing *two* heartbeats. Look here, Mrs. Pendleton," he said, pointing to the screen, "you're having twins! They're going to be fraternal, because there are two sacks…and it's too early to tell what they're going to be yet, but it's twins."

I guess some people want twins–you know, dressing them alike and all of that. I never had any twins in my family, but I always wanted to be a twin so I could skip math class and send my twin. Frankly, I wasn't thinking of dressing them up or the cost of raising them or even two kids in college at the same time. I was thinking about *the delivery*. It hurts to have a baby, and you have to go through it TWICE in one hour? Deal me out here. Let me off the rollercoaster. I got as big as a barn with one baby, so what would I be like with two inside of me? Dr. Hall had said I was older this time. I was already getting wrinkles, and I thought I'd seen a blue vein in my leg that morning.

Marty was looking at me and getting all excited, jumping up and down. Sure, she didn't have to push two watermelons through her manmade twinkie. I wanted to slap her because she was so happy, and I wanted to slap this kid, Zach, just because he was a man, and I wanted to punch George in the stomach, because he deserved it.

"Lizzie? Are you okay?" Marty asked, reading my expression.

"Sure," I said, "It's not every day that you find out you're going to have twins that you weren't expecting anyway. They'll be born in February, right in the middle of sweeps."

"Huh?" Zach said, looking at me.

"Ratings period. February is a big ratings period for people in television. Liz works at Channel 8," Marty said, translating. He turned to me, "It'll be okay, maybe they'll come early!"

I turned my head away, fighting tears. Zach gave a final once over and made some more clicks with his machine. He pushed a button and little black pictures with white images started spitting out of the other side of the machine.

"Their first pictures!" Marty exclaimed as she took them.

"I'll print you a duplicate. The doctor will need these," Zach said kindly. He glanced in my direction one more time.

"Mrs. Pendleton, is there something else I can get you? Something to drink?"

"I just drank almost a gallon of water and have to pee like a racehorse. May I get up now?" I asked.

"Sure," they both said, staring at me. I must have looked wild-eyed and crazy. Marty helped me get off the table and I headed straight for the bathroom. After taking care of business, I washed my hands, ran a brush through my hair and put on some lipstick. I decided I wasn't coming out of this little bathroom. I'd stay here where I was safe and warm, and I could pee anytime I wanted. No demands would be made on me in here.

"Liz, you have to come out now, someone else needs the room," Marty said softly.

I opened the door and glared at Marty. That was my leave-me-alone look. Marty had experienced it over the years and knew it was best to back off and give me some space.

I passed the next patient as Zach was WHEELING her in the door. Her face, arms and hands were bloated beyond human recognition. I thought she might have two suckling pigs underneath her dress, but I realized those were her breasts and her stomach looked like she'd swallowed a car before she'd gotten here. She carried an empty water jug.

"I drank it all," she moaned. "I'm so thirsty and hungry all the time. Can we get this over with? I have to pee."

"Poor guy, he has to listen to this all of the time," Marty muttered in my ear.

"Will we be able to tell if the twins are girls or boys today?" the lady asked. "I want to pick out a border for the walls and get the crib sets."

I turned, staring at the woman in horror. Twins? This woman was having twins?

"Marty? What am I going to look like?" I said, truly terrified, once we were out of earshot.

Marty put an encouraging arm around my waist and walked me quickly down the hall. "Not like *that*, I promise."

Marty opened my door and helped me in the car.

"I'll be there every step of the way if you want me to, Lizzie," Marty said, getting in the car and starting the ignition. "Have you given any more thought to looking for a house together?"

"I've thought about it. No decisions yet."

It had taken a week for cleaning and painting crews to take care of my house. I had my sofa restuffed with down and recovered. Marty had her friends at a local nursery redo the backyard. I had turned over the $3,000 from Glam to Marty, but she wouldn't take it. She insisted I put it in my account. Her business was doing really well. She'd opened another location in Brookside and spent time going back and forth between the two stores. I was proud of her.

My cousin Tommy-the-attack-lawyer was poised for action, but I was waiting, for what I didn't know. I knew I couldn't live with George, but for some reason I felt like I should wait a while to do anything legal. Every time I tried to think about it, I cried, so I knew I wasn't ready.

George had done the send-two-dozen-roses-to-my-work thing. I had seen him drive by when I was out shooting a story. One of the other "photogs," as we were nicknamed, pointed out he had driven around the block three times. A couple of his friends had called asking me to please go back with George because they'd never seen him like this. I'd even gotten a note of apology in the mail at the station from Brenda, full of misspellings of course.

When Marty brought me home, I saw Kendra and Michael in the front yard talking to George. That was something you didn't see every day. Marty pulled in the driveway.

"Do you want me to say something to him?" Marty asked.

"Marty, it's okay. I can handle George. You get back to the store."

"Aren't you coming in?" Michael called out to Marty.

"No, I've gotta run back to work. I've been off with your mom at the doctor's office." Marty said, waving him off.

"Is she okay?" Michael approached the car looking concerned. We had decided not to tell him yet.

"Yes, she is, it was just a checkup, buddy," Marty said. Michael was close enough now for Marty to ruffle his hair.

Michael seemed convinced and came running over to me as I got out of the car.

"Mom, George came by to visit. He played catch with me out in the front yard."

"That's great, buddy. Can you and Kendra go inside for a minute while I talk to George?"

"Kendra, Mom wants us to go inside while she talks to George," Michael complained, but he complied and went inside.

"Hi, you look great," George said.

"Thanks, you do, too." Of course he did, but his eyes looked different, puffy and sad, and he was thinner.

"I'm sorry for just dropping by but I saw Ray Hall in the corridor at the hospital and he suggested I give you a call. He said he saw you today."

"He did."

"Well, are you all right? Is the baby okay?" he asked.

"Yes, I'm fine and so are they."

"They?"

"Your family gene pool. I'm having twins."

"Oh, well, that's great!" He smiled. "Listen, I have some news, but I have to show you this for you to believe it."

"What do you mean?" I asked, not understanding.

"I have something to show you that you won't believe. Please come for a drive with me. I promise I won't touch you, well, unless you want me to…"

I gave him *the look*.

"I understand. I just want you to come with me."

George may have been an adulterer and a liar, but I knew he wouldn't hurt me. Still, I felt weird getting in the car with him after so much had happened between us. A car is a pretty small space for two people to be in who have had huge issues come up between them. I conceded. George gave money to Kendra and Michael for pizza and we left.

We drove a while in silence.

"Where are you taking me?" I asked.

"It's a surprise," he said, smiling.

"George, please, just tell me."

"Just wait," he said. "I've thought a lot about this, now just wait."

I waited in silence, looking out the window. We drove past George's house, winding through the Utica Square area, past large houses with thick trees that would soon turn golden hues. I breathed in the heady aroma of his cologne. We drove up to a wrought iron gate with brick columns on either side. The house sat back on a cul-de-sac and looked forlorn and forgotten, almost like something out of a story waiting to unfold.

On either side of the brick columns was a black wrought iron fence covered with honeysuckle vines so thick you couldn't see the house. The brick mailbox was also covered with vines and the door to the mailbox was slightly rusty and missing a hinge. George reached into the glove box and pushed a button on a remote control. The gate swung open.

"Who lives here, George?"

"You, if you want to," he replied.

TWENTY-ONE

"**A**re you crazy? Did you *buy* this house George?" I sputtered. "*Things* don't fix what's wrong with us, George." "Calm down, Liz," he said, putting a hand on my leg. I flinched. "I didn't buy this house. I *inherited* it."

"What?"

"I *inherited* it," he said, almost laughing.

"But I thought your parents were..." I said, confused.

George eased his car up the circular drive in front of the entrance.

"Not from my parents," he said, "from a patient. Mildred London. This was known as the old London estate, I guess. Millie married Robert London over fifty years ago. They never had children. Robert left her a widow some twenty years back and she lived here until she died about a week ago."

"How did you know her?" I asked.

"I was her doctor and I think one of her few friends," he said simply.

"Tell me more," I said. I couldn't help but be curious.

He put the car in park and turned off the ignition.

"Millie came in the ER a couple of years ago with chest pains. I treated her and then saw her for some follow-up care. I had recommended she walk because she had become pretty sedentary. We had talked about living in the same area and she asked me if I would walk with her early in the morning because she didn't feel safe walking by herself. So I agreed."

"George, that was so nice of you," I said, genuinely surprised.

He shrugged modestly and continued, "We started walking two or three times a week for about an hour. We walked slowly, of course, and we'd sit on the benches around the neighborhood and rest for a few minutes. I have to tell you, it was the highlight of my week. Millie was delightful. She'd been a photojournalist, like you, and she loved the visual arts. She had worked for a newspaper back in New England and had that Yankee spiritedness. Her philosophies, charm, wit, and intelligence were all there, even this late in her life. I learned a lot from her."

"Why didn't you ever introduce me to her?" I asked, wishing I'd met this wonderful character.

"I was going to. I had told her all about you when we were first dating and she wanted to meet you. She was thrilled I had found someone I could love and trust."

I couldn't believe this was the same George. This was like the George I fell in love with. And why was he talking about love and trust? Was he grasping at straws?

"Anyway," he said quickly, reading my silence as the prelude to an explosion, "I had set up a visit for all of us and when I was about to tell you, I saw her come into the ER. She was in cardiac distress and went into a coma. She's been in a coma ever since and died last week. I went to the funeral. There were only a handful of us there. Her attorney pulled me aside after the service and gave me this letter."

He pulled a wrinkled envelope out of his shirt pocket and handed it to me. The letter had an embossed letterhead in the upper right-hand corner in gold script reading Mildred J. London and this address. It was addressed to George Pendleton. When I opened the letter, it smelled of lilacs.

Dear George,

I can't begin to tell you how much I have enjoyed our walks and talks. I never told you this, but I lost a baby the same year you were born, and I always felt like God sent you at the end of my life to walk me into the next one. I know my son will be waiting for me, along with his father, but you have been the son I lost so long ago. You were always evasive about your family, and I knew whatever memories you had were painful, but I can't imagine your mother not loving or being proud of you. So if you never hear it from her, I want you to hear it from me. I am proud of your accomplishments. You are a good doctor and most of all, I want to thank you for your friendship.

I have been a lonely old lady. Most of my friends have died or are in nursing homes. I have no family. I'm leaving the money to the University, the church and various charities, but I want to leave the house to you and your bride. I know you have a wonderful house, but it's a masculine house. This is a house where a woman can be at home and I know your Elizabeth, uh, Liz, will love this house. There are plenty of trees for Michael to climb, and should you have more children, they will love living here. The house is free and clear, so there won't be any expense to you. The mortgage was paid off when my husband died and I paid the taxes forward for this year. I'm also leaving all the furnishings in the house to you. If there's anything you two don't want, just give it to the church or some needy person or family. Don't sell it. You don't need the money and I want people to have my things who will appreciate them.

I'm sorry there's so much clutter. I was a saver. You two will probably find lots to talk about when you go through all my treasures. I led a very full life.

One more thing, George. Cut yourself some slack. You are very disciplined, which is how you got as far as you did, but I want you to enjoy life. Take the time to look into Liz's eyes and tell her how much she means to you. Be a good role model for her son and both of you find a church. If your marriage isn't based on a belief in God, you won't stand a chance.

I had a beautiful life with Robert and many, many happy years here. I hope you will have many happy years here as well.

Much love,

Millie

I wiped the tears from my eyes and returned the letter in its envelope to George.

"I wish you'd read that a couple of months ago," I said, "maybe this would have played out differently."

"Just come in the house with me and keep an open mind," he said, getting out of the car. He moved quickly to open my door.

I followed him reluctantly, but my curiosity got the best of me. The house was totally my taste on the outside. The brick was weathered, not the fake kind, and I counted six chimneys. The double paned windows were large with thick, white shutters. There was a deep front porch almost as wide as the width of the front part of the house and white Adirondack chairs. I counted eight in groups of two across the front. Spiders had made homes in a few of them, but the paint still sparkled. Millie must have loved plants because white wrought iron planters sat in front of the windows.

George fished for a key in his pocket. He opened the heavy white storm door and inserted the key in the red front door. My mother always said a red front door was the best way to say hello.

"Remember, she's been in a coma a long time. The cleaning crew came once every other week, but nobody's lived here in over a year."

I nodded, on the edge of being overcome with emotion.

He pushed the door open, and I followed him inside. The brick entryway was softened with a thick round oriental carpet in blues and creams. There was an elegantly carved side table near the front door with an ornate antiqued white mirror over it. A bowl of potpourri and a vase of silk flowers sat on the table alongside a wooden bowl where Millie must have tossed her keys. An umbrella stand was next to the table with a Burberry plaid umbrella.

The wide staircase didn't spiral, like in George's house; it was more sensible, with a split stairway that held potted silk plants with a soft oriental runner. Glass doors with crystal knobs led into the living room on the right, giving way to a bright room painted a light creamy yellow with stark white woodwork. Millie had chosen soft, comfortable furniture with polished chintz fabric in shades of yellows, greens, and blues. The brick fireplace was deep and oversized. I could have walked inside it behind the ornate screen. The mantel was marble with delicately carved shelves on either side of it.

The ceilings were tall in this room, matching the others I would discover, with a vintage ceiling fan that had big, wide blades.

Off the living room were tall double doors of heavy solid wood with brass handles. They opened into a round room, revealing a two-story library with a brass ladder on wheels and a spiral staircase to the second-floor landing. There was a rounded window above two double glass doors behind a large carved wooden desk. The woodwork in this room was a light cherry, and the desk was the same. Millie's writing papers and fancy pen were in a paisley fabric covered box. The calendar was old, last year's. On the desk were two framed pictures, one of Millie and Robert in their younger days and one of George and Millie in their walking clothes.

The room smelled of books and polish. The wood floors barely looked worn, like they had all been refinished. The fireplace on one wall wasn't as large as the one in the living room, but must have made the library cozy in the winter. Beneath the large window were double paned glass doors opening to an outside screened-in porch covered with potted plants. The furniture was comfortable yet functional.

"This is all so beautiful, isn't it?" I asked, following George back into the house.

"Uh, huh," he agreed. "Wait until you see the kitchen."

We walked through the living room, across the entry way, and into an enormous dining room, which had something you don't see every day: two large round cherry mahogany dining room tables almost identical in carvings and style, sturdy as a rock. The chairs to match were covered in a stripe which complimented the traditional Waverly wallpaper with colorful birds and flowers.

On the entry side wall of the dining room and the opposite wall were built-in lighted China cabinets with serving spaces under them. The China cabinet was well stocked with Wedgewood, Lenox, and Waterford.

The swinging door led into a kitchen with beamed ceilings, a large white tiled island peppered with hand-painted tiles of Pennsylvania Dutch style. The woodwork was white in here with more glass doors. Across the large island was a black wrought iron pot rack complete with polished stainless steel and copper pots.

"The only thing that hasn't been updated in here is the refrigerator," George said. "Millie didn't have an icemaker. She didn't want to spend the extra fifty dollars at the time."

There was a sitting area in this kitchen with rocking chairs and a loveseat nestled in front of a brick hearth fireplace. The doors opened into the breakfast room, which had windows all around that looked onto an amazing yard with a pool below and sculptured landscaping.

"This place is incredible," I said, drinking it all in.

"I know, just like Millie was and just like you are."

I wanted to stop and go back to the car because this really was system overload. But I was here, and I wanted to see the master bedroom. As it turned out, there were two!

One master was downstairs with a fireplace and an elaborate dressing room and bath with a closet the size of my bedroom. Millie's furniture was simple and lovely: honey maple with lots of white throw pillows and, of course, another fireplace. We discovered a little hall that led back to the study with a bathroom off the study and enough space to make a darkroom.

Upstairs was another master, almost as large as the one below, with a door to the upper-level study, another fireplace, and a door to its own private deck. There was also a large dressing room, bath, shower, and closet. The two master tubs had been converted to whirlpool tubs.

The four other bedrooms upstairs were oversized. Each had its own bath and walk-in closet, and there was an incredible playroom at the end of the hall with a vaulted ceiling, two ceiling fans, more built-in shelves, an antiquated pool table, and a dart board. The floor in there was polished black-and-white tile.

"I forgot to show you the family room off of the kitchen," he said, snapping his fingers. "And there's a guest house out back near the pool with a greenhouse and a dog run."

"How big is this place?" I asked.

"I don't know," he said, "probably over five thousand square feet, and it's on about two and a half or maybe three acres."

"Well, you'll love living here," I said, "anyone would."

"How about you?" he asked.

"George, it's getting dark. I should be getting back to the kids."

"The kids are fine," he said. "Let's go get a bite to eat and talk about this."

"George, I don't..."

"Okay, listen to me. I love you and I'm miserable without you, but I'm not proposing we move in here together right now. I'm proposing that you, Kendra, Michael, and Marty, if she wants to, move in here."

"Huh?" I said, doing a double take.

"I have a lot of things to work on and I've found a good therapist. I've been broken for a long time and I need help if I'm going to ever live a normal life. I want to be good enough for you and I haven't been. I promise you I will never cheat on you again and that if we can't make love, I will live a life of celibacy until a decision is finally made about our marriage. Give me until the twins are two years old to get my act together. If you promise not to divorce me until then and just not do anything, I will sign over this house to you this week. Whether we decide to stay married or divorce, this house will be yours."

I had stopped breathing. All I could do was stare at him. This was an amazingly generous offer, one I could live with. It would give me time to get myself together. I didn't care about dating, and maybe George could turn himself around. It seemed fair and reasonable.

"I'm not going for sympathy here," he said earnestly. "I have never really faced why I am the way I am, I just accepted it. Millie's letter made me see a different side of myself and so did you. I know that guy exists in me who is good and loving, but I've got to get rid of the other guy, the one who is so angry on the inside and can leave his kids. See, I left them because I didn't want to be the father my father was."

"Then why did you have them?" I demanded.

"I thought I'd be different, but with Kendra and her brother, I found out that I couldn't tolerate children. I had no patience then and I couldn't look myself in the mirror."

"Why did you marry me?" I asked in a panic, thinking of Michael. "What about Michael?"

"With Michael it was different. He was my patient first, and I could be a friend to Michael. He had a dad, well, not a dad, but another parent."

"I guess I see," I said. My head was starting to hurt.

"And I fell in love with you. If you'll just not hate me and try to find that thread of a feeling you had for me to hold onto, I promise I won't make any physical or emotional demands on you. You can move in here and get ready for the babies."

"Okay," I said, and we shook on it.

This car ride changed my life. Little did I know that this house would be a home to many people I hadn't even met yet.

TWENTY-TWO

"You're right about going to church," Marty said after I told her the big news and asked her if she wanted to move in with me. "I've been praying every night that we find the right house to make a better home for Michael. And look what God dropped in our laps!"

"That's interesting," I said, "because I've been praying about if I should divorce George, and what to do about a house, and should I move. And finally, last week, I just gave it to God."

"Well, there you go. We'll start this Sunday. Let's try a few churches before we decide."

I was relieved to be doing something instead of wading through my days trying to figure out what to do. I was taking action. The timeframe was long enough that I didn't have to make an immediate decision. George and I might have a chance, though I had my doubts. I'd have some help with Michael and the babies. Kendra might be able to build a relationship with her dad. And I would be living in a house that looked like it jumped out of the pages of *Better Homes and Gardens*, albeit a long time ago.

We decided that Marty would keep her house and rent it because it was her grandmother's. In case George and I got back together she would have a home. Besides, neither of us could sell Granny's house. Marty rented it to an older woman who had moved to be near her children and wanted a quiet neighborhood.

After I put a sign in the yard, my house sold in two days. We closed on it about a month later. We moved into Millie's house in mid-October.

I gave Marty the upstairs master and I took the downstairs master. Michael chose the room in the middle of the hall because he liked the closets. The nursery was upstairs, but the babies would sleep in cradles in my room for awhile. Kendra chose the bedroom at the end of the hall in case she wanted to play music or talk on the phone. The other bedroom remained a guest room. Michael filled the playroom with his toys. There was a wonderful attic room with a big window and a skylight that George and I had missed on the tour. We made that Marty's studio.

George had the cleaning crew go through the house and do a thorough job. Marty's painters had come in and touched up and repainted a few of the rooms upstairs and made the creamy yellow color in the living room a bit deeper. George took a few of Millie's things out of sentiment. I kept her big desk and the two round dining room tables, the chairs, and of course, all her dishes. I liked her sofas in the living room and kept them too.

We all went through Millie's things. The cleaning staff emptied the refrigerator, but we replaced it with mine and put hers in the garage for overflow. You can imagine the enormity of the task. Luckily, I didn't have to buy much. She had linens for the beds and very nice towels.

I donated her clothes to the women's shelter. I kept a few vintage pieces of jewelry and some of the nicer stuff. I gave her diamond ring to Kendra and let her pick whatever else she wanted. I saved a few things for my mother.

I replaced her books on the lower shelves in the library with my books but found it fun to read her books as well. George took some and we donated some textbooks. We kept some of her paintings and donated others. We put Marty's paintings throughout the house, along with my photographs. We stored some items in the storage area off the guesthouse, which we pretty much left alone for now. We were making the place ours, little by little.

George kept his word. He was going to therapy, which I occasionally attended—with and without him. He was busy at the hospital, and he was rebuilding his relationship with Kendra. She and George had invited Hunter, Kendra's brother, to come for Christmas. I was busy getting ready for the ratings period in November and of course, the babies were growing.

I had discovered a lot more about George. He occasionally suffered from depression. He dealt with it through solitude; his therapist prescribed an anti-depressant. At times there was a pretty strong edge to him that he seemed to fight. He also refused to go to church with us.

So that people at church wouldn't ask a lot of questions or think we were lesbians, we introduced Marty as my sister. I realize it's not good to start off relationships with a lie, but most people wouldn't understand the changes Marty made. It wasn't on anybody's radar at the time. We told Michael this was a private thing, and if Marty wanted people to know, Marty would tell them. Michael understood. In fact, I think he was relieved.

Michael loved going to church. We chose the First Methodist church downtown because it looked like a cathedral and because it had lots of programs for children. Michael made some new friends and knew some of the kids from his old school. (We put him in a private school.)

Marty decided to join a Bible study. Marty also got involved in painting sets and walls in the children's area. I had learned I was having girls and decided to wait until they were born to get involved in a church group. Gestation was a big enough job for now.

One thing you don't realize when you move from a house on a small lot to a house on over two acres with trees is autumn and its leaves. We had piles of them everywhere. I wasn't too good at raking because of my size, so I sat and watched a lot. Marty, George, Michael, and Kendra all raked for most of one Saturday. Glam still felt bad about trashing my house. She came over to help, but she left Daisy and the veterinarian at home. Fred and Gloria joined us in the afternoon. We were all proud of the work. It was my favorite time of the year: a crisp fall breeze, a bright blue sky, and family and friends. It was a perfect day for a big fire in the fireplace.

This turned out to be a bad idea. Unfortunately, I hadn't thought to have the fireplace checked. I figured everything else was in good shape, why worry about it? Fred had brought the logs into the living room from the back porch area and Gloria had opened the damper and started a fire. Then she went into the kitchen to help Marty start the chili.

"Mommy? How come there's smoke in the living room?" Michael called.

We rushed in to discover Michael coughing and the living room filling with smoke.

George thought quickly. "Marty, get a bucket. Kendra, open the front door. Michael and Liz, get out of here. Fred!"

Marty ran and got a bucket from the laundry room and filled it with water. Fred came running to help.

"I can't figure it out, I know I opened the damper," Gloria said, coughing.

Smoke billowed everywhere.

Sirens. Who had called the fire department? The gate was open because of the visitors and the bright red fire truck came barreling through, racing up the driveway toward the front of the house where smoke was streaming out the front door. I stood there watching, looking like an elephant in bib-overalls.

Six big guys jumped off the truck. All of them were pretty hot looking, except for one old guy who looked like he might be pushing retirement. One of the firemen grabbed me and moved me farther out in the yard. Another one grabbed Michael and moved him.

What is it about firemen? Is it the uniform? The danger? The big red trucks? I must admit a few impure thoughts crossed my mind when this hunk grabbed me. Is it pretty sick for a pregnant woman, who in a few short months would give birth to twins, to think like that? Oh well, a girl can dream.

"Ma'am, please stay out here away from the house. Robert, get her a mask and give her some oxygen," he ordered. "How many more in there?" he asked, gesturing toward the house.

"Six," I said, counting off the names on my fingers.

"Cory," my fireman yelled, "we got six more in the house."

There was lots of confusion. George and Fred were protesting, saying they had this under control. The firemen were pushing through. Somehow, the youngest hottie on the truck found a hydrant and turned on the water.

Loud shrieks followed as Fred and Gloria came running out. One of the firemen carried out Glam, who winked at me through her apparent faint. Another one had hoisted Kendra over his shoulder. She hadn't wanted to leave the house. Apparently, insulation was found in the fireplace, a by-product of Millie's frugality. The firemen put it in fireproof bags and dragged it outside.

The firemen checked the roof and the other fireplaces in the house and pulled out more insulation.

"It's a good thing we got here so fast," the one called Cory said. "You would have had a real problem on your hands pretty soon."

George came around the side of the house scowling. He must have felt embarrassed by having the firemen here. I was kind of enjoying their visit, except for the damage I knew had incurred to my furnishings. It could have been a lot worse.

We invited the firemen in, but they had to get back to the station. They had opened all of the windows to let the smoke out, so it was pretty clear, but the smell lingered.

I surveyed the damage. It looked like someone put Niagara Falls in my living room. Water was everywhere. Luckily, my cameras had been in the study behind closed doors. I carefully waded through the living room with a little help from Fred. I started taking pictures of the damage. Glam and Kendra were mopping up the water to try to save the floor. A few lamps had been knocked over. Fred was picking those up and drying them off, blowing on the plugs. Some of my pictures were cracked and a vase had gotten broken. Kendra retrieved a stack of towels from the laundry room. Gloria helped her as they dried as much as they could.

I sat in the living room on the only dry chair available and watched the circus. We were all there working together. Even little Michael was picking up things around the room in his little red boots … everybody except George. George was outside walking around the house.

He stormed in the front door.

"Who called the fire department?" he said, his face beet red.

"I did," Kendra said in a meek voice. She was down on her hands and knees with a wet towel.

"Why? That was stupid. Fred and I could have handled it. We had it under control and now it's your fault there's this huge mess!" he yelled.

We sat in stunned silence for a heartbeat. Kendra gulped and started to sob.

"George," I said, "that's not fair. This isn't her fault, and if she hadn't called the fire department we all might be sitting on the lawn watching the house burn. Nobody got hurt, this is just stuff."

"It's nice stuff. You don't appreciate it because it was just handed to you," he sneered and walked out the door.

I powered up and pushed myself from the chair and waddled after him.

"Not so fast, buster," I said, standing in the doorway.

"I'm leaving, Liz. I can't stand being here."

"Well, that's fine, Dr. Please-Give-Me-Another-Chance-Wait-Two-Years-George Pendleton. This is *my* house based on our agreement, either way it goes, and I won't have you throwing this in my face. I had a house and I sold it. Now go cool off somewhere and get yourself together. You're acting like a baby."

"Well, you and your little motley crew can just keep cleaning. I'm going to the hospital," he said, climbing into the car and slamming the door.

"You might change your clothes first," I yelled after him.

I turned and saw Kendra, Glam, Gloria, Fred, Marty, and Michael crowded in the doorway. These were my motley crew and I loved them.

"Oh girl, I'm thinking you're not going to ever be able to live with that man again," Gloria said.

"I'd say," Fred agreed.

"He was just a jerk," Glam said, putting a protective arm around Kendra, who was still sniffing.

"I'm sorry I caused a fight, Liz," Kendra said, her words almost a moan.

"You didn't cause a fight," I said quickly. Everyone agreed. "George caused the fight because George is George. You saved the day by calling the fire department!"

"Yeah, George is just a butthole," Michael said.

"Michael!" I said, shocked. Everyone looked at him in surprise. "I've never heard you say that!"

"Well, that's what he is, Mom," Michael said moodily, crossing his arms.

"I don't want you talking like that," I said, shooing everybody inside, "and I never want to hear you speak disrespectfully to or about George or any other adult, is that clear?"

"Yes, ma'am," he agreed.

After cleaning up the mess as best we could, we retired to the kitchen to fix dinner. The fireman said it was safe to start a fire in the fireplace and would probably help dry things out. Fred opened the damper and lit the fire. He volunteered to stay in the living room and watch the fire to make sure everything was okay. He was also watching the television, which was fine with me.

Marty and Gloria got that big pot of chili rolling and Glam made the cornbread. Michael and Kendra had picked some apples from one of the trees in the backyard and made two pies together.

We gingerly started the fireplace in the kitchen, and it worked perfectly.

Assured that "everything's okay now" with the fire, after his game was over Fred joined us. We sat around the kitchen, some at the table, some in rocking chairs. I was stretched out on the loveseat with my feet up. I looked like a beached whale, but I didn't care. I was with the people I loved the most.

I would probably pay for eating the chili, but it tasted great. I put lots of crackers in mine and ate two pieces of cornbread. Gloria had made a pot of coffee and brewed some decaffeinated tea just for me.

After the dishes were cleaned up, we went into the den where Marty's grandmother's piano was. Fred played and we all sang songs. Michael sang the loudest.

Marty and Kendra got Michael to take his bath and get ready for bed. I was just too exhausted. Glam rubbed my shoulders and back, which were in a terminal ache. Glam had taken a massage course when she was studying to be a physical therapist. Glam was always taking courses. She was certified in everything and yet she never did these jobs very long because they bored her. She announced she was going to OSU in Stillwater, taking courses to be a veterinarian. We approved.

Michael kissed me goodnight and went upstairs. I sat in the overstuffed chair in the den and put my feet up on the ottoman. Kendra and Marty came back downstairs, and we all chatted, carefully avoiding mentioning George or the turn the day had taken.

We reminisced about childhood until about ten o'clock. I could barely keep my eyes open.

We kissed and hugged goodbye and Marty saw them out.

"Are you going to bed?" Marty asked with a concerned look.

I nodded.

She checked all the doors, set the alarm, and turned out the lights downstairs, except for the one in my room and a little light in the hallway.

"Goodnight, sweetie, I love you," Marty said.

"I love you, too," I said sleepily. "And Marty?"

"Yes?" he said.

"George *is* a butthole," I said, mimicking Michael.

"Yes, he is," Marty chuckled. "Now get some sleep."

TWENTY-THREE

1988

There are four times a year when people in television media go crazy: February, May, July, and November. These are ratings periods when programs are made or discarded, and networks live and die by the numbers. November is huge, and that's what I had just finished, a grueling ratings period with some ten- and twelve-hour days and late nights. It's kind of like an accountant's life in April.

We had done well. All of our newscasts were number one again, and that meant bonuses for everybody. The station gave them out on December 1, after Thanksgiving, so people would have extra money for Christmas.

Christmas was coming! This year, Michael was going to be a Wise Man in the Christmas pageant at church. Marty had drawn and painted all the sets; it looked like a stage play from New York. It was incredible. I made sure the station came out and did a story.

Kendra was so excited about her brother, Hunter, coming. We planned for him to stay with us with the option to go to George's house. We had lived here only for a few months, but we had settled in. George hadn't exactly apologized for the fireman fiasco. It threw him way back on the road to recovery with both Kendra and me. I did get Michael to stop calling him names though.

We met Hunter's plane. It was still a time when you could go all the way to the gate and wait as someone got off the plane. George said he had to be at the hospital, so Kendra, Marty, Michael and I braved the sleet and cold and waited. His plane was two hours late. Michael and I played fourteen games of Go Fish. I won a few times. It's not easy beating an eight-year-old.

I could have picked him out of any crowd. Hunter looked exactly like a seventeen-year-old George. He was tall and kind of gangly. His hair was long, and he was tanned (of course) because he lived in Florida.

We all hugged him. Kendra held on the longest. She was so happy Hunter was here. She chattered to him all the way to the baggage carousel.

As we waited for Marty to bring around the car, I glanced at my reflection in the glass window. With my dark green coat on and my bright yellow knitted hat Michael had given me, I looked like a portly pine tree. We piled Hunter's suitcases in the back of Marty's Jeep.

"Mom sent all the presents in the big suitcase," he muttered.

"That's okay," I said in my best reassuring tone. "We mothers know how to pack a suitcase." It didn't really make sense, but I was trying to set up a bond between his mother and me beside the fact that we'd both been married to the same man, and I was carrying his sisters.

Awkward silence.

"Do you like Christmas programs?" Michael asked excitedly.

"I haven't been to one in a while," Hunter said, smiling at Michael.

"Well, I'm going to be in one tonight at our church. I'm going to be one of the three wise men. I get to carry a jeweled box. Mom and Kendra made my crown and put jewels on it. My robe is gold and purple with sequins and glitter on it. Marty made it."

"That sounds cool. I bet you'll be the best one," Hunter said.

"You look like George when you smile. I like you," Michael said, taking Hunter's hand.

Hunter got choked up. Luckily, we'd reached the house.

Hunter was amazed by it. Kendra had already explained the situation to him about his dad and why he didn't live here. Kendra gave Hunter the grand tour, which ended in his room.

Marty had spaghetti sauce cooking all day in the crock-pot. All we had to do was make a salad and pasta and put some bread in the oven. There was homemade chocolate cake for dessert. Kendra had baked it that morning. She said it was Hunter's favorite.

Hunter showered and dressed in more comfortable clothes. I could tell he felt better. His hair was slightly damp when he came to dinner, but it dried quickly in the warm kitchen.

"We don't have a fireplace," he said, "this is really cool."

We said grace and dug in. Hunter had two helpings of everything and devoured the chocolate cake.

"We had to eat a little early because of Michael's program," I said, apologizing.

"It was great," Hunter said. "I was starving on the plane. None of my flights had food on them and the airport food is never very good."

Marty excused herself to get Michael ready. We had to leave in a little while. Kendra and Hunter rinsed dishes, loaded the dishwasher, and put the food away while I freshened up. I'd gained fifty pounds and I still had January and part of February to go.

We piled into Marty's Jeep and headed for the church downtown. The roads were icy and slick. Marty was a good driver and went slowly, letting the other guys run into each other.

We took our little wise man to his appointed room with other chattering children. Glam was putting make-up on the little actors, giving them all rosy cheeks and lips. She put a little eye shadow on the girls. She and the veterinarian had started coming to the church and wanted to help.

It was chaos, but the director got the children into a line and ready to go on stage.

Marty, Hunter, Kendra and I took our seats, leaving an aisle seat for George. The set was gorgeous. Everyone oohed and aahed and told Marty what a magnificent job she had done on the set. She gave the credit to everyone else, of course.

The play began and there were giggles across the room as various players came on the stage. Fathers and some mothers were lined up on either side of the aisles videotaping the event. We were almost on the front row, so I had a pretty good shot from my seat.

The children said their lines in loud voices met with tittering and chuckles. The play began with little Mary and Joseph traveling to the inn where there was no room and then getting lucky to find the manger. They settled in with various children around them in sheep, cow, and shepherd costumes. Now here came the Three Wise Men.

"We are going to see the baby Jesus," Michael said loudly.

"You will find him in Bethlehem wrapped in swaddling clothes and lying in a manger," said the little angel boldly.

Michael was trying to say his next line, but the chunky Wise Man next to him, who Michael had often complained about, was whispering something to him.

"Shut up," Michael said, and shoved him.

The third Wise Man tried to save the day by shouting his line but was interrupted with more shoving. Michael took his jeweled box and hit the bigmouth Wise Man in the stomach. That kid started to cry, then there was sympathetic crying from some of the other children, more shoving, and one of Marty's set pieces started to tip when the angel on the ladder, who had been so composed earlier, decided to join in the fight. She was Michael's self-appointed-nine-year-old girlfriend, and she wasn't going to let him go down.

Parents were shouting their children's names, metal chairs were clanging and dropping to the floor, some dragging the chairs with them as the parents tried to get on the stage. It was an absolute free-for-all. I was in a panic for my child.

Marty ran up on stage to try to retrieve Michael and was met with a hot, "Leave me alone!" He ducked under a few kids and ran off. Marty was swept backward with the crowd and I lost sight of her. The director announced that because of the weather, the play was cancelled tonight and everyone should go home now. This was sort of a lie, of course. The weather was awful, but the bigger disaster was on stage.

I sat next to George's empty chair and put my camera away.

"I don't know why he reacted that way," Marty said, returning. "He looked at me like I was some kind of monster. I don't know where he is."

"Kendra is looking for him. She'll find him," I said. I turned to Hunter and said, pleasantly, "Well, how did you like the pageant?"

Hunter smiled. "That was something!"

Kids everywhere were crying. As parents were putting their coats and hats on, they glared at us and walked by without saying a word. I didn't think it was because I looked like Mount St. Helens ready to pop, either. It was because Michael had ruined the Christmas program.

Luckily, Kendra knew where to find him. She found him in the music room, all alone, crying. She brought him back to me, his head down. Most of the crowd had cleared by now. His little robe was torn; he held his trampled crown in his hands, and his box was gone.

"What happened, Michael?" I asked gently.

He sniffed a response.

"Can you talk about it?" I asked.

Kendra indicated she knew the problem but didn't want to talk here. We drove home in relative silence with only the noise from sleet and windshield wipers to serenade us. It was hot in the car, too. Well, I was hot. I was having my own personal summer. My hair was wringing wet.

When we got home, Michael took a hot bath in my whirl-pool tub for a little comfort. I wrapped him in a big, fluffy towel. I noticed he was kind of modest in front of me, so I averted my eyes. There were mirrors all around the bathroom and he seemed ashamed.

"Michael, what did that boy say to you tonight that made you so angry?"

"He has always been mean to me ever since I came to the church, but the other kids were nice, so I ignored him. He started in again about Marty. Before Mrs. Taylor lined us up, he told me his dad knew Marty in high school. Then, after we were on the stage, he told me that Marty had his peepee cut off and is a girl, so I p-punched him," he said, tearing up.

"Oh, Michael," I said, holding him to me. He cried and cried. We both did.

Marty tapped softly on the door.

"Get out, you freak!" Michael screamed and began to wail.

There it was. It had festered way down below the surface and had erupted when one kid pushed the right button.

"Well, what happened to Marty was really unusual. Remember, we talked about it? Marty had a problem at birth that nobody knew about."

"What if I'm like that, Mom? What if I'm a girl too?" he cried, tears dripping from his long eyelashes.

"You're not like that, sweetheart. You're all boy. Nothing is wrong with you. You are my little man," I said, wrapping my arms around him. He shivered.

"Mom, can I sleep with you tonight in the big bed?" he asked.

"Sure," I said, "*if* you promise not to snore."

He smiled. "*You* promise not to snore, Mom!"

He put his pajamas on and crawled into my big bed. I washed my face and put on a gown and robe. I went out into the living room to say goodnight.

Hunter, Kendra, and Marty were sitting on the sofa. Hunter was looking wide- eyed and slightly shocked. Marty eyes were red and teary. Kendra had briefed Marty about the chain of events and explained to Hunter how Marty became Marty/Martha.

"I'm so sorry, I thought we were past this," Marty said, wiping her eyes.

"There will always be cruel people, Marty," I said. "We just have to help Michael deal with it and come to terms with it."

"I thought he was."

"He's eight," I reminded him. "It's not going to be a done deal. He'll get used to it as we all have, but it takes time, Marty. You're still adjusting too."

"I should have moved away, so it wouldn't hurt him. I guess I was selfish," Marty said, shaking her head.

"No," I said, picking up her chin and looking her square in the eye. "You were brave. You love Michael and you wanted to be there for him. That's love."

I felt Hunter watching me.

"Hunter, I'm sorry you have all of this on your first night here and I'm sorry George didn't show up," I said.

"It wouldn't be the first time, I'm not surprised," he said, dejected.

"Well, he's head of the hospital's ER and they keep him pretty busy, especially on a night like this," I said, not knowing why I was defending George, but I was trying to make Hunter feel better. I was trying to make everyone feel better and, personally, with the Pendleton twins punching each other's lights out inside of me, I wasn't feeling so hot myself.

The three in the living room decided some hot chocolate would hit the spot. Marty checked the damper several times with a flashlight before lighting the fire. We had strung lights everywhere outside, in the trees, along the fence, and along the front porch, and we had wrapped thick red ribbon around the columns to make them look like candy canes. We had saved decorating the Christmas tree so Hunter could be a part of it.

I went back in the bedroom to check on Michael. He was a dark little spot on a stark white eyelet pillowcase.

"Mom, are you coming to bed?"

"Not just yet, I was going to have a little hot chocolate. Would you like some? Marty, Kendra, and Hunter are making it."

"N-no," he said, hesitating. I could tell he was wrestling with the hot chocolate idea, which he loved, but he wasn't ready to see Marty.

"You know, Michael," I began, searching for the right words. "What happened to Marty was very, very rare, and most of the men in his situation move away, because it's easier to start a new life. They leave their families because their families won't love and accept them for the people they are, not just whether they were a boy or a girl."

"You mean, like how Grandpa Bill won't talk to Marty?" Michael asked, trying to understand.

"That's a good example. Marty has been my best friend since I was a little girl, just seven years old. I love Marty for who Marty is and I won't stop loving Marty no matter whether Marty sits or stands when going to the bathroom and whatever Marty is wearing."

"That's good, Mom," Michael said after giving it some thought. "I love Marty, too, it's just hard, Mom, because it's not like other dads and people don't understand."

"Well, we're not supposed to understand everything on this earth, Michael. Only God has it all figured out. We're just supposed to love and accept one another and keep praying. How about we pray about this? Maybe we'll feel better."

"Okay," he said, shutting his eyes tightly. "God, help me feel better about all of this please and help Marty feel better. I'm sorry I got in a fight with that kid and ruined the Christmas play. Please forgive me and help me be a better boy. Help George be nice to Hunter and Kendra and help Grandpa Bill love Marty again. Bless Mommy and my new baby sisters and also, please help us have a great Christmas. Amen."

"I know God heard that one," I whispered and kissed him on the forehead.

"*I* did and it was a good one," Marty said, standing at the door holding a cup of hot chocolate.

"Is that for me?" Michael asked meekly.

"Yes," Marty said, "but you have to brush your teeth afterward."

"I promise," Michael said, looking at Marty intently. "I'm sorry about tonight."

"I'm sorry you had to defend me, but I appreciate it, buddy," Marty said, guiding Michael out of bed to a little chair and side table. "Drink it here."

Michael was drinking his hot chocolate when the doorbell rang.

I glanced at the clock. It was almost ten.

"It must be George," I said. "I'll get the door."

I walked into the living room, my robe flowing behind me, the silk tight over my swollen belly. Hunter and Kendra were in the kitchen and met me in the entryway. The porch light was on. I had left the gate open for George. I didn't think robbers would venture out on a night like this.

George wasn't at the door. Instead, two uniformed police officers were there. One was young, with boyish good looks. The other one was probably pushing sixty.

"Yes?" I said, staring at them though the glass.

"Tulsa police, ma'am," the older one said. They flashed their IDs.

I opened the door to an icy blast.

"Please come in," I said, feeling my legs start to weaken and my lip tremble.

"Come in and sit down, officers." I indicated a place for them to sit on one of the sofas. I took my place in an easy chair. Kendra, Marty, and Hunter sat on the other sofa.

"This is Marty Greene and Kendra and Hunter Pendleton," I said, introducing them to the officers.

"Pleased to meet you. I'm Officer Trent and this here is Officer Darcy."

"Is there something wrong?" I asked, knowing there was.

"Yes ma'am. We're sorry to bother you at this late hour, but your husband has been in an accident," said Officer Trent.

"Is he all right?" I asked, fear making my voice tremble.

"Well, we don't know. He was alive when the ambulance took him to the hospital, there were a lot of cars involved with the ice and all and we just got him pried out of that little car of his. There were ten cars involved in that accident and it was a mess," the young one, Officer Darcy, said. "We came to drive you to the hospital."

The older officer helped me to my feet, which was no small task, getting me out of that chair. I went into my bedroom and quickly slipped on a sweater and some jeans, the kind with the big panel in the front. I put on some thick socks and low-heeled short boots with thick treads so I wouldn't slip. I brushed my teeth, ran a brush through my hair, and put on some lip-gloss.

Marty helped me on with my dark green coat and I put on a white knitted cap this time. "Where is he?" I asked.

"St. John's. It's the closest."

"I know. He's in charge of the ER there. Let's go."

TWENTY-FOUR

Have you ever ridden in the back of a squad car? Me, either. I've had to sit in one before when a cop was investigating an accident that wasn't my fault, but I've never really ridden in the back of one. They ran the siren and everything. If I hadn't been upset or as big as the Great Wall of China, it might have been a kick. As it was, kicking was involved, but it was all *inside* my belly.

"So, when are you due?" Officer Darcy shouted over the siren noise. Maybe it was the boyish face, but I think he couldn't have been more than twenty-three.

"February, but with twins, they say you never know," I said loudly.

"Oh, that's why you're so big," Darcy said. Officer Trent punched him.

"That's okay," I shouted, feeling on the verge of explosive tears anyway. "I am big, but that's because there's two babies in there."

"My wife and I are expecting," Darcy said proudly at the top of his voice.

"Oh, that's nice," I said. I doubt he heard me.

"We're having another boy. This is our third."

"Really?" I said. "You don't look old enough to have that many kids."

Deaf again.

"We started young. We got married at eighteen. Our kids are three, one-and-a-half, and now this one."

"Better figure out what's causing that. It ain't in the water, you know," Officer Trent said, chuckling at his own joke. I knew they were just trying to make me feel better, but I didn't. I felt lousy and I was afraid something terrible had happened to George. I was feeling it in my gut, as much as I could feel with two babies on a perpetual roll.

The lights of the hospital loomed in front of us as Trent eased into the Emergency Room entranceway. Darcy jumped out and helped me out of the car. He walked me in to the admissions desk.

"This here is Mrs. Pendleton," Officer Darcy said. "She needs to see her husband."

"Hi, Liz," Susan said from behind the desk. She'd been the main nighttime receptionist for years.

"Remember, my husband works here, officer," I said gently. "But thank you for helping. Tell Officer Trent thanks again for me."

"Will do," he said, smiling, and went back out into the cold night air.

"Where is he?" I asked.

"They're taking him to surgery right now. You might be able to ride up on the elevator with him," Susan said, pointing down the hall.

I raced. Well no, I waddled as fast as I could to the back hall to the patient elevator. Rick Palazzo, one of George's groomsmen, was at his side. He was another ER doc.

"Rick!" I called, walking toward him.

"Oh, Liz. Good, I'm glad you're here," he said. "We've been working on him and now we're on our way to surgery. You might not want to come any closer."

"I have to see him," I said with determination.

George looked, in a word, awful. Most of his face was bloody and bruised, swollen almost beyond recognition. His right hand was packed in ice, and I could see he'd severed some fingers. They had wrapped his hand, but the bone was sticking out of his right arm and there was blood everywhere. I stopped looking. Beyond that, I remember seeing a sea of red on his leg and his foot was twisted around in a hideous position. That was it. Here came dinner; I was throwing up on the floor.

"Nurse!" Rick shouted as the elevator doors opened.

Someone grabbed me from behind and put a wastebasket in front of me.

"Get someone to clean this up and get Mrs. Pendleton some tea," a voice said. It was Sally Hatfield, the ER's head nurse.

George hadn't moved or responded to me. I saw the utter sadness on Rick's face as he looked down at George. That was the last thing I remember before a geyser erupted between my legs. I looked in horror as my jeans and shoes were wet and a pool of water was forming on the floor.

"Oh no," I moaned, "they're not due until February!"

"Wheelchair," Sally ordered. "Alert Ob-gyn. Mrs. Pendleton is going into labor and we're going to need to get her to delivery. Hold on, Liz. Who's your doctor?"

"Dr. Ray Hall. Is he on call?" I asked.

"He is now," she said, grabbing the house phone and alerting the operator to find Dr. Hall.

While my husband was on the operating table fighting for his life, I was in a delivery room that resembled the Hilton: soft music, tasteful art, cabinets hiding scary looking hospital stuff, bedding in soft pastels, dusty rose pink walls and a light. It was part of the new birthing room craze across the country.

"Is there someone you'd like us to call?" Sally asked, as she helped me out of my wet clothes, dried me off, and put me into a warm, dry hospital gown—with no back, of course. She put the clothes in a plastic bag.

"Marty. Marty Greene," I said, "the number is…"

"I'm right here," Marty said, walking in the door. "They told me I could come in."

"Good, you can keep her company," Sally said as she hooked up the fetal monitors and took my blood pressure.

"How bad is it?" Marty said with concern.

"The pain here or the pain in my heart? The pain here is somewhat tolerable, but the pain in my heart is pretty bad. I don't see how they're going to put him back together again," I said.

"We're going to take good care of you, Liz," Sally said reassuringly.

"They're good surgeons," Marty said. "Let them do their job. You have a job to do, kiddo. The girls are on their way!"

"Is Dr. Hall? That's my big question," I said, sucking in a breath as a tiny foot jabbed my lower intestine.

"I'm going to go check on his status. You're dilated to a five, so you're moving along pretty well here," Sally replied.

"Sally?" I asked, touching her arm.

"Yes?"

"Did you see him before they took him up? He looked awful," I said, choking back the tears.

"I was here when he came in. We worked on him quite a bit before we sent him up."

"Was he ever conscious?" I asked.

"Briefly," she said. I could tell she was fighting tears herself. She was young, my age, with a face that could appear stoic, but her eyes betrayed her emotions.

"Did he say anything?"

"Yes," she said, hesitating.

"What?" I asked, fighting the pressure in my belly.

"He said to tell you and the kids that he was on his way when the accident happened, he was sorry he missed the play and that he loved you."

Hot tears trickled down my cheeks and the sob that I had wanted to let out before so badly finally came out, along with its friends. I sobbed and sobbed. Marty held me and motioned for Sally to go find Dr. Hall.

"Shh, there, there," Marty said, holding me firmly. "Calm down, Lizzie, calm down."

"It's not fair, Marty. It had only been a few months. He was just making progress. He was going to see his son tonight. He and Kendra were just starting to make a connection. He hasn't seen his babies yet!" I cried, the words tumbling over one another.

"He's not gone yet," Marty said, "we don't know anything."

"*I* know," I whispered, recoiling in a fetal position, pulling a pillow next to me for comfort. "I *know*."

TWENTY-FIVE

If you've ever had a baby, you know it's no picnic. Having two babies at the same time is doubly delightful. What's that old joke about if you want to know how it feels to have a baby, take your upper lip and pull it over your face?

There's a sense of accomplishment when you deliver a baby, like you've climbed a mountain or scrubbed your kitchen floor by hand, but then, after the first one is delivered, when you're having twins, you've got to get another one out.

I had thought I'd probably schedule a C-section—you know, have my nails done, get a pedicure, get a good haircut and be ready to roll. I hadn't expected sleet and snow and crisis. This had been a very long day anyway with airport time, a ruined Christmas program, and now George's accident. I couldn't possibly have these babies tonight. There was a huge fatigue factor working here and besides, Michael wanted to sleep in my big bed tonight.

"What about Michael?" I asked.

"Kendra's got it handled. Hunter, Kendra, and Michael are all going to sleep in your bed. Kendra made a fire in the fireplace, they're toasting marshmallows and having a camp-in," Marty said. "Good idea, huh? Michael's so excited that he's put all of this out of his mind."

"Oh, good," I said, blowing out short breaths to the count of ten. "She'll bring him up tomorrow when the girls are here."

"You don't suppose they could put a cork in me or something and let me wait awhile, do you? I'd just like to take a nap."

"The anesthesiologist is coming to put in the epidural," Marty said matter-of-factly.

Oh, goodie. Don't get me wrong, epidurals are God's gift to women, but *getting* the epidural is not fun. The needle is a mile long and they insert it in your spine. You have to sit perfectly, we're talking *perfectly* still, or you can be paralyzed for life or something. The process is delicate. You sit up and bend over, holding perfectly still, which isn't easy with two monkeys in your belly doing the jungle dance. The epidural feels like a large hot brick shooting up your spine, and then everything is fine.

Marty kept telling me everything would be okay, to just relax. Maybe Marty shouldn't be here, because I did want to shoot her at that moment, and those aren't good thoughts.

Dr. Hall breezed in.

"How are you holding up?" he asked, patting my hand. I started laughing.

Dr. Hall looked at me and smiled quizzically. Then he looked at Marty, trying to figure out why I was laughing.

Marty just nodded knowingly at Dr. Hall as if he would understand, as if either of them would understand. The twits. Had they ever delivered a baby from *this* end? I think not. Were they worried sick out of their minds?

Then somebody had the bright idea to give me an enema. This is part of the humiliation process, kicking a dog when she's down.

"Let's give her something to relax her," Dr. Hall said to the nurse. "She's under a lot of stress and it's putting a strain on her heart. Her blood pressure is up."

You think?

Suddenly, a warm rush of something was flowing through my body and I was melting into the sheet. Somebody did insert something into my backend whatsey, but I didn't care. Marty had the good sense to leave the room and the nurse took care of the fallout. I was thankful I was out of my mind. Had I not been, I would have been ticked.

It seemed like everything was compressed in a little capsule of crazy. Labor pains, enema, epidural, labor pains again and again, heartache, indigestion, indignity, thirst like I've never known it, and just wanting to get through it.

I was ready. Dr. Hall had decided I would have a C-section. I was on board with this plan. I didn't particularly care for the drool on my face from all of the ice chips Marty (she had returned) kept shoveling in my mouth.

I was being draped and there were mirrors and lights. Dr. Hall and the nurses were frantically working. Marty sat next to me and held my hand.

I remember seeing Dr. Hall's eyes light up, and there was this gorgeous little girl with dark hair who was obviously hopping mad because she was screaming at the top of her lungs.

"There she is! You're a big girl for coming so early. One out, one to go. What's this one's name? Do we have a name? I guess just put Pendleton Baby 1," he instructed the nurse. The pediatrician was standing by.

"No," I rasped, my mouth feeling like cotton despite having swallowed sixteen thousand ice chips. "Georgette, she looks like George," I said. "Georgette Noel because it's so near Christmas."

Everyone oohed and aahed and they took her to the table to be weighed and cleaned up.

"Seven pounds, two ounces, eighteen inches long," the nurse said, chuckling.

"Imagine what she would have been if you'd had her on time," Marty said with a big grin.

Ha, ha, ha, everybody. I'd carried that bowling ball, and her sister was coming out soon, I hoped. Dr. Hall had his arm inside of me trying to get the next little girl out. This probably would have hurt like all-get-out had I not had drugs pumping through my veins.

My hair was ringing wet and I could feel the sweat rolling down my armpits. This was not a pretty moment for me. I just wanted to get this baby out.

"Dr. Hall pulled the second twin free from my body. "Gosh, she's pretty, too, but look how fair she is compared to her big sister!"

I could see her. She was beautiful, and she wasn't screaming like her sister; she gave a quiet little cry.

"Gretchen Grace," I said softly.

"Oh, that fits her," Marty said with a big smile.

"Well, little Gretchen Grace is the runt of the litter," the nurse said. "She's only six pounds, four ounces, and sixteen inches long."

"Healthy, healthy babies," Dr. Hall said, looking at me. "You did great, kid. We'll wash everything down. Let me stitch you up and we'll be all done."

They brought the babies closer for me to see. I was freezing and shaking so hard, I was afraid to hold them. I stroked their faces and kissed their hands and told them I loved them. Marty held them both and everybody had a fit over them. They were perfect.

"Marty, how's George?" I asked, downing more ice chips.

"I don't know, sweetie. I've been with you this whole time."

"Can you find out?" I asked. "It's been quite a long time."

"I'll try," Marty said and left the room.

The nurses were incredibly attentive and busy. They were cleaning me up, discarding stuff, and buzzing around me like little bees.

"Would you mind rubbing my back?" I asked Lyn, the shorter one of the two. Her smile was contagious. "It's cramping."

"Sure," she said agreeably. She gently turned me on my side and rubbed while Julie, the other nurse, did the caretaking thing. I wished I had ice cream. Chocolate ice cream, the soft, creamy kind, but I knew my fate. Ice chips for a little while.

I think they were finished long before they left. They seemed to be just filling the time. Julie toweled my hair dry. Lyn took a warm washcloth and washed me down, then rubbed lotion on me. I could have kissed her; I was so grateful. I hadn't had this kind of treatment with Michael. Maybe it was only for women who had twins? Or maybe they were being kind because of George.

The door opened and Marty came through, followed by Rick Palazzo, George's friend who had accompanied him to surgery, and Ned Hardy, the top surgeon in the hospital. Marty looked sad, the other two looked sad, and I knew it was bad news.

"Congratulations on the girls, they're beautiful," Rick said sweetly, taking my hand.

"Thank you," I responded automatically, reading their faces, dreading what I knew they were going to say.

"We did everything we could, Liz," Ned said sadly. "There was just too much internal bleeding."

"Was he in a lot of pain?" I asked, arrows piercing my heart.

"It was like he waited until the girls were born," Rick said in a soft voice. "He died exactly the minute Gretchen was born."

I closed my eyes and wished everything could reverse itself. I'd go through all the labor again, but this time George wouldn't be working late, he'd have met the plane and seen the Christmas pageant, and he would have been here, laughing and holding his girls. He wasn't dead, he couldn't be dead, it wasn't fair, he had more time to get his act together.

But the joke was on me. I wasn't in charge. None of us are. George was dead and I was a widow with three children.

TWENTY-SIX

Nobody likes funerals. You don't wake up and think, "Hey, I get to go to a funeral today, or I get to wear that little black dress I've been saving for that special occasion." Nope. You just go through the motions and hope you don't embarrass yourself by saying the wrong thing to the bereaved like "Hey, George looked good," or "nice dress," or "Were you planning on serving food?"

In this case, I was the bereaved. It had been two blurry days at the hospital. George's death and the twins' birth coincided about one-thirty on December 18. This was the twentieth and I didn't have all my holiday shopping done. Oh well, here were my gifts to the world, wrapped in pink blankets.

Marty and Dad were taking care of the arrangements for George because I couldn't. My mother stayed with me and was sweet and sincerely nurturing.

"I brought you a pretty robe so you wouldn't bare your bottom to the whole world," she said cheerfully. She whisked it out of the sack and held it up to herself.

"Mother!" I gasped.

"Well, it was the only one I could find in black and you're in mourning. It's not appropriate for you to wear bright colors and this was all I could find. It's December 20; things are pretty picked over. I was lucky to find this one," she said defensively.

It was black *crushed* velvet, like someone had scrunched it all up in a little ball and then hung it up. It had a big wide gold zipper up the front with a gold tassel attached to it. Around the cuffs and the hem were gold-embossed balls with scattered gold sequins, and on the back (which just *made* the robe according to my mother), was a large Christmas tree made of the same gold balls. I looked like King Tut.

"Mom, I'm not sure the hospital will let me wear this," I lied.

"Oh, of course they will. And I brought you some pretty nursing gowns," she said, fishing in the bag.

"Are they black too?"

"Don't be silly. Nobody looks at your gown. I got you different colors and they have slits in them so you can nurse," she said, pulling out gowns that looked somewhat reasonable in pastel shades.

My mom was a pistol, with her red teased hair, her Christmas-green outfit, and her black fur-lined boots. She had painted her fingernails bright red for the holidays, and she was wearing her light brown round glasses, which softened her eyes and made her look very smart, which she was. Any woman who read five books a week, played weekly duplicate bridge, was scorekeeper, and taught Sunday school class was no slouch.

"Your father and Marty are at the funeral home right now," she said.

"I told Marty I didn't want an open casket. I'm having him cremated because of the accident."

"Have you seen him yet?" she asked, almost in a whisper.

"No," I said, feeling my eyes water. "The last time I saw him they were taking him to surgery and then they took me to the delivery room."

"Well, he didn't have any family," Mom said.

"He had lots of family, Mom. I don't know what happened to them. He left home at seventeen and didn't look back. I think he tried to talk to his mother, but that was about it."

"How sad," she said. "I'd be devastated if you didn't talk to me."

The statement kind of rocked me for a moment. Maybe it was the hormones and the fact my husband had just died, but it really moved me that my mother cared so much. I thought she had always favored my sister. Well, she did favor my sister, but I guess we got along okay, too. I put on the black robe. It was a gift. She meant well.

"Your sister is moving," she said, as if to say my sister had bought a pair of shoes.

"Where?" I asked, expecting her to say next door to them.

"San Diego. He's got a great job offer and they're moving. It makes me really sad to see her go." She teared up.

"Mom, you'll have a great place to visit. Planes go there, you know."

I tried to think of other nice things and then a little resentment elbowed its way in. Why was I trying to make my mother feel better when I was the one who just gave birth to twins and lost her husband in the same minute? This was the dance, though. Mom would worry, and I'd cheer her up. That was my job.

"You're right," she said, reading my face. "I'm supposed to be comforting you, not the other way around. It's hard because you're the happy one and I don't know what to do to make it better."

"Just being here helps, Mom. And Dad helping Marty get the funeral arrangements done helps enormously. I feel like there are lots of things I should be doing."

"Well, you just rest and take care of these beautiful little girls," she said, putting on her paper mask, washing her hands, and handing Georgette to me. "She's going to be tall; look at those legs." Mom laughed softly. "I think Gretchen is going to be shorter and she's so fair."

They were as different as night and day in looks and personality. Georgette was aggressive. She nursed like someone was putting a vacuum on my breast; Gretchen was hesitant and almost shy. Both babies were just beautiful.

"Are you going to let that Kendra stay with you now that George is gone?" Mom asked. "She's not your responsibility you know."

"I know that, Mother, but she's helping me with Michael and the girls. She is their sister. I like having her around. She can stay as long as she wants and don't you say anything to her about leaving."

"I won't," she said defensively.

"Excuse me, Mrs. Pendleton?" a handsome man, medium height, with a gray mustache and beard, lightly tapped at the hospital door. "I'm Garrington Bass, George Pendleton's attorney. Please call me Gary. I'm sorry to bother you like this."

"Oh, you're not bothering me, Gary," I said, trying to pull Georgette discretely off my mountain of a breast. I zipped up the robe. The ROBE. Why did I have to put on the robe? I pulled the sheet up so he wouldn't see how hideous it was. I handed the baby back to my mother. Gretchen was sleeping.

"This is my mother, Helen Littleton."

"So nice to meet you!" my mother said, proudly holding the baby. My mother always lit up when a handsome man came into a room. Gary wasn't wearing a wedding ring, so no doubt she was scoping out a prospect for me.

"Nice to meet you. I'm sure you're enjoying these new babies," he said warmly.

"Oh, yes! Elizabeth has beautiful babies. I have a grandson, Michael, I adore, too."

"Well, I can see you're busy. I wanted to offer my condolences and give you my card. I know you have your hands full with babies and trying to deal with George's death. I just thought we should talk at some point when you feel up to it to settle his estate."

"Yes, of course," I said, trying to appear intelligent, or at least coherent. My hair was rumpled from delivering babies. I had on no makeup, and I was wearing this ridiculous robe. It wasn't my best moment.

"The bulk of everything will go to you. He did make provisions for his children, and he left something for his mother."

"His mother? Was he in contact with her?" I asked, surprised.

"I think he knew where she was. She's in an assisted living center in Salt Lake City. George left enough money to provide for her living expenses. We'll go over all of this next week."

"I was planning to cremate him," I said calmly, "and scatter his ashes at Philbrook, where we were married."

"He preferred cremation," Gary said, "so that would be fine. In fact, I think he'd like that. You'll have to get their permission, of course, but I think there's a garden for that kind of thing. Well," he said, looking at me with some sadness in his eyes, "I better get going."

"Is it still bad out there?" my mother asked.

"It's snowing and blowing," he said. "I better get back out there; I've got to get back to the office."

We said goodbye and Gary left.

"I hope your father and Marty are okay."

"They'll be fine. They took Marty's jeep with its four-wheel drive."

"Oh, good."

As if on cue, Marty and Dad came in with wet boots and red noses.

"It's pretty cold out there, Ma," my father said, kissing my mother on the cheek. "Marty and I picked up some coffee down the hall to warm us up though."

Marty took off her black coat and cream-colored scarf and hung them on the hook behind the door.

"How's the little mama feeling?" she asked, taking a spot on the corner of my bed. "New robe?" she said, noticing.

"Mom got this for me."

"Very festive," Marty teased.

"It's black. She's in mourning," Mom defended herself.

"Were you able to get everything done at the funeral home?" I asked.

"Yes, we made the arrangements, but you have to sign the papers before they can proceed with George. I explained the situation. One of the representatives from the funeral home will stop by this afternoon with them. Kendra's mother and stepfather are making arrangements to come in for the funeral, but the airport is closing. When do you want to have the funeral and where?" Marty asked.

"Let's just have it at the funeral home, I'm not up for going back to the church just yet," I said.

"My feelings exactly. I thought we'd have Fred do the service and Gloria sing," Marty said.

"Oh, good idea."

"Is that choir going to sing?" my mother asked. "I liked that choir at the wedding. They were good!"

"I don't know," Marty replied.

"Well, Dr. Hall said I can be out of here tomorrow."

"Let's have the funeral at ten on the morning of the twenty-third," Marty suggested. "This is the twentieth. That'd give you a little rest at home before the funeral. A morning funeral is nice so people can visit, have a little coffee and croissants, maybe some fruit and then get on with their holiday. Your mom and I can take care of getting the food there, can't we Helen?"

"Oh sure," Mom agreed. "We'll make it look very pretty. How many people do you expect?"

"Honestly, I don't know," I said. "I imagine people from the hospital and people from the station will come. Maybe we should have it at the church. There'd be plenty of parking. George had some friends."

"I hate to have to walk in the snow," Mom said.

"We'll have a limo," Marty reassured her.

"Yes," Dad chimed in. "We thought that would be easier with everybody. We booked two limos. He was standing by the babies, watching them sleep.

"Well, the funeral home has a rather large gathering room for guests and their chapel is pretty big. I think it would be fine. People may just send flowers or cards and not want to get out in the weather," Marty said, looking outdoors.

"Are the kids at home?" I asked, missing Michael.

"Yes, with plenty of food. They've been decorating the tree as a surprise for you when you get home. Hunter and Kendra got that tree down from upstairs. All of the ornaments were in the green and red boxes, so it wasn't hard to identify them. I thought decorating the tree and the house would give them something to do and take Michael's mind off of missing you so much," Marty said.

"Thank you. I miss our little boy. Can they come up today?" I asked.

Marty grinned. "Sure, have jeep will travel."

Gretchen woke up and was hungry. They started clearing out so I could nurse her. Dad was ready to go home, and Mom wanted to start making arrangements with the bakery for the funeral reception.

"Oh, one more thing," Marty said, softly. "I got the paperwork for the obituary. I figured you'd want to write it."

"Yes." I managed a nod. Gretchen nursed for a bit and fell asleep. I held her close to me and kissed her forehead. "Here, take her and get me a pen and some paper, please."

Marty laid her back in the hospital bassinet and covered her with a blanket. Georgette was still asleep. Marty left the room briefly and returned with a legal pad and a pen. She said, "The nurse says there are flowers downstairs but no one to bring them up because the volunteer aids are off for the holiday. I'll go down and get them."

She left and I was alone with the sleeping babies. I looked at the blank yellow page looming up at me. How should I begin? How do you chronicle a life you knew so little about? I would put what I knew down and call the hospital to have them fill in the rest of the professional accomplishments. I began.

"George Andrew Pendleton was born in Salt Lake City, Utah, on November 6, 1948, and died tragically from injuries suffered from an automobile accident on December 18, 1988. At the moment of his death, two little angels were born, his twin baby girls, Georgette Noel and Gretchen Grace. He also leaves his wife, Elizabeth Greene Pendleton, his oldest son, Hunter Pendleton, his oldest daughter, Kendra Pendleton, and four other children he'd never seen, and I have no idea who they are."

I'd have to mark through that last part and add a bunch more stuff, but for now, I was just too tired. The world could wait an hour while I took a nap. That was all I could manage to do, even wearing this ugly robe.

TWENTY-SEVEN

You know how when you don't have much sleep or the sleep you have is interrupted you feel punch-drunk? I'm not sure where the expression originates, but that's how I felt—like I could barely hold my head up. And when I was with people and everyone else was talking, I'd just fall asleep.

Kendra had slept with me the past few nights. She said it was to help me with the babies, but the first night I was home, she'd curled up in my bed and cried in my arms.

"We were just getting to know each other," she sobbed. "We needed more time. Why didn't God understand that?" she wailed.

"I don't know," I said sadly. "I've thought a lot about this and asked myself the same question and asked God that question. He's stubbornly silent on this one, yet I feel tenderness when I pray about it."

"That's weird that you say that," she said, "because I do too."

"Here's what I've come up with, or maybe God has helped me come up with it," I said.

"What's that?" she asked, her dark eyes wide like saucers.

"Well, maybe George's death was God's grace. I don't know about the accident. I still haven't read the reports or anything. I think his car slid out of control and I know there was quite a pile-up, but as I understand, George was the only one who died."

"Go on," she said.

"Okay, we both know that we would have liked the good side of George to prevail, but we don't really know all of the demons he faced. What if George couldn't have gotten better? Maybe God spared us that and wants us to remember the best of George, which is in you and Hunter and the girls, maybe in the others too. Or maybe he spared him and it was just his time to go."

"Hmm, maybe so," she said, rolling over and staring at the ceiling. "I hadn't really thought of it that way. Speaking of the others, I contacted them and they're coming to the funeral. Mom and her new husband, Drake, want to come too."

"Ohh," I said.

"Are you mad?" she asked, her face wrinkling in concern.

"No, not mad, just feeling overwhelmed. Long week, I look like crap, I don't feel well, and it's a lot of people to meet all at once. Would your mom like to stay here?"

"No, I suggested they go to a hotel. They can afford it and that would be a little awkward for you. They have a cruise to go on Christmas Eve, so they'll be flying out that night."

"Well, that was nice of your mom to come."

"She said she was doing it for Hunter and me, that Dad had never missed a payment, and she had loved him once."

"Well, that's nice," I said. I wondered what the etiquette was here. Was I supposed to have these people to dinner? "When are they flying in?"

"They'll fly in later tomorrow afternoon. I thought Hunter and I would borrow Marty's jeep if that's okay, meet them at the airport, and we'd just eat at the hotel."

"No," I heard myself saying, "let them come here. Marty can cook. We'll have to ask Marty, of course, but we have plenty of food in that freezer, Marty can make something. We can do something simple like spaghetti. We have plenty of wine, we've got some bread, we'll make a salad, and you can bake one of your famous cakes. How would that be?"

"That would be so much nicer! Would you mind?"

"She's your mom, how bad could she be?" I asked with a smile.

"She's really not bad, just sort of absorbed by Drake right now, but she's actually pretty nice."

Marty agreed of course, and Kendra, Hunter, and Michael helped with dinner. The babies and I sat in the loveseat and supervised. Michael buzzed around the babies, but he seemed afraid of them, and he didn't mention George at all. Marty said when he told Michael about George, Michael was quiet and thoughtful for a moment, but didn't cry or anything. I figured he didn't really understand or maybe it didn't seem real to him. This was a lot to process at his age.

Audrey and Drake arrived around six-thirty by cab. I knew Audrey was taking in everything, all the decorations outside, the Norman Rockwell-ish Christmas tree the children and Marty had decorated, and just the magnitude of the house itself. I figured she was uncomfortable because of the situation. After all, her daughter had been asked to leave and was living with me, which was a bit dicey. Hunter spending Christmas with us might not have helped either.

I looked okay. I had showered of course. After blow-drying my hair I'd heated up the curling iron for a few minutes and kind of ran it through to make my hair take shape. I had put on some makeup, but I couldn't hide the dark circles under my eyes.

I did not wear the robe my mother gave me, but I did put on a long black sweater and a pair of stretchy black pants. This was safe and made me look thinner than I was. I sprayed on a little perfume and felt ready to roll.

Audrey looked like an older version of Kendra, except for the eyes. Kendra had George's eyes. Hunter looked exactly like his dad. He had only a few of his mother's facial expressions. She was very pretty, tall and thin, but not standoffish or uppity.

Once they were in my living room, I didn't feel weird about the whole deal. They were just people. Drake was a lot older than Kendra's mom. She was around forty, although with dark hair streaked with gray she looked a little older. Drake was probably late fifties, early sixties, with enhanced blond curly hair. I thought old Drake might have a bit of a roving eye. Ironically, the roving eye wasn't roving my way, it was roving toward Marty. This threw calm, cool, and collected Marty into a panic.

"He pinched my butt," Marty whispered when I came into the kitchen to check on things.

"What?"

"He pinched my butt! Drake did. When I came in here to check on the spaghetti sauce, he followed me to see what I was doing and pinched my butt!"

"Well, see," I said, "all those hormone shots paid off. What'd you do?"

"I told him he better not try that again or I'd knock his block off." Marty said, "Keep him away from Kendra."

I giggled. "Okay, but maybe he only has eyes for you."

"He just married her mother!"

"It's their business, and they'll be gone tomorrow. Just be nice."

I left Marty in the kitchen to collect herself and get the dinner ready. Drake had engrossed himself in a football game in the study where the TV was on. I returned to the living room and sat in my favorite soft chair.

"Has Marty worked for you long?" Kendra's mother asked.

"Oh, no, Marty isn't the maid, she lives here, and we're, uh, cousins."

"I see," Audrey said.

"We're not partners. I am married, uh, was married to George," I said defensively.

"I didn't mean to imply … it's just that George lived in another house and people have all kinds of arrangements these days."

"Mom …" Kendra said, looking annoyed.

"We were separated," I said quietly, resenting the implications.

"I understand," she said.

Okay, I was ticked. This woman's smugness was getting to me. I was filling up with milk and having trouble sitting in one position for any length of time, the weather was nasty and cold outside, and I wanted to take a nap in front of this roaring fire. Instead I had to entertain Mrs. Smug and Mr. Pinchbottom.

I glanced at Kendra and Hunter; they both looked miserable. Poor kids. I would put down my sword and start again.

"So, tell me about this cruise. I've never been on one," I said pleasantly.

"Oh, we're going to sail through the Caribbean," she said. "We have a cabin with our own private deck. It's very exclusive, with lots of amenities."

For some reason, I pictured a dilapidated cabin sitting on a boat deck with Drake and Audrey in overalls sitting in rocking chairs.

"Mom, you don't have to put on airs. Liz and Marty are just regular people that lived in normal houses until Dad gave Liz this house," Kendra said.

"I'm not putting on airs," Audrey said, looking defensive.

"Drake has money, or at least the appearance of money," Kendra said dryly. "Mom's child support was about to run out."

"I can't believe you're saying these things, Kendra, in front of our hostess! I work. We can't all be in television, you know."

That's when things erupted. Kendra went flying across the room at her mom. The two of them were in a catfight, rolling around on my living room floor, calling each other names, and pulling each other's hair. I sat there with my mouth open.

"Hey, stop it!" I said, not all that loudly, because I was somewhat fascinated with the fight.

Marty came out of the kitchen and started yelling. Drake joined the fray and Hunter was in the middle of them trying to pull them apart. Michael, who had been upstairs playing, came running down the stairs to see the commotion.

Many long moments later, Hunter pulled them apart. The appetizers Marty had fixed were on the floor and Audrey's wine had been knocked over. Both Audrey and Kendra were breathing hard, and Hunter's expression was angry.

"You two are ridiculous. I can't believe you'd do this here!"

"Does this happen often?" I asked, horrified.

"Just once before," Audrey said quietly, "which is why she doesn't live with me anymore."

"I don't live with you because your husband is a creep and you're a b—"

"Careful! Little pitchers have big ears," I interrupted.

Kendra looked at me apologetically. Her hair was a mess. Her shirt was torn, and she was bleeding.

"I'm sorry, Liz," she said sincerely.

"Go upstairs, clean up and change," I told her. "Audrey, there's a powder room under the stairs if you need it."

Audrey needed it. Kendra had gotten in some good licks. Her hair was scraggly, and her sweater was spotted.

"If you wish to have the rug cleaned, please send me the bill," Audrey said with dignity.

"Oh, it'll probably come up," I replied, glancing at Marty, who already had a towel, soda water, and carpet cleaner in hand.

"Mommy, your sweater is all wet," Michael said, crawling into my lap. It was true. I was soaked, and I could hear the girls waking up.

"I'm going to have to feed the girls, buddy. Are you okay? That was quite something, wasn't it?

"Yeah, Kendra socked her mom good."

"Well, Kendra was wrong to do that, Michael, because that's her mother and no matter whether she agrees with her or not, she shouldn't have done that. You don't solve anything by physically fighting with someone. Do you understand that?" I said.

"I guess."

"You remember you got mad and pushed somebody and things got out of hand, didn't they?" I asked.

He lowered his eyes. "Yes."

Well, that's not the way to let your feelings out."

"Okay, are we going to eat now?" he asked, looking at Marty.

"Yes, everything is ready." Marty nodded as she cleaned up the last of the wine.

"I'll feed the girls quickly and then we can eat. If you want, you all can start without me."

"Are you kidding?" Marty said. "We need you there."

I fed the girls, changed my bra and sweater, and went into the dining room where everyone was seated and not saying a word.

I looked from Kendra to Audrey. "As I was telling Michael, punching and fighting isn't the way to solve things, wouldn't you agree?"

"Certainly," Audrey said. She had combed her hair and put on lipstick.

"Agreed," Kendra said, head down.

"Well, the two of you obviously have issues, but wrestling in the living room isn't the way to do it. Marty has made a great meal. We have a sad task to go through tomorrow and I would appreciate it if everyone would suck it up and get along!"

There were some embarrassed smiles, and the food was passed. Small talk started and everyone seemed fine. Audrey didn't eat much, but I gave her credit for coming to the table. She did have some of Kendra's chocolate cake. We all did, and by the time it arrived, we were having somewhat normal conversations. I had put on my journalist hat and was asking lots of questions about where they lived, what things were like there, and what they liked to do.

Drake was a bit of a bore, but he wasn't horrible, although he did wink at Marty once during dinner.

Afterward, Kendra and Hunter helped Marty clear the table. Michael and Drake went into the den to watch something on television. Audrey and I went into the living room, which had been restored to its natural habitat.

"I am sorry about earlier," Audrey said sincerely. "I don't know what it is with mothers and daughters," she added, shaking her head.

I laughed. "Oh, don't scare me, I just had two of them the other day."

We sat down on the sofa in front of the fire. The room was comfortable, and the Christmas tree made it look almost magical.

"I think I've been really upset about the news about George," she said, clearly thinking out loud.

"It has been upsetting," I agreed.

"He was my first real love," she said. "We were young, just twenty when we met. We got married at twenty-one. We had both just graduated from college, a small community college in Massachusetts, and he'd been accepted to medical school at Tufts with a full scholarship. Our future looked so bright. We had Kendra. Hunter followed about eighteen months later."

I sat watching this woman transform from the guarded person she had been when she walked in the door to someone much softer, much younger. It was as if the memories were making her young again.

"Kendra was five and Hunter was four when he left. We got along okay. It was the children he couldn't handle. He loved them, but he would get upset with them for one reason or another, look in the mirror and then leave the house. One day, he just didn't come back."

"He just didn't come back?" I said. "You must have been terrified."

"I was. I notified the police, checked the hospital where he worked, and called the highway patrol. He was just *gone*."

"Where did he go?"

"He had taken a position at another hospital in another town. He sent me a letter a few days later along with divorce papers. He said it wasn't my fault or the children's. He just couldn't be a father. He hated his father, and every time he looked in the mirror, he saw his father and he couldn't live with himself."

"He wouldn't go to therapy?"

"He wouldn't hear of it. He said this was best for the kids and everybody. That was that."

"Oh Audrey, how sad."

"I never remarried. I dated some but I kept hoping George would walk back into our lives one day. Then, a year or so ago, I found out about the other women and the other children. I decided to start dating and met Drake."

You could have done better, I thought, but I didn't say it.

"You must really resent me," I said, "especially with Kendra here."

"I did, but I realized after meeting you and uh, after tonight, that you are just trying to be kind to my daughter and, a lot of years have passed."

"I still think he tried to deal with it; that's why he never married any of the mothers. I got pregnant after we were married, and it freaked him out. I don't know. It's sad and we'll probably never know all the answers. But I want you to know that Kendra is welcome here—if there are no more fights in my living room!"

"Agreed," she said with a smile.

"And I'd like to keep the lines of communication open between us. Our children are siblings. Hunter is welcome here too."

"I think that would be nice. They've missed having a big family."

"Do you know about his family at all? How did you find out about the other children?" I asked.

"I work for a legal firm in Florida. Someone came there from Tulsa and asked me if I was related to George. His sister is the mother of the twins; she had run into the other woman who had the other set of twins. I contacted them and we talked briefly. They didn't have much to say and didn't want to get together." She shrugged.

"Small world," I said, pulling my knees up and hugging myself. I felt a chill, even though it was warm in the living room.

"Did you ever try to contact his parents or siblings?" I asked.

"No. I thought about it. They live in Salt Lake City, or they did. I was afraid to do it. George was so vehemently against it, and he always paid me every month, so I didn't want to rock the boat."

Marty and Kendra joined us in the living room. Hunter went into the den with the boys.

"Does anyone want coffee?" Marty asked.

"No," Audrey said, "it keeps me up and it's been a long day. Drake and I better get back to the hotel. Will you call a cab?" she asked.

"I could take you," Marty said.

"Oh, that's too much trouble."

"I have a jeep, it's no problem. Hunter can go with me. Kendra can stay here to help Liz with the babies."

They said their goodbyes and got in Marty's car. Marty had thoughtfully turned on the heat. She forgot her gloves and ran back in the kitchen.

"I can't wait to meet the *others*," Marty said. "This should be one heck of a funeral, tomorrow."

After tonight's conversation, I had a feeling Marty was right.

TWENTY-EIGHT

I couldn't sleep, so I was up about 5:00 a.m. The babies had their breakfast, and I was feeling drained—literally and figuratively. I'm not a coffee drinker, so I started the fireplace in the kitchen and curled up on the loveseat with a blanket and a cup of hot chocolate so I could think. But as mine was a house full of people, someone joined me.

"I didn't expect anybody to be up," Hunter said. He was in flannel pajama bottoms and a ratty old T-shirt. It resembled several of my sleeping ensembles.

"I couldn't sleep," I said flatly.

"Neither could I," he said sadly.

I studied him for a moment. We hadn't really gotten to talk much since he'd been here. He was so quiet; I didn't know him very well. There was so much about him that reminded me of George: his voice, his height, his face, his hands, and the way he moved.

"We had quite an evening," I said.

"Yes, I hate it when those two get together because they always fight." He dropped his tall frame in the easy chair adjacent to my loveseat. "I mean, they used to be pretty close. I was always the outcast because there was no man around. I used to hang out with my uncle some, my mom's brother, but he had his own kids."

There it was, loud and clear. The thing men don't get when they run away from their responsibilities, the thing they don't get when they abandon their children, is how much the kids suffer. It's not just sad one day when they leave, it's sad when there's no father at little league or soccer or swim meets or at a school program. It's sad when only one parent goes to back-to-school night and when boys want to ask questions about their bodies and sex and they don't really want to ask their moms.

George had missed all of this with his son, and he'd missed the dances, the programs, and so much more with Kendra. I don't know if he'd ever even seen the other children.

My body started getting the "sad aches" again. It may have had to do with having two babies that week, but I thought it was all the sadness, too.

"How do you feel about today?" I asked him, trying not to yawn.

"He shrugged. "It's not going to be easy. It'll be kind of like going to the funeral of a stranger."

I knew what he meant.

"I mean, I don't exactly remember him. I've seen pictures and I remember a tall man who played with me, but I don't remember much else. I remember my mom crying for a long time after he left, like for weeks. I'm just mad because at least I could have met him. I never even had a chance to tell him off, you know? At least Kendra had her chance to scream at him."

"What did she say about that?" I asked, sipping my hot chocolate.

"Well, she said it was like he heard her, but was in denial about it and just told her she didn't understand. He never blamed my mom though, I'll give him that."

"It wasn't about your mom," I said. "It was something inside himself."

"I just think if a guy doesn't ever want to be a dad, he needs to think about that before he sleeps with somebody. I'm going to get married and that's it. And I'm not sleeping with anybody I wouldn't want to marry—period."

"That's wise, Hunter," I said. "Do you have everything you need for today?" I asked.

"Yeah, my mom made me bring a sports coat and tie in case we went out to eat and I have some khakis."

"Okay, that's fine. I just feel bad that I haven't spent much time with you for us to really get to know each other."

He smiled. "Well, you were having babies and that's a pretty good excuse! Don't feel bad. You and Marty have been so nice. She's really nice. Most of the time, I forget she was ever a guy. That's sort of a weird deal to me, but she's such a nice person, it doesn't matter."

"Well, it was kind of a weird deal for me, too, at first," I said with a half-smile.

"I guess so," he agreed.

"But Marty was always my best friend and no matter what he wore, Marty is still Marty on the inside and now Marty feels like Marty feels she should feel on the outside."

"I never heard of this before," he said.

"I'd never heard of it either, but we've adjusted."

"I bet it's hard on Michael. I mean I understand what it's like growing up without a dad."

"Well, Michael has two parents who love him who both happen to be women. Marty and I have remained best friends. She was wonderful when I married George—and now of course."

Hunter seemed to take all of this in and then closed his eyes. I saw tears streaking down his face.

"Hunter," I said, reaching across and laying my arm on his.

He sniffed loudly and looked at me. "It's just, there's so much *crap*." He put his head in his hands.

"I know. It's not fair and you didn't do anything wrong. Your dad was in the wrong. I do think he was trying to get better. I know he was looking forward to seeing you because we'd talked about it. I think that whatever happened in his household growing up, George got a warped sense of what it meant to love. I think he was terrified of becoming a father. Instead of getting the help he needed, he just ran. His father must have been a pretty lousy father, and someone should have told him every day of his life "You're not your father." He looked like him, I guess, so he was afraid of becoming him. I will tell you this, Hunter: you are not your father. You have his good looks and, as far as I can tell, his intellect, but that's where it stops. You can be a great husband and father. Those two things take commitment and love."

"I can do that," he whispered.

"I know you can," I said, squeezing his hand. "Now, how about you and I make some breakfast for this crew who will wake up shortly?"

"I make wicked good eggs."

"You got it, buddy," I said, smiling.

We made breakfast for everybody and got ready for the funeral. My parents came by to take care of the girls. I nursed each of them for a long time before the limo picked us up. Michael stayed home to help. There was no reason for him to come out in this weather, and he was pretty young for the funeral.

I wore a lose-fitting long black dress with black boots and a black jacket. Three little white roses graced my lapel to represent Georgette, Gretchen, and Michael. I also wore a gold heart George had given me for Valentine's Day. He had engraved "Love always, George" and the date on it. I had curled my hair and put on makeup. I looked nice and formal, ready to meet the entourage. I was still as big as a barn, but hey, I'd just given birth.

We were late. I wouldn't be late to my own funeral and, in this case, George's funeral, but the limousine got stuck a couple of times and had a terrible time making the corners. We got there a few minutes after ten and the place was rocking. I noticed the two buses from Fred's church were parked in the parking lot of the funeral home.

"What's all that noise?" Hunter asked, climbing out of the limousine.

"Just wait," I said with a big smile. "You've probably never seen anything like this."

Someone took our coats when we went inside and we were escorted into the chapel. Lining the walls was the choir, with extra members up front. Every one of them had showed up, and I think they brought some of their friends and their kids because they were all singing, gospel style, "Amazing grace, how sweet the sound that saved a wretch like me…."

Everyone stood when we walked in. I was amazed at how many people had braved the weather. The place was packed. There were my friends from the station, George's friends from the hospital, neighbors, and relatives. Seated on the second row down front were two attractive women next to men I assumed were their husbands. One woman had a set of four-year-olds with her, both little boys. The other woman had a set of what looked to be about nine-year-olds, a boy and a girl. All of them looked like variations of George and the women who were their mothers. Glam and her veterinarian sat next to them. Glam smiled and patted me as I sat down.

Kendra and Hunter sat next to Marty and me in the front row. Audrey and Drake were at the far end of the row with the children between us. I acknowledged them and each of the people in the row behind me by shaking their hands and introducing myself as the choir sang the last verse. When we were all seated, the choir finished and Fred began to talk about George. As he read all of George's accomplishments in life, the choir hummed. Marty had found several nice photographs, one large one from the hospital, and had placed them in the front of the chapel and in the outer lobby. There we all were staring at handsome pictures of George surrounded by Christmas greenery. The chapel smelled wonderful, which was a blessing, because usually a bunch of flowers kind of made me sick and there were flowers everywhere. Marty began sneezing, but then stopped.

Rick got up and spoke about George, what a great doctor he was, what a good friend he had been, and how valiantly he fought to stay alive. He addressed the family and said that George had loved us. One of the older twins snorted, and I could see him looking at his mother out of the corner of my eye. Kendra and Hunter were silent.

Gloria stood and sang "The Old Rugged Cross" with the choir backing her up.

It was perfectly beautiful. Fred began to preach. His style might have surprised this mostly all-white audience. Fred was fiery. He thumped his Bible. He waved his hands and punctuated his sentences with extra syllables at the end. Sometimes, for effect, the organist would strike a few chords to emphasize Fred's points. Several of the choir members shouted approval, agreement, and a multitude of "Amens."

Fred read the 23rd Psalm and the section in Revelation that describes heaven. He told us that George was greeted by a host of angels and all his long-lost relatives. His suffering was over. I hoped this was true.

When Fred was finished with his prayer, which was lengthy, Gloria started to stand up to sing the final song. For some reason, I stood up. I don't know why. I certainly didn't feel like it, but I did. I thought I heard a few gasps in the room and frankly, when I turned around and saw all of those people, I felt a little lightheaded. But I had something to say.

"I know it's not customary for the widow to say anything at her husband's funeral, but I wanted to thank all of you for coming out in this weather today to support my extended family, George's family, and me. As Fred mentioned, in our minds, George was taken from us prematurely. But I know God has a plan for every-thing. Had I not met George, I wouldn't have two beautiful new baby girls, and I never would have met Kendra and Hunter, his two oldest children.

"George touched many lives, he was absent from others, and ironically, those lives should have been the most significant to him. I may not have known George as long as some in this room. As many of you know, as brilliant as he was in the Emergency Room, he was struggling in parts of his personal life. I loved George Pendleton, but I realize there was a lot I didn't know about him. He was kind, compassionate, and loving, but he was also resistant when it came to facing his demons and moving past them. I hope that doesn't happen to you today. I hope today we can bury George Pendleton and truly give him to God and let go of any sadness in our past.

"Let's not hold onto our anger and bitterness the way George did, because even though a car accident killed him, it was his brokenness that kept him from progressing in any of his relationships. I pray our heavenly father has welcomed him home and may George finally rest in peace."

The room burst into applause, which my mother would have said was totally inappropriate, but I felt honored that they'd accepted what I said. I don't know where my words came from, but what I had said needed to be said. I was exhausted when I sat down next to Marty. She was crying, of course, because she was so proud of me.

Then the choir began a round of singing "Amens" and clapping. Soon, Fred invited everyone to join the family for food in the gathering room after the service. He prayed, and Gloria sang the solo part of "On Eagle's Wings" with the choir.

It was incredible and uplifting and everyone was teary and smiley. As the family stood to leave, the choir broke out with "When the saints come marching in…" and the four-year-old twins danced down the aisle. I felt like stepping pretty lively myself, but I tried to remain somewhat dignified. The choir sang everyone out of the chapel, which perked up the mood quite a bit.

Mom and Marty had arranged for hot coffee, hot tea, hot chocolate, croissants and cinnamon rolls, cheese cubes, and fresh fruit. They had planned an abundance of food for everyone, including the choir. People mingled pleasantly. Many of them came by and offered their condolences with hugs and handshakes.

Sarah, the attractive red-haired mother of the four-year-old twins, came up to me before I realized who she was.

"We're going to have to head out. The kids are getting restless. I wanted to thank you for including us and saying what you did. You're right. I've had a lot of anger toward George for not being there and missing their lives, but it was his loss."

"Yes, it was. Your children are beautiful," I said.

"Here's my card. Maybe we could get together for coffee or talk sometime. I live in Pryor now," Sarah said. "I got married about two years ago."

"Sure," I said, feeling a bit awkward.

"I guess the child support stops now," she said with a laugh.

"I don't honestly know any details, I've been busy this week," I told her. "I'm sure the attorney will contact you next week."

She nodded. "Oh. Okay. Again, thank you, and I'm sorry for your loss". Her husband pulled their minivan up to the door of the funeral home and she left in a blur.

"I'm Natalie." A short, petite blonde stood looking at me. "I'm the mother of George's *other* twins. I know we met during the service, but I thought with all of these people, I'd better introduce myself again."

"Natalie," I said, shaking her hand, "thank you for clarifying that."

"My kids have been horribly hurt by George because he never saw them. He had the doctor do the bloodwork to prove he was the father, and the rest was between the attorneys. I never saw him again," she said, bitterness evident in her voice.

"I'm sorry for that. I can't really answer to that, because I didn't even know about any of his children until Kendra walked into our lives last summer. Perhaps we can stay in touch since our children are siblings," I said.

She snorted. "I don't think so. My children have a different last name because my husband has adopted them. I just brought them because I thought they might get one glimpse of him and frankly, if there had been a casket, I would have stuck a pin in him to see if the S.O.B was dead!"

"Lady, this isn't the time to unload your crap," I heard Glam say from behind me. "Get your kids and leave. Liz didn't do anything to you. Call your therapist in the morning."

Natalie started to say something else, then turned on her heel and left. Her kids were already in the car with her husband. I thanked Glam, who put a strong arm around me. Glam was right; it wasn't my deal. I had my own problems to worry about, like two hungry babies at home.

Kendra, Hunter, Audrey, Drake, Marty and I said our final goodbyes. The funeral staff gave me George's wedding ring. Drake and Audrey waved and got into a limousine to drive to the airport. The choir and most everybody else had left. The few remaining cars in the parking lot belonged to funeral home employees.

A short, blonde-haired woman in a red coat walked quickly by me. In an instant, I recognized her. She turned and looked at me with tears in her eyes. It was Brenda, George's former secretary for the short-term.

"I didn't know whether I should come, but I wanted to. I'm sorry for your loss and for any hurt I caused you," she said, shivering in the cold.

I couldn't say, "That's okay," because it wasn't, but it was nice of her to come, so I said so. In fact, I thanked her for coming and told her to drive home carefully.

As the limousine pulled away from the funeral home, I was thankful it was all behind me. I had decided to scatter the ashes in the hospital's memorial garden.

All of us were quiet, lost in our own thoughts. The ache in my heart was still there, matching the ache in my body. I'd meet with the attorney after Christmas, and we'd get all the legal stuff handled. Next week we'd go over to George's house and start the process of sorting through his stuff.

I wondered what I would find in that attic and in the confines of his desk drawers that I had never been allowed to open.

TWENTY-NINE

Christmas was bittersweet. Michael and Marty had made homemade gifts for everyone. Hunter had built identical wooden cradles for the girls. Kendra had painted their names on them and had crocheted little baby blankets for them. Who knew the girl could crochet and when had she found the time?

They had made Michael a doghouse because Marty had thought Michael needed his own baby. Santa brought Michael some toys, but under the tree was Bob, a Bassett Hound puppy. He was adorable and very busy, keeping us entertained throughout the day.

We decided to start going through George's house between Christmas and New Year's Day because Hunter would have to return home January 2. It wasn't easy for any of us. Hunter had never been there, and Marty, Kendra and I hadn't been there since July. Marty stayed home with the girls and Michael.

There was a pile of newspapers on George's front porch. They were frozen solid. We gathered them up and put them in a trash bag. The mail overflowed out of the box. I reminded myself to forward the mail and stop the papers. We went inside. The house was welcomingly warm, but not too hot. Everything was perfectly neat and in its place, but just a little dusty.

I could see Hunter taking everything in as his eyes darted from the ceiling to the bookcases to the art on the wall. His reaction was much the same as mine when I first saw the house: Wow!

We went upstairs and went through the rooms. When we opened the project room door, we all gasped. Sitting in the middle of the floor were two cradles in almost the same shape and shade as the ones Hunter made the girls for Christmas.

Hunter went over and rubbed his hand along the wood.

"These are like the ones I made," he said, shaking his head.

"It looks like we see where you get your aptitude," I said, smiling.

On the table were two beveled mirrors. One was square and the other oval shaped. They had been lovingly carved, sanded, and stained. George had painted Hunter and Kendra's initials in the corners of each one. It was obvious these were meant to be Christmas gifts. Tears ran down Kendra's cheeks and she hugged Hunter. They had lost so much.

We wandered around the upstairs and I showed Hunter the master bedroom. This was pretty rough on me. I could visualize George coming out of the bathroom in the morning and kissing me goodbye or us curled up in bed at night talking about our day. His scent still lingered in the room, especially when I opened his closet.

"Hunter, look through here and see if there are things you might want. George had good taste and really expensive clothes. I've been a discount shopper my whole life, but George only shopped at the best places," I said, inhaling George's fragrance.

Hunter joined me and began looking through the closet. He found a couple of jackets he liked and a few sweaters. Kendra looked too. She pulled out a couple of his sweatshirts and handed me one. I understood. We would both wear them, honoring the good memories.

We meandered around the room a bit and then went up a little winding staircase outside the master bedroom door. It led to the attic. It was chilly up there because there wasn't any heat. Kendra and I put on George's sweatshirts and Hunter pulled on George's favorite sweater.

Everything was neat and orderly for an attic. How like George. I hoped he was up there stacking boxes for Jesus right now. There was a cedar-lined closet full of out-of-season clothes; there were various pictures and magazines, a large ice chest, several pairs of old hiking boots, some fishing rods, and a tackle box. There were stacks of boxes, but I wasn't sure what was in them, although most of them looked like college textbooks, that kind of thing.

"Hey, look at this old trunk!" Hunter said excitedly. Kendra blew the dust off and began flipping the fasteners, but the lock wouldn't open. "Let me carry it over to the window where I can see better," Hunter said. "Maybe I can figure out how to open it."

As he lifted the trunk with a loud grunt, something clanged on the floor. George had kept the key under the trunk, probably figuring nobody would find it. Kendra grabbed the key and waited until Hunter gently set the trunk down. He was sweating; it must have been really heavy.

Kendra opened the trunk and a picture fell out. It was full of pictures and trophies. There was a bowling trophy with the name of George's church on it and several little league championships for a team called the Salt Lake City Cougars, all dating back to George's youth. There was a ceramic animal George might have made in school and a wooden box he must have made in junior high woodworking class, because it had "George" burned on the top.

We started pulling out the pictures. There was George, looking just like Hunter, only with a burr haircut, standing next to a bunch of kids who looked like younger versions of George in male and female form. There were a couple of blondes in the bunch. In the middle was a man with a stern expression who looked just like an older version of George and a blonde, blue-eyed woman seated next to him. She had a soft, kind face. Something in her expression reminded me of the good George.

"This must be our grandparents." Kendra said what we were all thinking. "And Dad's brothers and sisters. Gosh, there are a lot of them."

"Look here," Hunter said, pulling out another picture. It looked like a class at school or maybe a group of students from a church, but we realized it must have been George's siblings from all of his mothers. There were three women standing behind large groups of kids. All the children looked like younger versions of George's dad, mingled with some softer features.

"Weird," Hunter said. "How weird would that be?"

"Really weird," Kendra agreed. "No wonder he left."

"According to George, your grandfather could be very cruel. Maybe that's why your grandmother left or divorced him."

"She divorced him?" Kendra looked surprised.

"Or he died, and she took back her maiden name, but that doesn't seem likely. He may have died and she remarried, because her last name is Carson now," I said.

"How do you know she's even still alive?" Hunter asked.

"Your dad was paying for her to live in an Assisted Living Center in Salt Lake City," I said. "The attorney told me."

"I wonder if she still has her mind," Kendra mused.

"I know. I've thought the same thing," I said. "Hunter, when you graduate in June, what would you guys say to maybe all of us flying to Salt Lake City and meet her?"

"What about the girls and Michael?" Kendra asked, wrinkling her forehead. "And Marty?"

"Marty may or may not want to go. I think it would be easier to fly instead of drive, and it would be nice to get away. I'll book the reservations for early June, but first, you'll have to ask your mother," I said.

"She won't care," Kendra said quickly.

"She might have something else planned," I said, choosing my words carefully. "Let's try to mend some fences and build bridges in the next six months, okay?"

"Okay," she agreed.

Hunter nodded. "Okay."

We went back downstairs, and I used the tiny key on George's key ring to open his desk. The checkbooks were here and all his files. He had a file on each child and their mother. He had copies of birth certificates and pictures that the school or the mothers had sent. I wondered how many times he looked at these late at night.

Hunter and Kendra seemed to be getting impatient and I was feeling a need to get home and feed the girls. They must be getting hungry.

We bundled up, locked the doors, and flipped on the porch light before we left.

"What are you going to do with Dad's house?" asked Hunter, glancing back as we drove away.

"What do you think we should do with it?"

"I don't know." He shrugged. "Sell it, I guess."

"That's too bad, I think it's a nice house," Kendra said.

"Well, I was thinking," I said slowly.

"I love it when you think," Kendra said, smiling at me from the back seat.

"It's really hard to be a mom without a dad around," I began. "What if we checked with some churches and created a house for single moms with their babies or small children?"

"How many would live there?" Kendra asked, interested.

"Well, there are four bedrooms. We could have two or three, I guess, depending on the children. We'd have to screen them and make sure they would take care of the house—keep it clean and not let the children destroy it. No pets or anything. This would be a place they could live rent-free and maybe just pay the utilities for a set amount of time until they got on their feet."

"Yeah, because if you give them everything, they won't appreciate it," Hunter said, grinning. He laughed. "I can't believe I just said that. My mom always says that."

"It's true," I agreed. "Well, we'd have to figure out all the parameters and also draw up some legal papers to have them sign for liability and all of that. But I think it would be a help to some people to get them started in life."

The girls were making hungry cries when we walked in the door. Marty was worn to a frazzle because Michael had broken a neighbor's window and the neighbor had been furious, screaming at our doorstep. The girls were crying, and Marty had to punish Michael. She sent him to his room to figure out ways he was going to pay for the window.

As I was feeding the girls, I reflected on how all of our lives had changed. I was sad to see Hunter go home, but he would be back. We were going to be taking a terrific trip in June, one that would provide us some answers. I hoped it would allow us to meet the family George had left behind over two decades ago.

Six months can go by quickly when you're busy, and we were a busy household. Kendra had enrolled in a photography class. I arranged with the station for me to do only specials for sweeps and work on a contract basis. They gave me a small office at the station that stayed locked most of the time.

The girls were starting to crawl. Georgette was loud, chatty, smiley, and aggressive. Gretchen was quieter and a good audience, smiling and laughing at everything Georgette did. They were both a delight.

We decided to leave them home with Marty and my parents. Before we made our reservations for Salt Lake, I called the retirement community.

"Greenfield Gardens," a cheerful voice said.

"May I speak with the director?" I asked. There was a series of clicks, a smattering of some canned music, and she answered.

"Fiona Flowers, may I help you?"

"Ms. Flowers, this is Liz Pendleton in Tulsa. George Pendleton was my husband. He died in December. I wonder if you all had been notified, and if his mother had been told?"

"The attorney did call here, but Mrs. Carson passed on Christmas day."

"Oh, no!" I said, shocked.

"It was a blessing, dear. She saw the angels for days before she passed and right before she died, she did speak quite clearly."

"What did she say?"

"She said, 'Oh, George, it's so good to see you!' I guess he came and got her and took her to her heavenly home!"

I was speechless, but I knew I had to say something. I thanked her for taking care of George's mother and for that information. She told me one of Mrs. Carson's children had come and packed up her stuff. She gave me a contact list of her family members.

Apparently, the Carson clan felt the same way about George as he felt about them. I contacted all the people on the list. They made me feel like a phone solicitor. I did hit pay dirt for more information from the last name. Ironically, it was an ex-sister-in-law, Claudia. She gave me the scoop on the family.

George's dad had died several years earlier, which started Betty (his mom) on a downward spiral. The kids were all grown by now, and Betty couldn't be left alone. She'd leave the stove on and forget to close the doors, that kind of thing. She also wandered the neighborhood and let people's dogs out of their backyards.

Claudia's theory was that Betty had been ill for years. She also said George's dad was a royal jerk who had a temper, would say terrible things, and got violent when he drank. He had several wives, and all the kids left and rarely came back, even to see their mothers.

Betty had always been sad that George had left. George did write her letters and called once in a while, but never returned. Claudia had been married to the brother just below George and had two sets of twins (these guys must have had a sperm bank the size of Chase Manhattan) before he left her. Her twins were just two years apart and her husband had taken off before the last set was born. Oh, and the big surprise? George was a Carson like the rest of them but had legally changed his name when he left home to Pendleton! I got her address and phone to keep in touch.

None of us saw any reason to go to Utah.

"How about we fly to Denver, rent a jeep and go exploring?" I suggested.

We were at the airport the next week and off to the mountains. The kids got a kick out of Vail, with its quaint shops and Swiss village ambience. We stayed in a condo that had carved wooden bears and light fixtures that looked a lot like elk horns.

Our first day was spent adjusting to the elevation. After that, we went horseback riding and river rafting and saw a couple of movies. We shopped and ate and were ready to go home a day before schedule. We were missing the girls and Michael. We were missing home.

We found Mom and Dad in the kitchen with Michael cooking dinner. The girls were in their room asleep, and the baby monitor revealed their soft breathing sounds.

"Mom!" Michael said, hugging me hard. He hugged Kendra. Hunter pulled him up on his shoulders.

"Did you bring presents?" he asked excitedly.

"Yes, we'll get them later."

"Well, I wish you'd let me know you were coming," my mother sputtered. "I didn't make enough food."

"That's okay, Mother, we can throw something together," I said.

"Well, you should have called," she scolded.

"Mom, this is *my* house. I wanted to come home and so did the kids."

"What difference does it make? They're back and we can go home!" Dad said with a grin.

"Your father misses his chair," my mother said, rolling her eyes. She finished chopping the celery and added another tomato to the salad and more lettuce.

"Where's Marty? Is she still at work?"

"Maybe. We-don't-know," my mother said, trying to get the dressing out of the bottle, shaking it hard with emphasis on each of the last words.

"Well—" Dad began.

"Jack, it's none of our business. If Marty wants to tell her, let Marty tell her," Mom said, tossing the bottle in the trash.

"Tell me what?" I asked, opening the fridge and rummaging for some deli meat.

"Well, all right," my mother said, as if I'd been begging for hours for her to tell me, "Marty met someone."

"A *man*," my father said, rolling his eyes.

"A really nice-looking man, too," Mom said, "which surprised me."

"Marty's nice-looking," I defended her.

"Yeah, but she was a man. You can never really change the hands, and Marty has very long fingers and they look even longer with those fake nails. If she wouldn't paint them such a bright color, people wouldn't notice. But as they are, I bet somebody notices Marty's hands. I know what I'm talking about, Jack. I know hands because I've looked at them all my life," my mother said.

"I always thought Marty's hands were okay, even when he became a girl," Dad replied. "You're making too much out of this, Helen. Just keep your opinions to yourself."

She glared at him.

"What do you mean you've looked at hands all your life? You never even worked," I said.

"Well, I've always looked at people's hands," she said. "I'm fascinated with hands."

"I'm not hungry, excuse me," Michael said and left the room.

"It upsets him to see Marty going out," my mother whispered.

I thanked her for making dinner and told her it would be a few minutes before I could come back and help her since I'd just got home. I followed Michael upstairs. He was in the bathroom, so I checked on the girls and waited. When he came out of the bathroom, his eyes were red.

"Hey buddy," I said, offering a hug, my arms open.

"What, Mom?" he said tersely, stomping into his room and shutting the door in my face.

I tapped lightly on the door. "Michael?" I said.

"Go away," he said, his voice muffled in a pillow.

I went into the room and sat quietly on the bed.

"You're not supposed to come in if somebody says not to, I could have been getting dressed or something. You always said that, Mom. Why can't you mean what you say?" he cried, punching his pillow.

"Michael, tell me what's upsetting you so. Is it Marty going out with somebody?"

"I hate Marty, stupid faggot."

"Michael! Where did you hear that?"

"Louis. Louis said guys who dress like women are faggots," he said.

"Well, your friend Louis doesn't always know everything and that's an ugly name that we don't use. In this case, the case of Marty, he is a woman and always was, he just had a birth defect."

"I'm never going to understand this, Mom. I just pretend it never happened and Marty is somebody else and never was my dad. It's like my dad is just dead."

"I understand," I said, slowly, trying to find the right words to say. "But he didn't die. Marty, the person, whether he has a penis or—"

"Mom, please don't say stuff like that," Michael said, wrinkling his face.

"It's part of life, Michael. It's part of the human body."

He frowned at me. "Yeah, but I don't want to hear my mom say stuff like that."

When had he gotten so much older?

"Okay, well, no matter whether Marty is wearing a skirt or a pair of jeans, I will always love Marty," I said. "And Michael, I hope you will too. I hope you didn't mean that about hating Marty."

His brown eyes teared up. "Sometimes I do. I'm worried, Mom, I don't want to be like him, uh, her."

"You won't be. What happened to Marty is a genetic disorder. It's pretty rare, but it happens. If it makes you feel better, I'll take you in for a checkup at the doctor and they can run a test. It's time to get your shots for next fall anyway."

"Okay, but what if I am like Marty?" he asked, full of fear.

"I can promise you that you won't be. You're very different from Marty. Remember, I knew Marty as a little boy, and he was much different than you."

"How come you married him, Mom?"

"Because he was my best friend and I loved him."

Michael obviously thought about this for a moment. "I guess that's a good reason. How come you married George?"

"Well, because he was nice to you, treated me well, was gorgeous, fun, and I fell in love with him," I replied.

"He was sort of two people. Like one time he'd be nice and then another time he'd be grumpy."

"Yes, he was," I agreed, adjusting my diamond ring. I had moved it to my right hand.

Michael glanced at it. "He sure gave you a pretty ring."

"Yes, he did," I said sadly.

The girls decided to start singing their "I want dinner song."

"I think the girls are waking up. Would you like to help me? I'll take them downstairs and we'll see what your grandmother has fixed for dinner."

"She's not that great of a cook, Mom," Michael said truthfully, "but she makes great pies and she baked one for me tonight. It's lemon with a bunch of white stuff on the top."

"Meringue? Don't you like that part?"

"Un-uh," he responded in the negative. "I just take that junk off.

Kendra and Hunter joined us. We changed the girls and took them downstairs. Michael had composed himself and appeared to be feeling better. I was looking forward to picking my mother's brain for more answers about this new mystery man.

C H A P T E R

THIRTY-ONE

As it turned out, Marty's new man was an absolute dud. It was a conclusion Marty came to after two weeks of intense dating and some mild passion. He never bothered introducing me to him and severely regretted his brief introduction to Mom, Dad, and Michael. This experience did awaken something in Marty though: the idea that men could find her attractive. She began to think of herself differently.

Sometimes I think that women think of themselves differently when they become parents. You have to look a certain way to go to the little league games; the moms who show up with manufactured tans and halter-tops aren't usually welcomed by the other moms. Marty didn't have *that* problem of course. The other parents didn't know our situation and accepted Marty. It was just that Marty hadn't given much time to thinking about being single because, in a sense, she was still living with me.

The dud never knew Marty had been a man. It didn't get that far and, according to Marty, if it had, the dud wouldn't have been able to tell. I didn't want to go there. That was Marty's business. I had made it clear that it didn't happen in our home. We both had that deal, though there certainly wasn't going to be any action in my wing of the house. I figured I absolutely was not capable of picking a normal man, if there were such a thing, so I gave it to God and asked Him to pick the right one for me, whenever that might be. I would have a long wait.

215

Marty and I ran the household together for five more years. Looking back on those years, they were pretty calm. Hunter graduated and moved to Tulsa. Both he and Kendra had gone to T.U. Hunter was now in Oklahoma City, starting OU Med School, and Kendra was working at the same television station as me, shooting the news. She still lived with us.

Michael had gotten into a few scuffles at school, but nothing really bad. The girls were just precious, as different as night and day. Georgette was taller than Gretchen, with her father's dark good looks. Gretchen looked like a blend of the two families, but more like George's mom, with blonde hair and cornflower blue eyes. Both girls were talkers, but mostly with each other, as twins often do. Georgette was the speaker for the two and the dramatic one, while Gretchen was the one who wanted to study the bugs outside and had her father's interest in anything to do with science and how things worked.

It was fall, with lots of new starts. Michael was starting his sophomore year at Cascia Hall Boys Preparatory School. He was fairly tall and had been asked to try out for the basketball team. Michael, an extremely aggressive teenager, was excited about the opportunity. His voice had dropped, and he was becoming moody and wanted to stay in his room a lot.

I needed advice about this because I didn't know what boys did. Marty turned out not to be one, and George and I hadn't discussed his teen years much. My parents had two girls. Glam had animals, but no kids. That left Gloria, who had three boys, all tall and full of energy. Two were older than Michael, so she'd already been there, and one was a year younger.

"You just have to ride herd on them," Gloria advised.

"Fred is probably the disciplinarian in the family, right?" I asked.

"Fred? Nah, he's cream cheese. He bellows from time to time, but I'm the one with the hairbrush and the ear pulling."

"*Ear* pulling?" I exclaimed.

"Well, they're so dang tall, that's the only thing I can grab when I get mad," she said, laughing.

I could see that. Gloria had always been a fireball. Her boys were tall and Fred was no shrimp. I liked Fred. We'd been going to his nondenominational church for years. When they were looking for a new church location I helped them find an abandoned warehouse downtown near Boulder Street. It had plenty of parking and turned out to have pretty good acoustics.

Fred had read some churches were using guitars and video in their services. He had started this style of worship in his church. I was able to help donate time, money, and talent toward this project. The congregation quickly drew folks from across Tulsa. It started rivaling the big boys in congregation size. It became a "seeker" church; people who normally wouldn't go to church found their way to this one. It was called Boulder Faith Street Church. Many lives were changed and renewed by going there.

My faith had deepened. Maybe it was all my life experiences, maybe being in my forties. I don't know, but I was definitely older and wiser.

It was a new beginning and fresh start for all of us. Mom was in her eighties. She'd lied about her age on my birth certificate, fudging five years, and she'd lied to Dad about her age. He was three years younger. Mom's fresh start was having a facelift. She thought it would make her look like she did as a girl. She did look younger, but her face swelled up and it was extremely painful. She couldn't wrap her mouth around a hamburger for about six months!

Vanity was my mother's middle name, well, not literally, but you know what I mean. There wasn't a picture made of her that she didn't have her nose and chin in the air. The woman had her hair done once a week at the beauty parlor, then wrapped toilet paper around her head every night to keep her hairdo fresh. How could hair be fresh after it was sprayed with a can of Aqua Net and then not washed for a week? Sometimes when we were little, she'd fly out of the room with her white train of toilet paper trailing on the floor. I always wondered what my dad thought of it, but it was a place I didn't want to go.

The girls were starting kindergarten. I had mixed emotions about this because they were my babies, but they were excited. We were sending them to private school, too. I could still afford it because George had left me quite a bit of money, and I wanted them to have a great education. Both schools the kids went to were Catholic. So I thought, having never been to private school myself, they'd be more strict and better schools. I suppose this was true.

I would become well known in the main office at the schools as I was often summoned there.

The girls were adjusting to the new school, but Georgette infuriated the kindergarten teacher. She was young and new and often late due to some other duty at the school. Georgette would hand out pretend assignments and then be in the bathroom putting on plays for Gretchen.

Gretchen didn't get into trouble exactly, but she was a co-conspirator in some of these escapades and would fiercely defend her sister if she got into trouble. Both had a strong sense of what was fair and often felt this delicate balance was threatened.

Michael just flat out got into fights at school. He'd become obsessed with video games that involved war and wanted to see every Sylvester Stallone, Arnold Schwarzenegger, Bruce Willis and any other tough-guy film that came along. I knew this was a reaction to Marty's big change. But often, knowing the reason for things doesn't always change the outcome. Michael was still a sweet kid, but angry and moody had replaced happy and cheerful.

I was in over my head here. I didn't want to drug him. I didn't want to beat him, and I didn't want to yell at him all of the time. Marty wasn't much help. In a sense, Marty couldn't help because Marty was the problem.

Marty was the problem on several levels. Marty was a woman and had started dating someone seriously. Michael had caught them kissing in the kitchen and threw up on the floor. I admit, this might have been an overreaction, but it was honest. Michael might have thrown up if he'd seen *me* kissing someone, because he was fifteen. Still, it was time for a change.

We all went to therapy. The therapist suggested Marty move out—not to give Michael all of the power in the house, but to give Michael some room to change his behavior. We weren't married anymore, and Marty's living there could be suspect. I was surprised by Marty's reaction because she was fine with this.

Marty did move out, but she didn't go too far. In fact, she moved back to her granny's house because the tenant had died and there was no mortgage. It was close to work, church, and not that far from our house. It was decided she would come for dinner a couple of times a week.

This seemed to calm Michael down a bit. He had not wanted to have friends over because people thought Marty and I were lesbians. The fights were less frequent. The school counselors, coach, and I decided Michael would be allowed to be on the basketball team if the fighting stopped. He became their star player. Michael Greene was extremely aggressive in the game, and when he had his game face on, it scared even his own mother.

THIRTY-TWO

1995

The school counselor recommended Michael's energies be channeled so he didn't end up hanging out with the wrong kind of kids. He was still active in church, so that was a good thing, but I decided to help focus some of this energy. I enrolled him in Tae Kwan Do, which he loved. The school counselor recommended he consider ROTC, which was music to Michael's ears.

Meanwhile, we had two weddings happening in the family: Kendra's and Marty's.

Marty had met the second love of his life, and I was really happy with this one. Marty had been through a whole slew of guys since the dud, and this one seemed to be the best fit.

Ben Fielding taught film history at T.U. and had met Marty at the video store. He couldn't believe Marty was an old movie buff. They had spent hours talking and talking before they ever went out on a date. Ben wasn't really what you'd call handsome, but he was nice looking. He was older than us, having just turned fifty. He was tall and on the slender side, probably a runner. He had gray hair and sometimes sported a mustache. He had three grown children who all objected to the marriage, not because Marty had been a man, but because Marty wasn't their mother, dead for fifteen years.

The important thing was Marty adored him and he adored Marty. Ben told her that he didn't care what she had been; he knew who she was now. They dated for about a year and a half before they decided to get married.

Because of the conflicts with the children, they decided to elope. Marty wanted me there as his matron of honor. I asked Ben if he would mind, and he said he would be honored.

Kendra watched the kids and I drove over to Eureka Springs on a Saturday morning. Marty and Ben had driven over early the day before to get their license. Marty presented her birth certificate from New York. Ben presented his from Kansas. It took fifteen minutes to get the license. The wedding was in the afternoon. When it was over, I just drove back home. I like to drive because it gives me time to think, and I rarely get time alone.

I didn't have second thoughts about Marty's marriage to Ben because I felt like it was right, but still, it was kind of odd when I watched Marty standing beside Ben in her floor-length white chiffon dress she'd always dreamed of wearing. She was next to her Prince Charming in his black three-piece suit. She carried a simple bouquet of white roses and baby's breath. As she said her vows to Ben, I remembered how she'd said the same words to me. Well, she didn't say *exactly* the same words because they'd made up some kind of flowery vow in addition to the regular ones.

A female preacher from Arkansas married them. The service lasted about thirty minutes. We had a little cake, and I was out of there, leaving the newlyweds behind for a honeymoon without me.

Kendra was marrying a wonderful young man who was one of Fred's youth pastors at the church. He played guitar and sang. He was actually Fred's nephew, who was the result of a mixed-race marriage. Dan's skin was the color of coffee with cream. He was about six feet tall and had broad shoulders. He and Kendra looked good together.

Audrey was against it; she thought the mixed-race thing would be a problem for the grandchildren. I didn't see it as a problem and neither did the kids, so it kind of set the tone for challenges on the wedding scene.

We had decided to have the wedding on the lawn at our house. We were taking a huge gamble here because Tulsa in April is anybody's guess for weather. I had ordered two large tents that would accommodate everyone. We planned to have tiny white Christmas lights strung around the trees and golden globe lights throughout the tent. We were hoping the magnolias would bloom, but had a backup with lots of white roses and some tropical flowers mixed in. We ordered lilies to float in the pool. The idea was to make it look magical and romantic.

Dan took care of the band. He used some members of his band mixed with a few others. Of course, we were going to have that great gospel choir. The music would be a mixture for all ages.

It was a given that the girls would be the flower girls. Georgette wanted to wear sparklers in her hair instead of flowers, but Kendra won that argument because it was her wedding. Georgette also wanted to wear a white princess-type dress and of course, so did Gretchen. We shopped and shopped and finally ordered some we saw in a catalog.

Michael was actually excited about the wedding and even liked Dan, which was surprising. I think he always thought he'd grow up and marry Kendra, but he couldn't quite catch up with her. Dan had wisely asked Michael to be one of his groomsmen, and Michael was thrilled. We had to explain to him what a groomsman was because this was his first wedding since my marriage to George.

Hunter was giving Kendra away. That had been decided between them a long time ago, when they were kids, long before George died. This was just a further reminder of George's absence.

Since Kendra's colors were in pastels, I decided on the peach suit. You can't go wrong with peach; it's fresh and springy looking. Forever practical, I would wear that suit over and over.

We were set. I had found the perfect caterer and we had nailed down the music, the clothes, and the tent. The bride and groom designed their own invitations. We mailed over a hundred invitations before it was all said and done.

Everything was perfectly planned. The wedding was set for April 22, 1995.

Little did we know that one of the worst acts of terrorism in our nation's history would shatter Oklahoma that very week. On Wednesday, April 19, Timothy McVeigh bombed the Murrah Federal building in Oklahoma City, just a short ride down Turner Turnpike, less than two hours away. It would be the biggest story of the decade, and as Kendra and I were both photographers and worked for a news station, we had to go.

C H A P T E R
THIRTY-THREE

If you were above the age of six in April 1995, you saw the images of the devastation caused by the Alfred P. Murrah Building bombing on television. It might have been some of our work. This was the biggest story of the decade and the worst act of terrorism on native soil until September 11, 2001. One hundred and sixty-eight people died in the bombing, nineteen of them children. The images of that building looking like an ugly, exposed beehive, the stench in the air, and the noise of the rescue workers feverishly trying to save those people will be imprinted on my soul forever.

Kendra and I worked for two days until we realized we'd better be relieved and go back to the rehearsal dinner that night. We didn't feel like laughing or dancing. We were drained.

We drove back most of the way in silence.

"Part of me doesn't want to go do this tonight," she said sadly, "but the other part of me wants to cling to Dan and never let him go." There were tears in her eyes.

I understood. We had cried in each other's arms more than once in the past two days. Every time a family had been told, every time we thought there was a live rescue, it was our job to bring it to the viewers. We also shot a lot of footage for the documentary we would do of the tragedy.

We went home, showered, and went to the rehearsal dinner, where they played the video I'd made of pictures of Kendra and Dan as they were growing up. Kendra always introduced me as her stepmom. I tried to make sure Audrey and Drake were included in everything. Drake still had a crush on Marty and seemed a little disappointed to meet Ben.

"He pinched my bottom again!" Marty whispered, outraged.

"You loved it," I said, grinning.

"Disgusting! How old is that guy?"

"I don't know, but he sure has a crush on you," I chuckled. "Just stay with Ben. He won't mess with you with Ben around."

The next day was full of excitement. One of my cousins had a Christmas decorating business and on the off-season, they decorated trees and landscaping for weddings and special occasions. He had his crew working for days getting the yard ready. They put lights on the front gates, all the way up the drive and wrapped around the trees in the front and the back. Everything was pearl white. It looked like a magic forest when they were finished.

Marty and her sister Missy, who owned a flower shop, carried in bags of ribbon and tulle. She had beautiful arrangements delivered from the shop.

Kendra, Audrey, Kendra's best friend from high school, three of Dan's sisters, and the twins and I spent the day at the spa. We had massages, which made the twins giggle. Then we had our hair and makeup done. We had flower rings for the girls for their hair. Kendra wore her hair up with baby's breath woven throughout the curls. The hairdresser swept my hair up and made me look almost stunningly sophisticated. Nobody would recognize me!

Dan's family arrived early. Kendra stayed upstairs getting dressed. We put Dan and the groomsmen in my room. The sounds of doors opening and closing, little girls giggling, older girls laughing, Bob barking every time the doorbell rang, and Michael's stereo blaring, was enough to make anyone go crazy, but I loved it. It was full of love, laughter, and chaos. This was my wonderful life and family! After two days of death and so much tragedy, I drank in every drop of this moment.

Kendra's wedding was beautiful. Fred was in rare form. A ceremony that usually takes about thirty minutes from start to finish in most Protestant churches took an hour in our backyard. It was mostly pure entertainment with a special touch of grace and spirituality.

The grandparents were seated first. Dan's African American grandmother wore a canary yellow dress with sparkles down the middle and a matching yellow feather in her hair. His grandfather had on a special black tux with a yellow rose in the lapel. The other grandmother, who was blonde like her daughter, wore a tailored pink pastel dress. Her husband had on the same special black tux with a pink rose. Since Audrey's parents were deceased and George's weren't there, my parents had decided to be part of the ceremony. Mother wore a knit emerald green floor-length dress with a large rhinestone buckle and little green low-heeled sandals. Dad wore the same black tux as the other men, with a white rose.

Dan's parents were next. Dennis looked dapper in the same tux. Lilly, his mother, had on a soft yellow dress with matching jacket. Audrey wore an orange floor-length print dress (don't ask me why), and I wore my peach suit, which was long, but slit up the sides. Drake wore an orange rose in his tux. We all sat up front together.

The wedding began with music from the band and video projected on two big screens of Dan and Kendra when they were dating. Next were comments from the girls about Dan. They giggled quite a bit and told the camera they thought he was cute, and if Kendra hadn't married him, they would. There was footage of Michael and Hunter pretending to argue over who would get her room. They ended it with an "I love you Kendra and we'll come after you, Dan, if you ever hurt our sister."

At this point, Dan and his groomsmen entered in their matching black tuxes with white roses and white shirts. Dan had a big grin on his face and his groomsmen were smiling and waving.

Next was the gospel choir. They came down the side aisles singing the wedding song gospel-style that has the refrain, "There is love." They clapped and hooted and hollered with the band backing up every note. It was magnificent.

The twins danced down the aisle, having learned their latest steps from Little Miss Muffet dance class. Georgette tossed rose petals on the ground on the white aisle sheet and blew kisses to the crowd. During this shining moment, Gretchen did a pirouette and took a bow.

Dan's little brother, Chester, walked carefully down the aisle carrying a pillow with the two rings as if he were carrying an egg. His pants were a little short because he'd grown some since the fitting for his tux, which was white. Someone had forgotten to get him some socks; his had soccer balls all over them, worn inside shoes that were a little too big and squeaky.

The bridesmaids and maid of honor were next, all four dressed in shimmery pastel dresses with rings of flowers for their hair.

Nothing could compare to the glow on Kendra's face when she walked down the aisle. Bless her heart, she looked incredible, and Hunter looked so handsome at her side. It took my breath away how much he resembled George on our wedding day.

Fred accepted the young couple and guided them through their vows. He preached a bit about what it was like to be married, then joked about his own marriage, which he told the guests he would pay for later. Gloria just looked at him and laughed. She was seated next to Glam and her veterinarian. Fred directed all of us to stand by these young people and to be supportive of them in their faith journey and their marriage.

One of the women in the choir sang "The Lord's Prayer" as Dan and Kendra took communion. Then Fred pronounced them man and wife. He said as their first act as a couple, they wanted to give communion to the guests. Fred blessed the bread and wine, saying the familiar words, and we came forward as the couple served us communion. It was an incredible unifying moment that I'll never forget.

Afterward, the choir sang and clapped as the group recessed down the aisle. Then we all made our way to the large banquet and dance floor we had ready for the celebration.

Marty hugged me with tears in her eyes, overcome with emotion. Ben stood in the background and smiled, letting us have our time together.

"I think this was even better than our wedding," Marty said, sniffing and laughing, taking a whiff of her inhaler.

"Of course, it was," I said, "my mother wasn't controlling everything."

"She looks good tonight," Marty said, looking at my parents standing together across the room. "She seems a little unsteady though, did you notice?"

"She probably has on shoes that are too tight because she won't go to the next size or her girdle is too tight."

"Do people still wear girdles?"

"My mother does. Maybe she's just giddy and had a little too much to drink."

"You're going to have to face the fact that she's in her eighties."

"And still smokes like a chimney," I said. "Marty, I can see her trying to sneak a cigarette and I specifically told her no smoking tonight. I have signs everywhere."

"That won't stop Helen."

"Go tell Dad that my mom is smoking and making me crazy. I have to check on the caterers."

Of course, Mom didn't stop, and Dad didn't make her, but they bickered about it, like always. It didn't damper the evening though, what with white lights in every tree and great music under the stars, a perfect spring night for a wedding.

Everyone stayed for several hours until the limousine came for the bride and groom. Glam caught the bouquet, which was appropriate. I'm sure she'd explain to the veterinarian what that meant later in the evening. Knowing Glam, she'd probably wear it on her head while doing her explaining.

The kids left for their honeymoon. Drake and Audrey had booked a cruise for them, which was their wedding present. They'd be away a week, which would be enough time for us to get the guest house cleaned to perfection. It would be their home until they could save enough to buy their own house, so they wouldn't be too far away.

Selfishly, I wanted them close. I loved having them eat dinner with us and be part of our lives. I had grown so close to Kendra, and the girls adored her. I think Michael would always be in love with her.

It was midnight before everything was packed up and gone. The girls had fallen asleep around ten, which was very late for them. Marty and I had carried them up to bed. Michael was in his room with the lights out listening to soft music. A peek in the door revealed he was sound asleep.

I went downstairs to my bedroom. I took a long hot whirlpool bath in candlelight and thought about George. I wondered if I'd ever meet anyone to share my life and this family, and if there were a man out there who thought it was fun to just sit on the front porch and swing.

I would find him, but not yet. There were more hurdles ahead to jump, and I would have to face some of them without a husband.

THIRTY-FOUR

1998

Michael turned out to be very smart, which sort of surprised us because he rarely studied. He loved history, sociology, and psychology, and was quite good at math, which he didn't get from me. Dad had gotten him started on the Civil War, which he loved. He was also fascinated with military history in general. You wouldn't think a big basketball star would be into ROTC, but he was. Aggression was the name of Michael's game. He also was in the chess club, and he had worked his way up to black belt in Tae Kwan Do by his senior year.

This was our sweet little Michael, who, at slightly over six feet tall, had become a man overnight. His grandfather had taught him how to shoot a rifle. They'd gone to the driving range early on Saturday mornings while other kids were sleeping. He loved working out and he was actually teaching some younger classes in Tae Kwan Do. He even taught the twins some moves. In the summer, he was a lifeguard and could swim like a fish.

He wasn't messing around with girls (or boys). He still went to church, and when he socialized, he went out in groups. He was too disciplined to use drugs or drink because his body was truly his temple, and he wasn't going to screw anything up. He was highly self-disciplined, taking instruction from various male mentors with an intensity one wouldn't often expect from a typical teenager, which of course, he wasn't. Michael had always been old beyond his years.

It worried me. I was afraid he'd snap some day; I knew the drive was really a flight farther away from Marty. He was polite to her, like one would be to a distant aunt or company. He never went over to Marty's anymore, which might have been expected when Marty married Ben. He was rarely home when Marty and Ben came over for dinner. At the holidays, he strategically placed himself at the opposite end of the table on the same side so he wouldn't have to look at her. I knew all of this of course, but never said a word to Marty. If she picked up on it, she never said a word to me, but then we no longer lived together.

My living situation was interesting. By the spring of 1998, when Michael was graduating, Dan and Kendra were expecting their first child and looking for their first house.

The half-way house we'd started at George's house had been successful, but the last bunch of kids living there trashed the place. We decided it was time to sell it. Kendra and Dan didn't really want to live in a two-story house now that a baby was coming, so we fixed it up and it sold in the first week. Houses in that neighborhood were never on the market very long.

I gave a quarter of the money to Kendra and Dan to buy a house and put the rest in a money market account for Hunter, Georgette, and Gretchen. Kendra and Dan bought a very nice house in a up-and-coming neighborhood with sidewalks, a park, and lots of children.

The Hispanic couple I had hired years earlier to look after the house and the twins had returned to Mexico about two years earlier. I had tried other domestic help, but they never worked out. Fred asked me if I could house a Vietnamese couple who had moved here from California. They'd been in the country only two years and spoke broken English. They understood more than they could speak. His name was Dung. I know, you think I'm kidding, but I kid you not, it means "brave and heroic" in Vietnamese. You aren't supposed to say the "D." Her name was Dong, which has nothing to do with bells. It means "winter." I've never been good with foreign names. I'm that person who repeats the names several times and then never gets it right. I was so intimidated by these names; I just never used them much. This became confusing at times.

The girls thought their names were hilarious and would say them all of the time and quite loudly. Well, Georgette would say them loudly; Gretchen would just giggle. They stopped when Dung won their hearts. He was a kind little gentleman who did beautiful landscaping and could fix anything. Both adults were tiny, not much taller than the girls. The girls wore the same size shoe as Dong. She was rather severe, but she liked the children, was a great cook, and an immaculate housekeeper.

I haven't really talked much about my housekeeping, but I'm not good at it. I mean, I don't leave the trash piled to the ceiling, but I'm kind of a clutter muffin, as Marty used to say, and I don't like to do laundry. It's not that I mind putting it in the washer; it's just that I hate to take it out and fold it. There were always lots of piles of it around the house on various chairs.

Dong and Dung's last name was Nguyn. In 1998 they took up residence in our guesthouse. Dung became great friends with Michael. He called Michael "Chien," which means fighter of battles and combat.

When Michael graduated that spring, he headed for Annapolis, Maryland, for the Naval Academy. The first semester he was allowed only one phone call. He called me, of course; I'd been out of my mind with worry. He said it was tough, but he could take it, and he was learning from a lot of people there. He also told me with conviction what his goal was and how he was going to achieve it: Michael was going to be a Navy Seal. I guess most people would prefer their son be a Navy Seal to him drag racing and going to strip bars. But I was worried.

"You don't have to do this, son. You don't have to prove anything to me or to anybody else. You're a man; we proved you're a healthy male years ago with tests. You're fine," I said, feeling tears sting my eyes.

"I know I'm fine, Mom, and I'm going to be the finest Navy Seal."

"Give it time, Michael. Are you sure you want to do that?"

"I've never been surer of anything in my life."

"I pray for you every day," I said quietly.

"I know, Mom," he replied softly. "I know."

The rules were extremely strict. The discipline was pretty tough. This was a life decision and not something he would outgrow. I had seen and heard that determination many times throughout his short life and I knew arguing with him on this subject was futile. But a Navy Seal? They don't swim at the zoo. Those guys do missions halfway around the world, and let's just say I didn't think he'd meet the future Mrs. Michael Greene this way. Finally, there was this: when it was all said and done, they would be teaching my sweet little Michael how to become a killing machine.

THIRTY-FIVE

As the new millennium approached, people got crazier. Everyone said it was the end of the world. Our house had a wine cellar/basement which, since we lived in tornado country, we kept stocked with oil lamps, flashlights with extra boxes of batteries, bottled water, an old refrigerator, and a generator. Generators and survival gear were big sale items around the new millennium. Dad made me put a shotgun down there, unloaded of course, with plenty of extra shells. I did have canned food and some dried rations to please my father.

We decided to have the millennium party at my house in the basement—just in case the world ended. I never believed the world would end. About the only thing I did buy in preparation were extra bottles of water, which we use anyway. Dung and Dong spent New Year's Eve Day preparing lots of wonderful delicacies, both American and Vietnamese.

The twins decided to bake cakes and cookies in the shapes of 2000. At twelve, they were the delight of the 'tween crowd. Both wore braces on their teeth, which they deemed a disaster when trying to attract boys. With her long legs, Georgette towered over Gretchen by four inches. Georgette was about five-seven and Gretchen would stay five-three and shop in the petite department the rest of her life. Georgette struggled in heavy academics and excelled in the arts; Gretchen thrived on academics and succeeded in the sciences. Georgette lived for the stage, singing, and dancing, and Gretchen, who could dance gracefully, preferred a good book or an afternoon movie. Georgette loved to watch a movie with her but wanted to analyze it and star in it. Both girls could draw and had a flair for fashion design.

I had encouraged them to decorate for the party. They chose to place silver sparkles all over the house and big snowflakes. We had left the Christmas decorations up but added 2000s in cutouts on various tables. Marty had ordered and sold quite a few of those big Elton John type glasses that were big 2000s.

Michael was home. He'd helped by getting down the large punch bowl and he polished some of the silver trays. He looked so handsome. He had gone to see a few friends, but he didn't really feel like partying away from home this holiday. He was content to stay home with the old folks.

The party consisted of mostly family and a few friends. Hunter and his girlfriend, Sandy, a friendly brunette from Edmond, had driven in for the holidays. They split their time between our house and Kendra and Dan's house, with Gracie, their baby girl, who was now two and into everything.

Glam and her veterinarian, Vince, came. Fred had convinced them to get married a couple of years earlier, so they had eloped to Las Vegas and had gotten married in one of those drive-thru wedding chapels with an Elvis look-alike serenading them. Glam had on big 2000 earrings and her blonde hair was swept up with a rhinestone stick. She wore black velvet pants and a jewel-studded 2000 top. Vince wore a winter sweater with an Elk on it and black jeans with black cowboy boots. They brought homemade beef jerky.

Fred and Gloria wouldn't miss it. They'd brought food as well, a big pot of Fred's chili. Fred said if the world ended tomorrow, we might as well go out with Fred's chili and Rolaids. He and Gloria had on matching bright blue sweatshirts wearing buttons that said, "Jesus lives in the New Millennium."

Marty and Ben arrived early. They brought a bunch of new movies and homemade ice cream. They'd given us one of those big, flatscreen TVs for Christmas. It resided in the den and Dad had already turned it on.

Yes, I had invited my parents. I figured if the world did end, they should be here with us. Dad had turned up the volume on the television because his hearing aids weren't working well. He told everybody he had wax in his ears, but none of us were brave enough to look. My mother brought onion dip and chips and wore a bright green sweater with a long black velvet skirt. Dad wore a loud Christmas sweater with dancing reindeer across the front my mother had gotten him.

We all looked festive. I had gone with a lightweight red cotton sweater and my black pants. The girls had gotten me some 2000 earrings, so I wore those. A little dangle on the ear can perk up a holiday anytime!

We know how to party. Gloria played the piano, which had been part of Millie's legacy, and we sang lots of holiday songs plus some gospel music. Wine and song was our motto, but nobody got very drunk. We played charades and Pictionary. We started the movie marathon with an old favorite, "It's a Wonderful Life." Some people watched the football game in the den. With pre-teens, toddlers, and various-aged adults in the house, including two who spoke only mild conversational English, it was the comfortable chaos I had grown to accept and love.

I guess it happened shortly after midnight when we had switched briefly from wine to champagne for the New Year's toast. Mom had just gone out on the back porch to smoke a cigarette (I wouldn't let her smoke in the house), and Dad had fallen asleep in front of the television. We were all having such a good time. I wasn't focusing on her. I didn't know how long she'd been out there, but the girls had created a song-and-dance routine they wanted to perform for everyone for the new millennium and they wanted Mom to see it.

I told them to go get her on the back porch. Georgette sent Gretchen to fetch her grandmother. Gretchen shrieked and came running into the house. "Mama, help! something's happened to Grandma!"

Fred was closest to the door, so he rushed out to see what happened. Mom had dropped her cigarette on the porch where it was still lit. Fred stamped it out and surveyed Mom, who appeared to have had a stroke. He shouted at Gloria to come help and told me to call 911, which I did immediately, but have no recollection of this. Someone woke Dad up and he joined in the fray.

The ambulance and fire truck arrived. They resuscitated Mom and put her in the ambulance. Dad and I climbed in my car and came after her. Everyone else stayed behind to watch the younger ones and clean up the mess.

I realized while driving to the hospital that this could be it. I could be losing my mother forever. I was irritated with myself for not paying more attention at the party, but I was hosting the party and I had other guests, I thought defensively. I chastised myself for not checking on her. What else? Had I told her I loved her in a while? My parents were not big on saying that four-letter word too often. What would her death do to Dad? We always assumed he'd go first. Where would I put her if she did live? I wouldn't want her to live with *me*.

"Don't borrow trouble," she'd say. I heard her words echoing in my head. I also had flashes of her humped over a sewing machine making me a new party dress and the time she'd made all of the food for a big teenage birthday party for me and I forgot to invite the guests. We had eaten cake for days. I remembered her teaching me to pray as a little girl and showing me how to put my hands together and get down on my knees.

"You can talk to God anywhere, Lizzie," she told me. "But if you're asking for something and you haven't been too good, you need to get down on your knees and pray like this."

I'd been on my knees a few times in my life but now I didn't have the luxury of doing so because I was too busy following the ambulance. When I close my eyes, I can still see those flashing lights.

At the hospital, the doctor told Mom she'd had her last cigarette. She pouted for a while but she got over it. We would have to keep her in rehab for a month. When she finally got home, she would discover Dad and I had thrown away all the ashtrays and cigarettes. That went over like a lead balloon.

My sister was traveling abroad when this happened so I couldn't get ahold of her. It was up to Dad and me to figure out what to do with Mom. She had always been the one in charge. She wasn't too keen on anybody making a decision without her. This time, she wasn't going to get her way.

THIRTY-SIX

Mom was in the hospital for about a month, on the rehab floor. The stroke had affected her walk and her speech. She could still talk, more slowly than before. When she would try to tell us things she'd stop in mid-sentence and spell the word she was trying to say. I attributed this to her strong aptitude for reading, since she devoured multiple books a week.

"Liz, c-could you go to the h-o-u-s-e and get me my r-e-d robe? This is so frustrating. I can see the w-words and I can s-spell them but n-not say them," she stammered.

She talked like this for about three weeks while they worked with her on speech, motor skills, and some walking. Her walking was very slow compared with the quick-paced steps of the past. My father was at the hospital with her every day and looked on with encouragement as she shuffled for the rehab worker.

We had thought about having round-the-clock nurses, but because of their age, the hospital, and the cost, the hospital suggested a nearby assisted living center for Mom. Dad could go there every day, have at least a meal or two with her, and watch television, which was his routine.

We knew Mom wasn't herself because she didn't complain much. She didn't like being apart from Dad. Fifty-eight years of sleeping together is a hard pattern to break. But I think, in a way, she welcomed her new solitude.

I don't know if you've ever been in an assisted living center. The rooms are small and many of them have kind of a split living area where there's a *tiny* living room with a sink, a small square refrigerator, and a microwave for a kitchen, an open walkway hall wide enough for a wheelchair, and a bedroom space in the back. The living room might be able to house a small loveseat, a chair or two, and a medium-size television.

The girls and I fixed up her place with bright, cheerful furniture. Mom and I both love yellow, so a bright chintz loveseat and chair were delivered from my favorite furniture store, along with a pillow top double mattress and small dresser for her clothes. The closet was tiny, but her wardrobe would have to change. She now needed very casual, loose-fitting soft cotton dresses. I forgot to mention she had become incontinent during this experience.

Having a stroke liberates you from a lot of worry in some areas. She stopped caring about dying her hair and finally lost the toilet paper around her head. Redheads don't usually go gray. Her hair just got lighter, kind of a mousy brown with tendrils of gray at the temples. In her eighties, she looked younger than all the white- and gray-haired ladies around her. I imagined most of them hadn't had a facelift within the last decade, or Mom's tummy tuck.

We covered the wall with pictures of our family and put some of her favorite artwork—flowery pictures of English country-side—on the wall. Gretchen and Georgette made her a wreath for her door and decorated a small tree with hearts and lace on it for Valentine's Day. It was her "occasion" tree. They told her they would keep it up year 'round and decorate it with items for each holiday. We bought her a nice little television that had a slot for DVDs and videotapes, so she could watch either one.

My mother, like most women of her generation, had always taken care of my father. She ran the household, doing all the laundry, the cooking, and cleaning. My father didn't know how to turn on the dishwasher or the washing machine. I had to show him how to sort his laundry and fold the towels and sheets. Shopping with my father reminded me of when the kids were little.

"Dad, let's get you breakfast stuff so you can have that meal on your own and then sandwich and soup things for supper. That way you can eat the main meal at noon with Mom and if you don't make it for one of the other meals, you'll have something to eat."

"Good idea," he agreed.

Dad began tossing things in the basket as we walked down the aisle. I spent time reading the contents of the boxes and cans, trying to figure out a few things for him to have. When I turned around, the basket was half full of cookies, cinnamon rolls, brownies, ice cream bars, cheese-in-a-can, crackers, Vienna sausages, Beanie Weanies, and more junk.

"What's all of this?" I asked.

"Snacks. Stuff I like," he said defensively.

I realized my mother had never let my dad have much of this stuff, never kept it around, and now he realized he was free to have whatever he wanted. I grabbed a few carrots and some fruit so he wouldn't go into hypoglycemic shock. He picked out the chocolate milk and added some orange juice to please me.

Dad was lonely without my mother around, even though he went to see her every day. Long retired from his hardware store, he had always been a busy man, doing projects in the yard and more. I quickly realized this house was too much for Dad, so we decided to sell it and find something smaller. They had cottages on the same grounds as the assisted living center, so that was the plan.

Their house sold quickly, but it wasn't easy to liquidate their stuff. Dad wanted to save everything. He tried to keep bottles with a quarter inch of oil left, old paint from 1977, rusted tools, Christmas ornaments with missing parts, and one treasure, my mother's diaphragm from 1962. I couldn't believe my eyes when I opened the case. It was a little, um, dried-out after almost forty years.

The girls and I organized, threw out, and liquidated. We had a huge garage sale and gave the rest to charity. I was exhausted and sad when we handed the keys over to the new owners. The house held a lot of memories for me, and it was a door closed to part of my past.

We furnished Dad's new little cottage with a mixture of old and new. He had to have his green vinyl recliner, so I found a nice masculine sofa to go with it. He had bookshelves filled with books he hadn't read in twenty years but refused to part with. We went to the rescue center and found a dog for him, a mixture of golden retriever and something smaller and shorter. She was sweet and housebroken but chewed. Sometimes when Dad left Goldie inside while visiting Mom, he would return to find torn-up quilts or a destroyed pair of shoes. Where you and I might have killed the dog (not really) or at the very least, gotten rid of her, Dad mildly got after her and repeatedly forgave her.

He decided he'd always wanted pigeons, so he built cages on his covered back patio, where other residents had attractive little rooms or patio furniture. These were the kind of pigeons that puffed up and looked like little turkeys. He joined a pigeon club and drove to meet with other pigeon owners. Yes, I said he drove, because Dad still drove everywhere. Since everything was close, he seemed to manage this okay. It was parking that was a problem.

Whenever Dad parked his car, he usually didn't close his door very well and his battery died. Another problem he had: confusion. He often lost his car in big parking lots. Multi-level parking garages were a nightmare for him. The security guards at the mall knew him by his first name and would drive him around to look for his car.

I realized when he went out and bought an almost-new Ford Taurus with a spoiler on the back that Dad needed some help making decisions. I had located my sister and we talked him into letting me be his power of attorney. They had enough money from the sale of the house and some investments to last them a few more years, so we were probably okay, but I needed to stop the leaks and ward off any predators that prey on old people. There had been stories of people who lost everything, and they had to live with their kids.

I wasn't ready for that. I'm not sure anybody is ever ready for their parents to move in with them. We weren't exactly the Waltons (the family from the old TV series), and I couldn't imagine my mother and me living under the same roof, even though she was more docile these days. But, of course, that was coming. I just hadn't seen it at the time. I'd figured at their age they'd pass on before they'd move in with me.

God knew what I was going to be up against, and finally, He was sending me a partner to help out. I had given up on men and hadn't really dated much, but this one would come out of the blue, as they say. And he would be riding a white horse when he did it, just like in the movies.

THIRTY-SEVEN

2002

The girls were thirteen now. Mom and Dad were settled in their new house, and I welcomed the opportunity to do some work projects. I had taken on a new contract from the station where I produced a weekly show called "Traveling Oklahoma." Kendra and I both worked on this project. I was the Executive Producer, shot some segments, and put the show together. It was fun.

Most of the stories were about tourist destinations, which Kendra shot. I did the character pieces; those added the flavor and spice to the show. It's the part that has always made Oklahoma special: the people who live here. I called this segment "Oklahoma Spirit." Some of these segments were focused on spiritual Oklahoma— churches, synagogues, mosques, church camps, special missions, monasteries, ministries, and some native spiritual dances and exhibitions. I had gotten a call from a woman named Ida Simpson who lived on a ranch somewhere between Choteau and Pryor, which are due north of Tulsa. She told me I should shoot a story on Charlie Waters.

According to Ida, Charlie owned a nice little spread, about six hundred acres outside of town. It was an interesting mix of flat lands and rolling meadows with a heavily treed area at the top of the ridge where the house was. He had a manmade lake on it. The land had been in Charlie's family for generations. It had all been left to Charlie to ranch as he saw fit, she told me. He had a small herd of cattle and probably about eight horses, so it wasn't a big place.

Since it was October, the leaves were starting their color show, and the air was crisp. I had on my favorite old brown corduroy jacket with a pair of khakis and a soft green mock turtleneck. I thought I looked professional yet casual.

I called Charlie and told him who I was and that his neighbor, Ida, thought I should meet him. He joked that Ida never could keep her opinions to herself and that whatever she said it wasn't his fault. He invited me over for coffee and a cowboy cookout.

It was Friday afternoon. Ida had told me to come late that afternoon and stay for the evening, but she hadn't explained exactly what to expect. I eased up the pea gravel road and got out of my old army green Subaru. The house was a large log cabin with soaring glass windows. It looked like it had a tall cream-colored stone wall inside.

I was greeted by Charlie's big, stupid, tail-wagging, tongue-slobbering chocolate lab. I knocked on the door, but nobody answered. I heard hollering from a distance and the pounding of a horse's hooves on the gravel.

"Look out!" a man shouted. I could see a huge muddy-legged white horse with sweat pouring off of it and a slender, strong-shouldered man hunkered down on it, riding the horse extremely fast. He was obviously trying to get the animal under control. He rode past me in a blast of gravel and dust and sped halfway down the road at a hard gallop. Finally, the animal broke, slowed down, and became more docile.

Amazingly, the man turned the horse around and rode him up the hill in a calm walk, patting him encouragingly and talking to him in a sweet voice. By the time they reached me, that snorting stallion was mild enough to put a baby on his back.

"Teenagers!" he chuckled. "You just need to show them who is in charge! You must be Liz Pendleton. I'm Charlie Waters, sorry to meet you like this." He dismounted the horse and landed squarely on his feet.

"I had planned on getting cleaned up until Mr. Independence here decided to show off. We've been riding around for over an hour until he wore himself out. Nobody's been able to ride him until today. Excuse me a minute, and I'll take him to the barn. If you want, you can join me."

I followed this man with thick white-gray hair that was pulled back in a short ponytail. He tossed his cowboy hat farther back on his head, looked up at the horse and said, "Well, we had quite a day, didn't we, boy?" The horse seemed to understand and snorted a nod in response.

Charlie wasn't really tall, though the hat made him look a little taller, but I imagine he was just under six feet. He had a slender but solid build. He walked comfortably in his cowboy boots and jeans like they were part of him. Charlie stepped gently, with quiet confidence. He took the horse over for a long drink of water and tied him to a post. He had work gloves on, took them off, and rinsed his hands in the water. He asked Mac somebody in the barn to take care of the horse.

As he walked toward me, he grinned and took off his hat. This revealed a tanned bald spot on top of his head. He must have been about fifty, judging from his tightly curled white-gray hair, and tanned face from lots of outdoor days. He was handsome. His blue eyes twinkled with amusement and interest.

"Have you ever been on a working ranch before, Lizzie?" he asked, immediately familiar, as if I'd known him all my life.

"My Dad was a rancher long ago, so I have memories as a little girl, but we moved to Tulsa when I was seven."

"Did he ranch around here?"

"On the other side of Inola."

"Lots of places over that way have changed hands through the years," he said pleasantly. "Come in the house, if you don't mind, and I'll get you something to drink. You can look around while I take a quick shower and get some clean clothes on, just don't stand too close!"

He didn't really smell bad. He smelled like a mixture of dirt and clean soap, a manly smell that wasn't manufactured in a bottle.

"Oh, Cora's made some coffee. Would you like some?" he asked.

"I don't drink coffee, thanks, but I'd love some ice water, if you have any."

"I'll fix you right up," he said agreeably. He washed his hands with hot soapy water in the sink and dried them on a towel, which Cora probably wouldn't like. The kitchen was immaculate. He got some ice and water out of the door of the fridge. He handed me the glass with a paper napkin and led me into a huge living room with a massive two-story stone fireplace. There was a loft and an open area where the upstairs bedrooms were.

"Just so you'll know, there's a half-bath between the entry and the kitchen in case you need to freshen up. You're welcome to just sit here and relax or wander around if you like. I'll be upstairs. Should take about fifteen minutes or so. I'll try not to keep you waiting."

"Is it okay if I bring my camera and equipment in here to shoot an interview?" I asked.

"I don't really know what to talk about," he said with a smile. "But if I can help you, I will," he added modestly.

"Ida said you'd be modest, but she didn't want to tell me everything either. She just wanted me to see for myself if there's a story here, although she assured me there was."

"I don't know." He shrugged and shook his head, turned on his heel, and went upstairs.

I took in the furnishings. The room was a mixture of rugged brown leather and thick wood. There were Navajo rugs on the floor and the lamps were wound with rope at their base with a couple of horseshoes for decoration. The room smelled of polished leather, rope, and a bit of smoke from the fireplace, which someone had started. The style was rustic and masculine.

An older woman came into the kitchen through the back of the house. I heard a garage door go down behind her. Her mostly white hair was streaked with gray and pulled back in a bun, and she had quite a few lines in her face.

"Hi, I'm Cora," the woman said, smiling and extending a hand. "I made coffee for you; would you like a cup?"

"No thanks," I said, accepting her handshake. She looked much older than Charlie.

"Is Charlie in the barn?" she asked.

"No, he went to shower," I said, suddenly feeling uncomfortable, realizing Charlie and I had been the only ones in the house, and he was in the shower. This might not look good.

"Well, that gives us time to get acquainted," she said, unfazed by my comment and seemingly unaware that I was uncomfortable.

"You're from the TV station, aren't you?" she asked, with a look of interest.

"Yes, I produce "Traveling Oklahoma" for the entire state," I said. "And I do project work for ABC. I'm Liz Pendleton."

"Nice to meet you, Liz. Oh, that sounds like such fun work!" she exclaimed. When she smiled, I could see coffee stains on her teeth. She got up to get herself a cup. "I've done a little writing for the Chouteau paper, but that's nowhere near as exciting as what you do," she said with a sigh.

"Well, not much difference," I said kindly. "People read your words and they see my pictures."

She smiled her response.

"How long have you and Charlie lived here?" I asked.

"Oh, well, Charlie grew up on this land. He's part Osage and the house and land has been passed down for generations. *This* house has just been here about eighteen years. He built it right over the old house he grew up in. It burned down about twenty years ago. He had these logs brought in from Oregon and took his time, built it the way he wanted it. Mac and me, we came here about seven years ago. Mac is my husband. He helps Charlie run the place. His name is short for Macintosh, which he hates, but his mom was eating one of those apples before she went into labor and decided it sounded kind of stylish!"

"I guess that's just as good as any other reason. I've never met an Osage. I think my family's background includes a mixture of tribes, like most native Oklahomans. Do you do most of the cooking, Cora?" I asked. "You seem pretty familiar with this kitchen."

"Yes. Charlie's wife died about three years ago. She had cancer for four years—all over. Terrible thing. That man rarely left her side. He's a good man, Charlie Waters is," she said.

"Is someone talking about me?" Charlie's voice could be heard from the stairway. "My ears are burning."

He entered the room smelling of fresh soap and maybe a little Bay Rum slapped behind his ears. He had on a denim cowboy shirt, clean jeans, a brown leather belt with a silver and turquoise buckle, and a clean pair of brown cowboy boots. His thick hair had been washed and brushed back, and his gray mustache and beard had been freshly combed. He looked very nice. I could see the goodness Cora talked about in his face more clearly now as he teased her.

"Cora, are you tellin' lies about me, woman? You and Ida got this city girl to come down here from Tulsa to do an interview and I'm gonna get all tongue-tied trying to talk in front of a camera. I want to help you out, Lizzie, but I don't have much to say about anything that anybody would want to hear."

Cora snorted. She looked at her watch and then at me.

"Tell you what, you follow me. This man is going to be too modest to say anything that makes sense. Maybe if you see what Ida and I wanted you to see and do the interview, you'll understand."

"Okay," I said, grabbing my new video camera. "You lead the way."

"Now Cora, don't make more out of this, it's just no big deal," Charlie said as we walked outside. He looked embarrassed.

"It *is* a big deal. Now just hush, Charlie Waters, and let someone else talk for once."

I raised my eyebrows and smiled at Charlie. He looked a little sheepish. Cora checked her watch again. I took a long sip of my water, set down the glass, and followed her outside.

"Set your camera stand over here," she said, looking down the road and squinting.

I obeyed and set my tripod up, carefully placing my camera on it and tightening the screws. I looked in the viewfinder and focused ahead, not knowing exactly what I was supposed to see.

"Cora," Charlie said, shaking his head. "This is crazy."

"Dang it, Charlie, hush now. You'll break her concentration. Pay attention, Miz Pendleton," she ordered, "because here they come."

THIRTY-EIGHT

At first, I saw just one old truck, so dirty, I couldn't tell what color it was. Then I saw another and then another. A van followed the truck. The dust and gravel being kicked up made them look almost mystical or on fire, like they were in a cloud of smoke. More cars and trucks followed the van and I could see now there was a huge line of vehicles, one after another, coming toward the house.

"I told you," Cora said, elbowing me slightly, but not enough to knock off my focus.

The trucks and other vehicles began veering off to the left, pulling into a field that was free of trees, animals, and any other debris, one that had been neatly mowed.

"You ought to see that field after a rain and a Friday evening. What a mess," Cora said.

"Well, I need to have some of the boys bring in some gravel, I guess," Charlie responded, chewing on the thought.

"Why are they all coming here?" I asked, staring into the viewfinder, seeing the snake of cars making its way toward the house.

"Aw, they're just coming for Mac's chuck wagon cooking," Charlie said, walking away from the house, toward the crowd. People were getting out of their cars, but they weren't coming toward the house.

"I have enough of this shot," I said to Cora. I pulled up my camera and tripod and followed Charlie. Cora was right behind me.

"They're going to the pavilion," she said. "They come for a little food, but mostly to listen to Charlie."

Charlie seemed to shrug off this statement and watched the people, mostly men, along with some women and even some older teenagers walk toward a chuck wagon standing next to a large pavilion structure with benches and tables. There was a sturdy roof and open sides so the breeze could blow through.

Charlie turned to me and said, "Let me carry your gear. Be careful now that you don't turn your ankle in this grass."

He hoisted my tripod, but I held fast to my camera, which I always carried with a shoulder bag full of lenses. He eased off the video recorder, put it on his shoulder, and took my arm. We walked across the field toward the wagon, catching the heady aroma of old-fashioned barbecue.

A large table with a vinyl red-checkered tablecloth had been set up with napkins, an industrial size coffee urn, and another dispenser filled with iced tea. Styrofoam cups were next to the dispensers, and there were paper plates with bags of buns and three big bowls of little bags of chips. Several plastic dispensers of sauce were sitting on the table, two marked "hot," along with salt and pepper. A towering tray of brownies sat at the other end.

"They try to come early to get the food. The brownies go first," Cora said proudly.

"Do you feed these people every week?" I asked, hoisting my camera on my shoulder focusing on the table and people beginning to load their plates.

"Every week. And since the planes hit those towers in New York City a few weeks ago, there have been more people coming," Cora said.

"How long?" I asked, zooming in on a withered hand reaching for a bun.

"Oh, I guess Charlie started about a year after Carol died. It started with just a few folks. They'd meet in the bunkhouse. Then it got bigger and bigger and they moved to the pavilion and now, well, you can see."

"What about when the weather gets colder?"

"We have big tarps that come down on the sides to make that a tent," Cora said. "They're made of heavy canvas and we have mosquito netting in the summer. There are big ceiling fans out there that keep the air circulating. Charlie's thinking about just enclosing it, but heat and air would be expensive. He is going to have to gravel that field."

"Do they come every Friday night?" I asked, looking at Cora.

"Every Friday night, except when it's really icy or snowy. Even then, some of them come. We always make pretty much the same menu because we can feed a lot of people that way and we've never really run out, except sometimes they eat up all the brownies."

"*Why* are they coming?" I asked again.

"To hear Charlie," she said. "In addition to ranching, Charlie is a preacher. This is a Cowboy Church."

"Why don't they just go to regular church?" I said, noticing tattered Bibles in their hands. I also spied another table with simple black Bibles stacked on it and another pile with a sign that said, "Biblia en Español-Gratis."

The people who didn't have a Bible picked one up and made their way toward the pavilion to find a chair in which to sit.

"These folks are the unchurched. They've never been in church in their lives. Or they might have gone at one time, but they fell away from it. A lot of them feel they don't have the right clothes to wear, or they just don't fit in. Charlie doesn't care. He's reached out to them and wants them to know that God loves them," Cora said proudly.

"Would you like something to eat?" Charlie said, walking toward me with a cordial smile. "Mac makes a pretty good barbecue."

"Sure," I said, "in a minute."

I grabbed some more footage of people eating and conversing and some footage of Charlie walking around, easily shaking hands with people and making them feel welcome. Most faces were weathered, and some people looked old before their time. They wore work clothes and many looked like they'd just finished in a field or at a factory. The one common denominator was that they all smiled at Charlie and shook his hand.

The barbecue was the best I'd ever tasted. It could rival any place in Tulsa. Mac was a good cook. We met briefly and shook hands, but Mac was busy passing out food and making sure people were fed. Several other men attended to the drinks.

After everybody finished eating, they arranged their benches and chairs in a big semi-circle. Charlie sat in front of the group with a microphone under the lights and opened his Bible. I filmed all of this from a distance, zooming in whenever possible, trying to be a fly on the wall. Hats and ball caps came off as Charlie said a prayer and then he began.

There was no hell fire and brimstone, no snake dancing, nothing hocus-pocus, just a message of hope that had transcended the ages. I saw tears in some eyes and some asked questions. Charlie took his time, explaining the gospel in plain language, giving examples from his own life, how he'd been pretty ornery, running with folks he should have stayed away from (many nodded their heads like they'd been there), and how God changed his path. He encouraged them that God could turn their lives around.

I saw transformation on that cool autumn evening, and I saw a selfless man with a spiritual gift. Cora and Mac helped serve communion at the end of the service. There was no organ playing, only soft singing from the group as each person took communion. Charlie prayed with some individually as they kneeled at the railing. I don't think I have ever been so moved. Maybe it was the element of surprise, because I hadn't known what was coming. Or maybe it was the simple idea that this is what life should be all about: people helping one another. Jesus said we were supposed to glorify God, make disciples, and set the oppressed free, and that was what Charlie Waters lived. He was using his time and money to make a difference in people's lives. There was no plate passed, no donation jar. These people were just welcomed at the banquet table, and nothing was required of them.

The meal, service, or teaching time and the lingering fellow-ship that followed lasted about three hours. Mac had lit a fire in a big nearby pit and handed out marshmallows and metal sticks made from coat hangers. There were stacks of graham crackers and I suspected some chocolate bars for s'mores, a camping tradi-tion. I joined in for some of that and got some great footage of people enjoying the fire.

Charlie saw every one of them off as they left. He shook hands, patted their backs, and gave them words of encouragement. I watched as the last car pulled off the field.

As Charlie was talking to Mac, I asked Cora, "So, Charlie pays for all of this himself, nobody ever pitches in?"

"All by himself and he does it every week. He feels like God has blessed him and he's going to share it. By the way, Ida called. Her cat was having kittens tonight so she couldn't come, but she said to tell you hello and is sorry she missed you."

"I'm sorry I missed her, and I'm grateful to her that she called me. This is a great story."

Charlie came over and asked me if I wanted to come into the house for something hot to drink. I agreed because I was slightly chilled from the crisp night air. I glanced at my watch. It was get-ting late, but I couldn't let this go. The girls were spending the night with Kendra, one of their favorite things to do on the week-end. They were watching movies and having fun. Dung and Dong would feed Bob and make sure he was okay, so really, there was no reason for me to leave. Besides, I wanted to hear more of Charlie Water's story and his reason for becoming a Cowboy preacher.

THIRTY-NINE

You know all those old cowboy movies where the hero sees the city girl and they fight and then he bends her over and kisses her and they fall in love and ride off in the sunset? Well, this wasn't quite like that. I'm no Maureen O'Hara and Charlie wasn't John Wayne, but there was an element of that to it.

I had an introduction to country life when I was small; Dad had been a rancher for a brief time. It was enough for me to find solace in walking in the woods. Hearing the sweet music of crickets singing outside was like a song in my soul. I loved fresh air and I liked riding horses. I loved the kindness of country people and enjoyed their conversational style. There was nothing affected about them, and they never seemed to have any agendas. I liked that.

So a relationship with the Cowboy Preacher wasn't out of the question. We did live in different places, so that might be a challenge. I have to say, I was intrigued with this guy; he was unlike any other man I'd known. He had some qualities of Marty that I liked, meaning his kindness and his eyes, and when he looked at me, he seemed perpetually amused.

Now I'm also not Lucy Ricardo, but there is an element of comedy in my ability to be athletic. I said I *liked* to ride horses, but I'm not particularly *good* at riding horses. I tend to lean a bit. Once, riding with Charlie, I slid off. Another time, I was getting on the saddle and went flailing off to the other side. Instinctively, I rolled away from the horse, but it didn't matter. The horse took off and Charlie picked me up, trying to control his laughter.

He also had some of the qualities of my father: solid, loyal, and honest. He seemed to have enormous respect for me. We kept the relationship strictly professional in the beginning. I did the story and got it on the air. It remains one of the most popular stories we've ever done. People talked about the Cowboy Preacher for a long time and the response to Charlie almost overwhelmed him.

The Monday after the weekend the story ran, I got this message on my answering machine: "Ms. Pendleton, this is Cora Miller out at Charlie Waters's place. We sure liked the story you ran on Charlie. He was embarrassed, of course, but very pleased. Anyway, you wouldn't believe what happened this past weekend. The response was incredible. I thought maybe you'd like to come out and spend the weekend here with us and see the service. We have some great news, and since we have you to thank, we thought maybe you'd like a steak dinner to celebrate with us. Can you call me back at area code 918…"

Of course, I wanted to know what news they had! I called them back and Charlie downplayed everything, except that he'd like me to come out and stay in the guest room, of course. He even offered for the girls to come, but I thought I'd wait on that deal. I didn't know exactly how I felt about this guy, and I didn't want to drag the girls into it yet. They were pretty self-involved. And even though they were always trying to set me up with this coach or that teacher, I wasn't sure how'd they react.

I'd take my time. The girls had a church retreat that weekend, so I was off the hook on being the mom. I decided to throw a couple pairs of jeans, a sweatshirt, a sweater, and my cotton plaid pajamas and toiletries in my bag and head for the ranch. I also packed my Bible, which I had been reading lately.

Charlie seemed genuinely glad to see me. Cora had been baking brownies all day for the Friday night service. Mac was firing up the chuck wagon, and Hershey, Charlie's chocolate lab, was wearing a red bandanna.

This time I had jeans, a light sweater, and my denim jacket. I didn't have any western boots, but I had my pink running shoes on. Georgette had outgrown them and bonus: they lit up when you walked. Bob had "borrowed" one of my favorite sneakers, so I went with the pink.

Charlie, Cora, and Mac got a kick out of the shoes. Cora and Mac seemed giddy to see me and Charlie just kept smiling. I helped serve food at the chuck wagon. I'd brought my camera in case I wanted to do an update. The number of people who came to hear Charlie speak had doubled; they all seemed eager to listen to Charlie teach.

After the service, or class, as Charlie called it, I walked around and met some of the people. Many of them recognized my name from the show. Cora took me aside and thanked me again.

"Don't tell Charlie I told you this, but your story was an absolute godsend. Me and Ida, she's my best friend, called you because we thought Charlie needed some help," Cora whispered.

"Help? It looks like he is doing fine to me."

"Well, he is fine on his preaching. But the ranching business isn't what it used to be, and Charlie spends a lot of time counseling these people and feeding them. He won't take a dime for it. He was running out of his own dimes. The last few months, I noticed he was selling off some stuff. I asked Mac, who is pretty tight-mouthed about Charlie and his business. All Mac would say was that 'it could be better.'"

"So," she continued, "that's when Ida and I prayed about it and came up with your show. We thought if we publicized Charlie, then maybe more people would come and someone would step up and help him. And you know, that's what happened!"

"What?" I asked in surprise.

"Well, Charlie had spent quite a bit to build that pavilion. There's a feller from Claremore who saw the show and realized some of his workers had been talking about Charlie and going to Charlie's services. They were changed men. They stopped drinking and carousing and cleaned up their acts. This man said his business had improved because his workers became more conscientious. He owns an asphalt company. He's going to come over and pave that field for free so folks won't get their vehicles stuck in the mud."

"That's great, Cora," I said, pleased. This was the magic of television.

"Well, that's good, but it's not the great part. Another man who owns a little oil company down in Oklahoma City called Charlie and said he got to looking and wanted to put a couple of oil wells out on Charlie's land, the back twenty acres. He's sure they'll find oil. He said he'd pay Charlie twenty-five percent of the profits and also pay him handsomely to let them set up their rigs and stuff. They started coming out this week and building the site, so now Charlie's back in business!"

"Well, that's super. I just assumed Charlie was doing fine," I said.

"He's been doing okay, but his wife's illness left a big hole. She had some life insurance of course, which paid a lot of bills and built the pavilion, but the man had to build himself back after her death. This teaching has been the best medicine."

Charlie came up behind us, laughing. "Well, girls, I hope we have extra marshmallows 'cause we have quite a crowd tonight." He was walking with a young Native American who wore his hair in a long braid and a short Asian man. Charlie looked relaxed and happy.

Cora had bags of marshmallows and had cut more hangers for toasting. People shared, laughed, and talked. Some men were quiet, sitting on rocks around the fire, just staring into it, likely thinking about their lives. Others were laughing and talking, encouraging each other in their newfound faith.

After the fire died down and the people had gone home, Charlie, Cora, Mac, and I cleaned up everything and went back to the house. I was cold, but Charlie built a roaring fire inside and we all sat down with coffee (in my case, hot chocolate), and visited. Charlie was a storyteller. He had lots of stories from his youth and times he and Carol had traveled before she got sick. He talked about her easily, as if she were still part of him.

Their children, two sons and a daughter who all lived in Colorado, were older than Michael, around Kendra and Hunter's age. I saw pictures. They looked like a combination of the parents. Charlie still had a framed picture of Carol and him in his office. She was pretty. He had several, in fact, including one from their younger days when Charlie had all his hair.

I wasn't jealous and that surprised me. Why should I be? After all, my husband was dead too. Nobody should be jealous of a dead person, but it was more than that. I felt a kind of kinship with her. I understood why she had loved Charlie. I wasn't sure what this meant. At this point, I was just enjoying myself with a cup of hot chocolate in front of a fire with new friends. I wouldn't really start to feel the branches break until the next morning, when Charlie surprised me with breakfast in bed.

FORTY

"Knock, knock," said a friendly voice outside the bedroom door.

"Good morning," I replied, quickly trying to smooth my hair and open my right eye.

Charlie cracked the door open and peeked inside. I could smell the aroma of bacon, sausage, eggs, and biscuits with gravy. A frosty glass of orange juice on ice was on the tray with a rose in a vase, stolen, no doubt, from the large bouquet on the dining room table.

"Cora's not going to like it that you stole that flower from her bouquet," I said, smiling.

"It's not Cora's bouquet; I bought them for you," he said, smiling back. He gently set the tray next to me on the bed and sat in the chair.

"Thank you," I said, surveying the spread. "Wow! I don't think I've had breakfast in bed since I gave birth."

"Well, you deserve a little pampering. I wanted to thank you for that story. And though I think you exaggerated a bit about my good qualities, it really helped the ministry," he said sincerely.

"I didn't exaggerate a bit," I said. "You deserved every good word. I'm sorry I look so scary, no makeup and crazy hair."

"You're beautiful with or without makeup, and I like your messy hair. It looks fine," he said. "Do you want me to leave you alone or do you want company?"

"Oh, company of course, but what about your breakfast?"

"I ate hours ago. It's nine thirty. Around here, that's late. We're up early to feed everybody and take care of the animals." He grinned. "I've always been one to go out early in the morning and have my quiet time with God. That's when He downloads my best stuff."

"Do you hear a voice?"

"Sometimes, but it's more like the message is clear in my head. When you finish this great breakfast, do you think you'd be up to riding a horse or taking a hike around the place?"

"Sure," I said, taking a few bites, feeling it would be impolite to not eat most of these biscuits and gravy, even though I knew this meal was a heart attack on a plate. "Hey, do you eat like this all the time? You must have cholesterol through the roof."

"I'm on medicine, and no, we don't eat like this all the time, just for company. I've got to watch that stuff now, being an old guy. I get plenty of exercise and try to watch my stress level."

"I wouldn't think the stress level would be bad out here, it's so beautiful and everybody is so nice."

"That's true, but stress comes in all kinds of ways and forms, I just try to give it to God, especially at night. He's up anyway."

"Good philosophy. Okay, buddy. I'm sorry I can't eat all of this, and I know you're dying to see me in these sexy plaid pajamas, so I'm giving you a thrill here, and getting up."

"Whew!" He whistled and laughed. "You'd look great in anything. They're cute. Now I'll take the tray down and you get yourself ready and we'll go out on an adventure," he said, and winked.

Everything with Charlie was an adventure because it was all new territory to me. Over the next few weeks, we rode, we fished, we hiked, and we even rowed out in the middle of his lake and just sat and talked. We talked about everything from our past experiences growing up, to family, dysfunctional family, dysfunctional friends, our thoughts on child-rearing, our thoughts on parenting and grandparenting, and our dreams. Charlie had a master's degree in philosophy and was well read. We also talked about the Bible because Charlie knew so much on this topic. We even took a few stabs at politics, where we seemed to agree. We were both registered Independents. Charlie was more forgiving of people, where I was more demanding, but that didn't stop us from getting closer, which we did.

I couldn't always come out to the ranch because the story was done. Now it was just for fun and to see Charlie. I had wanted to wait for him to meet the girls and the rest of the family until I had more time with him, so we often met in town for an evening dinner and a movie, or sometimes we'd just sit someplace and talk for hours.

Once or twice, we went to a bar and we danced. Charlie could really dance, he could two-step with the best of them, which, if you're not a country girl, is country dancing to country music. I'm okay when it comes to dancing, but nothing like those gals that dance with a rose in their mouth. I'd only slow-danced with Marty and George, and I could follow. But I was going to have to do better in the dancing department to match Charlie.

Charlie had a brilliant idea: square dancing. I hadn't square danced since gym class. Charlie didn't care. We went into Pryor and picked the least offensive square-dancing outfit for me I could find, which involved me wearing red and denim. I think there were ruffles, but I ignored them. Charlie had plenty of western shirts, so he was fine. We replaced my pink running shoes with some little slipper type shoes for dancing, which were very comfortable. We also found a pair of nice leather boots on sale.

That night, after a steak dinner, Cora, Mac, Charlie and I went into Pryor to a square dance held in a big barn. I can't remember when I've had so much fun or exercise! There was real country picking on the guitar; one guy was even blowing on a jug. Lemonade and soft drinks were the only beverages, which was fine with me.

They also served cookies, brownies, and homemade ice cream for snacks. The hay would have really bothered Marty's allergies, but it didn't bother me at all. I was too busy clapping and do-si-do-ing.

We all collapsed after an hour or two and sat eating ice cream and watching the younger folks go 'round and 'round. That's one thing I liked about square dancing: they tell you what to do, so young and old can participate and no one feels any less qualified than anyone else.

I marveled at the callers. They were the ones with the real talent and never missed a beat. Several people took turns calling, which made it more fun.

"Let's take this city girl home, we don't want to wear her out," Charlie said good-naturedly. Cora and Mac agreed. They were tired. It had been a long day of fresh air, sunshine, and lots of activity.

There was a full moon on this night. After the animals were bedded down and Cora and Mac had gone to their house nearby, Charlie and I sat out on his porch swing with a blanket over us, just swinging and looking at the moon. Hershey was lying not far from the swing, and when it squeaked, he'd wag his tail and pass gas.

We were alone with a million stars, a chorus of crickets, and a farting dog, but that was okay—it was all perfect. I leaned my head on Charlie's shoulder and we rocked back and forth. I could feel those branches breaking again. This guy Charlie was pretty fun and consistently nice to everyone. I was falling for him, and I didn't care. I was enjoying myself in a way I'm not sure I ever had, because I didn't have to be perfect. Charlie seemed to think I looked good even in this square-dancing outfit. It didn't matter what I wore or what makeup I had on. He didn't care. George had loved me, but he'd often suggested I change into something suitable. Marty didn't care, but when he became a girl, she told me I didn't dress as feminine as she wanted to dress.

I had my share of pink clothes, but I liked pants and sweaters. I knew that had nothing to do with my femininity, because that's something you carry inside that is reflected in everything you do. Charlie saw that and he understood me. Eventually, as I would come to realize, he understood me the way no man ever had.

The challenge would be blending Cowboy Charlie into city family. The thought of this was exhausting. It made me want to sit on a porch swing with Charlie and never go home, but I had girls to raise and parents to contend with, and I wasn't sure how Charlie would fit in that world.

Of course, I wasn't giving Charlie much credit, because as I'd already witnessed by the group who came faithfully every week, Charlie was comfortable with Charlie. He could fit just about anywhere, with anyone. I didn't have any trouble keeping in step with Charlie, but could he keep up with me? What followed would be, as Charlie would always say, an adventure.

FORTY-ONE

2002

I t's about fifty-three minutes from Charlie's door to mine if it's not rush hour and there's no construction, which there always is. We made this trip back and forth to each other's homes for almost a year and a half, then decided to get married on New Year's Eve, 2002. Charlie said he wouldn't ever forget our anniversary that way, and we'd always have cause to celebrate.

We had the wedding at Charlie's house in front of the fireplace. Fred officiated, of course, because Charlie and Fred had become great friends and Charlie didn't care that Fred had married George and me. Charlie wasn't superstitious. In fact, very little bothered Charlie.

We decided not to dress up for this one, no tux, no long white dress, no big guest list, just family and a few close friends. Glam brought the veterinarian, who actually took a look at two of Charlie's horses and a cow before the ceremony. Gloria was there, of course, and my girls.

Teenage girls are their own type of wonderful. Georgette wanted to wear a backless dress that was skintight, which I vetoed, and Gretchen voted for jeans, which I would rather have had her wear than a sexy cocktail dress.

Georgette begrudgingly settled on a long skirt, which she wanted to wear down to the crack in her butt, again vetoed, so she settled on two layered shirts with sparkly jeans and boots.

Gretchen went with black pants and a soft blue sweater. Both girls wore their hair up because they wanted to look older.

I decided to sort of dress-up. I wore a black skirt and a lacey white blouse with puffy sleeves and pearl buttons. Charlie had given me pearl earrings as a wedding present.

My sister was in Europe. Dad was in the rehab center from a bad fall and Mom was at their retirement home. It was just as well. Big social gatherings were hard on them. Hunter and his new girl-friend came. We had liked the last six and we liked this one, too. Apparently, Hunter refused to get serious about any of them until he met "the one". That's a good plan. Kendra and Dan were happy to be there without a child. His mother was watching Gracie.

Michael had come home for the holiday and was leaving the day after tomorrow to go back to San Diego where he was in Navy Seal training. At twenty-two, he was such a man. He was power-fully built, not an ounce of fat on him, all lean muscle, and his stamina for running and of course, swimming, was amazing.

Charlie's kids had planned to come but the Denver airport was closed and so were most of the roads between here and their places in the mountains of Colorado.

Marty and Ben weren't there. They had booked a cruise a year in advance and although they had offered to cancel, I didn't want them to be out all that money. It was best. I didn't want any tension tonight between Marty and Michael. So it worked out.

Cora and Mac were there of course, and Ida, Cora's best friend. They had made us a lovely wedding cake and had spent all day making a large variety of food. Dong and Dung came to help with the food and brought Bob.

We got married in front of the fireplace and at the end of the ceremony, since our family was gathered around us, Fred had everybody put a hand on a shoulder and pray for us.

When that was over, we started the celebration off with a toast and began the feast! There was lots of food that involved pastry and there was plenty of fresh fruit and cheese. Mac had actually roasted a pig over a spit and that ham was the best I've ever tasted.

We ate and laughed and talked. Mac could play the fiddle and Gloria sat at the piano and began to sing. Charlie's big living room was so large; we actually had room to dance and did. Charlie had taught me a few moves, so I wasn't such a klutz. The girls got a kick out of dancing, and it turned out Glam's veterinarian could do quite a two-step. Of course, so could Glam. Michael surprised me. He got up and danced with both of his little sisters and seemed less stiff and formal than he had throughout the holiday. Maybe it was the champagne.

Feeling a little giddy, Charlie and I retired to "our" bedroom. We had decided to wait until we were married to sleep together, so we actually were really looking forward to our honeymoon. We had also decided to wait to leave until Michael left. Since we had booked a Bed and Breakfast in San Diego, we would be flying out with Michael.

I had bought some flimsy lingerie for the honeymoon and slipped into a silky short nightgown for my wedding night.

With just the moonlight coming in and voices still below us, we crawled under the sheets.

"Dang that Mac," Charlie said, "he went and put a snake in the bed."

"What?" I shrieked, recoiling and starting to bolt from under the sheets.

"Relax," Charlie said laughing, "it's only plastic."

He pulled the plastic snake from the bottom of his side of the bed and threw it in the corner.

"I'm not sure I can get used to country living," I sighed, rolling over and looking at him.

"It's too late, you're hitched," he grinned.

"Are you nervous about this marriage thing?" I asked, looking at those always smiling blue eyes.

"Nope, not a bit. I am a little nervous about what's going to happen here in a while," he said.

"Oh yeah? What makes you think anything's going to happen?" I said, coyly.

"Because it's almost midnight," Charlie said softly.

"Do I turn back into Cinderella at midnight?"

"No," Charlie said, "and you don't get to take your old name back, either."

"Well, what then?" I asked, slipping my hand around his waist, as if I didn't know.

"Well," Charlie started to say, but he couldn't talk because I was kissing him.

"There's uh, something you…"

"What Charlie?" I mocked interest and kissed him again.

"There's a, uh, tradition," he tried to say, and I wouldn't let him.

Then suddenly the loudest noise I'd ever heard erupted outside our door. Pans were banging, cymbals were clashing and the loudest cacophony of voices with no discernible pitch.

Charlie jumped out of bed and threw on his robe.

"That's what I've been trying to tell you!" he shouted. "That's why I knew we should wait."

"What? You planned this?" I yelled.

"Of course not," he yelled back.

He turned on a lamp and opened the door. I had managed to pull on my matching silk robe.

There they all were, banging pans, howling, singing, and every way to make noise they could.

"They're giving us a *shivaree*, kind of an old-fashioned serenade to newlyweds. They start out with this and then they usually end up singing."

As if on cue, our friends and family began singing, "Good night, Charlie. Good night, Lizzie. We want to wish you well," over and over. We both were at the door listening to this and thanked them, then Charlie shut the door and they went away shouting lone "Goodnights!" as they marched back down the stairs.

"Mrs. Waters, would you like to step out on this balcony for a minute and look at the moonlight before we retire?" he said, trying to sound like Rhett Butler and failing miserably.

"Why, my, my, my, Mr. Waters, I do think I'll catch my death of cold," I said, in a better imitation of Miss Scarlet. "But since I am your wife, I will accommodate your wishes."

He opened the door gallantly and brisk cold air blew into the room. I had on my feathery slippers and my silk robe, but they were no match for the outside. I gingerly stepped on the observation deck off the master bedroom and looked at the full moon. There was just a smattering of stars to be seen.

"May I kiss you under this moonlight, ma'am?" he asked sweetly.

"Yes, you may," I agreed. He kissed me in that warm, sweet Charlie way.

"Charlie, can we go inside now? I'm freezing."

"I was hoping you'd say that," he said.

Once back in bed, I snuggled up to Charlie.

"I'm freezing," I said, shivering.

"Good, that means you need me to warm you up," he said, his arms around me.

"Always," I said, softly. "The shivaree is over, isn't it? No more pans? We're alone?"

"Yes, ma'am, and the door is locked."

"It's been a very long time for me, Charlie, I may not remember how to do this," I warned.

"I'll remind you," he said.

"I've only slept with two men, you know. One of them is a woman now and the other one is dead. I don't know what that says about me, Charlie. Maybe I'm some kind of freak. I don't want anything to happen to you because of me," I said, genuinely worried.

"Shhh, Mrs. Waters. Nothing's going to happen to me. I would like something to happen here tonight if you're finished worrying."

"Charlie," I said. "Let the honeymoon begin."

CHAPTER

FORTY-TWO

When we came back from San Diego, it was time to get Dad out of the rehab hospital and take away the keys to the car. That was his last little bastion of freedom and we just had to do it. The blow to the head, plus his eighty-odd years of stubbornness, made him untrustworthy on the road.

Charlie and I had worked out that we would pretty much live in the city because of the girls' school and church activities and then have the weekends at the ranch. Charlie would drive to the ranch during the week and then return to Tulsa at night. Cora and Mac could run the ranch just fine and would keep things in order.

When we took Dad back to the retirement center and Charlie surveyed the two rooms they were living in, he said nothing. When Charlie had seen my parents, it had been at my house or out to dinner and he'd never seen them in their environment. He spent a long time talking to Dad about his Native American Art and his history books on war. Dad adored Charlie and welcomed the male attention because there weren't too many men left standing at the retirement center and very few of them even in wheelchairs.

My father could still walk, but he was unsteady. He hated using the walker and would just follow the railing down the hall or push Mom in her wheelchair. Mom had resigned herself to the chair and actually seemed to think she was entitled to everyone waiting on her hand and foot. The doctor had diagnosed her with Alzheimer's disease. She often called me her sister.

Alzheimer's disease isn't particular; it has felled past presidents and dignitaries. My mother gave it her best fight, but after the stroke, it weakened her system. Mom wasn't at the awful stage yet; she just stammered from time to time and had dementia and no filter, which had its moments of hilarity.

After we ate lunch with them, Dad wheeled Mom back to their room and I helped her get ready for bed. We left them for a nap and walked outside. Charlie opened the door on my side of his truck and helped me in. He hadn't said anything since we left the building, which for Charlie, was kind of unusual.

"Penny for your thoughts," I said.

"Liz, I don't feel right about your parents being in this place. You have me now to help you and I think it's time to move them in with us."

I had thought about this many times, moving them in with me, but I just didn't think I could handle it. I had two teenagers at home and a career.

"Charlie, we just got married."

"I know. So?"

"It's going to be challenging enough with teenagers and activity in the house. Do you think we need old people?"

"Nobody *needs* old people, Liz, that's the problem. Old people didn't do anything wrong, they just survived. These are your parents, and they need care. This place is fine, but the food is lousy and they're crammed in those little rooms. They need a house. You have Dong and Dung in the back that can help. There are two teenage girls in that house who can contribute and both of us have somewhat flexible schedules. This is family and they're part of my family now. Besides, it's the right thing to do," he said. His blue eyes weren't twinkling or amused. He was dead serious and determined.

I knew he was right. I had always felt bad about them staying there, but they hadn't wanted to live with me. They wanted to live on their own. I knew mother was getting worse and might have to go to a nursing home; this way they could be together at my house. They'd been together over sixty years and it would be a shame to split them up now.

I didn't have any problem with Dad living with me. Dad and I had always gotten along. We had shared the mutual amusement and aggravation of my mother, and our natures were alike. We both loved doing things for people and loved people. Mom had always loved the audience, but not so much the people. She had a few friends but didn't really invest herself in anybody but her family. She rarely visited her sisters who were scattered across the country. Her obsession had been reading, bridge, and sewing. The stroke took her ability to play bridge or read much and the sewing went by the wayside, too. I tried to find friends for her at senior centers and at the retirement home, but she "didn't relate to anybody."

As a person who finds most people in all walks of life interesting, intriguing, or amusing, I couldn't figure out how to deal with this, so I gave up trying. Besides, my therapist had told me it wasn't my job.

The thought of having my mother live with me twenty-four/seven scared me a little, but not as much as it would have ten years earlier. After all, I'd been alive almost half a century. I had survived a husband who was a woman and a death of a spouse. I could handle a ninety-year-old lady with Alzheimer's who called me her sister. There was another factor working here: Mom and Dad couldn't afford to live in this retirement home another two years. They were running out of money. They didn't take out long-term care insurance because Dad didn't think they'd live that long, and when 9/11 hit, their stocks went in the toilet and a lot of that money was simply flushed away.

I knew, deep in my heart, Charlie was right, and I had known it was coming; it's just that I wanted someone else to take care of it. I was in a new marriage, and I didn't want to have to deal with my parents every day. Where the hell was my sister through all of this? Why couldn't she take them half the year and we take them half the year? Lots of families do that. But it wasn't an option. She was busy hoping continents, and Dork liked to travel and not be tied down, plus he didn't seem to care much for my parents. The irony here was Claire was mother's favorite and I would be the one who ended up being stuck with her.

Don't get me wrong. I don't hate my mother. She was fun when I was little, singing me songs, teaching me how to pretend, developing my imagination early. She taught me to read before I ever went to school and encouraged me to write. She gave me her old Brownie camera and taught me how to look at a picture and take it. She let me do chores around the house to earn the money to develop the film.

So my love of the arts, reading, writing and my early photography experience all came from her. She made my costumes for dance recitals and plays and was truly involved in my life. But she was obsessed with weight. Had I known about anorexia, I might have been that, but I was too busy finishing all the food on my plate, which she insisted I do. She never could understand why I could fill out and gain a little weight and my sister stayed so thin, like her. That's because Claire never ate a plate of food in her life; she just pushed it around the plate. She was the pickiest eater on the planet. Mom would just roll her eyes and they would fight about it for a while and Mom would give up. To please Mom, I ate everything—sometimes even a second helping!

She made a few friends, mothers of playmates of mine, but she found fault with most of them and she rarely had them over. She did volunteer work or helped my father at the hardware store he owned in Sand Springs. It went out of business when they moved a Lowes in down the street.

It wouldn't be too hard to move them. Charlie and I could pack them up and have them moved in a day. We would have to sit them down, because their pride would keep them from wanting to intrude in our lives. Mother used to say she'd rather be in hell with her back broken than to live with her kids, but that was years ago before the stroke. She probably meant it, but she was out of choices.

The girls wouldn't be too happy about this. They had survived fourteen years of my parents. Mom had made over them when they were little, but when they became teenagers, she started picking on them about weight and it had affected them both. We'd all done a little therapy around this issue and the therapist said the problem was rooted in my mother.

Charlie had said our life together would be an adventure, but I was picturing safaris and trips to Europe, not moving my parents in with us. Oh, well. When I looked into those warm determined blue eyes, I knew with Charlie by my side, I could do anything. I could even move my parents in with me, even though mother thought all of us were too fat.

FORTY-THREE

"**W**here are my demitasse cups?" my mother asked irritably. "Why haven't you unpacked them? Those are my most important possessions."

I knew this. I hadn't unpacked them yet because they'd been in the house only three hours and we were busy rearranging furniture to get mother's hospital bed in the downstairs master bedroom along with Dad's double bed. Charlie and I had the movers rearrange everything (we had moved into the upstairs master). The rooms were about the same and both had fireplaces. I had removed the key in the downstairs master fireplace and put it upstairs, so Dad didn't decide to blow us all up one night.

Georgette and Gretchen kept Mom and Dad entertained while I messed with furniture and bedding, but fifteen-year-olds have a short attention span when it comes to friends calling them on the phone.

"Girls," I said, knowing my voice was a little testy, "would you please come down and unpack your grandmother's demitasse cups and set them up for her?" Demitasse cups are those little teacups half the size of a regular tea or coffee cup.

"In a minute," Georgette said, which was her standard line. If you held your breath for one of Georgette's minutes, you'd be dead.

"I will," Gretchen said. "I'd love to do that for you, Grandma."

"Who is that girl?" my mother asked my father. Does she live here?

"That's Gretchen, our granddaughter," my father said.

"Well, I've never seen her before, and I don't want her touching my things. I want my sister to unpack those cups," Mom said, nose in the air.

"Your sister isn't here. That's Liz, our daughter," Dad reminded her.

"That's not Liz; she's too old and fat to be Liz. Elizabeth always struggled with her weight, so it might be her, but surely Liz wouldn't have let herself go like *that*," Mom said, as if I weren't in the room. Dad looked sad and shook his head at me.

Gretchen was in tears as she went back up the stairs. I followed her and put my arm around her. "Honey, she doesn't know what she's saying," I whispered.

"Why is the only grandma we have *mean?* I hate her," Gretchen said, sniffing, "and I don't like the way she talked about you, Mom. You're not that big!"

"Well, I'm not small. Your grandmother has always been a size six and anything bigger than that is huge to her."

"Well, she isn't a six now. She's probably a twelve or fourteen since she's been in the wheelchair."

"I know," I laughed. "I love it that she's gotten bigger on the bottom. She hates it so; she's had such an obsession about it her whole life. I love the irony."

"Mom, that's kinda mean," Gretchen said, her tears stopping.

I chuckled. "I know, but it's honest."

She hugged me and went back in her room. The girls had each claimed their own rooms when the other members of the household moved out. Gretchen's was the softest shade of blue to match her eyes, and everything in her room was white. She had white Battenberg lace curtains with a matching dust ruffle and a soft Laura Ashley down comforter.

Georgette's room was white with one long black wall. I wouldn't let her paint all the walls black. She had a fluffy pink bedspread and a pink and black feather boa draped over her wrought iron headboard. Everything was rhinestones and stars.

I came downstairs just in time for Charlie to pay the movers. I could hear Dung and Dong chattering in their native tongue in the kitchen. They were snapping at each other, so that couldn't be good. Mom must have blasted them too. They understood English perfectly and could now speak it pretty well, though Dad could never understand them because his hearing aids rang too much.

I set up mother's curio cabinet in her new bedroom with her demitasse cups and put a small chaise next to it that had been in her room when she was young. I had inherited the chaise for my bedroom as a child; it wouldn't fit in Claire's room.

"Elizabeth," Mom said, obviously recognizing me now. "I like the one with the shamrocks on the second shelf," she directed, looking at it lovingly. "Your father gave that to me on St. Patrick's Day, and that evening we conceived your sister."

I could have gone my whole life without knowing that.

"Is there a cup for my conception?" I asked.

"Oh, I don't remember," she said, waving a wrinkled, blotchy hand at me. Her fingernails were still long and polished, thanks to the help at the retirement home. They were natural. "I told you, after I lost that one baby, I almost gave up. I didn't like being fat, but I thought God always p-punished me because I didn't want to get f-fat, so I lost that baby."

"Mom, God doesn't work that way. You lost the baby because the doctor was incompetent, and the baby choked on the umbilical cord."

"Well, your father wanted another baby, so that's what we did," she said, remembering. She was quiet for a moment, as if thinking about this. Then she turned to me. "Iris, is mother in the kitchen making dinner? I'm starving." In an instant, I became her sister again.

I patted her shoulder and said I'd check and see. I wheeled her into the bathroom that we had made handicap accessible and helped her take care of her business. I pulled off her soaked diaper and thought, *What have I done? This isn't going to be easy.*

When Mom was freshly changed, I washed my hands and wheeled her back into the kitchen. Dad was already there, visiting with Dung and Dong. The girls had come down as well. Charlie was perched on a stool telling everybody a story and Dad was grinning from ear to ear. I wheeled Mother in quietly and Dad looked at us, still smiling.

"Who are these foreigners in my mother's kitchen?" Mom said, fretting. "We can't have this."

I figured she meant Dung and Dong, but she might have thrown Charlie in there with them. And of course, she didn't know Gretchen and Georgette.

"Iris, call Mother and tell her not to come home until we take care of this mess. We have to get all of these people out of mother's kitchen. Oh, there you are, Jack. I didn't see you come in. You have to help us."

Dad rose unsteadily and shuffled over to Mom, his right arm shaking from his newly diagnosed Parkinson's disease.

"Jack, stand up straight and don't walk like such an old man, it's not f-funny," she ordered.

Dad silently turned her around and took her into the other room. I pulled the Xanax out of the cabinet, tempted to take one, but I didn't want to start now. I got a glass of water and gave her one. This was on instructions from the nursing home doctor and the staff.

Charlie was sipping a glass of cabernet, and I joined him. I could hear Dad talking to Mom in the living room, trying to change the subject when she became irritable.

"How are we going to do this?" Georgette said. "She's awful."

"She'll have her good days and her bad days. It is worse for Alzheimer's patients at night," Charlie said.

"How do you know?" Georgette challenged him. She liked Charlie, but she didn't trust any man over forty.

"My father had it," he said quietly. "I took care of him for a couple of years before he died."

New information. I didn't know Charlie had done this. I knew he'd taken care of his wife, but he never mentioned taking care of his dad, only that he had died. That would be Charlie, though. I hadn't asked about it and he wouldn't have told me. Cora was the person who had told me about Charlie's late wife. I was truly blessed here.

We decided to feed Mom and Dad early in the dining room. The girls put a pretty tablecloth and candles on the table, but we didn't light them. We figured until Mom was settled into a routine, we'd better simplify things.

"Oh my, how pretty!" she exclaimed. "I bet my sweet Gretchen and Georgette did this," she said. "Where are they?"

Shocked that she knew them and was being pleasant, they approached her with caution.

"You girls are so nice to do this for me. Tomorrow, I'm going to drive you girls over to Utica Square and get you some new clothes. Don't worry; we're not going to tell your mother. We're just going to do it. We'll eat ice cream afterward, too, because I like to have fun with my girls."

She smiled her childlike smile at them with glee in her eyes. Who could resist that? We would have many more of these moments with Mom, but we learned how to handle her better and I learned to give her Xanax when I anticipated she'd be around all of us, especially in the evening.

In the beginning, I figured that she wouldn't live very long, since the doctor had put her on hospice care. I could handle this for the short run. Little did I know, the short run would get longer and longer.

FORTY-FOUR

I was thinking about people who plaster their cars with bumper stickers. I was behind a car today that was loaded with them. Since we're in Oklahoma, you expect ones related to the state schools, but there are also ones that really show a person's attitude toward life. There are political stickers, social stickers, smiley faces, ying and yang, Christian stickers, Darwin stickers, and anti-everything stickers. Then there are the random sayings: "My other car is a Mercedes," "Baby on Board," "Stuff Happens."

The driver I was behind today was not a happy person. He drove an old Datsun—that's right, a Datsun, before Nissan. Its stickers read "Ticked Off" and "I love to hate" and one was a picture of a hand giving me the finger. Isn't that supposed to be illegal? Doesn't it violate some kind of decency law? When people are driving aren't you're not supposed to see obscene gestures? But is it obscene when it's just a piece of vinyl on a car? The middle finger had a string tied around it. I liked that, like he had to be *reminded* to give totally innocent people who could be driving with children or old people the finger.

"What's all that stuff on that man's car?" my mother demanded from the back seat. The girls were sitting on either side of her. Dad was in the front passenger seat.

"Oh great. Pass him, Mom, or drop back. That guy's a nut job," Georgette said, looking out her window.

He'd fit in here, I thought mildly.

"I can't pass him. It's a no-passing zone," I said, glancing in the rearview mirror, "hence the double yellow line in the middle of the road."

"Who paints those lines?" Gretchen asked in a worried voice. "Wouldn't they get hurt if they were painting a line and a car came?"

"They block off the traffic," Dad said.

"It's so nice of you to join us," my mother said pleasantly, patting the girls' legs. "You are such pretty girls. Tell me something, did your mother die?"

"No," Georgette said, "she's driving."

"Oh, that's not your mother, dear, that's Iris," my mother said emphatically. "I'm asking about your mother because I never heard if she died or not."

"She did," Georgette said, sniffing and looking for a tissue. "It was a long, painful illness." She actually manufactured tears. Gretchen held her hand over her mouth to keep from laughing.

"Oh, I'm so sorry. I thought that's what I heard, but at least you have your father."

Gretchen laughed out loud now.

"It's okay," my mother soothed her.

Dong was in the far back seat with a large picnic basket she had packed with the girls' favorite food. She had come to help handle mother in case I wanted to leave. Mother liked Dong only half of the time, but she had learned to put up with her. I think Dong felt the same about her. Dong was asleep with her head against the window—or pretending to be asleep.

The guy with the finger sticker on his car turned off. Dad sighed.

"How far is it out here again? I don't think Charlie goes this way when he takes me to the ranch. You can pass this car ahead, but watch him."

"Dad, I don't know how Charlie goes to the ranch, but this is how I go and I'm driving."

"I should have driven with Charlie. I have my *own* tackle box, you know. I've built up a pretty nice tackle box. I don't know what happened to my poles. You probably got rid of them when I was in the hospital."

"I don't think so," I said, trying to remember. "If I did, Charlie has plenty of fishing poles for everybody."

"A man likes his own rod."

Wasn't *that* the truth!

"You girls are nice and slender," Mom said.

Here we go.

"I wish I were nice and slender. I'm so fat. I look like an e-el-elephant between you two."

"No, you don't, you're beautiful," Gretchen said. "Just look at those legs!" she exclaimed.

"Oh, they're awful," Mom disagreed.

"You should be thankful you're even here," Georgette said, "How old are you again?"

There are two questions regarding age and weight you never asked my mother. If you did, no matter what decade of her life she was in, she would lie.

Dad and I held our breath.

"I'll tell you how old I am." My mother narrowed her eyes. "I'm older than I was last year and I'm younger than I'll be next year," she said with a nod of her head.

Gretchen and Georgette thought this was a pretty good answer and laughed.

"I know I've seen him turn off here before, you could turn off here," Dad said anxiously.

"What's that noise? Mom, do we have a flat tire?" Georgette asked.

Everyone in the car was quiet for a moment.

"It sounded like something was caught under the van," Gretchen said.

That muffled taping came again.

I pulled off the road and stopped the Sienna van. I got out and walked around it.

Gretchen heard it again.

"Oh," Dad said, sheepishly, "it's me. This tremor in my arm is making me bang against the door."

I got back in the van.

"Why'd she get out of the car?" my mother asked Georgette.

"She was just checking on things," Georgette said.

"Iris," Mom said, "is Mother at the ranch waiting for us?"

Iris is my mother's sister who lives in Oregon and is a size 3X.

"Charlie is at the ranch waiting for us," I said, smiling.

For some reason, Mom always knew Charlie.

We had decided to come out to the ranch for spring break. This was about the extent of a trip Mom could take, and we could have fun out here riding horses, fishing, and hiking. The water probably wasn't warm enough for swimming, unless it stayed hot for a few days.

"Well, we're finally here," Mom said as we drove up. I jumped out and ran around to the other side of the van. I opened Dad's door to help him out. Hershey was barking and jumping in excitement. Gretchen got out. She helped Dong out of the car and carried the basket in. Georgette was struggling with Mom's seatbelt.

Charlie came from the barn and gave everybody a hello hug. I brought around my mom's wheelchair and Charlie lifted her into the chair.

"I bet Mother's making biscuits." She winked at Charlie.

He laughed. "You never know."

You're not supposed to tell Alzheimer's patients that people are dead or what they're saying is crazy; it just upsets them all over again. Though my father frequently tells my mother she's crazy.

We all went inside, where we could smell the wonderful aroma of pot roast cooking. Cora was rolling out biscuits from scratch. I admired that. Dong began unpacking the big picnic basket. We all said our hellos.

The girls hauled their suitcases into their room.

"Dong, after you finish in the kitchen," I said, "would you mind taking Mother into her room to freshen up?" This was code for "change her." Dong nodded her response and didn't say anything.

Charlie was busy hauling in Mom and Dad's suitcase. We kept the Depends and bed pads in the bathroom in their room. Mom and Dad slept together here in a queen-size bed, but it had to be heavily padded, and so did Mom.

I loved it here. I think I always was a country girl at heart. Don't get me wrong; I love my conveniences and my shopping center close by, but I also love the sounds of the night in the country and the smell of fresh air.

The girls disappeared into the barn to visit the horses and talk to Mac. We settled Mom and Dad in the big living room. Cora brought out a tray of cheese and crackers and some glasses of wine.

"I don't like wine. Scotch is my drink of preference," my mother said, her nose once again in the air.

"Mom, you can't really have that with your medication," I said.

"What medication? Are you trying to kill me?" she asked, looking alarmed.

"No, to keep you alive, but don't tempt me," I teased.

She smiled. Mom still got jokes from time to time.

"Then I'll have celery juice," she said agreeably.

"Celery juice?" Dad said. "What kind of juice is *that?*"

"C-celery juice," Mom said, decisively.

"How about apple or cranberry?" I asked.

"I WANT CELERY JUICE," my mother shouted, slamming her hand on her knee.

"Well, Mom, I bet we're fresh out of that, but let me see," I said, opening the refrigerator. "Oh look, Cora got some at the store and I didn't know it."

Everyone watched as I poured green Gatorade into a glass and handed it to my mother. We held our breath.

"That's the best celery juice I've ever tasted," she enthused.

Just then, my cell phone rang.

"Oh hi, Michael," I said, pleased to hear his voice. "Is everything all right?"

"Well, yes," he said, "but I don't think you're going to be too excited about my news."

"Why, what's wrong?" I asked, frowning.

"Well, there's no easy way to say this, Mom," he said.

"What? Michael? Michael?" I said, not hearing an answer and then, as is typical of reception in an outlying area, the line went dead.

FORTY-FIVE

2003

I could barely eat Cora's pot roast while waiting for Michael to call again. I was so upset I ate only one biscuit instead of two. Michael called in the middle of the chocolate cake dessert, his favorite. He was going to Afghanistan, shipping out early in the morning. He couldn't talk much about it. He asked for our prayers, then talked to the girls, to Mom and Dad, and to Charlie and me. He told us he loved us and then he hung up.

"I don't know why they let little children go on long trips like that," my mother complained. "How can little Michael go to Afghanistan?"

Sometimes the Alzheimer's patient has a glimpse of sanity. That was my sentiment exactly.

"He's grown up now, Grandma," Georgette reminded her. Gretchen nodded in agreement, slicing a second thin sliver of cake for herself. Georgette gave her a "How about me?" look, and Gretchen sliced one for her sister.

"I don't think that's right," Mom said. Then she was on to more important things. "Girls, you'll get fat if you eat all that cake."

I agreed with Mom about Michael, not the cake. Don't get me wrong, I am proud of Michael. I am proud of our country and believe the things we are doing are right, but this was *my* Michael and what if he didn't come back? I guess every parent, spouse, or sibling worries about this, and we need to remember this when we see troops around the world.

After dinner, I excused myself, praised Cora, and asked Charlie to come upstairs. We sat on the glider on the deck off of our bedroom, held each other and looked over the meadow. The tears came, and so did the sobs. Charlie just held me tighter.

"He's well trained. He'll do a good job. He'll figure it all out," Charlie said.

"What if he dies over there?" I said, crying.

"Then he goes to heaven," Charlie said. "The last time I looked you weren't in control of the Universe."

"I don't like to think of him over there."

"He's twenty-three," Charlie said. "He's a man and he's about to grow up even more. We'll pray for him, and God will look after him. He's going there for a reason."

"I still can't get it in my head that Michael will kill people."

"I know," he said quietly, "but he's a trained specialist now and the assignments he gets will be dangerous, but necessary. He'll be saving lives, too. Just trust the process."

I didn't have any choice. Michael had made his decision. That's the way it is with our children's choices when they grow up. We have to roll with the punches and pray for them.

There was a knock at our bedroom door.

"Mom," Georgette said, loud enough for us to hear her. "Can you come downstairs? Grandma is throwing biscuits at Dong and yelling about Pearl Harbor, wherever *that* is." I heard her sigh and bounce down the stairs.

"Okay," I said, jumping to my feet. Charlie and I looked at each other and started laughing.

"If it's not one thing, it's another," Charlie said, still chuckling. "We better go save Dong from your mother."

I don't know Vietnamese, but I could hear Dong chattering in her native tongue as I came down the stairs. The dining room was littered with the remaining biscuits, silverware, and various other items my mother had found within arm's reach to throw. Gretchen, my peacemaker, was attempting to wheel Mom away, talking softly to her to calm her down, and gently patting her shoulders.

"Crazy, crazy," Dong said, shaking her head. Her face and dress were wet, so Mom had obviously doused her with a full water glass.

Cora was busy taking what Mom hadn't thrown on the floor off of the table so she could remove the wet tablecloth. Cora was obviously biting her tongue to keep from laughing. Georgette was helping her, rolling her eyes at me because I'd missed everything.

"Where's Dad?" I asked, looking around for my ally.

"He went to the barn with Mac," Cora said, wiping the table.

"Mom," I said, "Are you about ready to go to bed?"

"Yes, I am," she declared. "Where's Jack? I want my Jack," she said, looking frightened.

"Grandma, it's all right, let's go pick out a pretty nightgown to wear. Do you like the pink one?" Gretchen said sweetly.

"Yes, I like that one. I like the yellow one, too. Pink or yellow, I'm easy to please," she said, shrugging her shoulders and smiling her childlike smile.

Gretchen wheeled her off to take care of her. Dong went to her room to change her clothes. Georgette grabbed herself another piece of cake and Cora carried everything into the kitchen. Charlie headed for the barn to see how Dad was getting along.

"Georgette, please go help Cora in the kitchen," I said.

"I'd rather sit here," she said, eating her cake.

"There are lots of places we'd all rather be, just do it."

She gave me the sulky teenage look and went into the kitchen. Did I mention that Georgette would argue with God? Most of the time we got along, but if there is a limit to test, an argument to have, a point to disparage, Georgette would be in the middle of it. I think she was trying to make her mark, trying to define herself. Georgette was not the student Gretchen was. Gretchen devoured long novels, science and history. She loved to learn. You could take Gretchen anywhere and give her a good book and a comfortable chair and she was fine. I could read anywhere, too, if a book isn't boring.

Georgette didn't really like to read unless she was in the mood and then she'd have to go someplace quiet. Georgette would act everything out and sing for everyone. She frequently entertained us in this manner. Her grades were good in the subjects she liked and average in others. Georgette was clever and creative.

The girls were each other's allies. They spoke that special twin language that only twins seem to know ... the silent one where communication is on a different level. Each was protective of each other's weak side and proud of each other's accomplishments. When Gretchen won an academic award, Georgette was her biggest cheerleader, and when Georgette was in a musical, Gretchen was backstage helping her with costume changes.

Children are all different, especially when they have different fathers (in the case of Michael and the girls) and just being born a few years earlier or later can make a difference.

I didn't want to tell Marty about Michael's assignment over the phone. I knew Michael wouldn't have called her. He never did. He'd send a card and a neutral gift, like a vintage video or maybe a cool piece of art that he thought Marty might like; sometimes it was a book. He never wrote anything about himself or asked about Marty. He would just write "from Michael." This always made Marty a little sad, but she took comfort in the fact that at least Michael remembered and was trying.

Since our marriages, Marty and I had naturally drifted apart. Charlie didn't care if Marty and Ben came over for dinner or if they came to the ranch for the day. He didn't mind them being part of our holidays. Charlie was not a jealous person. Of course, I never gave him any reason to be jealous, although I knew men who were often jealous. George had been jealous if I talked to a busboy.

I didn't think of George too often because it was still painful. Georgette looked just like him to me, but then she looked like me, too. At certain angles, Gretchen favored him slightly. It was like that part of my life had washed away, like waves going out to sea, and I was walking in the opposite direction.

I settled myself in a big oak rocking chair on the front porch and looked over the ranch as the sun was setting. I was so blessed to be part of this life and have this time. I loved my family and extended family. I thought about my oldest baby boy getting ready to go to a country most people couldn't even spell, much less have seen. Michael had never been out of the country before.

I had a pain in my chest. It wasn't a heart attack or anything. It's the pain one feels when you've been hurt or suffered a loss. That heavy feeling in your chest that makes you feel like the weight of the world is on you. It was starting to settle in my chest and in my heart.

I knew this feeling. I had felt it when Marty and I had split up and I felt it when George and I had split up and he later died. I didn't want it again. I didn't want to live with dread. Charlie would tell me to give this worry to God, so I did. But like most women, I would take it back a few times to refine it and I would shoot up repeated prayers—just to make sure God heard me.

FORTY-SIX

"**O**h, God, Jack, Marty's wearing a dress and holding hands with a man," my mother said, as Marty and Ben walked through the front door.

Dad shakily stood up from his chair and offered a hand to Ben. Dad was of the vintage where you didn't shake a lady's hand. Even though he used to shake Marty's hand, he had stopped.

"Hello, Helen, how are you?" Marty said, ignoring her earlier comment.

"Why are you wearing that ugly dress? What happened to your voice? You sound like a girl, Martin."

Marty looked like he was debating whether to go over the big change in his life with my mother. Ben looked mortified and left the room to use the bathroom.

"Sorry," I said to Marty, wheeling Mother around and taking her back toward her room. "Dong, can you help Mom freshen up?"

"I don't need to fr-freshen up," Mom said irritably. "And why is Marty wearing a dress? Is he queer with that man? Who is that man? Don't tell Lizzie, it'll break her heart, Iris."

"Mum's the word," I said. Dong took over the chair and pushed Mom back to her room. I noticed this wasn't easily done. Mom had put on a few pounds and Dong was so tiny.

Ben was sitting in the room with my father and Marty had seated herself in another chair. Marty knew my dad had finally accepted her change, but still, she didn't need to throw it in his face. None of them were saying anything. Dad had gone back to reading the paper and Ben was examining his cuticles. Marty looked up at me and smiled, the smile I got nowadays, the one that says, YOU-POOR-THING-YOU-HAVE -TO-DEAL-WITH-SO-MUCH smile.

"I'm sorry, Marty. She doesn't remember anything. I'm afraid every time you see her now it's going to be unpleasant."

She smiled. "It's okay. It freaks Ben out a little, but I'm okay."

"Did you all want to ride horses?" I asked. We say "you all" here even when there are just two people involved.

"We thought that might be fun. Is there a gentle horse or a big one both of us could ride?" she asked.

"Charlie and Mac are in charge of all that," I said with a wave of my hand. "Can you and I take a walk outside first?"

"Sure," Marty said, trying to read my face. She knew when I had bad news; I could never keep it inside long.

We walked out back and made our way to a bench facing the lake.

"What's wrong, honey?" Marty asked.

"It's Michael," I said, tearing up. "He's going to Afghanistan. He left this morning. I got the call last night."

"Oh God, no!" Marty said, covering her face. She pulled her hands away after a moment and put her arm around me. "Did he give you any details? How long will he be there?"

"Nothing," I said, shaking my head. "I don't think they tell them everything. He asked us to pray for him and said he'd be fine. This whole thing scares me. He's never even been out of the country. He hates the heat. Remember when he was a boy, he always wanted us to turn up the air conditioner?"

"It's hot as balls in here, Mom," Marty said, making her voice deep. We both laughed. "I guess that's when he was a little older."

"It happens too fast, Marty. Kids grow up too fast and then they're gone, and you wonder if you told them enough times that you loved them or how important they are to you. You wonder if you taught them right from wrong, so they'll make the right decisions and you wonder if your sweet, sensitive little boy is still in there somewhere in that tough man."

"I know. They have all grown up fast," Marty agreed.

"I remember the parties and the special holidays, but I also remember ordinary days. Sometimes I wish I had chronicled every minute of every day so that I wouldn't forget," I said, my voice a whisper.

"We can't forget, Lizzie. Even if we consciously forget, the information, the images are all still there in our subconscious and in our hearts."

"I guess so," I said, feeling a little numb.

"You don't have any of your bad feelings you get about things, do you?" she asked. From time to time, I did have feelings about things that seemed to come true, but it wasn't that big of a deal.

"You mean like when Charlie said, 'Let's move your folks in with us?'"

We both laughed.

"How is it going?" she asked. "Seriously, we haven't talked about it in a while."

"We haven't talked in a while. It's going fine some days and perfectly awful other days. She has bowel movements the size of Texas about every three days. Dong refuses to deal with this part of it, so that leaves me. Dad tries to help, but he really can't."

"That's gross. You need to hire a nurse."

"Well, I've thought about it, but most of the time she's sleeping, and I hate to pay someone to just sit around. I can handle it for the time being. Actually, I've gotten used to it. Changing her every morning and cleaning her up is kind of like unloading the dishwasher. It's a chore you have to do, and you just don't think about it."

"That's my Lizzie, the glass is always half full," she said, patting my leg. "How are you and Charlie getting along?"

"Great. Charlie is a godsend. Nothing bothers him, and he handles Mom and Dad beautifully. He jokes with Mom. And when she gets crazy, he just laughs it off and he takes Dad places so he won't get too bored."

"He's the son Jack always wanted," Marty mused. "I know I was always a disappointment."

I didn't know what to say, because Marty had been a big disappointment. Dad had taken the news of Marty's change very hard.

"Do you think that Michael is trying to, uh…" she searched for the right words, "trying to prove he's not like me?"

"Honestly?" I said, looking at her. "Yes, I do. I think that's what this whole macho ride he's been on since puberty has been about."

"I hate that. I hope he doesn't hate me, and I hope you don't hate me for it."

"I don't think Michael hates you. I don't hate you for it, but I admit, there have been times I've been pretty frustrated about it. We know Michael on the inside. I hope this whole Navy Seal thing hasn't killed that in him. I know he needs to be tough, but I hope he's still compassionate."

"I don't know," Marty said, "I've hardly seen him in the past five years. He's like this phantom person to me."

"I'm sorry," I said. "I know it's been hard on you."

"Mama!" Gretchen yelled, running toward me. She looked frightened. "Charlie wants you to come to the house. Grandpa was walking out to the barn. Hershey was trying to play, and Grandpa tripped over him and hit his head on a rock. He's not making any sense when he talks."

Marty and I were both running, with Gretchen ahead of us. Charlie and Mac were on either side of Dad on the ground.

"The ambulance should be here any minute," Charlie shouted. "I didn't want to move him."

"I want to go with him to the hospital." My mouth could hardly say the word. This was too much, first Michael and now my dad.

"What about your mom?" Charlie asked.

I looked at Gretchen and Georgette. They were both terrified. They loved their grandpa.

"Can you girls keep an eye on Grandma until I get back? Don't tell her anything has happened to Grandpa," I said. "I'm serious; she'll go nuts. Tell her we all went into town with Charlie to shop."

"Okay," Georgette said, "I can do that."

Gretchen looked at me and nodded. "We'll take care of things, Mom."

"You're good girls," I said.

The ambulance blazed down that gravel road and came to a screeching stop. Hershey was going nuts. Mac put him in the barn. The EMTs set about checking on Dad and put him on a gurney. They hoisted him inside and jumped in the ambulance.

As Charlie and I followed that screaming ambulance back down the driveway and out onto the road, I said a prayer for Dad, for Michael, and for myself. I needed to have the energy and the courage to deal with whatever was to come. And of course, I thanked Him for the kids and Charlie.

CHAPTER
FORTY-SEVEN

They flew Dad in a helicopter to Tulsa, where he stayed at St. John's Hospital for about a week. It was probably the worst spring break we'd ever had, but it was one we would never forget. The girls helped Dong take care of Mom, which was no easy task. Charlie and I took turns hospital-sitting with Dad. They moved him into a rehab hospital for about six weeks. He needed speech therapy, physical therapy, and plenty of rest.

School let out and Dad came home. The girls were thrilled to have us all under one roof again. We had to put another hospital bed in Mom and Dad's room to make it easier to maneuver him. We took the other bed out and gave it to Kendra for her spare bedroom.

I was glad to have Dad home, but I realized I needed help. I had a Home Health person come in and help Dad every morning to get him showered, shaved, and ready for the day. He was still too wobbly to do it on his own; his injury had weakened him considerably. Oddly enough, the Parkinson's had subsided for a bit; the tremors weren't as strong as they had been. Charlie took care of Dad at night, getting him ready for bed and helping him do his evening rituals. Dong and I took care of Mom.

You think it would be like getting a child ready for bed, but it wasn't. Children get to where they can do things themselves and, as time goes on, are more and more helpful. Mom and Dad could do less and less. Although they *wanted* to go to bed, it took a while to get them there because of the pace at which we had to do the tasks. They undressed slowly and wanted to do it themselves. Dad couldn't stand for anybody to undo and do his buttons, and it was painful to watch him try. There are dignity issues here. You would like to think that someone would let you do the simple things for yourself. As a caregiver, you want to jump in and get it done so you can go do something else, but that's not always possible because you don't want to rob them of their last little ounce of pride.

Dad always complained I was cutting his wings. I had taken his car and his checkbook. And though I'd hung up some of his artwork, I couldn't tolerate some of the gorier work hanging in my home. The quality wasn't so bad. It was the content of the pictures—paintings of bears devouring their prey or Indians on a prairie killing a buffalo. It wasn't pretty or serene or soothing. I wouldn't put it in their bedroom because I thought it wasn't the best thing for an Alzheimer's patient to see before she went to sleep.

So the tasks themselves aren't hard to do, but the responsibility and tedium of the tasks can wear one down. Charlie and I often fell into bed, exhausted. We had the responsibility of two households: teenagers, old people, and a great deal of livestock.

Another weight was added to our load: our financial situation. George had left me money and I'd sold my house, so I had that money. I had gotten this huge house as a gift, and that was great, but it had been fifteen years. I had put Michael through an expensive college, I had sent Michael and the girls to private school, and I had invested in Enron and some similar companies that had gone away. After 9/11, my portfolio was in the toilet.

Charlie had struggled on and off to continue ranching. He had given so much away to the community. The oil wells on his land had paid some and had helped him climb back, but oil production was slow right now.

We also employed people we didn't want to lose and felt we couldn't fire. Mac and Cora were like family and they lived on the ranch. We couldn't let them go. Dung and Dong lived in the guesthouse and had only ever worked for me. I needed their help.

We weren't broke, and of course, we could always sell this big old house and scale down, but I didn't want to do that yet. The taxes were expensive, but I could maintain those. There was just a lot of overhead. So I was taking on more and more projects.

I had bid on a big project funded by one of the local oil companies. The CEO's father had Alzheimer's, and he wanted me to do a documentary that would show what caregivers and patients have to go through, what they both have to endure. I was paid pretty well to shoot this, which would help with some bills on the ranch and the house. The documentary would premiere at a private showing at one of the elegant hotels downtown, preceded by a sit-down $100-a-plate dinner. The invitation list would include some of Tulsa's old and new high-end households. They'd be encouraged to pledge big for the Alzheimer's Association to find a cure. This had to be good.

I had decided to shoot at a few facilities, with family permission of course, and see patients at different stages of the disease. I got a line on other patients who were being cared for in private homes like ours, and I made a list of caregivers and their families to interview.

Throughout this process, I felt like I was searching for answers too. I was hungry to talk to these people. Did they ever just want to jump in their cars and drive off? Did they just not get out of bed one day? I wondered what techniques they used to cope. Above all, besides chronicling their thoughts and feelings, I wanted to encourage them on their journey.

The news director had agreed to air the documentary after the premiere. The sales department could easily line up sponsors, and instead of running it like a regular television show with lots of commercial breaks, they decided to air it in its entirety with sponsors at the beginning and at the end of the program. The local educational channel had agreed to run it statewide after it ran on ABC.

This was a lot of pressure. The head of the station anticipated if the documentary were good enough, we'd submit it to the Emmys for consideration and go for some other documentary awards. I tried to put all of that in the back of my mind instead of the forefront. I was going to do what I do best. That is, to tell a story with my camera. The people would tell the story; I'd just try to convey their circumstances and emotions through pictures.

Our new accountant lectured Charlie about changing things around a little. We wrote off the costs to maintain Charlie's ministry—the food, the upkeep of the pavilion, the website, the Bibles, and other materials. Charlie didn't want to do it, but our accountant convinced him it was the best way to go and entirely legal.

Donations came in from time to time. Charlie kept track of every dime and turned it back to the ministry. Many made their checks out to "The Cowboy Preacher," so Charlie opened a special account and listed his name and "The Cowboy Preacher" underneath.

Like most married couples, we were working together to pay the bills and run our households. We did most of the painting and repair work ourselves, along with Cora, Mac, Dung, and Dong. I knew it was probably impractical to keep the big house, but we loved it. I had transferred the girls to a public school. They were still getting a decent education and it was much cheaper.

Summer was here. The girls would be home doing their activities. We could all flow in and out of the house and make sure someone was always around to cover besides Dung and Dong. I had wristband alarms for both Mom and Dad in case they got in trouble. Mom kept complaining that she couldn't read her watch because there were no numbers on it.

I felt excited about the documentary. I wanted people to feel something when they watched it, and I wanted it to be a tribute to the caregivers. So many families take care of elderly parents and grandparents without any help. This disease is insidious. It can rob people of their memories and even their present existence. Often, the patient isn't always aware of what is happening. It is the family, the loved ones, who have to be the witnesses. They became my heroes.

FORTY-EIGHT

The Fourth of July 2003 rolled in on a typical Oklahoma heat wave. Since Charlie had come into our lives, we'd always gone to the ranch. He would buy an obscene number of fireworks, the biggest box available, and we'd all shoot off firecrackers. We'd eat barbecue ribs, homemade potato salad, and smoked sausage on a real outdoor smoker, biscuits the size of your foot, and homemade vanilla ice cream from the old crank kind of ice cream maker. Sometimes Mac and Charlie made two kinds of ice cream. The second one was always homemade peach. There was chocolate cake for Dad and Kendra's birthday.

All our family and friends always came for the Fourth. Kendra and Dan loved it. So did little Gracie Jean, because she was the only child. At four, that can be tons of fun. We were getting ready to have more fun because Kendra and Dan were pregnant again and expecting in December.

Hunter drove up from Norman. This time he brought Joelle, who was, of all things, a comedian. She performed all over the southwest in churches, community centers, assisted living centers, and college campuses. She was blonde with blue-green eyes that lit up when she talked, and she could make her face contort into all different shapes. Her almost six-foot frame was like a pretzel. She was so limber, and she made us laugh. More importantly, she made Hunter laugh. I had never seen him look at a woman the way he looked at her, It made me so happy. I could tell Kendra felt the same way.

"What do you think?" Kendra whispered as we were scooping out ice cream.

"Joelle?" I whispered back. She nodded. "I think she's fantastic."

"I think he's crazy about her," Kendra murmured. "Finally!"

"Liz?" Hunter said, pulling me aside later. "Could we talk somewhere inside for a minute?"

"Sure," I said, and we walked across the yard and went into the kitchen.

"Do you like Jo?" he asked, his eyes smiling.

"Of course, I do. She's adorable, Hunter," I said.

"She's the one. She's my best friend and I can totally be myself with her. She makes me feel things I've never felt with anyone before," he said.

"That's wonderful. Have you bought her a ring yet?" I asked.

"Well, that's what I was going to talk to you about. Do you think I could have some of that money from that trust fund to buy her a ring and put a down payment on a house? My internship is going to be at St. John's, and I want something close."

"Of course, it's your money. I also know a wholesale guy who can get you a deal."

He grinned. "Of course, you do. I thought maybe you and I could look this weekend and I'll surprise her."

"Would you like the diamond ring your dad gave me?" I asked, feeling my eyes tear up. "I'd be happy to give it to you for Joelle."

He was stunned at my offer. We both knew the ring was probably worth about sixty thousand dollars.

"I don't wear it anymore." I shrugged, smiling. "Charlie didn't have the money to beat that deal and I'd never asked for that much ring. Your dad just did it."

"I'd love to give it to her, but I don't think it's Jo. I think she'd want something simple."

"You might ask her to marry you and let her pick out the ring," I said, thinking out loud. "After all, she's going to wear it the rest of her life."

Hunter grinned and hugged me. He almost danced me out the door.

"Does your mom know?" I asked.

"No, she's out of the country again. They travel a lot."

The girls were shooting off firecrackers and laughing wildly. Gretchen was a little scared, but loved it, and Georgette was in her element, whooping and hollering. Charlie was out there too and so was Mac.

Mom flinched at the loud noises, but she loved fireworks that lit up. Dad loved Kendra as his birthday twin. We thought Mom would enjoy watching the girls shoot the Roman candles. Mom was so childlike at this stage in life; she loved Christmas lights and fireworks. Dad had improved so much since his fall. He was actually walking with a walker. Hallelujah!

Fred and Gloria arrived with their crew. Dan's little brothers climbed all over everybody and chased little Gracie around the yard as she squealed in delight.

Glam and her veterinarian, Vince, came too. They never had kids, but had recently acquired two more miniature pigs, one of which they had brought on a leash. I have never understood this craze and wondered why anyone would want to domesticate a pig, unless maybe they didn't have a garbage disposal in their house.

Sometimes we went to the barn dance in town they held before dark. They usually had a barbecue and a square dance and crowned Miss Fourth of July. Georgette was excited because next year she could compete for the title. Technically, she lived in the county part of the time. Gretchen wanted no part of a pageant.

"Would I have to wear red, white, and blue?" Georgette complained. "I mean, who wants to wear those colors?"

"You have them on now," Gretchen observed.

"Well, duh, it's Fourth of July," Georgette replied.

"Well, duh, you'd be competing for Miss Fourth of July!"

"I know." Georgette frowned. "I don't want to wear white because it would make me look fat. Navy is too boring. Maybe red. Red would look good."

"Maybe you could have sparkles on your suit," Cora suggested.

"I like the sparkles idea," Georgette said, as she danced with an unlit Roman candle.

"Wear high heels," Gretchen gushed, "all the models wear heels with their suits."

"What's wrong with flip flops?" Georgette said. "Nobody wears heels to the pool."

"You're not *swimming*," Gretchen said, "you're *competing*."

"I don't even know if I want to do it now," Georgette replied, flipping her long brown hair over her shoulder.

I was about to respond when I saw a pair of headlights way down at the end of the road. The car made its way toward us, and we all watched in silence.

"Charlie, are you expecting anyone else?" I asked, feeling sick to my stomach.

"Dung and Dong are back at the house in Tulsa, aren't they? Unless it's them, I can't think of anyone. Marty and Ben are still on the cruise."

We waited.

The car inched its way up to the front of the house. Even though it was dark, the car was visible because it was stark white with "U.S. Navy" written on the side door. My stomach flip-flopped and I held my breath. We were all quiet.

A tall, middle-aged man in full officer's uniform emerged from the passenger side of the car. He was military handsome, tight faced, with short hair and an almost "at attention" posture when he got out of the car.

"I'm Captain Nathan Bates," United States Navy, and my driver is Private Brandon Griston. Which one of you is Mrs. Elizabeth Waters?" he asked.

I couldn't stand up. I could barely speak. My voice came out in a squeaky whisper.

"I am," I said, my heart sinking.

"Would you men like to sit down and join us?" Charlie said, good-naturedly as he moved behind my chair and rested his hands on my shoulders.

"We can sit, but we've eaten, thank you," Captain Bates said graciously.

"What's happened to my son?" I asked, my lip quivering.

"Well, ma'am," he said, removing his hat. "I'm sorry to tell you that Michael is missing. We don't think he went AWOL, but we don't know what happened to him yet. Naval intelligence reports they think he might have been hit in the leg during his last mission and we're hoping he escaped."

"Could he have been captured and held prisoner?" I asked, my tongue like lead.

"That's always a possibility," he conceded.

"Well, they damn well c-can't have him," my mother's angry voice rang out in the night.

My sentiments exactly, except I was too busy crying. The girls were both crying. Cora was in tears and so were Glam and Gloria. The men's faces were grim. Dad put his arm around Mom and patted her shoulder. She held his hand.

We thanked them for coming. Charlie offered them more food, but they declined and left. They said they would update me and to "sit tight." What does that mean, exactly? Are you supposed to cross your arms and hold yourself? WHY DO PEOPLE SAY THAT?

I didn't want to sit tight. I wanted to run. I wanted to run and run and run all the way to Afghanistan and rescue my sweet little Michael and bring him back home with me.

I wouldn't run to Afghanistan, of course, I had too many responsibilities at home.

No, it was a waiting game, the Navy's little war game. Even though I had not wanted to participate in this, I was in the middle of it. I had no choice. I would just have to pray and sit tight.

FORTY-NINE

We heard nothing about Michael, not a word. By Labor Day, I had lost fifteen pounds. I didn't look like Twiggy, because I'd needed to lose about ten pounds, but the extra five made me somewhat thin. I couldn't eat very much, and I threw up from time to time when I thought about Michael. I kept picturing him wounded somewhere, fearful that he'd had to cut off his own leg or that he was dying in some hole.

My knees were raw from praying. Charlie and I prayed several times a day and at every meal, we always included prayers for Michael. I had the entire church praying for him. People were very kind, periodically sending me notes of encouragement. One woman, who had been out of the loop, sent me a note that said: "I haven't seen you all summer because we were in Maine. You've really lost weight and look fantastic. What's your secret? Could you send me a copy of your diet?" I thought about sending her a copy of the article about Michael in the paper, but I asked Gloria to call her instead.

I tried to keep busy, which wasn't difficult. We had two households to run, two parents to watch over, two teenagers, and our work. Luckily, my work was demanding, and this assignment revealed to me just how blessed I was.

When I began to feel sorry for myself, I thought of Barbara. Barbara lived in a little house on the north side of town.

Her husband had left her for another woman, and she moved in with her mother, who was diagnosed with Alzheimer's just two months later.

"I remember I went to court that morning and the judge decreed the divorce," she said, "and that afternoon, I took Mom for her assessment. We knew she'd been forgetting things, but we never expected this because she's so young. That was three years ago."

Barbara's mother, Linda, was only fifty-eight. It was an early onset of the disease and she was rapidly declining. Barbara was only thirty-five, but she looked fifty. She had a little girl, Christel, who was eight. Barbara worked at the Wonder Bread factory at night. During the day she took care of her mother. She didn't get much sleep. In an odd way, because people sometimes look younger with brain damage, Barbara's mother looked like her sister—or even her daughter.

Medicare paid for her mother to have a caregiver at night because her mother had no money left and Barbara had so little. Her house was tiny, with only two bedrooms. Barbara let Christel sleep in her own room with her toys and a homemade dollhouse that Barbara had lovingly put together and painted.

Barbara shared a room with her mother so she could better care for her. Barbara had a twin bed for herself and a hospital bed for Linda. Her mother also had COPD/asthma, so she had an oxygen tank nearby and various medicines on a tiny table. Linda, was totally bedridden now. She had forgotten how to get into an automobile or even what one was. She didn't know her little granddaughter. Most days, she didn't know Barbara as her daughter. She thought Barbara was a nurse. As the ability to speak and recognize things was slipping away, Barbara did all the talking for them both. Barbara was as jolly as she was burdened and her outlook on life was one of unquestionable faith.

She was an inspiration to me and to others. On sunny days, she would wheel her mother around the block for fresh air and would read to her every day, which her mother obviously enjoyed. Barbara had taken a massage course and gave her mother a therapeutic massage twice a week.

As inspired and warmed as I was by Barbara's loving spirit, I also felt a huge amount of guilt, like I was going to DAUGHTER HELL for not taking care of my mother in the same manner. I was nice to my mother. I occasionally read to her and I always prayed with her at night, but I didn't give her as much attention as Barbara did her mother. Maybe Barbara's mother had been nicer. I wasn't ignoring my mother; I just didn't want to spend every waking moment with her. I needed to work to keep my sanity. I think there were lingering issues I should have worked out years earlier; maybe didn't realize this until this stage in my life. I don't think I expected Mom to live this long and be like this. It wasn't her fault or mine, it just happened. I knew that she loved me and always had. I knew she was and is proud of me. I just don't know if she ever really understood me.

I sound like a whiner and it's all about me. Maybe I didn't understand Mom either. I sometimes think under all her little "look at me" petite personality, Mom didn't have that much confidence in herself. She never had a career, but it wasn't important in the times in which she lived. In fact, it was almost frowned upon. Her accomplishments were her two daughters, taking care of Dad, dinner on the table, laundry washed, ironed, and folded, and a clean house. Those *are* accomplishments; don't ever let anybody tell you they aren't.

Our mothers and grandmothers had the luxury of running the house and not having to work. They didn't have to prove themselves, and most women in my parents' generation didn't have to worry about a man walking out, because the divorce rate in their generation was almost nonexistent. NOBODY got divorced when I was growing up. I never knew a single soul whose parents were divorced until I went to college and the girl I knew whose parents were divorced was from New York.

I did get some insight into my mother's thinking one night as I was putting her to bed. As she often did, she thought I was her sister.

"Iris, come sit down next to me and let's talk in the dark like we did when we were girls," she said, her face full of childlike wonder.

"Okay," I said, wondering what I was getting myself into this time. I pulled up a chair and sat down.

"Iris, do you think mother understood us?" she asked.

"I don't know, I guess I never thought about it," I said, trying to be neutral. "What do you think?"

"I think she did. She was a fun person. I tried to be a fun person like her." She said the words slowly. "I always liked to have fun."

"Yes, you did. You were always a fun person. Everybody said so," I replied.

"Did they? I wanted to be like Mother. I don't know if my girls ever wanted to be like me though," she said, deep in thought.

"Why do you say that?" I asked, feeling my voice choke.

"Well, Claire looks like me and acted like me, but I think she always resented me for it."

"What about Liz?" I whispered.

"Oh, Liz is just like her dad, and I'm so glad. She got all the good stuff, the brains, character, and common sense. The only thing poor Claire got were good looks, which are fading now. The girl has no strength of character; she's just not a strong person, I'm sorry to say."

"Do you think Liz is pretty?" I asked softly. Why was this so important to me?

"She's *almost* pretty, more attractive. But what makes Elizabeth so striking is what's on the inside, Iris. She's like Mother was," she said, yawning. "Iris, you've talked my head off, now I have to go to sleep!"

I couldn't say a word because I was a puddle of emotions and tears. My mother fell asleep the moment after she stopped speaking, but I just sat there in the dark, thinking about all the years we had battled. She had never told me these things and she wasn't even telling me now; she was telling Iris. That was another thing … her lucidity. Sometimes, late at night like this, she could carry on a conversation clear as a bell; the next morning her speech would be slurred and she could barely stammer out a sentence.

I thought about Barbara, across town in a house possibly smaller than my living room, putting her mother to bed and then going to work. I prayed for her, for all the daughters and sons taking care of their parents, for all the caregivers taking care of loved ones, and I prayed for myself—to be given the strength to carry on.

As always, I also prayed for my sweet Michael and asked God to bring him home alive and fully functioning, and wherever he was tonight, to please, please protect him.

C H A P T E R

FIFTY

I t was raining, pouring down rain, and it had been raining off and on for days. My favorite season is fall, and this October's rain felt so good. The leaves had already been falling and when you stepped outside, you could smell that wonderful aroma of someone burning logs in their fireplace, wet leaves, and cool, sharp air. I loved it.

In our house, the minute it started raining one of the girls would call me and ask me to make chili. Charlie had all the fireplaces going because of the brisk air, and I had invited all of the gang over for chili and an evening of charades. It was a Friday, but Charlie had already spread the word that due to the storms, his meeting was cancelled this week. We decided to celebrate the vacation.

Fred and Gloria loved charades and were particularly good at them. Charlie was okay, but he kept forgetting to act out the clue. He wanted to tell us the clue, which is against the rules. Gretchen did pretty well, but she hated to get up in front of people. Georgette, of course, loved being center stage. Kendra and Dan liked to play. We put Gracie in one of the girl's rooms to watch her favorite video and fall asleep when it was close to bedtime. Glam and Vince liked to join in the game, too, but Vince also hated to get up in front of everyone.

Usually, we did this after Mom went to bed, but if my parents wanted to, we let them watch. Dad got a kick out of everyone performing and would sometimes try to make a guess himself.

We had stuffed ourselves on chili and were in the throes of a good game of charades in front of the fire when the doorbell rang.

"Did somebody leave the gate open?" Charlie asked.

"We might have," Glam said, frowning.

Charlie went to the door. The front porch light was already on. Ben was standing there, squinting to look inside. He was drenched.

Charlie opened the door and beckoned him in.

"I didn't mean to intrude on your evening," he said hesitantly.

"Hi Ben," I said, smiling. "We have leftover chili and the girls baked a cake. Would you like some?"

"No-no thanks," he said. "I know you have company, but I came by because I can't find Martha. She usually shows up on Friday nights at the store, but she hasn't been to the store all day. She hasn't been coming home some nights and when she does, she's been drinking."

"Marty?" I said, shocked. "Marty has never been a big drinker," I said, shaking my head.

"Well, she is now. It started when Michael went missing. It's been getting worse and worse. She used to drink a couple of glasses of wine before she went to bed, but then she switched to the hard stuff, and she'd start at dinner and drink all night. Lately, she started drinking at noon. The other morning, I caught her mixing her orange juice with vodka."

"She blames herself," I said quietly. "Did you confront her?"

"Mom! Come on, we want to finish the game," Georgette yelled from the living room.

"Georgette, Ben, Charlie and I are having an important conversation. You guys go ahead with the game," I said, stepping into the living room, irritated.

"Well, you're ignoring your guests," Georgette hissed.

I gave her *the look*. She gave me another look back and they all returned to a quieter version of the game. Charlie, Ben, and I went into the den.

Ben took off his wet jacket, threw it in front of the fireplace, and sat down.

"I just don't know where to look for her," he said, sighing. "I've looked in the bars around the store. I don't know if she went home with someone…" his voice broke off.

"Have you called all of your friends?" I asked.

"A few, but I really don't want people knowing our business, and I knew if she ran to anyone it would be you. She wouldn't have gone home. I just don't know."

"What about the church? When people are broken, they usually turn to God and Marty believes in God. Maybe she went to church," Charlie suggested.

"I hadn't thought about that. It wouldn't be open this time of night, would it?" Ben asked.

"No, but there's a prayer room that has an outside door for people to go in and sit when they need prayer," I said. "Do you want us to go with you and look?"

"That would be great, but what about your guests?" he said.

"Why don't you go, Liz. I'll stay here with everyone and serve cake," Charlie said, giving me a quick hug. "Or do you want me to go?"

"No, I think maybe this time I better go alone with Ben."

Ben drove an old Volvo. We hopped in and took off toward the church downtown. When we got there, we drove around the block, but didn't see any sign of Marty. We parked the car and went in the prayer room. Still no sign. Ben started to leave, but I stopped him.

"Wait a minute. We need some divine help here. Come here and kneel with me."

Ben did as he was told, but his body was stiff, like a kid in an ill-fitting new suit. I could tell he was uncomfortable. Ben wasn't a churchgoer, and he wasn't a believer.

"Father, God, we need your help to find Marty. Wherever she is, she is hurting, and we ask that you help us find her and let us help her. We pray for your guidance and understanding, and we pray for wisdom to handle this situation. Please help us to bring her some peace and restore her to the person she truly is. Please heal her, Father. In Jesus's name, amen," I prayed out loud.

Ben was visibly shaken when he got up. He helped me to my feet, and we left.

"Where should we look now?" he asked.

"It'll come to me," I said, "just give me a minute."

"What do you mean?"

"God will send it to me, I've just got to open my mind and heart and be patient. I just need to clear my own thoughts and be receptive," I said matter-of-factly.

"Whatever," he said. He sounded irritated.

"You'll see," I said with a smile.

We got in the car and rode in silence with only the sound of the windshield wipers going back and forth and the rain beating the windshield.

"Let's pull over and drive through Starbucks and get a hot chocolate," I said.

"Is God at Starbucks?" he said sarcastically.

"That was unnecessary, Ben."

"Sorry, I'm just worried about Martha."

"I understand."

He ordered two hot chocolates with extra whipped cream. He handed me one and pulled into a parking place.

"Where to now?" he asked, sipping his hot chocolate loudly.

"I feel like she's at the church where we got married."

Ben gave me a look like he didn't know whether to scowl, laugh, or cry, so he clamped his mouth shut, threw the car in reverse, and drove. It took us about twenty minutes to get to our old church in the rain. Marty's jeep was the only car in the parking lot. She was lying in front of the doors of the church, soaked to the bone.

Ben started to cry and so did I, but for different reasons. Ben was relieved to find her. So was I, but I was thankful that God led me here. I thanked God as we raced toward her. She was passed out cold.

We managed to each take an arm and lift her down the slippery steps. This wasn't easy, because she was deadweight and even in the rain, she reeked of liquor.

We put her in the back seat of the car, shut the doors, and got in the front.

"Let's take her to St. John's hospital," I said.

"Oh, she'll be all right at home. She can sleep it off."

"No, Ben, she won't be all right. She's soaked to the bone, is probably getting pneumonia, and needs to dry out, physically and emotionally. They can assess her and get her into detox. She needs real help."

"I'm her husband," he said crossly. "I know what's best for her."

"Listen," I said, turning in my seat and getting in his face. "You may be her husband now, but I've been Marty's best friend for forty years. We have a child together who is missing, and I won't let Marty die because you're too proud to get her help."

"You don't have control over this situation," he said, his eyes narrowing.

I shot up a prayer because I was in deep water here. I hadn't realized the depth of Ben's jealousy toward me, and I hadn't counted on his being such an ass. Ben was a nice guy; he was just threatened by our unusual situation. I waited and calmed myself for a moment.

"Ben," I said, choking up. (What man could resist tears?) "I am so sorry. I didn't mean to be anything but your friend. Please, let's help Marty get the help she needs so she can go back to being the Martha you love."

He considered this for a few moments, then nodded in agreement. We drove to St. John's in silence. Marty's breathing was shallow and extremely labored, and she was wheezing terribly. She sounded like Mom's COPD on a bad day.

We pulled up to the Emergency Room doors and were met by two guys in white coats with a gurney. They carried Marty out of the car, put her on the gurney and wheeled her inside. We were instructed to park and go in the regular entrance.

I called Charlie and told him where we were and that I thought it would be a while. He assured me everyone was eating cake and just fine. Ben and I sat in the waiting room and didn't talk much. We tried to watch a little television to take our minds off of Marty. Finally, a doctor came out and said Marty had pneumonia and her blood alcohol level was off the charts. He was moving her to the ICU.

"Oh, I'll need you to fill out her information sheet to keep in the ICU unit. We'll need your insurance information of course and medical history. Any significant operations or medical conditions?" he asked.

Ben and I just looked at each other. I don't know why, maybe because of all the tension and our exhaustion from the labors of the night; we started laughing. We were doubled over. Every time we'd look at each other, we would break into laughter again and neither of us could stop.

"This is why I hate the night shift," the doctor said rolling his eyes and dropping the chart on the counter. "The full moon always brings out the crazies."

Ben and I laughed so hard at this that we each had to visit the restroom. The things the doctor said helped.

I shot up a familiar prayer to the Almighty: *Dear God, bring Michael home safely, and please care for Marty.*

FIFTY-ONE

I had finished the documentary a few days before Halloween. It had to be in by October 31 to be judged for an Emmy. My boss at the station, Gregory Roberts, thought I had a real shot. He'd worked at CBS in Washington years ago and had taught me so much about journalism and how to find the story within the story. He planned to quietly retire at the end of the year. He'd get a watch from the company, an ABC jacket, and a lot of good memories.

The show would air on December 14, the Saturday night after the premiere banquet. We'd know by the banquet, December 7, if we'd won anything. I had narrowed it down to three stories for the fifty-eight minutes: Barbara and her mom; Gerry, who took care of his wife, Pat. And a woman named Jenny, who took care of her grandmother, who was in her nineties. I'd done a montage of faces of a multitude of patients at the end, showing them when they were young, in their prime, and now. The names appeared under each face and that entire segment played out to the credits. I had included Mom and Dad in there as a personal tribute.

It was the best thing I had ever done and the most emotionally and physically draining. Maybe if my son hadn't been missing in action in the middle of it, my parents hadn't been living with me, and Marty hadn't been in rehab, I would have had a little more energy. I did feel driven to do this project though, not by anybody else but myself.

Kendra had worked with me on it, feeling equally driven. It was like if we did this, if we made it really good, our reward would be Michael. We never said this, but it was there.

I still kept my office at the station. One day, a letter arrived. It was from a Sergeant James Matthews. I held my breath when I opened the envelope. I pulled out a letter and a folded envelope. The letter was written in handwriting I didn't recognize.

Dear Mrs. Waters,

I am sending this letter to the television station because I have lost your home address. But I remember Michael talking about how you worked for the local ABC station and that you were a photographer.

Michael gave this letter to me to give to you before he went on his mission the day everything went wrong. He had a feeling he might not talk to you for a while and wanted to say some things to the family. I was wounded and have been in the hospital all this time and frankly, I forgot about the letter until they gave me back my things when I went home.

I understand Michael is still missing. If anybody could survive, it would be Michael. You raised a very special person. He was the toughest soldier I ever saw. He was smart, quick, and absolutely lethal. I saw plenty of these guys on our Special Forces team, but they didn't have something that Michael had, which was a heart for his fellow man and a very strong faith.

I was a womanizing, cussin' sailor when I met Michael. He never corrected me or got mad at me for the way I was, he was just a perfect gentleman. He opened doors for everyone, men and women, and I never heard him swear. When I asked him about it, he laughed and told me a story about when you caught him swearing when he was little and you told him that anybody could say bad words, but it was the smart guys who said the good words.

He was smart, too. I never saw anyone figure numbers faster in his head, beat everyone at cards, and assess a situation quickly and take action. I also saw him pray before every assignment and he often read his Bible he kept with him in down times.

I don't know if you knew we were reassigned to Iraq. We were taking out some guerilla soldiers who had been pillaging the area, torturing women and children for fun and killing their husbands. We discovered an orphanage where the children were being housed. The guerillas had taken the food and moved on, leaving these people with nothing. One of them tossed a grenade behind him. It exploded at the orphanage door.

We saw all of this from a distance but couldn't get there in time to stop the soldier. Michael stopped him though, forever, and took some of his friends out with him. Then he began pulling the children out of the building. I helped, along with some of our team.

Michael worked the fastest. We tied rags over our faces to cover our mouths to battle the dust and fire. Michael carried the littlest ones out first, then we made a human assembly line, passing each child from man to man. It was a chaotic scene. I can close my eyes and still see it all… the smoke, the crying children, the women screaming words we didn't really know but understood. We got all of them out and took them to safety, but Michael went back to make sure there weren't any more guerillas in the area. That's when he disappeared.

I don't want to get your hopes up, Mrs. Waters, but I don't believe Michael is dead. It was like he just disappeared. Michael was too smart, too quick, and trained too well to let anyone get him. I believe he got away. Michael taught me to pray, Mrs. Waters, and believe me, I've prayed for him every day since he's been gone. May God bless you and your family this holiday and I pray God brings Michael home.

Sincerely

Sergeant James Matthews

I sat and cried for a few moments, blew my nose, and then unfolded the envelope that had obviously seen a lot of action. It was dirty and yellowed with wear and tear. I wondered how I would read perhaps the last thing my son would ever write.

"Dear Mom and Everybody,

We are going out on an extremely dangerous mission today and for some reason, I felt I better write this letter to you all because I don't have time to write individual letters. Being over here and seeing so much death and sadness has shown me quite a bit about my own life. I've been praying and God has revealed to me why He brought me here and some truths about myself.

I've been angry inside for a long time. It started when my dad went away and a woman came back in his place. As much as I wanted to accept it, I never did because I looked like my dad and walked like my dad and I wanted to be just like him. But when he turned into a woman, it scared me to death, down to the depths of my soul.

It wasn't until I saw human nature at its worst over here that I had time to reflect on the people in my life, and

God showed me the flaw in my thinking. I want to apologize, Marty, because I've been so angry and unkind to you for so many years. I realize you never changed on the inside; you just changed on the outside. I also realize that you did what you had to do to make your heart agree with your body. I forgive you for what I didn't understand when I was little. I hope you will forgive me. I know that you love me, and I know, despite trying not to, that I have always loved you.

To Kendra and Hunter, I always wanted a big sister and brother, and you guys are it. We are a family and I love you. If something happens to me, please look out for my mom, and take care of her. I understand Charlie does a pretty good job, but he surely has his hands full with this bunch. Charlie, I know you're a good man from your letters and from the reports I've heard from the others, and I love you, buddy, for loving my mom.

Georgette, stay out of trouble. You have a nose for getting yourself into outrageous situations and of course, you make everything funny. I love that about you. Pay attention in school and do your best. Keep singing, even if it's just in the shower. Stay in church and keep your faith. Always remember you have a big brother who adores you.

Gretchen, sweet girl, don't let your twin sister walk all over you. Stand up to her occasionally; it'll drive her crazy. Keep studying, keep your determination, and stay close to God. You'll have a great life. I'm very proud of you, and I will always adore you.

Grandpa, you taught me how to be a man with all the trappings. Thank you for being a great example to me of how a man should love his family. I love you.

Grandma, pretty lady, you always made me feel special, thank you. I love you.

Mom, there's not enough time or paper to thank you for all you've given me. You are a great mom and I carry your words and your laughter with me wherever I go. You used to say, "Make me proud," when I went off to do something. I knew that meant to behave and not do anything crazy or stupid. I hope I have made you proud. I know I haven't always behaved the best way. I got into a lot of fights, and you always dusted me off and hoped for the best the next day. Your optimism has been an inspiration, Mom, and so has your love.

I will always love you, Mom, now and forever.

I better go.

Love, Michael.

It was dated July 2, 2003, the day Michael was reported missing.

After reading this, I glanced through the rest of the mail, then set it aside for another day. I jumped in the car and went right to the hospital where Marty was. They didn't usually allow visitors this early in the program, but I begged her doctor to let her see me and read the letter from our son. I can be pretty convincing when I want to be.

Marty was sitting in the corner of a room staring out the window. She had just left a session. Her face looked drawn, like she had the weight of the world on her shoulders. I had never seen her like this. Maybe the letter would help.

I sat down quietly next to her. She looked at me in surprise. "When did you get here?" she asked.

"Just now," I said, smiling. "You look pretty today," I lied.

"I feel like crap. I just don't have any energy and I feel like hands are pulling me down to the ground. It takes an enormous amount of effort just to stand up."

"I got something in the mail today that may lift your spirits," I said, pulling the envelope out of my purse.

"What's that?" Marty said, her tone flat.

"A letter from Michael," I said.

"What?" Marty said, her eyes wide.

"It was written the morning he was missing before he went on his mission. Another soldier sent me this letter with it. Read the letter from the soldier first," I said.

Marty sat and read the letter slowly, tears rolling down her cheeks. Then she read Michael's letter.

"You don't need to drink anymore, Marty," I said. "You've been forgiven all the way around."

Marty cried for about fifteen minutes nonstop, then she grabbed the last of the tissues from a nearby box and blew her nose loudly. It was bright red.

"My dad came by today. It was part of my therapy. My mother was here the other day and today was his lucky day."

"What happened?" I asked.

"The staff here is very good. They drew him out. It was the first time he has actually looked at me in years. They made us do this, just sit and look at each other without speaking for several minutes. I slowly saw his resolve break down, all of his defenses. He looked sad. His eyes teared up and then he looked away."

"Really?"

"Yes. The counselor asked him why he looked away and he said it was because he couldn't stand to look at me. She asked why again. He said because he had failed me and he couldn't look at his failure."

"That must have hurt."

"It did. The counselor explained what had happened to me and that it wasn't my fault or his fault, it just happened."

"He said there must have been something wrong with him that he couldn't father a son."

"Did the counselor jump on that?" I asked.

"She did," Marty said, nodding, "but he wouldn't budge much. Then she asked what if one of the reasons I was drinking myself to death was because I thought he hated me and would never love me again?"

"Wow, good for her."

"This rocked him a minute. Then he said he didn't hate me, he hated himself for creating me and, while he didn't want anything bad to happen to me, he couldn't deal with me because it was too painful."

"That was honest," I said.

"It was, and I felt a little better. The counselor helped me realize after Dad left that he was probably going to remain stuck where he was and that he might never come around, but that wasn't my fault. She had me tell him how I felt about him. I did, I told him I loved him."

"Well good. So that's done. People can't change just because we want them to, Marty. I learned that a long time ago."

"I know," she said, "but it doesn't make it any easier."

"Are you getting better in here?" I asked.

"Yes," she said.

"Do you think you'll get out and drink again?"

"No, probably not. I was drinking to numb myself from the hurt from Michael and maybe a little bit from my dad. Whatever happens, I can live with myself now. I just need to get some more therapy, get stronger, and get out of here."

"When is the program over?"

"I have to stay here until December 1."

"Can you get out for Thanksgiving?" I asked.

"I think I can get a six-hour pass," she said.

An orderly came over and politely told me that my visit was over that Marty needed to go to another session, this time with her physician. I hugged Marty and followed the orderly out of the building, stopping at four locked doors before we got to the outside.

The air was wonderful, and my steps felt lighter. Just hearing from Michael and the things he said eased the pain for both of us.

I shot up a familiar prayer to the Almighty: *Dear God, Thank you for the letter and the help for Marty. Please bring Michael home safely. Please, bring him home.*

FIFTY-TWO

November was going to be a busy month. We had our traditional Thanksgiving with all our family and friends at the house in town. Hunter and Joelle were getting married Saturday in Norman at a little chapel on campus. They'd be coming down for Thanksgiving on Thursday, and heading back to Norman that night to get ready for the festivities.

Cora and Mac would be joining us from the ranch—and so would everybody else in the world. Cora was bringing the pecan and apple pies (she'd picked the pecans and apples from the trees at the ranch). Marty was being allowed out of the hospital on a six-hour pass, but Ben had to promise no alcohol and sign something saying he wouldn't let her out of his sight.

Fred and Gloria were coming. Their boys were all in the service, except for the youngest. He was away at college having Thanksgiving with his girlfriend's parents. Kendra and Dan would be here with Gracie. The baby was due in mid-December. Kendra's mom and the pincher were coming in for the wedding, so we invited them for Thanksgiving. Why not? Gloria was making sweet potato and green bean casseroles. Kendra was bringing a big vegetable and fruit tray. Glam and Vince were bringing the rolls, their specialty. They would be baking all day the day before. Vince would also bring berry pies he'd bake himself.

Claire and her husband were supposed to fly in Wednesday night but had both come down with the stomach flu, so they were staying home. I still loved my sister and had been exploring the rivalry we'd had growing up. I decided that it was time to put all that aside. I had bigger fish frying. My son was missing, and Marty was in rehab. I had a wonderful husband, two girls to finish raising, and two parents who needed my care. Her deal was her deal, and it had always been that way. Claire's world revolved around Claire, and I had felt some resentment because my mother had two daughters. I decided that Claire would have to live with her choices. When Mom and Dad did die I'd know I'd done everything I could for them and would have no regrets. It followed something my mother had taught me a long time ago. When you have jobs or chores to do, do the worst one first and the rest will be easy. But if you do the easy ones first, you'll be dreading that big job and may never get to it.

My Aunt Lucinda was coming, too. She was my father's youngest sister and one of my favorite aunts. If Lawrence and Lee, the famous Broadway writing team, had met my Aunt Cin, as we called her, they would have written a musical called "Cin" instead of "Mame." Cin had been married four times, which was something for her day, but she'd married the third husband twice.

Cin had traveled all over the world. I have a picture on my refrigerator of her riding elephants in Tibet. "My dearest Lizzie, I'm in Tibet, and look what I'm riding! I turned eighty today and it's been a pretty good day so far. Tonight, I'm eating cake."

Cin was eighty-six now. She'd been an artist all her life. She knew Andrew Wyeth and other famous artists of her time. She painted as flamboyantly as her colorful nature. Her paintings were quite popular, selling for thousands of dollars.

She wore her hair in a mass of curls on her head. Most often, her hair was blonde, but sometimes she'd go peach in the summer. I'm not kidding, it was peach, and she wore lots of floating pastel dresses.

Aunt Cin was an absolute ball to have around. She told funny stories about her many travels. Dad was always happy to see her. Aunt Cin attracted characters like herself, and they were always getting into mischief. Uncle Arthur had traveled with her but had died a couple of years earlier.

So Aunt Cin had come to see her brother and have Thanksgiving with us. I was in a bit of a tizzy planning dinner for so many people. But really, it was easy with everyone bringing food. I just had to make the two big turkeys and the stuffing, because my family had to have my stuffing with fresh cranberries and pecans chopped up in it, in addition to all the other goodies. I made the fresh cranberry rings like Mom always had and, of course, the mashed potatoes and gravy. Georgette and Gretchen made chocolate and coconut cream pies. Dung and Dong made Cha Gio (Vietnamese spring rolls), which was always a treat.

When the whole group was crowded around the two big round tables that would easily seat twelve with an added smaller round table for Mom, Dad, and Gracie, plus Gracie's big bear, we were ready for a feast. We were on our second helping of stuffing and mashed potatoes when the doorbell rang.

Charlie answered the door to see a man standing on the porch with a big bouquet of flowers in front of his face.

"Oh, how nice," Charlie said. "I didn't realize anybody worked on Thanksgiving."

"Delivery for Elizabeth Waters," the man said.

"Oh, Charlie," I said, coming to the door, "how beautiful. I'm Elizabeth Waters."

"Please sign here, ma'am," he said, handing the flowers to Charlie.

It was Michael. He was leaning on a crutch. He was much thinner, he had shaved, but his face was worn with a tan that looked somewhat faded, and he looked much older than when he left.

We all started screaming. Charlie carried in Michael's bag and the flowers and set them down next to him. I grabbed Michael around his neck, hung on for dear life, and cried like a baby. The girls were jumping up and down, crying, and Marty's arms were around both Michael and me. Kendra was crying, and so was Hunter. We could have started our own flood.

"Why are those fools hugging the delivery man?" Mom wanted to know. "Working on Thanksgiving isn't *that* big of a deal," she said, putting her hand to her cheek in disgust.

"That's not the delivery man," Dad said, pulling himself up from the table. "That's Michael! He's home!"

"Where's he been? She ought to tan his hide," Mom said. "Why, that can't be Michael, he's too old."

"Hush, Helen. Michael did you whip their butts?" Dad asked, grinning.

"Yes, Grandpa, I did." Michael laughed, coming over and giving him a hug. He hugged Mom, too. She smiled because she loved the attention.

"Am I in time for dinner?" he asked.

"Yes, Uncle Michael, you can sit where my bear was sitting," Gracie said sweetly.

Michael made the rounds, shaking hands and hugging the ladies. He was particularly glad to see Aunt Cin. We fixed Michael a plate of food. He sat down where Gracie's bear had been and dug in.

"Dibs on more stuffing," Michael said, sighing. "There were times I thought I'd never taste this again."

The room was silent, watching Michael eat.

"Well, the rest of you can sit here like a bunch of stumps, but I want some pie and a piece of Cin's cake," Mom said. "Iris, can you get me some pie?"

Gloria, Glam, and I started cutting the pies at the buffet table. We also sliced up Cin's chocolate cake. There was the general argument over the size of the pieces and what kind they wanted.

"Can you tell us what happened, Michael?" Georgette asked.

"Some of it," he said.

"I got your letter," I said. "Sergeant James just sent it to me a couple of weeks ago.

"Oh, I'm so very sorry; I thought he would have sent it in July. Well, you know we were at the orphanage."

"Did you save some kids?" Georgette asked.

"Yes, we did," Michael said, "then I went looking for the guys who had—"

"Careful here…" Kendra said, nodding at Gracie, who was listening with all her heart.

"I went looking for the guys who were bad. I did a stupid thing and walked into a blind alley. It looked empty, so I turned around, and I think one of them must have jumped me from a rooftop," Michael said, propping his leg up.

"Was he Spiderman?" Gracie asked, clapping her hands.

"It seemed like it when he jumped me, but he wasn't Spider-man, he was a bad guy and he had bad guy friends that I had to fight. I fought with those four guys for a long time; I'm not sure exactly how long it was. Finally, it was just this other guy and me standing, or barely standing. He had, uh, messed my leg up pretty good with his weapon and I had gotten him in the arm. Both of us were running out of oxygen in the sense that we were about to pass out, which we finally did. I lost so much bl—, uh, stuff, you know, they thought I was gone. I came to with a woman's face looking at me. She was a missionary nurse working in a small hospital over there and she had heard me moaning. They had stripped my clothes…"

Gracie giggled.

"Honey, why don't you go watch TV in the other room with your great grandma and eat your pie?" Kendra said, wheeling Mom into the living room. Gracie agreed reluctantly. Mom was thrilled to be with Gracie.

"Anyway, this angel found me, her name is Allison, but I call her Allie. She didn't know whose side I was on because I was so dark. They'd torn off my cross and had ripped the front pages out of my pocket Bible."

"Why didn't you tell her your name?" I asked.

"I didn't know my name. I had been hit on the head and had amnesia. I couldn't remember anything. I'd lost a lot of blood and I think I did almost die a couple of times. They thought I would lose the leg. I've been in the hospital this whole time. I've had one infection after another. At one point they brought in leeches and put them all over my leg. I ran a fever off and on for over three months."

"When did you get your memory back?" Gretchen asked.

"It started coming about two weeks ago. Allie was taking care of me; she brought me a treat from home. Someone had donated a case of Cokes. She poured it in a tall, frosted mug the way you used to, Mom, and I flashed back on my childhood. All of a sudden, I started to remember things. Allie wrote it all down and we started piecing things together. Then I finally remembered my name. She notified the Navy, and here I am!"

"Do you have to go back?" Marty asked, looking worried.

"No, I've been assigned to training and a desk job. This leg won't ever be the same. I can't be an active Seal anymore."

"It will be nice to have you home, Michael," Marty said, sincerely.

"You're alive, that's all that matters!" I said and hugged him again tightly.

We cleared all the dishes and everyone who didn't live here said their goodnights. Marty had to go back to the hospital and Ben took her.

Poor old Bob, Michael's now blind basset hound, had crawled up in Michael's lap and put his head on his chest to be stroked. It was quite a sight because Bob was a big dog. Charlie took a picture of the two of them sitting by the fire.

"Are we going to see the Christmas tree lighting at Utica Square, Mom?" Georgette asked.

"If Michael wants to," I said, "but if he's not up to it, I want to stay here with him."

"Me, too," Gretchen said.

"I guess, me too." Georgette sighed and then laughed at herself for being so Georgette.

Michael said he just wanted a hot shower and to go to bed in his old room. I put on fresh sheets and lit a candle in there. The room was neat, but a little dusty. I quickly gave everything the once over and vacuumed the rug while he was in the shower. I plumped his pillows and pulled back his covers.

Charlie had let Bob out to do the necessary, then carried him up the stairs to sleep in his dog bed on the floor next to Michael's bed. Bob looked happy his Michael was home.

When Michael came out of the bathroom, he had on a T-shirt and boxers. He limped across the floor with the help of his crutch. I gasped when I saw his leg. There were scars all over his leg, with a really ugly purple one on his thigh. In the garish bedroom light I saw a scar on his forehead. His arms were scared up as well.

"Mom, please don't say anything. I know it's hard to see, but I'm fine."

I choked up, still almost not believing he was actually here. I tucked him in bed, the way I used to, and he asked me to tickle his back. I used to grumble about this because I've never been a good back tickler. A back rubber I can be, but not a tickler. However, tonight I tickled without complaint and even went a full twenty minutes singing four songs until he was asleep. It's funny the things we hold onto.

In the morning, Michael discovered Bob had died in his sleep. He had waited until his beloved Michael came home so he could say goodbye. We buried him in the backyard. Charlie took some cement, made a frame, and poured Bob a little headstone that read: Bob the Basset Hound. 1988–2003." We let Georgette write on Bob's headstone with a sharp stick because she had the best handwriting.

Our house was whole again. This was a Thanksgiving we would never forget.

We'd turned a corner. Hunter and Joelle would get married in that sweet little chapel on OU's campus in Norman that Saturday and we'd give them a big sendoff. December was just around the corner. My project was finished, and the big Alzheimer's Fundraiser premier was next week. I had a new dress for the occasion. Now all I had to do was try to get Charlie to wear a tux.

Joelle and Hunter's wedding was just plain fun. Maybe it was because we were all so relieved Michael was home and we were ready to kick up our heels. Luckily, football season was over at OU, so there was plenty of parking for the guests.

The ceremony started off with music from the Indiana Jones movies. There was a video of all of Joelle's brothers being interviewed complaining about Hunter, like a reality show. One of Joelle's brothers was also a comedian, and her other two brothers were just as funny. The boys interviewed their parents like a therapy session where the parents were quibbling back and forth about napkin rings and the cake size. Finally, Joelle came on screen in her wedding gown and said, "This is ridiculous, let's just get on with the wedding!" She walked toward the camera and turned it off.

The music started right on cue. Hunter and his merry men walked out in front of the crowd. All of the bridesmaids came in carrying streamers instead of flowers and blew bubbles at the crowd, the big kind that popped over our heads. Kendra was the matron of honor. She looked like a stomach with a person following close behind. She just waved her bubble maker, probably because blowing was too much of an effort.

Joelle appeared with her dad. She'd been transformed from a fun-loving girl into an elegant woman. She carried flowers and had a satin bag over her shoulder bulging with chocolate kisses that she threw out to the congregation with a smile. When she got to the altar, she kissed her dad, bent down, kissed her mom, and joined Hunter.

Hunter was bursting with pride when he looked at her. They had written their own personal vows. Hunter's vow was sweet, sincere, and beautifully written. I could tell he'd spent a great deal of time on it. Joelle's was funny, tender, and loving, just like she was.

The reception was in a ballroom in the OU student union. They had it decorated to the nines, with lights in every artificial tree and big white ribbons everywhere. We had a blast dancing and visiting with everyone. The food was fabulous, and the girls especially got a kick out of the chocolate fountain. Charlie danced with all of the women in our family, including little Gracie. The band played everything from big band music to country, from contemporary Christian to rock 'n roll.

I had a great time getting to know Joelle's folks. Her mom did ask me about "the pincher" because Drake had managed to pinch her bottom as he was passing by. Marty would be crushed. She wasn't here because she was still in the hospital. I told Joelle's mom that Drake was just an old letch and not to let him get away with it. She raised her eyebrows and said that actually she had been quite flattered. Nobody had pinched her bottom in years!

Kendra and Gracie were seated next to me. Dan had gone to get the girls some punch. It was hot in here with so many people. Suddenly, my shoe felt wet. I leaned down to look at what was causing it and saw that Kendra's dress was wet. I pulled my head up and looked at her. She was bent over, holding her stomach.

"Kendra!"

"I think my water just broke."

I yelled for Hunter, Charlie, and Dan. Hunter was a doctor, Charlie was Charlie and fixed everything, and Dan was her husband. The men hustled into action. Dan lifted Kendra up and carried her to the elevator and outdoors with Charlie and Hunter at his side. Gracie stayed with me, which was the plan. Meanwhile, I took my shoe off and tried to blot it dry. The silk was ruined, but that was okay, I'd never really liked these shoes. They were beastly uncomfortable. The band continued to play. Hunter came back inside to dance with his bride, but he looked worried.

"Dan and Charlie are taking her to Norman Regional," he said distractedly.

"Hunter, don't worry about her," I said. "They'll take good care of her. It's not far. You need to stay here with your guests and dance with your bride."

"Yeah, you've got your honeymoon ahead of you, buddy!" Michael said, winking at him. Allie was at his side, a brown-eyed, brown-haired beauty with the sweetest smile. I loved the way she looked at Michael and he obviously adored her. I'd thanked her over and over for taking care of him. She said she was just doing her job, but I imagine she didn't look at all of her patients the way she looked at Michael. I hoped Miss Allie would be getting a ring this Christmas.

Kendra's mom and the pincher followed Charlie and Dan in their rental car. In the confusion, Gracie started to cry. She wanted to be with her mother. She crawled in my lap and asked if her baby brother would be here soon. I promised it wouldn't be too long now.

The bride and groom cut their cake, threw the garter, and tossed the flowers. It was over in three hours, and they were off for their honeymoon with a stop at the hospital. We migrated over there ourselves. Gracie fell asleep in her car seat. Charlie met us in the parking lot and carried Gracie into the hospital. We followed behind them with my squishy shoe and all.

Hunter saw his sister and said goodbye. They were flying to San Francisco that night in a friend's private plane. I'd never seen Hunter happier.

Kendra was dilated to a seven, so we all waited in the lobby, preparing ourselves to camp out for the night.

"What's wrong with your shoe, Mom?" Georgette said, looking at the squishy mess.

"Kendra's water broke on it," I said.

"Gross!" She made a face. "Why are you still wearing it?"

"Because it's December and I don't want to be barefooted, or hose-footed in this case."

"Can it be fixed?" Gretchen asked, always the curious one.

"I don't think so," I said, studying it.

"Yuck. I bet your foot stinks," Georgette said.

"Probably," I agreed.

Dan ran out excitedly. He said Kendra was dilated to a ten and the doctor was on his way to deliver the baby.

"That was quick," Drake, the pincher, said. He walked toward us with a can of Coke. "Does anybody want anything? Her mom is in the room with her. I don't know where to go."

"You can sit with us," Michael said pleasantly. The pincher complied.

We waited. The waiting room was not far from Kendra's door. We waited until we could hear a loud wail from Kendra's room followed by cheers and laughter. We all stood up, hugged each other, and moved outside the door.

Dan appeared carrying little Henry, weighing in at a paltry nine pounds, three ounces. He was as beautiful as his sister had been. I could feel the tears. I woke Gracie up to see her baby brother. She was still sleepy. She waved and went back to sleep.

We headed back to Tulsa the next morning. We had been up all night. Dan would be bringing Kendra home in another two days. Mom and Dad were excited to see us. They wanted to hear all about the wedding. We managed to tell them a little bit before we had to give it up and go to sleep. We slept all day. I took a couple of extra Vitamin C's before going to sleep. I couldn't get sick now. The premiere was coming up and that was one event I didn't want to miss.

FIFTY-FOUR

y big day had finally arrived. I was as nervous as a cat. Georgette, Gretchen, Joelle, Kendra, and I all went to Miss Jackson's salon to get our hair and makeup done that afternoon. Joelle had gotten back from her honeymoon a day earlier. Kendra had been home from the hospital for only five days, but she insisted on coming. Our dresses were waiting for us, hanging in plastic bags at home, with shoes to match. Mine was a lush, deep rich evergreen, floor-length like the others, with a fitted waist, since I finally had one, and a flowing skirt. It was covered with little sparkly things that shimmered when I walked and would look beautiful on stage.

The girls wore the same shade of crimson red in the same shimmery satin fabric. A little black was mixed in with red and they wore dressy black sandals. Both dresses were long, but Georgette's had an empire waist, fitting snugly under her bodice, while Gretchen's was nipped at her waist with a self-tie belt either in front or back. We gave them their early birthday presents, two teardrop garnet necklaces and matching garnet earrings with tiny diamonds attached to them. They looked stunning.

Kendra had been pregnant when she had tried the dress on, but it didn't matter, because it was an empire waist that flowed gently to the floor. It looked good with or without a stomach and hid a multitude of sins. We chose a simple black for her, fitted under her ample nursing bust.

Joelle had decided on a shimmery deep midnight blue that sparkled to the floor. Hunter had bought her sapphires as a wedding gift. She was still glowing from the honeymoon.

Michael had invited Allie, who wore a floor length chocolate brown dress with crisscross straps in the back.

Charlie, Michael, Hunter, Dan, Fred, Mac, and Vince all wore tuxedos. Charlie called them monkey suits, but I caught him grinning and looking at himself in the mirror. I told him he could eat a banana, but not in that tux!

We had decided to take Mom and Dad. They hadn't been out of the house in ages and Dad really wanted to see the documentary and me. We bought Mom a special gold dress and the girls fixed her hair and makeup. We'd gotten Dad a tux too, because none of his suits fit anymore.

I stuck three adult diapers in a bag and put them in the car, just in case we had a problem. Fred and Gloria were coming along and so were Glam and Vince. Gloria was wearing a long white suit, which was beautiful against her cocoa skin. Glam wore a silver lamé number, and looked like our holiday Glam. Marty wore a very simple high-necked, long sleeve black dress, and Ben wore a tux.

I had dropped by the ballroom at the hotel where they were showing the documentary. We tested the sound again and again and made sure it would run correctly. They had three copies and one backup machine in case something failed. How do you spell compulsive?

Charlie and I arrived early to make sure everything was okay again. The entourage followed about an hour later. That was fine. It gave me time to drink a bottle of water and go to the bathroom four times. People were arriving. We were sitting in the front. There were sixteen of us seated around two tables pushed together. Mom's wheelchair was nestled in tightly to Dad seated next to her.

"Who is that fat old slut in the wheelchair?" Mom asked, looking at her reflection in the mirror on the wall next to her. "She's sitting next to you, Jack, you ought to know her."

"Helen, you're the only woman sitting next to me and you look real nice tonight," he said sincerely.

"Oh gracious! Is that me? When did I get that *old*? I guess that gold dress doesn't look so bad, but who did my makeup?"

"I did, Grandma," Georgette said. "Don't you like it?"

"I look like a slut," she said irritably.

"I'm having second thoughts about this," I whispered to Charlie. He just winked and patted my leg.

"It's going to be fine. You look beautiful."

Dinner was served: either a filet mignon or chicken breast with rice, salad, and apple rings. The dessert was turtle cheesecake. Not exactly your one-hundred-dollar meal, but it was a charity event.

"Why do they call it turtle cheesecake?" Georgette asked.

"Because they crush turtles and put them on top of the cheesecake," Charlie teased.

"No, they don't, why do they call it that?" Georgette demanded.

"Isn't it like chocolate turtles, you know, that caramel candy chopped up?" Gretchen said, ever the scholar, especially when it came to chocolate.

"That's it," Kendra agreed.

"Well, I don't see a turtle," Mom said, looking around. "But if I did, I'd step on the little bastard."

"Why?" Georgette asked, "Don't you like turtles, Grandma?"

I shook my head slightly as an indicator for her *not* to engage Grandma in discussion.

"I damn sure don't," she said. "One time one of those snapping turtles nearly took off my toe."

I knew this story. It wasn't pretty.

"If Jack hadn't cut its head off before it got a really good bite on, it would have chomped off my toe. As it was, I had to have stitches and your feet have a lot of n-nerve endings. It hurt," Mom said, challenging anyone at the table to disagree with her.

I wasn't hungry anymore, and everybody else seemed to have lost their appetite when they heard about the turtle's head getting cut off. No matter, the head of the Alzheimer's association was introducing my boss.

"Good evening. I'm proud to introduce someone who has worked for me a long time. She has an ability to take on more than any person I know. She's been a widow, a single mom, a caregiver to both her parents and survived a son going off to war. She is one of the most amazing photojournalists I've witnessed. Her compassion and visual detail in this piece has garnered her two awards she doesn't know she's receiving. Two days ago, I received notice that she has won Best Documentary Film by the Oklahoma Film Task Force and, on a national level, she has earned her first Regional Emmy nomination for tonight's documentary. The station will be sending her to Kansas City in a few months to the awards banquet. Please allow me to introduce Elizabeth Waters. Liz?"

The crowd went wild, applauding and cheering. I was stunned. Charlie was hugging me, Georgette was whooping and clapping her hands over her head, and Gretchen reached out and squeezed my hand. Mom applauded along with the rest of them, and Dad's face was one big smile.

I stood to go up on the stage. My legs felt a little wobbly in my heels, but I managed to walk up the stairs without tripping. I waited until the applause died down.

"Thank you. First, I'd like to introduce my parents, Jack and Helen Littleton" (applause). My father stood up partially and waved. My mother waved because my father did, but she didn't understand. "My husband, Charlie Waters, and my family and friends seated with them (more applause).

"Thank you. Let me say that the credit for this film doesn't go entirely to me. I have a protégé and co-photographer for video and for this film project who has been working alongside of me since the day I met her sixteen years ago. She is my stepdaughter, and I couldn't have dreamed up a better person. She is talented, compassionate, and a wonderful mother to my grandchildren. Kendra, please stand up and be recognized." (More applause) Kendra, embarrassed, stood, nodded to the crowd, and sat down.

"This project probably saved me thousands of dollars in therapy. My son, who just returned home from Iraq" (more applause), "was found missing in action when I first took on this assignment. If I hadn't had this much work to do, I might have found myself sitting around too much and worrying.

"My parents moved in with us this year and I might have felt sorry for myself, being the only sibling taking care of them, and overwhelmed, if it hadn't been for my family and the inspiration of the people in tonight's film.

"What have I learned through this process? I've learned that God teaches us lessons through our trials and the main lesson is to lean on Him. I've learned that we have to see the people in our lives for who they are, not who we want them to be. I've learned that loving somebody can make this task of caregiving harder because we remember who our loved ones used to be, and we have to watch helplessly as they decline. This is a disease that can rob a person's abilities, but it is up to us to preserve their dignity.

"Every caregiver in this room is a hero. You've made a decision to take on something and someone that most people have forgotten or want to forget. It's not convenient, it's not easy, but it's the right thing to do. *You* are making a difference in someone's life. That's important, because you *are making a difference* in someone's *life*.

"Some of you in this room aren't the caregiver. You may pay someone to do this task because you live far away, or you may be fortunate enough to have a sibling who is the caregiver. To be honest, there have been moments when I have been angry that all the caregiving has fallen on my shoulders. Caregivers, if this describes how you feel at times, I can tell you that it is natural and normal to feel this way. I can also tell you that to dwell in this place only takes up space in your head for more important things, and it simply doesn't do any good, because it won't change anything.

"If you're not the caregiver, here are some suggestions to help you contribute to the cause. Call the caregiver often. After first getting a report on your family member, talk about lighter things—like movies, hairstyles, clothes, jokes, and funny memories. Above all, do not criticize what they are doing or how they are doing it. They are in the trenches! Let the caregiver laugh. Listen to the caregiver, whatever he or she needs to say or talk about. If you can, give them a break. Hire some relief, find a local reputable spa and buy them a gift certificate for a massage or a makeover, send them gift certificates to restaurants and movies, and make time to come see them and let them go away for a few days. Your loved ones will appreciate your efforts.

"I thank God for orchestrating this magnificent opera of events that brought all of you into my life and allowed me the opportunity to do this film. Thank you for inspiring this film and inspiring me to carry on a task that is both challenging and rewarding. I thank my station and the association for choosing my team to create this film. I hope you are as moved by this as I was putting it together. Thank you."

Warm applause filled the room and guided me back to my seat. The lights dimmed. I reached for Charlie's hand and glanced around the table at the family and friends I loved. Marty had tears in her eyes. Glam winked at me and Gloria gave me a thumbs-up. The girls had big smiles on their faces. Michael was grinning from ear to ear, sitting between his sisters with his arms around them both. My eyes rested on my parents. My father was holding my mother's hand. She was staring at him sweetly, and he was looking expectantly at the screen. I realized at that moment that every minute of every day this past year had all been worth it. I had been blessed beyond belief and I hadn't even realized it.

I looked at the screen and held my breath. Charlie squeezed my hand. The music started, and as the images unfolded, the title of the film rolled across the screen: "Goodnight, Whoever You Are."

◆　◆　◆　THE END　◆　◆　◆

GOOD MORNING, WHAT'S YOUR NAME?
(SEQUEL TO *GOODNIGHT, WHOEVER YOU ARE*)
BY VICTORIA COOKE

Elizabeth Waters has accepted a life of chaos: living with two hormonal twin daughters, her elderly parents, a wounded son (a Navy Seal just back from war), and a cranky Vietnamese live-in couple who provide domestic help. A photojournalist and an Emmy nominee for her documentary, *Goodnight, Whoever You Are*, Liz is struggling in a down economy. Her talents are many, but her dollars are few. Her husband Charlie, the Cowboy Preacher, owns a ranch an hour from town, but most of his profits go to feeding a growing congregation of dusty field workers and boot-scootin' cowboys on Friday nights.

Liz and Charlie's historic home in Tulsa, Oklahoma, is groaning with age and maintenance issues when Liz's world-traveling eighty-five-year-old Aunt Cin comes to visit—riding a baby elephant in their front yard! Little do the couple know that this won't be a short visit. While recuperating from a heart attack at Liz and Charlie's, Aunt Cin meets the new love of her life online, and that calls for a wedding! Liz gets help from her lifelong friends, Glam and Gloria, and much unsolicited advice from her resident parents.

The entourage spends their time between the city and the country. There are surprising heartaches with Liz's children, Charlie, her mother, and her best-friend-ex-husband-turned-female,

Marty. This extremely blended family reflects the times. Liz's sense of humor, her loving husband, and the grace of God carry her through the rough spots. In *Good Morning, What's Your Name?* Liz makes discoveries about herself and the people she loves that force her to say goodbye to her old life—and blaze a trail toward a new one!

AFTERWORD ...

I wrote the first draft of this novel when I was taking care of my mother, who had Alzheimer's disease. My parents both lived with us for several years in the early 2000s. Around the same time, my friend, Barbara, told me she had lost a son who became her daughter. She explained the process and how her daughter, Michelle, had become much happier. During this time, I saw a program on two friends who had gotten married and remained friends after his transition. I had never heard of gender reassignment, so I decided to write about it.

I consulted with Michelle, Barbara's daughter (thank you, Michelle) and did some research. I wanted to put the love I feel and have felt from my three best guy friends from my youth (Rick, Gary, and Ricky) in Marty and Lizzie's relationship. I hope you felt this, too. Unconditional love.

By the way, the Morman faith is NOT the villain in this story. I have several good friends, now known as The Church of Jesus Christ of Latter Day Saints, whose faith and practices do not resemble George's family. The bad guy in George's life was his dad, who was the self-appointed leader to his family cult.

This has always been Lizzie's story and her journey with her friends and family. We all suffer disappointment in divorce, death, and when our dreams die. I feel the secret is to keep finding new challenges, new directions, and your purpose in life. For me, faith has helped and is a huge part of that equation.

This book would be a lot wordier and not as clear or as well-punctuated without the help of my editor, Anita Salzberg. She is one of my heroes! She understood and appreciated my humor and she cheered me on when I had moments of doubt in myself. Anita is part of the incredible gang at 1106 Design who have helped prepare this book for publication. Owner Michele DeFilippo has put together a wonderful team who held my hand throughout the process and had such patience! What a talented team!

A big thank you to all of my friends and family who supported my journey along the way. You know who you are. Thank you for your suggestions, your thoughts, your love, and your friendship. I don't want to leave anyone out, so I'm not naming everyone, but you know who you are because you reside in my heart. —VC

QUESTIONS FOR BOOK CLUBS

1. The book begins when Lizzie is seven years old and then jumps to a slumber party when she was in sixth grade. Did you ever go to a slumber party or sleep over? What is your memory of this? Was it similar to Lizzie's experience?

2. Did you have a best friend in your childhood or youth? How is Marty and Lizzie's relationship like or unlike yours?

3. Were you surprised by Marty's announcement? Did this change your feelings toward Marty? How do you think Lizzie handled the news?

4. How did you feel when Marty and Lizzie told Michael about the changes that were going to happen in his life? Did you ever have to break bad news to your children or someone you loved?

5. Lizzie dates Dr. Gorgeous after Marty. What did you think of him when they were dating? Did you see any red flags? What about when they got married?

6. Lizzie has two girl friends who have been at her side since childhood. Describe Glam and Gloria. Do you have friends like this?

7. Lizzie has three children. Do you think it was harder for her to raise girls or her son?

8. Describe Lizzie's relationship with her parents. Would you say the parents have a good marriage? Can you relate to this relationship?

9. How is Charlie different than the other two men in Lizzie's life?

10. What does Charlie do that George probably never would have done?

11. Lizzie's work is important to her. What does she do? Is your work important to you or have you ever had meaningful work experiences?

12. The book's title could actually be said to three of the characters. Who were these characters and why would she say this to them?

13. What will you remember about this book?

14. Would you recommend this book to a friend? What would you tell your friend about the book?

We welcome your comments on our website: nativeredbirdbooks.net

Goodnight, Whoever You Are is the first book in the Liz/Marty series. Watch for *Good Morning, What's Your Name?* which is the second book in the series, coming to your favorite bookstore or online soon! ALSO, we are excited to announce that *Goodnight, Whoever You Are* has **been optioned for a television series!** Check our website for more updates!

BIO

A native Tulsan, Victoria now lives in the Oklahoma City metro area with her husband, Michael, and two goofy dogs. They share a beautiful blended family. Victoria started out teaching junior and senior high students, but switched to television and has been a producer, news anchor, reporter, radio talk show host, national voice talent, and has written hundreds of radio and television commercials. She has also written, voiced, and produced more than twenty-five documentaries. An Addy award winner, she graduated summa cum laude from Emerson College in Boston and did her honors graduate work in professional writing at the University of Oklahoma. A person of faith and a proud member of the Osage nation, she is often asked to give motivational talks. She loves to read, binge watch TV shows, play games, and spend time with friends and family.

For questions or comments, please reach out to Victoria at info@nativeredbirdbooks.net or visit her website at nativeredbirdbooks.net.

9 798989 493302